All the Things

K. A. Last
kalast@kalastbooks.com.au
www.kalastbooks.com.au

ISBN: 978-0-6480257-7-1

Formatting and cover design by KILA Designs
www.kiladesigns.com.au
Cover images: ©bigstockphoto.com

Editing by Lauren Clarke Editing
www.laurenclarkeediting.com

All the Things

Something - Nothing - Everything

K. A. LAST

www.kalastbooks.com.au

Also by K. A. Last

Fiction
Sacrifice – A Fall For Me Prequel
(The Tate Chronicles, #0.5)
Bound (The Tate Chronicles, #0.6)
Fall For Me (The Tate Chronicles, #1)
Fight For Me (The Tate Chronicles, #2)
Die For Me (The Tate Chronicles, #3)
Immagica
The Lovely Dark
Something (All the Things: part one)
Nothing (All the Things: part two)
Everything (All the Things: part three)
The Other Side of Me (All the Things: part four)

Non-fiction
The Tate Chronicles Notebook
Immagica Notebook
A Novel Idea! Colouring Journal for Writers

For my sixteen-year-old self.
If only I knew then what I know now.

For every girl who has ever had her heart broken.

For KSS. Just do it!

Something

All the Things: part one

The damage is already done

The words on the page in front of me blur, and I drop my pen onto my desk. It rolls off and lands on the carpet beside my foot. With a sigh, I swivel in my chair. I stare at the pen for a moment before bending to pick it up.

Study is the last thing I want to be doing on a Saturday night, but term three starts on Monday and trial HSC exams are in two weeks. I worked hard to earn my scholarship, and I don't want to disappoint Mum and Dad. They have big dreams of me becoming a lawyer or a doctor. I have to keep my grades up.

I roll the pen between my fingers and turn back to my history text, blinking a few times. Outside, a car door slams and a voice yells something, but I don't catch the words. I glance up at the clock. It's almost eleven-thirty pm. No wonder my eyes are blurry.

Usually when I hear a car outside I go to the window to see if it's Levi White. But tonight, I need to get through thirty more pages on Egypt and the pyramids.

Something crashes. I jump.

I put my pen down and go to my window anyway, glancing out to our front yard below.

Next door, the veranda light shines brightly into the darkness. Levi sits on the wooden boards, his feet hanging over the top step, staring at a pot plant lying broken on his front path.

I bite my lip. Levi's mum, Yvonne, is not going to be happy.

The front door opens, and Levi's mum comes out, pulling her dressing gown tight around herself. She says something to him, but I can't make out the words.

I unlatch the lock on my window and slide the bottom sash up.

Yvonne speaks again, and this time I hear her. "Did you drive home?"

Levi's car is in the driveway, but it wasn't there half an hour ago. I'd checked.

"No, Mum ... Jarred ..." Levi trails off. He's still sitting on the veranda, his upper body swaying from side to side.

"He better not have been drinking. You know—"

"He wasn't," Levi says. "I'm not stupid, Mum."

Yvonne glances up at my window. *Shit!* My heart beats faster. I dart backwards.

I don't want her to know I'm watching them. I'm pretty sure she doesn't want me to ogle her son and the mess he's made. Or hear their conversation about drink driving.

If Levi has been drinking, how can he do this to her?

His brother only died a year ago, killed in a car accident when he got behind the wheel drunk.

I miss him.

He was like an older brother to me, sometimes better than my own.

Mason would never have turned his back on me like his brother has. Ever since I landed that scholarship, Levi has been different. On my first day at his preppy private school, he pretended not to know who I was. It's like I'm his dirty little secret that no one can ever discover.

I move back to the window and pull the curtains closed, leaving a small gap in the middle so I can see what's happening.

Levi gets to his feet and turns away from his mum. His foot slips, and he tumbles down the stairs. He lands in the mess of the pot plant, sprawling onto the path and face-planting the concrete. I wince.

Yvonne shakes her head and swipes at her cheek. She makes her way down the steps to Levi, her mouth moving in a low whisper. She crouches and tries to help him up, but he shoves her hands away.

"You're bleeding," she says. "Come inside."

"Leave me alone!" Levi shouts.

I suck in a sharp breath and hold it, glancing around, expecting someone in our quiet street to react to Levi's loud yell. But most of the houses are dark. They stay that way, and no one comes outside.

Levi glares at his mum. Blood runs from a cut on his cheekbone.

Yvonne stands. "I'll leave the door unlocked," she says before going inside.

I grip the edge of the curtains and stare down at Levi. What's happened to him? His gaze flicks towards me, and I quickly step back, my heart racing again.

I stand in the middle of my room and twist my fingers together. I shouldn't be spying on him. He's drunk and injured, so I should help him, but he didn't want his mum's assistance, so why would I be any different? Besides, it's not like he's been nice to me the past couple of years.

A car door slams, and when I go back to the window, Levi is sitting on the lawn with his knees up and his head hanging between them. His fingers grip the neck of a bottle of bourbon. He raises his head and stares at my window, then brings the bottle to his lips and takes a swig. I should step back again, but I can't. My gaze is glued to Levi's face.

The pain in his eyes sears its way through my heart.

What happened to the boy I have loved my entire life?

How did he become so broken?

He shakes his head and looks away, then flops back onto the grass.

I want to go and see if he's okay.

But I don't.

I back away from the window and sit at my desk, my history book open where I left off. I try to concentrate on studying, but ten minutes pass and my thoughts keep returning to Levi. I can't stop glancing at the window and wondering if I should go downstairs and see if he's okay.

"Katie, are you still studying?" Mum's voice makes me jump, and I drop my pen on the desk.

"You scared me," I say.

"Everything all right?" She leans against my open

door and crosses her arms.

I shrug. "Levi's out on the lawn. He's drunk."

Mum frowns. "I heard the yelling." She goes to my window and peeks through the gap in the curtains. "Maybe you should go and see if he's okay."

"It's late, Mum."

"Yeah, but it's Saturday night." She glances at my clock and smiles. "Tomorrow is the last day of the holidays, and you have a bit over an hour before curfew."

"He's a big boy, Mum. I'm sure he'll be fine." I tap my pen on my desk.

Mum sighs. "He might need a friend to talk to, Katie. See you in the morning." She pulls my door closed, and I listen to her pad down the hallway to her bedroom.

I take my glasses off and rub my eyes. Maybe Levi does need a friend, but that *friend* isn't me. With a deep breath, I push my glasses back up my nose and return to the window, pulling the curtains aside.

Levi hasn't moved from his position on the lawn. His gaze locks with mine as if he's been expecting me to come back. He gets to his feet and staggers a couple of steps to his veranda, avoiding the smashed flower pot. I raise my hand and give him a half-hearted wave and a close-lipped smile. He scoffs and shakes his head, and I regret even looking at him. He puts a foot on the first step and clutches the railing.

I turn away from the window, go to my desk, and close my text book. I think I'm done for tonight. Levi's reaction has gotten under my skin, but I told myself a long time ago that there are worse things in life than people laughing at me.

My eyes are heavy, so I take my glasses off and set them on my desk. I flick my overhead light off and get changed into my PJs by the light of the reading lamp attached to my bedhead. The covers are cool when I slip between them. I lie back and stare at my ceiling, counting the stars my brother, Daniel, and I stuck up there when we were kids. They've been there so long they don't glow much anymore. I want them to glow again. Maybe I'll replace them.

I reach up to turn off the lamp when something taps on my window. The curtains move, and Levi sticks his head through the open section at the bottom, a frown on his face. I scramble to sit up and grab my glasses, putting them on.

Oh God, I'm in my PJs. I grip the edge of the covers and pull them up to my chest.

"What the hell are you doing?" I ask in a whisper.

He mutters something I can't make out, then he tumbles through and lands in a heap on the window seat before falling to the floor. My journal lands beside him with a thud.

Levi pushes himself up and sits with his back resting against the wall. His head lolls onto the seat cushion.

I have no words.

Levi White just climbed in my window.

He hasn't done that since the middle of tenth grade, when he found out about my scholarship.

Levi raises his head and studies me. "Stop opening and closing your mouth, Katie. You look like a fish."

I finally find my voice. "I ... what ... how did you not fall and kill yourself?"

He gets to his feet then plonks down on the end of my bed, almost falling off.

"I haven't forgotten how to climb—"

"What do you want?" I keep my voice low.

"You waved. I came." He smiles.

"I was trying to offer you a little support," I say. "Not asking you to scale the side of my house and fall through my window."

"Your trellis is still pretty sturdy … even after all this time."

I scoff. "I remember the last time you climbed it." My heart lurches at the memory.

"So do I," he says.

Levi's eyelids are droopy, and he closes his eyes for a second. I take the opportunity to stare at his face. Despite how he's treated me, he's still the boy next door who I fell in love with in kindergarten. And I'm secretly glad he's climbed into my room. *Maybe …*

I shake my head, refusing to entertain something that's impossible.

"That looks nasty." I point to the bloody cut on his left cheek.

"It didn't tickle," Levi says. "My hand hurts, too." He frowns and looks down to where his right hand rests on his leg.

"Wait here." I throw the covers aside and go to my door.

Levi smiles a lopsided, drunken smile. "Nice PJs."

I roll my eyes and inch the door open, escaping into the hallway, thankful Levi can't see me blush. Having him see me in baby pink flannel pants covered with little white sheep is embarrassing.

Dad's soft snores float down the hallway. Daniel is out, but I check the hall anyway, then go to the bathroom to grab a wet face washer and some Dettol.

Back in my room, Levi is lying on his side on my bed with his head propped up on his elbow.

"Are you going to tend to my wounds?" His smile widens.

Levi is muscular and gorgeous, and I want to do more than tend his wounds, but I'm not about to tell him that—especially while he's being an idiot.

"Don't be a jerk." I perch on the edge of the bed, pouring some Dettol onto the face washer. "Sit up."

Levi shuffles behind me and drops his legs over the side of the mattress, moving until he's beside me. I dab his cheek with the wet cloth.

"Ouch!" Levi's smile falls away, and he winces.

"You really should ice it ... to stop any swelling."

Levi grabs my hand and pulls it gently away from his face. "Why are you so nice to me?"

"I *try* to be nice to everyone."

"You shouldn't."

I stare at his hand holding mine, and I want him to be holding me in other ways, but it's never going to happen. Outside this room we can't be friends. Not anymore.

"What's the point in being mean to people?" I say. "It only makes you unhappy."

"Some people deserve it."

"That's true."

Levi's grip on my wrist tightens. "Katie ..."

I stare into his deep brown eyes. "Levi." I hold my breath.

He tears his gaze away from mine and looks at his fingers wrapped around my wrist. "Don't tell anyone about this." He lets go, and my skin is cold where he's been touching me.

"Don't tell anyone about your drunken fall down your front steps, or don't tell anyone you climbed in my window?"

"Both," he says.

I lick my lips and chew on the bottom one. "Who would I tell?"

I take his injured hand and look at his palm. There are some cuts on it, so I swab them with Dettol as well. He winces again.

"Don't be such a baby," I say, but I stop anyway.

We sit in silence. I fold the face washer and rest it on the edge of my desk.

"Your mum seemed upset," I say to try and break the tension in the air.

"She's always upset."

"Why? Because of … Mason?"

Levi scoots around me and flops back onto my pillow. "I'm not having this conversation with you. I don't want to talk about it."

"Then why are you here?" I ask. Right now, I'm not sure if I'm mad because he won't talk to me, or happy because he climbed in my window in the first place.

"I have no idea, Katie." He rolls his head to the side and closes his eyes.

"Well, it couldn't be because we're friends, now, could it?"

Levi opens his eyes but doesn't move. I blink a few times then look away, pushing my glasses up my nose.

"I miss you," Levi says. The words were whispered, but they were there.

I want to tell him I miss him, too. But do I really want to open old wounds?

I press my lips together. "Why are you drowning your sorrows in a bottle of bourbon?" I ask instead. "Drinking isn't the answer to anything, Levi. You, of all people—"

"Should know that? Yeah. I should. But you don't ..." He puts a hand over his face and lets out a long breath. "You have no idea."

There are a lot of things I could say to him, like *alcohol makes it worse*, or *you're not the only one with problems*. But how could I say anything like that when I really don't know what he's going through right now? As much as I loved Mason like a brother, I've never lost a real family member.

Besides, I have my own problems without having to worry about Levi's. He's the type of guy who's had everything handed to him. I have to work for everything I get, and being considered trash in a private school is pretty lonely. Mr Popularity, Levi White, is the last person who would ever understand loneliness.

Levi picks up one of the stuffed teddies on my bed and stares at it for a minute before handing it to me. I hug it to my chest. He sits, and shuffles back against the bedhead.

"You still like that kind of shit?" he asks.

I stare at the white bunny in my hands. It has big floppy ears and a pink tummy, and it's my favourite. I nod but don't say anything, putting it back with the others and going to sit at my desk.

Levi scoots to the edge of the bed and clumsily puts his feet on the floor. He grabs the book from my desk.

"History," he says.

"You should be studying, too." I pick up my pen and glance at my clock. It's well past midnight.

He laughs and puts the book back, then rubs his temples. "Study isn't really my thing."

"What is?" I put my pen down and swivel my chair to face him. I may have known Levi my whole life, and we may have been best friends once, but now, I don't *really* know him anymore.

Levi shrugs. "I don't know what I want to be when I grow up." He grins.

I ignore his stupid comment. "What are you good at? There must be something, other than everyone loving you."

Levi runs a hand through his mess of dark brown hair. I want to reach out and run my fingers through it, too. The thought makes me almost laugh out loud, and a blush heats my cheeks. As if I would ever be the one who got to do something like that.

"I don't know. Maybe ... science. Or marine biology." He goes quiet and stares at his hands. "It's stupid. I'm not smart enough."

"I could help you study ... if you like." I hold my breath, hoping he'll say yes because it will be an excuse to spend time with him.

"I probably won't remember this conversation tomorrow." Levi looks up.

I scoff, and suddenly, I'm mad. As if we could ever be friends again. It's obvious he's looking for an out. Well, if

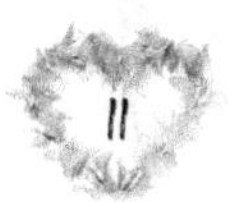

that's what he wants, I'll give it to him. "If you *really* want help with your homework, you'll remember. The window's that way." I point, before swivelling to face my desk.

"Do you want me to leave?"

"That would be good." I stare at my closed history book.

"Are you angry with me?"

I look up. "No, Levi. I'm not angry with you. Being angry is something a *friend* would do when their other friend behaved like an arse."

"You think I'm an arse?"

"Yes … a drunk one."

"Why?"

"Gee, I don't know." I stand and my chair spins. "Maybe because this is the first time we've had a real conversation in two years, and you want me to not tell anyone. And I get it. You're the popular rich guy, and I'm the scholarship girl who's poor and worth shit. You don't want to be associated with me."

"That's not true."

"The hell it isn't," I say. "Your parents should've moved you all to one of the ritzy suburbs instead of rebuilding here. Then you could hang out with the rich people twenty-four-seven."

"I like it here." He frowns.

"Yeah, well, since my first day in year eleven when you pretended you didn't know me, nothing has changed."

Levi rolls off the bed and sways towards me. "I am an arse."

"A drunk one."

"I'm sorry … I'll go."

I shake my head, and cross my arms in an attempt to seem pissed off when really, all I am is sad. He probably *won't* remember anything in the morning, and we'll go back to being neighbours who used to be best friends but now never speak to each other.

"Don't break your neck on the way down," I say.

He climbs onto the window seat and puts one leg through the open window, then pauses on the sill. "Do you want to know why I came up here?"

"I get the feeling you're going to tell me anyway."

"Of all the people I know, Katie, you always look for something good in everyone, even the people who hurt you. Maybe … maybe I need someone to see the good in me. And maybe I don't want to hurt you anymore." He turns and is out the window and on the trellis before I have time to think of a reply.

I watch him cross the grass and then step through the garden bed on our boundary. When he reaches the veranda, he glances back, and I move away from the window so he can't see my wet cheeks.

"It's too late, Levi," I whisper to the open window.

The damage is already done.

2

You never know unless you try

I don't see Levi again for the rest of the weekend. His car isn't in the driveway all day Sunday. I try to study for our upcoming exams, but I can't concentrate, so I resort to quality time with my iPod and my journal.

I don't write in it as much as I used to. These days I can't find many things I want to remember. Levi climbing in my window is the first note-worthy event that's happened in a while. My biggest thought is *how can he come up here and pretend like nothing happened, after all this time?*

Now, I'm standing on the corner waiting for the bus. Levi's BMW is parked on the street. It takes me a bus ride, a train trip, and a ten-minute walk to reach the back gates of school, a total of around forty-five minutes. Levi can drive it in twenty, but he's never offered me a lift.

"Hey, Katie." Jessica Hart from a few houses down the

street stops beside me, her school folder clutched to her chest. "Ready for first day back?"

"Not even," I say. "You?"

She shrugs. "I guess."

We stand together, our blue tartan skirts the perfect private-school length, just above the knee. Our white button-up blouses are freshly pressed. We both look the part, only I feel like an imposter.

Jessica and I are good friends, and like me and Levi, we grew up together. The only difference is she didn't ditch me when I started private school.

It's no secret my family is not as well off as some families in the street, but it's never mattered to Jessica. When she found out I would be going to school with her for our final two years, she was over the moon.

A blue Honda Civic passes us and Jessica's twin sister, Josephine, honks the horn, then flips us the bird.

"Charming," I say. "I can't believe she never drives you."

"That's because she's a bitch," Jessica says, so matter-of-factly that I laugh.

"I don't think I can disagree."

Jessica shrugs. "It's cool. She spent her eighteenth birthday money on a car. I'm saving mine for an overseas trip. And Levi never drives you." Jessica glances at me sideways. She knows how hurt I was when he stopped talking to me.

"That's because he's a jerk, *and* an arse."

Jessica laughs as well.

The bus pulls up to the kerb, and air whooshes as the doors open. We climb on and take our usual seats in the middle.

"You been studying?" Jessica asks.

I smile. "What else would I be doing?"

"You'll get dux. I know you will."

"That's the plan. I've already written my speech … Just in case."

Jessica grins back at me.

When we get to school, Jessica and I go to the office to scan our student cards that record our attendance for the day. The halls buzz with commotion as we make our way to our lockers. The first bell sounds and students dart in every direction. I switch out my English and math books for first and second period, then slam my locker shut.

"Hey," Karen, my best friend, says. "What exciting things did you get up to since I saw you last?" She leans against the lockers and bites into an apple.

"What could've possibly happened between Friday night and now?" I desperately want to tell her about Levi climbing in my window, but I told him I wouldn't say anything, even though he probably doesn't deserve my loyalty. "What do you think I did?"

"Made mad passionate love to Levi while studying." Karen smirks.

I stare at her as if she's grown horns. "You're the devil."

"I think she just did the study part," Jessica says.

"Whoa, speaking of the devil." Karen looks over my shoulder. "What happened to his face?"

I turn and follow her stare. The cut on Levi's cheek looks worse in daylight. It's scabbed over, but the edges of the wound are bruised and purple.

"That looks … sore," I say.

"Ouch," Jessica says, then she sighs. "How is he still

so pretty?"

Karen and I exchange a glance, and she laughs.

Levi saunters along the hall, his hands stuffed in his pockets, surrounded by his pack of loyal followers.

The in-crowd consists of the richest kids in the grade. Karen hates them, and not because they have more money than her, but because most of them aren't very nice people.

I try not to hate anyone, but some people make it pretty hard.

"What are you staring at?" Veronica Porter snaps. She hangs at Levi's side, keeping her distance from me, as if she's afraid she'll catch poor people.

Karen puts her hands on her hips. "The hole in your face that noise comes out of."

"Oh, bitch much?" Veronica's sidekick, Rachel, asks. "She's looking for trouble."

Josephine glares at Jessica but doesn't say anything.

"Did everyone have a great break?" Britney, our vice-captain, asks in her high-pitched voice.

We all ignore her.

"I'm not the one who's the bitch," Karen says.

I cringe and put my hand on her arm. "Don't. Please."

She doesn't listen.

"What happened to your face, Levi?" Karen says as he levels with us. "Veronica have a good chew?"

"Shut it," Veronica says.

Levi's mates, Jarred Lewis and Geoff Wilcox, walk up behind the girls. Levi steps around all of them and glances at me as he passes, but I can't read his expression. I have no idea if he remembers anything he said to me on

Saturday night, and knowing he is so much kinder than any of these rich snobs tears a hole in my heart. I want my Levi back—only I don't know where he's gone.

"No one said you could talk." Jarred gets in Karen's face, but she doesn't back up. She's tougher than I could ever be.

"No one tells me what to do," Karen says.

Jarred narrows his eyes.

"Someone should." Geoff pushes past her.

"Cut it." Levi glances back but doesn't meet my stare, even though I'm glaring at him.

Jarred clenches his jaw then moves away, walking a few steps backwards towards Levi before turning around and falling into step with him and Geoff.

I lock gazes with Veronica, unable to believe she's the girl all the other girls want to be. She steps towards me and rakes my folder and books from my hands. They scatter onto the hallway floor, papers falling from my folder and fluttering everywhere. Her friends laugh.

"Don't forget who you are," Veronica says before catching up to the boys.

Rachel follows, muttering words like 'trash' and 'slut' under her breath.

"I guess it's my job to try and control this situation," Britney says, rolling her eyes. She walks off in a huff.

Josephine is the only one who hesitates. "You shouldn't make her mad." She's looking at Jessica, but I know she's talking to all of us.

"Veronica is such a bitch." Karen kneels and helps me gather my papers and books from the floor.

"Just … be careful," Josephine says before walking away.

Jessica sighs. "I don't know why she's friends with them."

"Because she's a try-hard loser," Karen says.

I frown. "Don't say that about Jess's sister."

"It's true." She hands me my folder. "Jess is so nice. And Josie is just … as much of a bitch as Veronica. How is that even possible? They're identical. It's like Josie's personality got switched at birth or something."

"She's not that bad at home," Jessica says.

"You shouldn't react," I say to Karen. "It only makes it worse. You should know by now that reacting is what they want."

"You should react more," she says. "Stand up for yourself."

"I don't care what they think. I want to get good grades, so I can live my parents' dream, then get out of this hellhole." I stare down the hall after the group that rules the twelfth grade.

"I rest my case." Karen puts a hand on her hip. "You need to live your own dream."

I sigh. "Can we not talk about this now?"

The second bell blares through the sound system, and Karen, Jessica, and I make our way to first-period English. We take our seats in the front row as the rest of the class trickles in. Veronica sashays down the aisle to take her seat in the back, and I have to resist the urge to turn around and glare at her.

Moments later, a screwed up ball of paper hits me in the back of the head. As much as I'm curious to see what derogatory remark Veronica has written to me, I ignore it and take my books from my bag, setting them neatly on my desk.

Levi walks in, his backpack slung casually over his shoulder. He comes to the far aisle where my desk is and turns. I watch him go to the back of the room and take a seat beside Veronica. She smiles smugly, and I face the front of the room again. There's nothing going on between them as far as I know, but even though she's with Jarred I think she'd jump at the chance to be with Levi if she could. Every girl in the school would.

I turn again to glance at Levi. He's sitting back in his chair with his arms folded. He raises his eyebrows at me, and I look away quickly. There was no reason for him to walk down my aisle. He could have easily cut across the room, and the fact he didn't annoys me. What's he trying to prove? Does he want me to pay attention to him? Because if he does, he's going about it the wrong way.

Karen clicks her fingers in front of my face. "Hello ... Earth to Katie."

"Sorry." I blink and give her a tentative smile.

"Where did you go?"

I sigh. "Nowhere you can come."

"I hope it was nice."

Our English teacher, Mrs Wu, finally makes an appearance. She struts in, her skirt billowing around her legs and her glasses bouncing against her chest where they hang from a beaded chain. She puts her folder on her desk and sets her iPad on top. Before she speaks, the class waits as she makes a quick headcount and records it.

"Hello, class," Mrs Wu says. "Welcome to term three. Your trial exams start in exactly two weeks. Today, you will focus on revision. You know the texts we've covered.

I don't mind what you revise, but I don't want any noise, and I don't want anyone out of their seats." The class groans. "Face the front. Books out. No talking." Mrs Wu sits at her desk, puts her glasses on, and opens her folder.

I do as she says and open my copy of *The Great Gatsby*. I figure re-reading it is as good a place to start as any.

Five minutes later, another ball of paper hits me in the back of the head. It bounces off my shoulder and lands on the floor between my foot and the low shelves that line the window side of the classroom. I check Mrs Wu isn't watching before bending down, pretending to get something from my bag, and scooping the paper into my hand. With my hands under the desk I slowly un-crumple the ball then lay it flat on my desk.

I bite my lip as I read the words.

Truth or dare, Katie? V.

Great. Getting sucked into the in-crowd's stupid games is the last thing I need. The whole grade knows they play truth or dare on a regular basis, and if you're one of the less-popular kids, it's not good if they single you out. The only advantage to playing is I would get to go next, but I can't single out Veronica since she's truth-or-dared me.

Whatever she's trying to do, I'm not buying into it. I screw the paper up again and stuff it into the pocket of my uniform. I'm not playing.

For the rest of English class, the words *truth or dare* run over and over in my mind. I'm surprised no one has challenged me before, but I've heard stories about some of the stupid things people have done. I'm not sure what I'd choose if Veronica made me pick one. Or what would scare me most—the question she'd ask or the thing she'd dare me to do.

I have no desire to find out, either way.

"What did it say?" Karen asks as I leave English with her and Jessica.

I pull the note from my pocket and hand it to her without saying anything. She smooths it between her fingers, and Jessica looks over her shoulder.

"Oh no," Jessica says. "This is bad."

"I'm not answering it," I say. "Veronica can get stuffed."

"You have to answer." Jessica's eyes widen. "Or she'll make your life hell. You can't ignore a challenge to truth or dare."

"Veronica already makes my life hell." I raise my eyebrows. "And I can ignore her as much as I like."

"Remember what happened to Karen last year when she tried to ignore it?" Jessica says.

"Yeah, that was fun," Karen says. "Not."

Karen ended up being called in to see the school counsellor because they thought she had a drug problem. Veronica had spread a rumour that Karen was a pothead. She even planted a zip-lock bag in Karen's backpack.

Karen got suspended for three days and had to be interviewed by the police. It took a while for the hype to die down, even though the students knew it was a load of bull. The teachers took a bit more convincing.

"You don't want to get suspended," Jessica says.

"No one is getting suspended," I say. "Veronica can throw whatever she has at me."

"But you're set to be dux. She could ruin it for you."

Karen stops walking and grabs my arm. "This could be the perfect opportunity."

"For what?" I ask.

"To prove to Levi he made a mistake when he dumped you as a friend."

"I don't have to prove anything to anyone." I take the paper from Karen and rip it in half. "I'll see you at lunch."

I stomp off down the hall towards math class, which ends up being more of the same—revision for the upcoming trial exams. Thankfully, Veronica is not in my class, because there's no way I'm answering her note.

I spend most of the lesson thinking about what I said to Karen and Jessica, and I decide my words were true enough. The only person I have anything to prove to is myself.

But what if Jessica is right? What if Veronica decides to ruin my chances at being dux?

I push the thought away and try to focus on the text book in front of me.

At recess, I switch out my English and math books for history and art, then head to the library to renew my copy of *Gatsby*.

On my way to History, I flick through my text book to find where I was up to on Saturday night. My feet twist together. I fall. My history book flies from my grasp, lands on the hallway floor, and skids to the wall. The lockers bang as I grab for something to stop myself, but I cut my palm as it slides over one of the metal hinges. My right knee smacks into the ground before the rest of me follows. The impact knocks my glasses off, and they clatter to the floor.

I don't need to look up to know who tripped me.

Veronica laughs. "Oops. You should watch where you're

going, Katherine."

With my good hand, I push myself to a sitting position then grab my glasses and put them back on. My right palm is bleeding and my knee aches, but I get to my feet as quickly as I can. When I look towards Veronica, Levi and Jarred are there, too. Levi's brow is knitted, and he has his hands stuffed in his pockets. Jarred snickers.

"Karma's a bitch, Veronica," I say. But I'm not looking at her. I'm looking at Levi. How can he let her do this to me?

"Yeah, whatever. And so are you."

"Ronnie. That's enough. Let's go." Levi walks away with Jarred.

Veronica laughs and follows the boys. "You still need to answer me," she calls over her shoulder.

Like hell I do.

Jessica's best friend, Stacey MacDonald, comes over to me, her folder clutched to her chest. "You okay?"

"Yeah, I'll be fine."

Stacey smiles warmly. "Want any help?"

"Really, I'm okay. You'll be late for class. I'll see you at lunch."

I collect my book from the floor and head to the bathroom. The cut on my hand isn't bad, but by the time I clean myself up and get to History, I'm late.

Mr Jenkins glances up from his desk as I enter the room.

"Sorry, sir," I say.

"I don't want to hear your excuse. Take a seat, Katherine. We're concentrating on revision."

Veronica sniggers from the back of the room.

"Is there a problem, Miss Porter?" Mr Jenkins asks.

She puts her head down and doesn't answer. Rachel is sitting beside Veronica. She smirks at me and narrows her eyes. I quickly look away.

Levi isn't in his usual seat, and when I take a quick glance around the room, I can't find him. He must have skipped, which is odd, because he was there when Veronica tripped me.

I slide into my seat in the front row and open my text book to where I was up to. As hard as I try, I can't concentrate, and I can't stop thinking about Levi. He's the school captain. He can't skip classes.

Something must be wrong.

When the bell rings, I jump, and I can't get out of the classroom fast enough.

My knee throbs as I walk to Art. Thankfully, by lunch it's reduced to a dull ache. I find Karen, Jessica, and Stacey on the seats by the oval, already eating. I haven't had anything since breakfast, and I should put something in my stomach, but I've lost my appetite.

"Are you limping?" Karen asks as I sit down.

"It's nothing." I don't want to talk about what happened with Veronica.

"What's up with Levi's face today?" Stacey takes a bite of her sandwich. "What happened to him, Katie?"

"How should I know?" I say a little too defensively.

"Thought you might have heard something." Stacey shrugs. "You're his neighbour."

"That doesn't give me automatic rights to know everything about him," I say.

"It's a pretty big scrape," Karen says.

Stacey chews her food. "Maybe he got into a fight."

"With who?" I ask. "Everybody loves Levi. He'd never fight with his mates."

"I heard his parents fight a lot. Especially after what happened with Mason." Stacey looks at me. "Do they?"

I shake my head. "I don't hear them if they do."

Which isn't the whole truth, but I'm not about to tell them I've heard the odd argument. Everyone argues at some point, and it's none of my business. As far as I know, Levi's parents are great. Even though I haven't had a proper conversation with them in a while, I did grow up half-living in their house. I don't remember anything bad happening. Levi's dad was just, there.

"He probably fell over, drunk or something," Jessica says.

I press my lips together. "What makes you think that?"

"Josie tells me about the parties they go to all the time. He's always a total mess, stumbling all over the place."

I frown but don't say anything.

"Speaking of parties, we should start thinking about what we're going to wear to the formal," Karen says.

"What, now?" I ask. "It's almost two months away. They haven't even announced the theme yet."

"You know the committee likes to keep everyone in suspense," Karen says. "Who cares about the theme? It's a minor detail. We're not going dressed as fish or something. We need to be prepared."

"Fish? You're weird. And I'm hanging on the edge of my seat." I roll my eyes.

"We should try and get the best dresses before they

all disappear," Jessica says.

Stacey nods. "It's our last chance to make a statement."

"About what?" I ask.

"Okay, not a statement. But it's our last chance to get noticed," Karen says. "We can look just as awesome as Veronica and her bitches."

"You're all crazy." I laugh. "There's no way I'm even going."

Karen's mouth drops open. "Of course you're going."

"You have to go," Stacey says.

"We can go together." Jessica looks between each of us. "Has anyone, you know … been asked?"

I laugh. "I think you know what I'm going to say."

"Come on, Katie." Karen grabs my hand and kisses it like I'm a princess and she's the prince. "It will be a splendid night."

Really? My idea of a great night involves a packet of Tim Tams and a good book. Not fancy dresses and uncoordinated dancing.

My friends start talking about dress colours and styles, and I shake my head. I scan the seats around the oval, searching for Levi, but I can't find him in his usual place. Veronica catches me looking in her group's direction and she stands up, putting her hands on her hips.

Karen follows my gaze. "You know you're going to have to play eventually."

"She can't force me to do anything," I say.

"You should just get it over with." Jessica picks at her nails and doesn't look at me. "It's the best way."

"I'm not bowing to her," I say. "She can take her truth or dare and stick it."

Jessica sighs. "It's your funeral." She grabs her bag and gets to her feet. "I'm going to the library."

"I'll come with." Stacey jumps up and the two of them walk together.

Karen studies me. "You're not telling me something."

"I don't know what you're talking about."

"You've been funny all day. You're looking for Levi more than usual. I can tell."

Sometimes I hate that she knows me so well. "Maybe I'm worried about him. I'm allowed to be, aren't I?"

"Why don't you just talk to him, Katie?"

I stare at Karen and raise my eyebrows. "Veronica won't let me within spitting distance. And even if I do talk to him, what would I say?"

Karen shrugs. "You never know unless you try."

My answer is yes

After dinner with Mum and Dad, I head up to my room to study. A light breeze wafts through my open window. I take a moment to peek outside.

Levi's car is in the driveway, and the streetlight reflects off its shiny, black surface. I should ask him what Veronica's problem is, what his problem is, but there's no way I'm going over there.

I sit on the edge of my bed and stare at the books scattered all over it. I'm not sure where to start with study tonight. I'm finding it hard to concentrate again. My knee aches, and my palm is itchy. Since I got home, all I've been able to think about is what happened at school today with Veronica, especially the truth or dare challenge.

A door slams, and I go back to the window. Levi jumps down the front steps of his veranda. The mess from the smashed pot has been cleaned up, and there's a new ceramic tub in its place. Levi heads to his BMW.

The front door of the house opens again, and his dad comes out. "Don't talk to your mother that way," he yells.

Levi yanks the car door open and before he slides into the driver's seat, he glances up at my window.

I step back.

He caught me watching him on Saturday night and look where that led. Besides, I don't want him to think I'm spying on him.

Levi's car starts, and I move to the side of the window so I can peek out without him seeing me. He backs out of the driveway and his tyres squeal as he drives off down the street.

Levi's dad, Mark, stands on the veranda for a few minutes, staring after Levi's car. The way he has his hands clenched at his sides suggests he's not too happy with his son.

When he goes inside, I leave the window and grab my art history book from my bed. At my desk, I sit and turn to the section on Modernism, getting lost in the various artworks and making notes as I read. I can't concentrate for long though, and my mind keeps wandering to Levi, so I grab my journal, flip it open to a new page, and start writing.

I'm worried about Levi. He's … being weird. His parents are yelling at him. He's yelling at them. He's drinking. I wish we were still friends so I could ask him what's going on. If I can do anything to help.

Then there's Veronica. Truth or dare … such a stupid

game. I have no idea which one to choose. Maybe not thinking about it is best. Maybe I should just make a decision when and if I finally have to.

I sit back in my chair and stare at the page, chewing on the end of my pen. There are so many more thoughts I want to get down on paper, but my head is so full I don't know where to start.

The sound of a car engine brings me back to reality, and I glance at my clock. It's quarter past nine. I want to go to the window to see if it's Levi coming home, but I'm tired and I need to finish this chapter on Modernism before I turn in. I flip my journal closed and read for a few more minutes. I end up reading the same line five times.

I shake my head and laugh at myself. What is wrong with me? I've never been this distracted before when it comes to study.

I push my chair away from the desk and stare at the carpet beneath my feet. Using my toes to push off, I spin my chair around and around until I'm dizzy. Focussing on the dizziness helps me put everything out of my mind.

"I think the bougainvillea needs cutting back." Levi's voice startles me. His leg comes through the window, and he blurs as I spin. "It's hard to get my toes into the trellis."

I plant my feet on the floor and stop, gripping the sides of my seat. I stare at him and chew my bottom lip.

"Are you drunk this time? Because if you are, you can get out now."

"Nice to see you too, Katie."

"You could use the front door like a normal person." I scowl.

"That would take the fun out of it." Levi sits on the window seat with a goofy grin on his face. "Want me to spin you again?"

"What are you doing?" I stare at the open window behind him so I don't have to look into his eyes. They will undo me. "Why are you here?"

Levi runs a hand through his messy hair then stands and takes a step towards me. I roll my chair backwards until it hits my desk. Levi shoves his hands into his pockets and looks at his feet.

"Can we … I want to … Katie." His hand goes through his hair again and he lets out a long breath. "I want to apologise."

Levi looks up, and our eyes meet.

I take a deep breath. "Why?" My voice sounds small, like it has fallen into a huge canyon with me on one side and Levi on the other.

"Because … Veronica hurt you. I want to make sure you're okay."

"Since when do you care?" I ask. "You made it perfectly clear the day I started at *your* school what you expect from me."

A light tap sounds on my bedroom door and I look at Levi with wide eyes. I jump up and yank the wardrobe door open, shoving him inside. The hangers clink together as he falls into them. My parents aren't that strict, but they still don't allow boys in my room, especially at this time of night.

"Katie, honey?" Mum pushes the door open and I meet her at the threshold. "Is everything okay? I heard voices."

"Fine, Mum." I pull my phone from my pocket. "I was

talking to Karen." She looks at my hand and frowns. "We hung up."

Mum opens the door wider. "Okay. Don't stay up too late."

Dad comes up the stairs and stops beside Mum. "You girls off to bed?"

"What's this? A family meeting?" Daniel sticks his head out of his room across the hall.

"Just saying goodnight," Mum says. "I'll see you two in the morning." She gives me a quick kiss. Dad ruffles my hair and follows Mum to their bedroom.

Daniel watches me from his doorway, waiting for Mum and Dad's door to close.

"Who's in there, Katie?" he whispers.

I chew the edge of my thumbnail. "Would you believe me if I said no one?"

He shakes his head and comes to my door, studying my room. "Bed or wardrobe?"

"Daniel …"

"You forget I'm two years older than you. If you've done it, I've probably done it a hundred times already."

"Please don't say anything."

Daniel chuckles and kisses me on the forehead. "Don't do anything stupid, but tell him if he hurts you, I'll break him." He says it loud enough so Levi can hear.

The door makes a soft click when I close it.

"You can come out now." I pick up the books from my bed and stack them on my desk. I sit near my pillow and cross my legs, hugging my favourite stuffed bunny to my chest.

The wardrobe door opens, and Levi sticks his head

out. "That was close."

"You're lucky I have an awesome brother."

"I know how great Daniel is. He and Mason ..." Levi shakes his head and comes to sit so he's facing me, one leg on the bed and the other resting so his foot is on the floor. He's quiet for a minute, staring at his hands. I really want him to leave, but I want him to stay, too.

"Katie—"

"You should go." I put my bunny in his place against the wall.

I don't need to hear what he has to say. No apology from him will fix the way Veronica treats me, or the way he has treated me, so what's the point? And being near him is exhausting. I can't handle the way I feel about him, because I love him and I hate him at the same time. It's too much.

"Can I stay and just ..." He shrugs. "I don't know, talk?"

"About what? I have nothing to say to you."

Levi pulls his other leg onto the bed and crosses them, mimicking me. "You were nice to me on Saturday night, even though—"

"You climbed up the side of my house and fell through my window. Drunk."

Levi sighs. "You're right. I should go."

He gets up from the bed and I do, too, but he hasn't stepped back to give me enough space. I stare at his chest. His T-shirt hugs the curves of his shoulders, and it's not until he clears his throat that I realise I've been staring too long. I drag my gaze away from him and look to the side towards the window. Heat rises in my cheeks and I fidget with the hem of my top, waiting for him to move.

He doesn't.

"I really am sorry," Levi says.

"You can't control Veronica's actions. But you can control your own." I finally get up the courage to look at him again. "Why are you friends with her?"

"Veronica is a tough nut, but she really can be nice. And we've been friends since year seven."

I laugh then clap my hand over my mouth. "If you think what she did to me is 'nice', then you're crazy." I move away from him, suddenly unable to breathe properly. "I've been your friend since birth, and you ditched me."

Levi sits on the bed again and rubs his face with his hands. I sit in my desk chair. It doesn't look like he's going to leave, so I swivel around and open my art history book to where I left off. We sit like that, in the quiet, for a while. I can feel him watching me, but I don't look in his direction.

When I realise I've read the same page three times over, I take my glasses off and clean them on the hem of my top. From the corner of my eye I catch Levi smiling, but I ignore him and put my glasses back on.

"You look nice without your specs," Levi says. "They hide your eyes."

Heat floods my cheeks and I let my hair fall across my face. "If you insist on staying, please be quiet."

Levi lies on the bed, his head on my pillow, and picks up my bunny. He plays with its ears, flopping them back and forth, before setting it back in its place. He folds his hands behind his head and stares at the ceiling.

"The stars up there," Levi says, "do they still glow?"

"I said, quiet."

"Okay, okay. I can handle quiet. It's a refreshing change."

The tone of his voice hints at sadness, and I wonder what's getting him down.

There seems to be something going on with his family, but how do I ask him if he's okay when we haven't been close for so long? It's been a while since Mason died, and we never talked about it, because when it happened, Levi had already cut me off. Maybe he just misses his brother. Even though I'd gone to the funeral, and I'd wanted to offer him my condolences, I didn't know how. I figured he wouldn't have wanted to talk to me anyway. Maybe I should talk to him about it now, because if it was me and I'd lost Daniel, no amount of time would ever fix the pain.

"Where were you this afternoon?" I ask, keeping my eyes on my text book.

Levi rolls onto his side and props himself up on his elbow. "Headmistress's office. Then I came home."

When I look at him, his eyes are cast down at the doona cover. He runs his finger around the edge of one of the butterflies in the pattern.

"Mrs Pritchard questioned me about ..." He raises his head and points to his cheek.

I sit back in my chair and swivel to face him. "What did you tell her?"

"I fell over and face-planted the garden path." He drops his gaze back to the bed. "I don't think she believed me."

"But that's exactly what you did."

"Apparently, they think I was in a fight, or someone hit me."

"That's ... crazy. Isn't it?"

Levi locks his gaze on mine. "Not so crazy if you've been through what my family has."

"Do you want to talk about ... you know?"

"You mean Mason?"

I stay quiet. Yes, I mean Mason, but I don't want to push him. I'm glad we're talking again, even though it is in secret, and I don't want him to clam up on me.

"It's okay. We don't have to talk about him." I rub my knees with my hands, then twist my fingers together. Levi stays silent. "Did Veronica tell you what else she did to me today?"

"There's more?" Levi sits and swings his legs over the edge of the bed.

"Truth or dare." I stare at him.

His mouth opens. "She didn't."

"She did."

We stare at each other, and I have no idea what to say next. I want to ask him if he'll play with me now. I have so many questions I want answered, but I don't think he'll agree.

"What did you tell her?"

"I haven't told her anything," I say. "And I'm not going to."

Levi stands up. "No, Katie. You can't do that. You think Ronnie was bad today? You have no idea what she's capable of."

"Yeah, I do. I was there when Karen got suspended. Remember?"

"You have to choose." He sits down again.

"I don't want to."

"Now is not the time to be stubborn."

"Come on, Levi," I say. "What's the worst she can do to me?"

"She can ruin your reputation."

I laugh. "What reputation?"

Levi goes quiet and stares at me, his brow knitted. He presses his lips together and rubs his face with his hand.

He sits on the edge of the bed, his back straight, and puts his hands on his knees. "What would you choose if I asked you?"

"What? No. I'm not choosing."

"Come on, Katie. Truth or dare?"

I stare at him, my mouth slightly open, unsure what to say. A moment ago, I wanted to play with him, but this could go in my favour or it could all go terribly wrong. On the other hand, if he truth or dares me, then I can do it back to him.

"I'll do this on one condition," I say. "You play, too."

"Okay." Levi waits, and his eyes bore into me.

"Dare." My heart pounds. *What have I done?*

Levi raises his eyebrows. "Is that what you would have chosen for Veronica?"

"I'm not answering that. Now dare me to do something."

"Stand up." Levi gets to his feet and takes my hand, pulling me from my chair. "I dare you to kiss me."

A puff of air leaves my mouth and I go tense. I pull my fingers from Levi's grasp. *What the hell?*

He smirks, and I want to punch him.

"You want me to kiss you?"

"No. Yes. Maybe." Levi laughs. "I want you to think your way around the dare. There's always an out. A way for you to complete the dare, but not in the way the person who dares you is expecting. So … Kiss me.”

I bite my lip and step towards Levi. His lips are slightly parted and the white of his teeth peeks through. I've fantasised about kissing him a million times, and now he's dared me to, I want to so badly, but I also know that it's not the real reason he's dared me to do it.

I push up with my toes and plant a soft kiss on his cheek. His stubble scratches my lips, and his pine scent makes me a little dizzy. I grab his forearms to stop myself from falling into him.

“Does that count?” I ask.

“That totally counts.” He grins, and I can't help grinning, too.

I sit back in my chair before my knees buckle and I fall over.

We're quiet for a few minutes. I try to take even breaths because my heart is hammering so fast Levi must be able to hear it.

“I should say dare to Veronica,” I say. “But what if it's something I can't get around like I did … kissing you?”

“You could always take truth, and then lie.” Levi shrugs. “She'll want to embarrass you no matter which way you go.”

“But I'm a terrible liar. And what if she asks me something I can't lie about?” I press my lips together. “I'll think on it. But now it's your turn. Truth or dare, Levi?”

He lies back on my bed, taking up the same position as before with his hands tucked behind his head. He crosses his legs at the ankles and looks up at the ceiling. “Truth.”

I sit up straighter. I wasn't expecting him to choose truth. I figured he'd go with the dare because he'd think I was too nice to ask him to do anything horrible.

I sift through my thoughts, and all the questions I've wanted to ask him over the years, trying to find the one I want answered the most. This could be my only chance to get something from him. Something other than rejection.

I take a deep breath, and finally ask, "Do you ever think we can be friends again?"

Levi turns to look at me. A small smile plays at his lips and I want to look away because I'm embarrassed, but I hold his gaze.

"I thought you'd ask me why I did what I did to you," he says.

"I know why you did it, Levi."

I hold my breath, waiting for his answer, and I realise I'm not really sure what I want it to be. But maybe it's not a question of what I want, but rather, what I need.

"Yes, Katie." Levi's smile widens. "My answer is yes."

4

That bitch will never see you coming

The rest of the first week back at school goes by quickly. Veronica pretty much leaves me alone all week, bar a few snide comments and occasional death stares, and Levi does, too. The latter I'm not very happy about, especially since he told me we could be friends again.

I'm guessing he didn't mean straight away.

Levi doesn't climb in my window again all week, and the most I get from him in the halls is a nod or a close-lipped smile. The more I think about him, the more things I find to be annoyed about. He obviously doesn't remember the conversation we had when he climbed in my window drunk, because he hasn't asked for any help with study. And now, it's the weekend, and only one week until trial exams.

A bang pulls me from my thoughts.

"Katie?" Dad says.

I shake my head and stare at my father, then at the garden rake resting at a funny angle against the side of the house.

"Sorry, what?" I bend and retrieve the tool I'd been using.

Dad chuckles. "Where did you go? Lost you for a minute there."

"Just thinking." I rake some bougainvillea clippings away from the side of the house.

"Tell me again why you want this thing cut back?" Dad hacks at a particularly stubborn branch.

"They scratch the house at night," I say. "It's … creepy."

Which is the best excuse I can come up with. I'm not about to tell Dad I want easier access for Levi to climb up to my bedroom. *If* he ever does again.

A door slams, and I turn towards Levi's house. He's standing on his veranda, watching Dad prune the plant that clings to the trellis on the side of our house. Levi jumps down the steps in two leaps and heads towards us, a lopsided grin on his face.

"Morning, Katie, Bill. Need any help?" he asks.

I stare at him with wide eyes. What the hell is he doing?

Dad stops cutting and holds the sheers at his side. "I think I've got it covered. How are you, Levi?" Dad's forehead creases, and he throws me a questioning glace before turning back to torment the bougainvillea.

"Fine, thanks." Levi rocks on his heels. "Katie, can I talk to you?"

I don't want to talk to him. He's avoided me most of

the week, and I'm not about to let him think he can just come over here and be all 'oh, we're friends again' when none of his mates are around to see.

I chew my lip and frown, then turn and walk away before my mouth opens and something comes out that I'll probably regret, or that I shouldn't say in front of my dad.

Levi follows me to the front door, and when I try to close the screen he jams his foot in the gap.

"Katie, what's the matter?" he asks.

"Please leave." How can I explain to him that I'm hurt and angry when he probably won't even know why?

"Did you ask your dad to cut the bougainvillea back?"

"You haven't spoken to me all week," I say.

"I ..." He frowns. "It's not that simple."

"Really?" I yank the screen door so it squashes his foot.

A silver Subaru pulls into Levi's driveway, and the driver honks the horn. Levi glances over his shoulder then pulls his foot from the door. It slams shut because I'm still pulling on the handle. I glare at him through the mesh.

Jarred gets out of the car and leans against the bonnet.

"Go on," I say. "Better not let him see you over here. Who knows what rumours might spread?"

Levi turns back to me, his jaw clenched. I can't look at him, so I slam our heavy front door in his face.

"What's all the noise about?" Mum calls from the kitchen.

"Nothing." I race upstairs to my room and slam that door, too.

From my open window I look down onto the yard. Levi talks to Dad, then helps him put a few branches into the garden bin. He jogs over to Jarred who has moved to the veranda steps. They clap each other on the back in that stupid way guys do. Jarred says something while looking up at my window, and I quickly draw the curtains before stepping back.

The room is darker, but I don't mind. It matches my mood. I flop onto my bed and grab my bunny, hugging it to my chest. Why do people have to suck so much?

My journal is sitting on the edge of my desk so I reach over and grab it. It's funny because I'm not sure what I want to write down, but when my pen hits the paper the words come more easily than I thought they would.

He tells me we can be friends again, then he ignores me! What a joke. Why did I even bother getting my hopes up? I don't fit in Levi's world anymore. Did I ever really fit there in the first place?

The whole 'truth or dare' thing is eating at me, too. Why do they make such a big deal of playing a game where the only objective is to humiliate people? If I choose truth, what will Veronica ask me? What if it's something I can't lie convincingly about? What if it's Something about Levi? I'm not sure if I could ever be prepared to answer any questions to do with him. If I choose dare, it might be embarrassing, but at least I won't have to bare my soul.

My phone vibrates on my desk and I reach over to grab it. Karen's name flashes on the screen with a picture of her I took when we went bowling a few months ago. I'm not sure I'm in the mood for talking at the moment. All I feel like doing is wallowing in self-pity.

I swipe the screen anyway. "Hey, you."

"Hey. I was about to hang up," Karen says. "Why so gloomy?"

"Levi was just here."

"Get. Out! Why?"

I'm not sure how to answer. She sounds as surprised as I was when Levi fell through my window a week ago. We've been best friends for a long time. Karen knows all there is to know about what's happened and hasn't happened between Levi and me. Except for the stuff I haven't told her about this week.

"He saw Dad cutting the bougainvillea back and came over. Then he offered to help."

"Why is your dad cutting back ...?" Karen squeals. "Oh my God. Did he?"

"Did he what?" I ask, knowing full well what she means.

"Did he climb in your window?"

"He ... might have."

Karen squeals again. "Oh my God!"

"Stop saying that. It's not as big a deal as you think. The guy's a jerk."

"So, you didn't talk to him just now?"

"No," I say. "I told him to leave me alone, and then I slammed the door in his face."

"Oh, Katie." Karen sighs.

"Jarred turned up, and he saw Levi talking to me. The minute that happened, Levi changed back to the rich kid who's too good to be seen with me."

Karen groans. "I really don't like Jarred."

"You're using nice words. That's unlike you."

"I'm saving all the bad ones for the next time he's a dick to you."

I smile. I love how Karen can make me feel so much better just by talking to me about stupid stuff. But I also can't help wondering why some people are like they are. Why do people like Jarred and Veronica single out people like me and Karen? I guess it's a power thing, but I just don't get it. What did I ever do to make them hate me? I mind my own business, but because I'm not rich like them I'm a target.

"Why do you think Veronica hates me so much?" I ask Karen.

"She's jealous."

"That's funny. Of what? I'm not rich. I don't have a car. I'm hardly a supermodel—"

"Stop right there," Karen says. "You're beautiful. And you're smart. And Levi is your next-door neighbour. There are plenty of things for Veronica to be jealous about. You know, because you've got me as a best friend, too."

I burst out laughing and fall back onto my bed, putting my hand over my mouth. "Yep, she'd definitely be jealous of that."

Mum used to tell me people picked on others because they liked them, but I stopped believing that by the time I got to high school.

"What are you doing today?" Karen asks.

"Apart from butchering my favourite plant, studying."

"Get ready—we're going out. I'll pick you up in fifteen."

"What? No. I don't want to go anywhere."

"Come on, Katie," Karen pleads. "We'll go to the shops. I'll buy you a hot chocolate. We'll window shop. It'll be fun."

I roll over on my pillow and rest my ear on my phone. The last thing I feel like doing is following Karen around the shops. But I could use the company, and I'm not sure I can focus on study anyway, not after my encounter with Levi.

"Okay," I say. "I'll see you soon."

I stand in front of my wardrobe for ten minutes and still can't decide what to wear. Late July is always chilly, but I know I'll get hot traipsing around the shops. I opt for the jeans I already have on, and the prettiest top I own—a turquoise number with little pink flowers on it. It's sleeveless, so I grab my favourite cream cardigan and hope I won't be too cold.

I rip the elastic out of my hair and fluff it a bit so it sits around my shoulders, then I coat my lips with gloss, and adjust my glasses, wishing I didn't need them.

I take them off for a second and stare at my face in the full-length mirror on my wardrobe door, remembering what Levi said about my glasses hiding my eyes. With a sigh, I put them back on. There's no reason for me to listen to him. It's not like I need to impress him. He's not my boyfriend.

A car horn honks, and I run to the window. Karen is sitting behind the wheel of her mum's car, stopped at the kerb. I shove my feet into my worn black Converse, grab my tote, and slip my wallet, phone, and cardigan inside, then run downstairs to the kitchen.

"Mum? I'm going to the shops with Karen."

"Okay, honey." She looks up from where she's sitting

at the kitchen counter, reading a magazine. "Have fun."

I grab my house keys from the bowl on the hall table and head outside. Levi and Jarred are leaning on Jarred's car, talking. They stop as soon as they see me, but I don't make eye contact with them.

Dad puts down his pruning shears and meets me at the kerb. "Where are you girls off to, Katie?"

"We're going to the shops." I glance around the yard. "You don't need me?"

"Nah, you go and have fun. Just be home for dinner."

"Hey," Karen says through her open window.

"Hi, Karen," Dad says. He smiles, then pulls his wallet from his back pocket, taking out a twenty and handing it to me.

I'm aware of Levi and Jarred watching us, but I resist the urge to look at them. "Dad, no. I don't need any money."

"You're the strangest teenager, Katie. Take it. You can buy yourself some lunch."

I give him a kiss on the cheek and stuff the money in my tote bag. I hate taking money from my parents. We don't have much, and everything that's spare they use to make up the difference for my education. The scholarship only covers so much. But I don't want to make a scene in front of Levi and Jarred. I resist the urge again to look in their direction. Levi's stare melts me, like hot lava. Or at least it feels that way. I have no idea if he's actually looking.

"Someone's checking you out," Karen says as I slide into the passenger seat.

He's looking!

"He's not checking me out. He's probably plotting

something humiliating. Something to dare me for when I finally answer Veronica."

"You're going to accept the dare? Not take truth?" Karen asks.

I look at my best friend and try to catch a glimpse of Levi from the corner of my eye. "I don't know what I'm going to do yet."

Karen blatantly looks in Levi and Jarred's direction. "He's totally watching you."

"Is not."

"Is too. Because you're hot."

"I'm cold, actually." I pull my cardigan from my bag and slip it on before buckling my seatbelt. "And Levi never felt that way about me. If he did, he never would have dumped me as a friend."

"Then why is he looking at you as if he could eat you up?"

"Karen! I am the last person Levi wants. Would you just … drive?"

Karen frowns and puts her mum's Suzuki Swift into first. "Okay then. Let's get some retail therapy. Shopping fixes everything."

It takes us twenty minutes to get to the closest Westfield shopping centre. Karen cranks the music and we sing along at the top of our lungs.

Karen parks the car and we make our way through the steady stream of shoppers, past the smaller shops and outside to the mall towards our favourite café. We grab a takeaway hot chocolate each before heading back inside.

"We should look for formal dresses," Karen says.

"I thought we were going to do that with Jess and Stacey."

"They won't mind." Karen slips her arm through mine. "We can all go shopping again another weekend."

I follow Karen around for an hour. She lives for this kind of thing, but I can never really get into it. What's the point when I can't afford to buy anything anyway?

I let Karen ooh and aah over all the pretty dresses. She tries a couple on, and my stomach growls as Karen changes out of a deep purple pencil dress.

She opens the stall door, her eyebrows raised. "Lunch?"

I nod. "I'd love to find a dress that colour for the formal. Or something with purple in it at least."

Karen puts the dress back on the hanger. "This cut won't suit you. But we'll find something else."

We give the dresses back to the sales lady, who frowns, and giggle as we leave the shop.

"Not sure we should go back there," I say.

"Yes, we will. There are a few dresses I think you should try on. But first, food." Karen pulls me in the direction of the food court. When we get there, most of the seats are taken. We spot one free table in the middle, so Karen runs off to save it while I line up.

At the pizza place, I pass the few minutes I have to stand there by glancing around the food court. My heart beats faster when I spot Levi and Jarred on the other side, lined up for burgers. I wipe my sweaty palms on my jeans and face the front of the line, hoping they haven't seen me.

I'm almost at the front when I feel someone's presence behind me.

"I hear the pepperoni is really good," Levi says.

I turn to look at him.

Levi rocks on his heels, one hand gripping a takeaway paper bag, the other stuffed into the pocket of his jeans. He glances over his shoulder, his gaze darting around as if he's looking for someone.

I stare at him in disbelief. "Are you feeling okay?" I ask before I can stop myself.

"Fine. Why?"

I glance around. "Aren't you worried Jarred will see you talking to me?"

"He's gone to the bathroom."

I eye Levi sideways. Just because Jarred is in the bathroom doesn't mean he won't see us. Boys pee really fast. I'm pretty sure he'll be back soon. I have no idea why I'm so worried though. It's not like *my* reputation is on the line.

I step up to the counter and order two slices of vegetarian pizza and some garlic bread. Asking Levi what he wants is on the tip of my tongue, but I stay silent. Right now, I don't really trust myself not to say something stupid or mean. And I don't want to be either of those people.

After paying for my food, I walk away from Levi towards Karen. Levi follows, and I'm not sure what to do. Telling him to go away crosses my mind, but I decide to let this play out and see what happens.

Karen's eyes widen when she sees who is walking behind me, and I give her my best 'please keep your mouth shut' look, hoping she'll understand what I'm asking of her from my contorted facial expression. I slide the tray with our pizza on it onto the table and sit down across from her.

Levi glances around again, his jaw clenched, and his lips pressed together. My stomach churns with anger and I don't feel so hungry anymore.

"If you're worried about someone seeing you with us, then why don't you go away?" I ask.

I hate that he can make me feel this way, and I wish it didn't affect me so much. I want things between us to be like they used to, but I need to wake up, because it's never going to happen. Levi was everything to me. Now he's just a guy I used to be friends with. I can't keep kidding myself and thinking everything will magically go back to how it was. I want him back, but at the same time, I want him to go away so I can breathe.

"What do you want, Levi?" Karen asks, then takes a bite from her pizza.

Mine sits in front of me untouched. I grab my garlic bread and tear a piece off, but I don't eat it.

"Um ... I ..." Levi sets his paper bag on the table and runs a hand through his hair, making my insides flip. "Katie, I ..."

"Oh my God, spit it out," Karen says.

Levi pulls a chair over from the table next to us and sits down. "Exams are next week. I was wondering if ... you know?"

"You want me to help you study?" I don't look at him. I stare at my garlic bread and the film of butter on my fingertips.

"Only if it's no trouble."

I finally look at him. "Sure."

"Okay then. Thanks." Levi stands and grabs his lunch.

"You better shoo before Jarred catches you talking to us and the world ends." Karen waves her hand at him, then goes back to eating her pizza. Levi walks away, and Karen watches him from the corner of her eye until he's out of hearing range. Then she turns on me. "What the hell?"

"You know how I told you—"

"Levi climbed in your window?"

"Yeah … well, I also offered to tutor him for History." I shove the piece of garlic bread in my mouth so I don't have to talk anymore.

Food in her mouth doesn't stop Karen. "That means you can spend more time with him," she says through a mouthful of pizza.

"It's not a big deal." I wipe my hands on a paper napkin.

"You're kidding me, right? Has he climbed in your window more than once?"

I raise my eyebrows. "Maybe."

Karen sits forward in her chair. "You're going to tell me everything, and we're not moving until you're done."

"Twice. He's climbed up twice. The first time he was drunk, and … it's a long story."

Karen glares at me. "I don't care if we have to sit here until tomorrow. Spill."

"You know how he hurt his face? Well, he fell down the veranda steps. His mum was pretty upset." I stop and think back to the night Levi climbed up the second time. He hadn't been drunk, but he had been angry. "The second time I think he'd had a fight with his dad. There was yelling."

"Did he tell you what the fight was about?" Karen asks.

"No … but we did play truth or dare." I stare at my best friend. "He dared me to kiss him, and I asked him if we would ever be friends again."

"Get. Out!" Karen hits me on the arm, then sits back in her chair. "What did you do? What did he say?"

"I kissed him, and he said yes."

Karen's mouth hangs open. "You kissed—"

"Don't get too excited—it was on the cheek. He wanted to prove a point."

"Being?" Karen rolls her hand through the air.

"That there's an out for every dare. You just have to think of a way to do what you've been dared to do, but not how the darer is expecting."

Karen raises her eyebrows. "Veronica?"

I nod. "I think I'm going to choose dare."

Karen laughs. "That bitch will never see you coming."

5

The bed can be
Switzerland if you like

Levi didn't climb in my window on Monday night like I expected him to. A little bit of hope fell away on Tuesday when he didn't show. On Wednesday, I tried to ignore the empty feeling in my stomach when I turned my light out at ten pm and he hadn't come. By Thursday, I'd given up completely, and I spent the night at Karen's place, studying with her.

On Friday, I was pretty pissed off with Levi.

And Veronica had been giving me hell all week, pushing me for an answer. The more she pushed, the more I didn't want to give her one.

Now, the last bell for the day rings and I pack up my math books. Double Math on a Friday afternoon is pure torture, especially when all we've been doing is revision for the past two weeks. Exams start on Monday, and I think I'm ready, but I'm nervous, too. Everything I've worked so hard for starts now. Everyone keeps telling me I'll get dux, but I've been so distracted that I'm not as confident as I have been in the past. Maybe writing my speech was a waste of time.

I shoulder my bag, and head out to meet Karen.

"Why so blue?" she asks as I walk towards her. She's leaning against a tree on the nature strip outside the gate.

"It is that obvious?" I hug my folder to my chest as if it's a shield.

"Your face is all screwed up."

"Thanks." I laugh.

"That's better. Come on. I don't want to miss the train."

We hit the footpath to start our ten-minute walk up the hill when a horn blares.

"Hey, Katie," Veronica yells.

I turn towards the sound of her voice. She's across the street, hanging out the back driver's side window of Levi's BMW.

I take a deep breath and stop on the kerb. "Yes, Veronica?"

"Get in." She thumbs over her shoulder to indicate I should cross the road and get in the car.

She's crazy.

"I'm fine, thanks." I slip my arm through Karen's and start walking again.

"What are you doing?" Karen whispers. "Get in the car."

I stop. "What? No."

"Katie." Levi's voice travels across the street.

"He wants you to get in," Karen says.

"I'm not getting into his car." I clench my teeth.

"He hasn't climbed in your window all week. So yes,

you are." Karen spins me around so I'm facing Levi.

"You want a ride?" He raises his eyebrows, and my stomach flutters.

Why does he have to look so hot? And be so irresistible?

"If you give Karen a lift, too, then yes," I say.

"Sure. Hop in."

I pull Karen across the street.

"I really don't need to come," she says.

"I'm not leaving you here."

We reach the other side of the road, and Jarred gets out of the front passenger seat, a scowl on his face. He leaves his door open and puts his hand out for me to get in. If he didn't look so angry, I would have called it a gentlemanly move. He yanks the back door open and climbs in.

Karen stoops so she's staring at Veronica. "I'm not sitting in the back with her."

"Get in, bitch," she says.

"Just … get in, Karen," I say.

I dump my bag in the foot well, slide into the front passenger seat, and pull the door closed. I look at Levi and he smiles. I shake my head. His smile drops away.

I turn and look at Veronica. "You call Karen a bitch again and I'll—"

"What?" Veronica asks. "What will you do, bitch?"

"Ronnie, that's enough," Levi says. He gives her a death stare in the rear-view mirror. It makes me feel a little better, but I'm itching to say something back to her.

On the way home, I gaze out the window because I don't want to look at Levi. When I'm this close to him, my anger is replaced with hope. If I look at him, that hope will probably turn to longing, and then I'll be done for.

I catch sight of Karen in the side mirror. She pulls a funny face and I giggle.

"Care to share?" Veronica asks.

"Not with you," I say.

Karen bursts out laughing.

"What?" Veronica asks. "What's so funny?"

I turn in my seat, and the scowl on Veronica's face makes her look ugly. She's quite pretty, and if she smiled more it would do her the world of good.

"Wouldn't you like to know?" I say.

"Can you drive faster, Levi? I need to get out of this car," Jarred says.

He's squashed between Karen and Veronica, and seeing how uncomfortable he is makes me laugh harder.

"I'm not having much fun either," Karen says, through fits of giggles.

"Sounds like you are." Levi glances at me.

I stop laughing and go back to staring out the window.

Levi turns off the highway down a wide tree-lined street, taking the first right and then the next left. He stops outside a house that would fit mine in it three times.

"Catch you bitches later." Veronica throws her door open. She gets out and comes to my window, rolling her hand for me to wind it down.

I press the electric button and the window whirs. "What?"

"Truth or dare, Katie?"

"Give it a rest," I say. "You'll get your answer when I'm ready."

"I want it now." She leans down and puts her hand

on the car, gripping the edge of the door through the open window.

"Well, we don't always get what we want." I stare at her. I'm tired of letting her intimidate me. It's time to give her a taste of her own medicine.

She clenches her teeth. "When, then?"

I tap my cheek as if in thought, raising my eyebrows. "After exams."

"That's two weeks away!"

"Yep."

"Take it or leave it," Karen says from the back seat.

"This is *not* how it works." Veronica straightens. "Tell her, Levi. We don't play this way."

"I do," I say. "If you want my answer, you'll have to wait."

"Let it go, Ronnie." Levi grips the steering wheel.

"Whatever." Veronica turns around and walks up the path leading to her house, or rather, her mansion.

We drive again, taking a few more right and left turns until I'm lost, and we drop Jarred off. His place is just as flashy as Veronica's, complete with swimming pool and tennis court. My house looks like a shack in comparison.

Since I started private school, I've learnt that there are three kinds of people: the rich ones, the not as rich, and then there's me. Levi is somewhere in the middle of the rich and the not as rich, but he has looks and charm, so everyone loves him. Karen is at the lower end of the not as rich, and I'm the one who could only afford private school on a scholarship.

Thinking about the class distinctions upsets me, so I go back to staring out the window, waiting for this stupid car ride to be over. Suddenly, I don't want to be anywhere near Levi, and I can't believe I ever got into the car with him in the first place.

"Can we just go home, please?" I lean my elbow on the open window and rest my head against the seat.

We turn back onto the highway. Karen's place isn't far from mine and Levi's, and it's on the way. When we stop at the kerb, she unbuckles her seatbelt and leans forward between the two front seats.

"You need to stop being a dick, Levi, and pull your head out of your arse."

Levi and I both turn to the middle to look at my best friend. My mouth hangs open, ready to give her a serve, but Levi talks first.

"You're right." He glances at me. "I am a dick, and a jerk, and an arse, too." He smiles.

"Okay, then." Karen opens her door and gets out. She walks backwards up her path with her bag hanging from one hand. She points two fingers at her eyes, and then at Levi.

"I have no doubt she's watching me," Levi says, quietly.

"She's always had my back." I lean my head against the seat again and close my eyes. I don't want to see the expression on Levi's face, but I hope he gets that I'm angry with him. I have to take a deep breath, because thinking about it and being so close to him makes me really sad. Can I ever trust him? If we do fix our friendship like he said we could, how will I know he won't hurt me all over again? Am I setting myself up for another disaster?

The car turns and comes to a stop. "We're home."

I open my eyes and stare at Levi's house. "Thanks for the lift."

He kills the engine and jumps out, coming around to my side of the car before I've managed to get my bag and folder sorted. Levi opens the door and takes my bag from me. I frown but let him help me out of the car.

We stand on the driveway, looking everywhere but at each other.

"Can I have my bag?" I clutch my folder to my chest.

Levi hands it to me. "You, um …" He glances at his front door. "Want to come inside?"

I look over to my house, and I feel like running straight up to my room, and never speaking to him again. I want my safe place, and right now being with Levi is not it.

I push my glasses up my nose and tuck my hair behind my ear.

"We can study," Levi says.

I laugh. "You want to study now? Exams start on Monday. It's a bit late."

"History is my worst subject. I should be fine with the others."

"Well, you should've come study with me before."

Levi smiles, but it doesn't reach his eyes. "It's okay. I can do it on my own." He turns and heads for the veranda. I wait until his foot hits the top step.

"Levi," I call out. "Mum and Dad won't be home until later. I've got an hour or so."

He turns, his smile widening. "Okay."

"Okay."

I take a deep breath and follow Levi into the foyer of his house.

His mum has it decorated like a show home. It's always been like that, but it's been so long since I've stepped foot inside that the clinical feeling surprises me. There's no warmth. It doesn't feel like a home. It's just a house.

I glance up the stairs to the second storey. Levi's bedroom door is open. I try to remember the last time I was in his room, and I can't.

"Want something to drink?" Levi asks.

I nod and follow him into the kitchen, dumping my bag on the huge timber dining table that sits in the open-plan family room. Levi opens the fridge, and I pull up one of the bar stools at the kitchen bench.

"Coke? Lemonade?" He looks at me around the fridge door.

"Water, thanks."

Levi brings out a jug of chilled water and a can of Coke, then sets them on the bench. He pops the can and takes a swig, grabs a glass from the cupboard in the corner, and pours me a water. We stare at each other across the bench, and I can't help thinking that even though we're so close physically, he still feels so far away. I want to close the gap, but I'm not sure how.

I sip my water. "So … why do you struggle with History?"

Levi puts his can down and leans on the bench with both hands. "I can never remember all the details."

"It's not that difficult. You just have to associate what you want to remember with something already familiar."

Levi raises his eyebrows. "How?"

"It's called the Roman Room method. You choose a room in your house you know really well, then you pick an object and use it to associate certain pieces of information."

Levi stands up straight and folds his arms. "A room in my house?"

"It can be any room. For instance, my bed is Pompeii, and my pillow is Vesuvius. And each of my soft toys is assigned a piece of information."

"You made your bed Pompeii?"

I laugh. "It's a really easy and effective technique. You should try it."

Levi walks to the door that leads back into the foyer. "Come on then. Let's go make my bed Pompeii."

I hesitate and bite my lip. "You don't want to study down here?"

"My room is the room I know the best." He leans against the doorjamb. "The bed can be Switzerland if you like."

6

Bring it, bitch

We didn't end up going to Levi's bedroom. I told him I was more comfortable studying at his kitchen bench, and he didn't push me. For some reason, the thought of being in his room was different to having him in mine—maybe because it's out of my comfort zone.

Exams fly past in a two-week haze of study at night and information regurgitation during the day. The weekend in between is filled with more study, and Levi has mastered the climb up the trellis. He comes over most nights, and we fall into a routine of two hours on the books followed by an hour of talking.

Levi also drives me to school some mornings. He offers to do it every day, but I tell him I'm not about to completely ditch Jessica and Karen. I secretly hope he finds some meaning in that. Veronica is horrified on the mornings

I'm in the car before her, but she mostly leaves me alone. Other than reminding me I owe her an answer after our last exam.

I haven't forgotten.

Now, it's the last day of exams, and thinking about Veronica is making me ill. I don't want today to end, because I don't want to choose. But I will, because I'm not afraid of her, and I said I would.

Dad watches me from across the table.

"Why are you looking at me funny?" I take a bite of my toast.

"No reason." He adjusts his morning paper and it rustles. "What's the deal with you and Levi?"

My mouth hangs open. "What do you mean? We're just friends."

"Maybe. When you were ten. I've seen the way he looks at you. I was a teenager once, too, you know."

I look at Mum, but she shrugs and takes a big gulp of coffee, raising her eyebrows over the top of her cup.

"Well, there's no *deal*. We're—"

"Just friends?" Daniel saunters into the kitchen and grabs a banana from the fruit bowl.

Dad sips his coffee and feigns thoughtfulness. "Cutting back the bougainvillea had nothing to do with access to the trellis then?"

I almost choke on my toast. "I ... what? ... No!"

Mum tries to hide a smirk with a hand over her mouth.

Dad sets his paper down and places his hands on the table. "Katie, honey, I know he's climbed in your window more than once, and he's lucky I haven't strangled him."

"But ... he used to do it all the time when we were

younger.”

“That was before he started looking at you like …” Dad takes a deep breath. “Do we need to have the facts-of-life talk again?”

“Oh my God, no!” I say. Daniel laughs, and I glare at him. “Did you tell them?”

“You knew about this?” Dad stands.

Daniel’s eyes go wide. “Dad, calm down. We should trust Katie.”

“Yes, we should,” I say. “There’s nothing going on other than study.”

“Well, this is my warning, Katie.” Dad points a finger at me. “He’s a teenage boy, so if he comes over he has to use the front door. And if I catch him in your room when I don’t know about it, there will be hell to pay.”

“Your father is right,” Mum says. “Climbing in your window isn’t the right thing to do. But it is romantic.”

“Whose side are you on?” Dad asks.

“I’m just saying.” Mum smiles. “He obviously likes you, Katie.” She stands and clears our breakfast dishes, taking them to the sink.

“We’ve all known Levi for a very long time,” Dad says. “He’s a good kid, but he’s been through a lot, and he’s hurt you in the past. I want you to be careful.”

“I will.” My voice is small, because Dad is right.

Dad takes his work jacket from the back of his chair and puts it on. “Do you have a crush on him?”

What can I say? I’ve never been a good liar. “Yes. But Dad, we’re just friends. He doesn’t think of me like that.”

“Oh, let me assure you, he does. Now, I’m going to work.” Dad kisses Mum on the cheek and gives me a kiss on the head on his way past.

I pick at my fingernails and wait until Dad leaves before talking again. "Mum, how can I tell if he's really interested?"

"Climbing in your bedroom window is a sure sign." Daniel takes a bite from his banana.

Mum sighs and leans against the bench. "I know that look he has, Katie. I've seen it in your father's eyes. We don't want to have to put restrictions on you, or tell you who you can and can't see. We trust you, honey, but he needs to use the front door."

"Okay."

There's a knock at the door, and Daniel goes to get it. A second later, he calls out, "Katie, Levi's here."

Mum and I exchange a glance and she smiles. "Good luck today." She comes over and gives me a hug.

"Thanks, Mum." I grab my bag on the way out of the kitchen.

Levi stands on the threshold, leaning against the doorjamb with his hands in his pockets.

"Big day today, Katie," he says. "You ready?"

"If you're talking about exams, yes." I shoulder my bag and we walk outside to Levi's car. "If you mean Veronica, then no."

"Are you going to tell me what you've decided?" Levi opens the front passenger door for me.

I slide into the seat and dump my bag in the foot well then look up at him. "That would also be a no. Stop asking me. You've asked a million times over the past couple of weeks."

"You're no fun." He closes my door, goes around to the

driver's side, and gets in. "I won't tell anyone."

"You'll find out when she does." I smile. It's nice to have something over him. "Not long to wait."

Levi starts the car. "You've drawn this out longer than anyone else has ever gotten away with."

"I won't let her intimidate me. She needs to learn she won't always get what she wants when she wants it."

"She's nicer than you think, you know."

Levi backs out of the driveway and we start the drive to school. I frown but settle into the seat and try to focus on something other than Veronica. She'll be in the car soon, and I should probably be as calm as possible.

We pick Jarred up first. He grunts when he gets in, and I think that's the extent of the conversation I'll have with him this morning. Levi stops outside Veronica's place a few minutes later, and she yanks the door open.

"I want the front seat back." She flops into the car and pouts.

"Good morning," I say.

"It'll be better this afternoon when you give me my answer."

I turn in my seat to look at her. "It's killing you, isn't it?"

"You know, I could've burnt you by now."

"Why haven't you?" I raise my eyebrows.

Veronica's gaze flicks quickly to Levi, she smirks then stares out the window and doesn't answer. I turn back to face the front. What did the look she gave him mean? Is he involved somehow? He has pestered me quite a bit to tell him what I'm going to say.

My stomach fills with a sinking feeling, and by the time we reach school, I think I'm going to vomit. What if Levi is in on whatever Veronica has in store for me? What if him being nice is all just a show so the letdown will be worse for me, and far more fun for everyone else?

I open my door before Levi has the chance to turn the car off. "I'm going to find Karen." I jump out and cross the street before he can stop me.

I walk quickly up the back driveway into school, and don't look to see if Levi and the others have followed. Karen reaches our lockers a minute after I do—just enough time for me to empty my bag of everything I don't need for our last exam.

"Hey," Karen says. "I miss anything this morning?"

I slam my locker shut. "Just the usual."

"Veronica?" Karen asks.

"I don't really want to talk about it." All I want to do is focus on getting through today.

"I could beat her up for you."

I laugh, and look Karen up and down. "No, you couldn't."

"Well, I could try."

"Please don't. As annoying as you are sometimes, I actually like you."

Karen grins and we head to the hall for our last trial exam. If we get there before Levi and Veronica, I can find a seat at the front and put my head down with no distractions.

Karen and I walk through the big doors at the back of the hall and make our way to the front row of seats. There are already quite a few students in here, and we're lucky to get the last two desks on the side at the front. I chuckle to myself because only I would think getting a seat at the front is lucky.

No sooner have I sat than I can sense his presence. I don't know what it is about Levi, but I always feel him when he walks into a room, or if he's close by. It's like I'm tuned in to him, and I don't want to be.

He sits one seat behind and across one row. I don't think I've ever seen him sit that close to the teacher before. He usually sits in the back.

A low hum echoes through the hall and I take my notes out, ignoring everyone around me, including Karen. There's nothing like a bit of last-minute revision right before an exam. I think I'm good for this one though, like I have been for all the others.

When I finally do glance over my shoulder, Levi is staring at me with a frown on his face, and I quickly look away. Even with his forehead scrunched between his eyes, he's still so hot.

I do not need this distraction right now.

A piece of screwed up paper hits me in the back of the head, and I hear Veronica snigger. What I wouldn't give to have her disappear out of my life. I ignore her attempt to get my attention.

"All right, class. Settle down." Mr Jenkins shuffles the pile of test papers in his hands. "I trust you've all studied hard." He walks up and down the aisles, placing a test paper on each student's desk, face down. "You have two hours. No talking during this exam. And no cheating on your phones. Don't think I can't see you, Miss Porter." He looks down his nose at Veronica, then sits at the desk at the front of the hall. He looks at his watch. "You may start in three ... two ... one."

The room fills with the sound of rustling paper.

The exam is okay, and I feel pretty confident that I'll do well. When I sit back in my seat and look around, pretty much everyone still has their heads down. Even Mr Jenkins is staring at his desk. I turn to risk a glance at Levi, and he looks up, his mouth set in a firm line. I quickly face the front of the room again.

Moments later, another piece of screwed up paper lands on my desk. My breath catches in my throat. What if Mr Jenkins sees? I could get in big trouble and be accused of cheating. When the teacher doesn't look up from his desk I exhale slowly and flatten out the note.

It doesn't say much, but I'm angry Levi would risk getting caught for something so stupid. I want to yell at him, but I can't do that in the middle of an exam.

The note reads: *What are you going to tell her?*

I risk another glance at Levi, chewing my bottom lip until I taste blood, and frowning at him. He looks back to his test. Neatly, underneath his messy handwriting, I tell him what I would have said if I could open my mouth.

You're an idiot.

I drop my hand to my side and line my throw up with the space at Levi's feet. I flick my wrist and hope the piece of paper lands in the right place. A minute later it's back on my desk.

I un-crumple it and stare at the piece of flattened paper in front of me.

The suspense is killing me.

Levi's reply makes me smile, because I can imagine the playful tone in his voice. I pick up my pen and write back to him.

You're still an idiot.

When I look up, Mr Jenkins regards me with a stern expression. "Your time is up. Pens down please."

I fold the paper into my palm, praying he hasn't seen it. Mr Jenkins walks the room, like he did at the start of the exam, to collect our papers. He reaches my desk, and I hold out my test so he can take it.

"Miss Sullivan, may I have the note as well, please?"

I stiffen in my seat, and a million thoughts run through my head. My first instinct is to lie, and deny having a note, but I'm not a liar. I have no choice but to give it to him.

"I'm sorry, sir."

My teacher takes the note and reads it, then looks around the room at every student in turn, paying close attention to those sitting near me. Karen is staring at me with her mouth open.

"Who else wrote this?" Mr Jenkins holds up the piece of paper. "This kind of behaviour will not be tolerated, especially during a trial HSC exam. Katie, go and see Mrs Pritchard immediately."

My cheeks flame with heat. I've never been sent to the headmistress's office before. I've never so much as been in trouble for anything at school before.

My teacher strides to the desk at the front of the hall, dumps the pile of exam papers on it, and opens his folder. He fills out a slip of paper and comes to give it to me.

"But sir, I—"

"Save it for Mrs Pritchard, Katherine. And as for the rest of you ..." Mr Jenkins looks around the room again. "If the other culprit does not own up in the next two minutes, I will fail all of you."

I take the piece of paper from Mr Jenkins and stand,

adjusting my bag on my shoulder.

"That's not fair," Veronica says. "Why should we fail because of *her?*"

For once, I actually agree with her.

Levi sits hunched over, tapping his pen on the desk. He raises his head and his gaze locks onto mine. His mouth opens, and my eyes widen. I shake my head once, no. He can't own up. He's the school captain. He'll get crucified for passing a note in an exam.

"I did it," Karen says, and I spin in her direction. "Send me to the headmistress, too."

My mouth drops open and I go to say something, but Levi beats me to it.

"No, sir. It was me." He grabs the strap of his backpack and stands from his desk. "Karen has nothing to do with this."

The class lets out a collective gasp.

Veronica scowls, and her look cuts through me like a knife.

I glance from my best friend to Levi. I know it wasn't Karen, but I love her for wanting to help.

"Very well." Mr Jenkins looks down his nose at Levi before filling out another slip. He staples our note to it.

I adjust my glasses and wait for Mr Jenkins to hand the piece of paper to Levi.

We walk to Mrs Pritchard's office in silence, and I'm not sure if I'm angry or happy. I think I'm both. In reception, Levi and I hand our slips to Ms Smythe, the office lady. She offers us a weak smile before going through a door to the left where Mrs Pritchard's office is.

Ms Smythe comes back to the counter. "Off you go."

She nods at the headmistress's door.

Levi goes first, and I follow him in. Mrs Pritchard takes her glasses off and sits back in her chair.

"To what honour do I owe the school captain and our star pupil?" she says.

Levi and I both know she knows why we're here. We say nothing.

"Sit." Mrs Pritchard points to the chairs that face her desk. "Passing notes in an exam—I have to say, I'm very disappointed."

"It's not Katie's fault," Levi says.

Mrs Pritchard clasps her hands together on the desk and leans forward. "Ah, but she participated. If she hadn't done so, Katie wouldn't be here."

"Are you going to fail us?" I ask.

Our headmistress looks at Levi and me in turn. "No. It's obvious what you were talking about had nothing to do with History."

I let out a long breath. "Thank you."

"However ... you both acted inappropriately, so you will both lose five marks from your score on the exam you just took."

Lose marks? I close my eyes for a second. This isn't good. What if my mark isn't high enough to cope with the loss? This could ruin my chance at dux.

"Can I ask you to go a bit easier on Katie, please?" Levi says. "I passed the note first. I should receive more punishment."

"You definitely haven't set a very good example in this instance, Levi. I should strip you of your position. However, I would like to believe that this boils down to an error in judgement rather than an attempt at cheating." Mrs Pritchard looks between us again. "But Katie will receive the same punishment. I hope your efforts have been worth it."

Heat rises into my cheeks and I look at my hands.

"Okay, thank you," Levi says.

"Dismissed." Mrs Pritchard picks up her glasses and puts them back on.

Levi stands and touches me on the shoulder. I follow him out of the office, and we make our way across the yard towards the back driveway. Trial exams are over, so we're free to go for the day, and it seems like most of the year twelves already have.

When we reach the back gate, Karen is waiting for me on one side, and Veronica and Jarred are waiting for Levi on the other. Veronica is sitting up on the brick wall that encloses the school grounds. If I had a knife I could carve the tension in the air. Veronica and Karen glare at each other, and I wonder what we've missed.

I raise my eyebrows at Karen. "What's going on?"

"Nothing," she says. "What the hell happened to you two?"

"We lost marks," I say.

"Five each. Off our score for that exam," Levi adds.

"And you're okay with losing marks?" Karen stares at me.

"Not exactly." I glance at Levi, and adjust my bag on my shoulder.

"Great. Love you and leave you then," Karen says to Levi. "Let's go, Katie."

"Not so fast." Veronica jumps down from the wall and

walks towards me. "You owe me an answer."

I take a deep breath. "Yes, I do. But I get to go next."

"Yes," Karen says, pointing a finger at Veronica. "She gets to go next."

"Of course. That's how the game works." Veronica crosses her arms. "What's it gonna be?"

I lick my lips and glance at Levi before looking Veronica straight in the eyes. "Dare."

She laughs. "Oh, this will be so much fun."

I smile. "Bring it, bitch."

7

Now it's my turn

Mum watches me push peas around my plate. Dad has his eyes trained on his food. I've already had the lecture, and I've wracked my brain for a way to figure out how to tell Mum and Dad I want to go out tonight. Usually getting in trouble at school means not going out and having fun five minutes later.

Veronica hadn't dared me to do anything straight away. Instead, she'd invited me to a party. Apparently it's an end-of-trial-exams celebration, but I'm not sure if it was pre-planned or if she just made it up on the spot. I would've thought I'd have heard about a party over the past two weeks.

The last thing I want to do is go, but I can't back out of this one, and Levi is picking me up at eight. Now would be a good time to get grounded.

Mum sets her fork down. "Really, Katie? The head-mistress?"

"I told you, it's not that big a deal."

"You do realise which house you're in?" Daniel asks between mouthfuls.

Dad remains silent, eating his dinner slowly and sipping his wine. His silence is worse than Mum's look of disappointment.

"We passed a note," I say. "It's not the end of the world. And we didn't cheat."

"You don't pass notes in an exam." Mum picks up her fork again and stabs her steak. "Losing marks could affect your chances at dux. And you need the best grade possible to get into a degree in law or medicine."

"Have you decided what you'd like to do yet?" Dad asks.

I shrug. "Not yet." *I want to do a fine arts degree.*

"Well, just don't do it again, okay, honey?" Dad pats my arm.

Daniel shakes his head. "If it were me, I'd be grounded for a month."

"What's the point in grounding her? She doesn't go anywhere," Mum says.

"I do so … sometimes."

"Sweetie, I'm teasing you." Mum smiles. "Finish your dinner."

"Actually, I want to go somewhere tonight." I look from Mum to Dad and back again. "One of the girls at school is having a party to celebrate the end of trials."

"Where is this party?" Dad asks.

"It's at Veronica's. You remember Veronica? Levi is

going to drive us." I pull my phone from my pocket to check the time. "We're supposed to be leaving in about an hour."

Mum frowns. "Okay. But be home by one o'clock. No later."

"What?" Daniel says. "You're letting her go?"

"Yes." Mum glances at him. "Katie can go."

"So unfair," Daniel mutters into his plate.

I actually agree with him.

We finish dinner in silence. Daniel and I clean up while Mum and Dad go out to the lounge room. I stack the dishwasher and wipe the benches while Daniel washes the frypan. He keeps looking at me from the corner of his eye.

"What?" I ask.

He flicks soap suds at me. "Can't believe they're letting you go out after stuffing up like this."

I shrug. "I have an untarnished record. Or at least I did."

Daniel chuckles. "So, Levi. Still just friends?"

"Yep." I concentrate on moving the sponge in circles across the bench.

"The guy you've been in love with for like, forever."

"I'm not in love with him." I grab Mum's pen off the counter and chuck it at him. "Next time, I will stab you."

"Katie, it's okay to like him." Daniel puts the frypan on the sink to drain.

I laugh. "No, it isn't. Girls like me should not have the hots for guys like Levi."

"Everything okay at school?" He leans against the bench and dries his hands on a tea towel. I chew the side of my thumb. "I'll take that as a no."

"I can take care of myself." I punch him on the arm. "Don't worry, I'm fine."

Daniel wraps me in a brotherly hug, resting his chin on the top of my head. "If you say so. But let me know if you need anything, okay?"

"I need to get ready. You can let go of me now." I pull away from my brother and head out of the kitchen.

"Katie," Daniel says, and I turn in the doorway. He presses his lips together. "Be careful. Okay?"

I nod. "Stop worrying. I'm fine."

I take the stairs two at a time and go to my room, closing the door. It's been a long day, and my mind is so full I feel like it's about to explode. I grab my journal off my desk and sit on the edge of my bed. Maybe if I get some stuff out, I'll feel a bit better.

It's truth-or-dare time tonight and I'm nervous. I've tried not to think about it too much. I've chosen dare, and I'm totally freaking out. What will Veronica ask me to do? And what will happen once it's my turn? Who will I truth or dare, and what will I ask them?

I don't know any dirty secrets about anyone, so my question would be lame. And I can't think of anything to dare anyone that they probably haven't been dared before. Do I have it in me to make someone do something awful? Has this whole thing turned me into a horrible person? I hope not. Besides, the only person I would really consider doing something mean to would be Veronica, but even so, I don't want to hurt her.

Levi is probably my safest bet. If he chooses dare, I can just think of something on the spot. Something lame to get it over with. But if he chooses truth, maybe I can ask him a question where the answer will tell me if he actually cares, or if it's all a show.

There's a tap at the window. A second later the bottom sash slides up and Levi sticks a leg through onto the window seat.

"What are you doing?" I ask, closing my journal and putting it back on my desk. "It's not time to go yet."

"No," he says, plonking onto the seat. "But this is your twenty-minute call. And I came to see if you wanted any help getting ready."

I raise my eyebrows but don't reply. My wardrobe doors are open, so I go stand in front of them and stare at my meagre fashion range. What am I supposed to wear to a party at Veronica Porter's house? She lives in one of the richest suburbs on the North Shore, so I'm not sure jeans and a jacket will cut it.

The hangers click as I search for something that doesn't say 'poor Katie', but I have nothing. I drop my hands to my side and sigh.

"Jeans will be fine," Levi says.

I look him up and down. He's wearing dark blue jeans, an ice-blue T-shirt, and a black leather flying jacket. He comes to the wardrobe and looks in, taking a pair of my jeans out and handing them to me. He rifles through the hangers and takes out a cream three-quarter-sleeved top with navy stripes. Then he grabs my grey chunky-knit cardigan. It's probably the nicest piece of clothing I own.

I screw my nose up. "That top doesn't really go with that cardigan."

Levi raises his eyebrows. "Why?"

"I wear white or black with grey. Not cream and navy."

He hands me the cardigan and puts the top back, choosing another simple black one. "This do?"

"Perfect," I say. "Now can you leave so I can get ready? And can you use the front door like a normal person?"

"Fifteen minutes?" He climbs out the window.

"I'll do my best."

I watch as Levi makes his way down the trellis. When he reaches the ground, I shut the window and pull my curtains closed. I'm not much of a makeup kind of girl, so it doesn't take me long to get changed and ready. I fluff my hair and leave it loose around my shoulders, then apply some gloss to my lips. I pull my only pair of heels from the back of the closet—short black leather boots with a suede section that slouches around my ankles, and buttons up the sides. I don't wear them much because I find high heels hard to walk in, so they look almost new.

I grab my favourite clutch purse, shoving my gloss, house keys, and phone inside on the way out of my room. A knock sounds at the front door as I'm walking down the stairs.

Mum answers it before I reach the bottom.

"Hi, Sonja," Levi says.

"Levi, how nice to see you." Mum opens the door wide.

Dad and Daniel appear from the lounge room.

I stop at the bottom of the steps and take a deep breath. This is the first time I've ever been right where I am now—with a gorgeous guy standing on my doorstep waiting to take me somewhere. I want to pinch myself, and then I remember where we're going and who else is going to be there. I take another deep breath.

Levi smiles at me. "You look nice. Ready?"

"Sure." I nod, my cheeks turning hot.

Dad steps forward and looks at Levi. "I trust you won't be drinking tonight?"

My stomach clenches and I bite my lip. Of all the questions he had to ask, it was the drinking one. I feel like yelling at him. Does he think Levi is that stupid? After what happened to his brother?

"No, of course not," Levi says. "Just a few of us watching a movie and having pizza to celebrate the end of trials." Levi smiles.

Daniel crosses his arms over his chest, and I think I'm going to pass out from all the deep breaths I'm taking.

"I'll be home by curfew." I move to the door and stand between Levi and my family.

Dad opens his mouth to say something, but Mum gives him a look. "Have fun," she says. "Call us if you need anything."

I gently push Levi off the threshold so we can get out of here, and close the door. Once it's shut behind us I look at him and laugh. "Sorry about that."

"S'okay." He shrugs. "They care about you."

We walk across our boundary, stepping through the garden bed to Levi's car, which is parked in his driveway.

The night air is chilly, and I rub my arms. He opens the passenger door for me and I slide in, pulling my cardigan tight around me. Levi gets in and starts the car. The BMW's engine rumbles to life. I fidget with my sleeve as we drive to Karen's place, nervous about what's going to happen tonight. I'm so glad she's coming with us. I don't think I would be able to do this on my own.

Karen is waiting in her driveway, and she has the back door open before Levi even comes to a full stop.

"Hey," she says as she climbs in, slamming the door.

I turn to look at her and smile, even though I feel so sick I think I might vomit.

"You look good, Karen," Levi says.

She blinks a few times. "What do you want?"

He chuckles. "Can't I give you a compliment?"

Karen sits back and fastens her seatbelt. "Didn't think you did compliments anymore."

"Maybe I'm turning over a new leaf." He glances sideways at me before he reverses back onto the street and takes off towards the highway.

I'm not sure what to make of his comment. There are so many things I'm confused about at the moment. What if his intentions aren't what I'm reading them to be? What if I think we have something, but we really don't? The thought makes my stomach twist into more knots, and by the time we reach Veronica's house, I really do think I'm going to be sick.

Levi parks on the street across the road from Veronica's. Cars line both sides of the road. When Levi told my parents 'just a few of us' were going to this party, I assumed he meant maybe ten people. The sounds coming from inside the house suggest a lot more than that. Like the whole of year twelve.

Karen gets out of the car, and I stare at her through my window. The lights from Veronica's place shine into the darkness. About five people are outside on the veranda that runs the length of the front of the house. More bodies move around inside, visible through the huge glass windows. Music pumps into the night, and I wonder what the hell I'm getting myself into.

Karen opens my door. Levi is beside her, looking down at me.

"You okay?" he asks.

No, I'm not okay. I don't want to move. "Sure." I smile up at him. "Looks like fun." *Looks like hell more like it.*

I swing my legs around and get out of the car, slipping my hand through the strap on my purse and clutching it to my chest. Karen pushes my door closed and links her arm through mine. The BMW's lights blink, and it beeps when Levi presses the button in his hand. I scan the street. Maybe I can make a getaway now.

"How the hell are we going to survive this?" I whisper to Karen.

"We'll be fine." She tugs me across the street and Levi follows. "We're better than every single one of these snobs."

I want to believe her, but I don't.

The three of us walk up the driveway towards the huge house. I recognise the people on the porch as kids from school, but I'm not friends with any of them. They stop talking and watch as Levi takes my hand and walks through the front door. I don't let go of Karen, so I'm sandwiched between my best friend and my ex best friend.

The lounge room on our left is crowded, with people sitting on every seat available, and others dancing to the music coming from the iPod dock in the corner. Levi keeps walking and takes us through into a gourmet kitchen, big enough to host a dinner party of twenty at the long timber table. We keep going through a set of double French doors and out to the backyard.

There aren't as many people here, and I take a big gulp of fresh air.

"Where are Veronica's parents?" I ask.

Levi lets go of my hand. "They'll be upstairs in their room. They let her have parties all the time. Although this is bigger than usual."

"Of course it is."

I glance around at the expansive yard. There's a recently mowed lawn leading to a swimming pool, then a tennis court up the back. The banana lounges are occupied, some of them with more than one person. I know everyone here by first name at least, but I wouldn't call most of them friends.

Over to one side is a big outdoor setting, and I spot Jessica sitting at the table with her sister, Josephine, and Jarred, Veronica, Geoff, and a few others. My gaze meets Veronica's, and she smirks. I catch Jessica's eye, but she's not smiling like Veronica is. I pull my arm from Karen's, even though I could use the support, because I don't want to look like I'm clinging onto her for dear life.

"Katie," Veronica calls. "So glad you could make it." She jumps up from her chair. "Now that you're here we can all go inside."

My stomach flips at the way Veronica is looking at me. I glance around the backyard. I'd much rather be outside in the open air, but everyone gets up, one by one, and follows Veronica towards the house.

"Be careful, Katie," Jessica says when she reaches me. "I don't know what she's got planned for you, but I think she's told some of the others."

"Don't worry," Karen says. "Veronica thinks she's smart, but she's got nothing on Katie."

I hope Karen is right. Veronica will either outsmart me and I'll get crucified in front of the entire year, or I'll get one over her and give her a very good reason to hate me even more.

"Just … be prepared," Jessica says.

"How the hell do I do that?" I ask.

Jessica shrugs.

Levi looks at me. "You okay?"

"Sure." I wish he'd stop asking me that because no. I'm nervous as all hell. I try to smile.

"Just remember what I told you." He grabs my hand and pulls me towards the house.

"This is not going to end well." Jessica rubs her arms, warding off the cool air.

"That's the spirit, Jess," Karen says.

I let out a half-laugh. "She's going to crucify me."

"I won't let that happen." Levi lets go of my hand when we reach the French doors at the back of the house.

We make our way into the kitchen. With a deep breath I grab a bottle of water from the stash on the bench, cracking the lid to take a sip. I pause in the doorway to the huge lounge room at the front of the house. The music has been turned down, and no one is dancing anymore.

I have a pretty big audience.

There are three three-seater lounges arranged in a U-shape around an open fireplace. I'm glad it isn't lit. If it were, I'd be sweating more than I already am from nerves. In front of the fireplace is a coffee table filled with cups, glasses, and bottles of alcohol. At least half the kids here are eighteen, so can legally drink, but there are a few with cups in their hands who I know are underage, and I bet they're not drinking water like me.

"I saved you a seat." Veronica points to the couch cushion beside her. She's sitting up on the arm with her feet on the lounge.

I stand tall and face her, promising myself that whatever she throws at me I'll be able to handle just fine. And then, I'll throw it back at her like a force-ten hurricane. She'll never know what hit her.

I make my way over, set my bottle of water on the coffee table beside a bottle of lethal-looking spirits, and sit down. Karen and Jessica follow, taking up positions on the floor near my feet. Karen leans against the big arm of the couch, and Jessica crosses her legs. Levi hangs back at the doorway, a drink in his hand.

The room buzzes with low conversation, and I stare at the carpet in front of me. I don't want to look around at everyone. I'm already nervous. Why the hell did I choose dare? I must be an idiot.

Karen slips her arm behind my leg and hugs it, resting her shoulder against my knee. I'm so glad she's here. At least I have her and Jessica on my side.

"Is everyone ready to play?" Veronica asks.

The room erupts with cheers.

"The real party starts now," someone yells, and a few people laugh.

"Remember the rules," Karen says. "Katie gets to go next."

"I wouldn't dream of breaking the rules," Veronica says.

"Come on," I say. "What's my dare?"

"Okay, Katie." Veronica looks down at me from her perch on the arm of the lounge. "I dare you to drink five shots."

More cheers erupt around the room.

Five shots? Is she crazy? I'll fall into a coma.

Karen stiffens beside me. "Are you trying to kill her?"

"Just trying to have fun." Veronica smirks again and takes a sip from her cup.

I stare at the table, and that's when I notice the shot glasses already lined up in front of several different bottles of booze.

"You can pick your poison," Jarred says.

"Five shots of anything on this table." Veronica looks at me with a smirk.

Behind the five shot glasses are bottles of bourbon, vodka, rum, and scotch. Any one of those is going to have me flat on my back seconds after the fifth shot hits my stomach, if not before.

"Okay." I scoot forward to the edge of my seat.

I take a deep breath and let it out slowly. There has to be a way around this. I kneel then shuffle the two steps to the edge of the coffee table. The room has gone silent, and I stare at each bottle in turn, trying to decide which will do the least damage. I really have no idea though. I don't drink, and I've certainly never been drunk before.

Levi drinks bourbon, so maybe it's not that bad.

I pick up the bottle of Jim Beam and pour the first shot. I reach for the small glass of amber liquid, and cheers erupt around the room. Before I can chicken out, I bring the drink to my lips and tip my head back. The bourbon burns my throat on the way down, and I grimace.

"Blerk," I say. "That's horrible."

Laughter rolls around the room in waves.

"Four to go," Veronica says.

I find Levi and lock gazes with him. He's smiling, but it's not touching his eyes.

I lick my lips and pour another shot. My belly is warm from the first one, and now that the burning in my throat has gone, I feel kind of good. Maybe I'll come out of this okay. I throw back the second shot to more cheers and laughter.

My head spins a little as I pick up the bourbon bottle.

Or maybe I'm about to end up in the hospital. *Come on, Katie, don't let them beat you.* I lick my lips again and lean on the coffee table. My elbow brushes my bottle of water, and through the slight fuzz in my head I remember what Levi told me. There's always a way around a dare. You just have to find it.

I stare at my water for a few seconds, then put the bourbon bottle down beside it. I pick up the water and take the cap off.

"What are you doing?" Veronica jumps up.

I pour water into the three remaining shot glasses. "You said anything on this table."

"I didn't put that there." She glares at me.

I throw back the three shots of water. "But it was there when you told me the rules. Now it's my turn."

8

As it falls back into place

The room erupts with shouting. It's so loud I can't make out any words. Veronica's mouth drops open, and she stares at me.

"You can't do that." Rachel gets up from her seat on the couch opposite us. "That's cheating."

"Cheater, cheater, cheater," everyone in the room chants.

"No, it isn't." Karen gets to her feet. "You're all sore losers."

"Bitch," Veronica says.

I laugh and stand, swaying on my feet a little. "Is that your best comeback?" But my voice gets drowned out by the noise.

Veronica narrows her eyes and clenches her fists at her sides. Jessica stands, and I now have her on one side of me and Karen on the other. I follow Jessica's gaze around the room where it stops and rests on Josephine.

Jessica's sister shakes her head and rolls her eyes.

Levi jumps onto the coffee table, knocking over a few cups and a bottle of vodka. Thankfully, the lid is on.

"Stop!" he yells.

The room quietens to a murmur, and I look up at Levi. He glances down at me, a half-smile touching his lips. He goes to say something, but now that the noise has died down, Karen beats him to it.

"When are you going to get over the fact that Katie is smarter than you?" Karen's voice travels around the room. She folds her arms and glares at everyone.

Veronica takes a step towards me, but I stand my ground. Karen and Jessica do, too.

"You cheated," Veronica says, pointing a finger at me.

"Katie drank her shots." Levi jumps off the coffee table and lands in front of me. "It's her turn."

Veronica grits her teeth. "This better be good." She takes up her seat again on the arm of the couch.

Karen sits where I was, and Jessica squeezes in beside her, but I stay standing. I do not want to be sitting for this. In case I need to run away really quickly. Running away seems like a good idea, actually, because I don't want to do this.

"Levi, truth or dare?" The words are out of my mouth, and a second later I want them back.

The room erupts with chatter and cat-calling. Someone lets out an ear-piercing wolf whistle, and I cringe.

What the hell am I doing? What am I going to ask him if he says truth? What will I dare him if he doesn't? I thought maybe I was prepared for this, but it turns out I'm not. All eyes are on me, staring at the boy in front of me. The one I've been in love with my entire life. The one I have so many questions for, but they're ones I don't want to ask in front of a room full of rich-kid snobs.

I should never have come to this party.

Levi sits on the coffee table and stares up at me, that lopsided smile still playing on his face. He rests his hands on his knees and licks his lips.

"Truth," Levi says.

My mouth opens, and I close it again. Truth? *Shit!* What am I going to ask him that isn't too personal and won't reveal how much I like him? But I want to ask something that I get a decent answer for, otherwise this is all a waste of time and effort. Should I ask him something about his past? His brother?

No, that would be mean.

"What's your favourite childhood memory?" I blurt. *Lame.*

"Seriously?" Veronica says. "That's your question?"

Laughter erupts through the room.

Levi runs a hand through his hair and my knees go weak. He smiles wide, looking around at all the faces. "Come on, everyone. It's a good question."

I stand there and twist my hands together, unable to look at him, so I stare at my feet. My boots have a scuff mark on them and I make a mental note to polish them tomorrow.

"It's a sucky question," Rachel says.

"Why? Because it's not about sex?" Karen scowls at her.

"I have more than one," Levi says, "but do you remember the day Mason and I wanted to pull down the treehouse?"

I suck in a breath and look up, catching Levi's stare.

"Yes," I whisper.

"Mason thought we were all too old to have a treehouse. You got mad because it had taken us so long to build that thing. You didn't want us to pull it down, but I guess we were going through a destructive phase. If we could break it, we would."

A few chuckles roll around the room, and it seems like everyone is suddenly hanging onto every word Levi says.

"I told you we had to keep the purple flower curtains, because I'd made them myself." I smile. I have so many great memories of spending time in that treehouse.

"Yeah." Levi smiles back at me, and rubs his legs with his palms. "You also said if we tore it down, you'd never speak to either of us again. You were so angry, and I remember thinking, you're really pretty when you're angry." He stops and takes a breath.

I have the chance to say something, but I don't. Levi just admitted in front of everyone that he thought I was pretty. But we were only fourteen then. Does he still think the same now? The room is silent, and I wait for someone to say something, but no one does. My heart pounds, and I stare down at my twisted hands again.

"But my favourite part about that day happened later," Levi says.

"I bet you got some," Jarred yells, and I cringe.

"You and me in the treehouse, Katie. There's more than one memory that's my favourite."

"Woohoo," someone yells.

"It's always about sex," another voice calls out.

"You did it with *her*?" Veronica asks.

Levi doesn't say yes or no, and the room erupts again.

I stare at Levi with my mouth open. What has he done? Here I was thinking I'd asked a simple, innocent question, and he's turned it into something where everyone thinks we were together.

He's made something from absolutely nothing.

There is nothing going on between us. As much as I've always wanted something with Levi, it's never happened.

"Is this some cruel joke?" I ask. "You want them to think we did it in the treehouse?"

But I don't wait for an answer. I do what I wanted to do the moment we first pulled up to Veronica's and I got out of Levi's car.

I run.

I run through the people clogging the lounge room and out onto the porch. I run down the driveway to the street.

I can't believe he's letting everyone think those things. I've never even kissed anyone, but I know exactly what they *are* thinking back in that house.

"Katie, wait," Levi calls, but I don't turn around.

I keep running.

The train station isn't far. I'll jump on the next train home and walk the half an hour to my house. Another set of footsteps sounds behind me. Levi grabs my arm and pulls me to a stop.

I reef myself from his grip. "Don't touch me!"

The streetlight casts a glow over his face. "Katie—"

"What the hell was that back there? We never did anything in that treehouse."

"I know we didn't."

"Then why did you let them believe we did?"

"Because I want everyone to know that I like you."

My breath catches in my throat. I stare at him and shake my head. "And this is the way you do it? You're an idiot!"

"Katie?" Karen yells.

She runs along the footpath, Jessica behind her.

"Over here." I step from the shadows, so she can see me in the streetlight.

Karen's feet pound the ground. "Get away from her, you arsehole." She stops between Levi and me, and I take a step back.

Jessica reaches us a few seconds later. "He's more than that! You're … you're a dick, Levi. How dare you make everyone think you and Katie …" She stops and puts her hands on her hips. I've never heard Jessica speak to anyone so meanly. She's usually so quiet, and always nice.

"We should never have come." I take Jessica's hand and pull her away from Levi. "I'm going home."

"If you want to go, I'll take you," Levi says.

"Like hell you will." Karen steps towards him.

"Okay." He raises his hands and backs away.

"I have Josie's car." Jessica pulls her phone from her pocket. "She can get a lift with *you*." She quickly types a text to her sister, then re-pockets her phone. "Come on."

Karen and I follow Jessica down the street, and I feel Levi's presence behind us. We find Josephine's Honda. Jessica pushes the button on the remote and the locks pop. I go to open the passenger door, but Levi beats me to it.

"Would you go away?" I say. "I'm really angry at you."

"Doesn't mean I can't be nice." He smiles, and it's so infuriating.

"Go away, Levi." Karen gets in the back, slamming her door.

Jessica sits behind the wheel and starts the engine.

I climb into the car, rest my purse in my lap, and pull my cardigan tight around myself, refusing to look at Levi. Here I was worried about falling on my face because of Veronica's dare, and instead I've been humiliated because of a stupid question *I* asked. One Levi answered truthfully. But which also suggested I'd slept with him when we were fourteen. How could he embarrass me like that?

I grab the door and pull it out of Levi's grip, slamming it. Jessica drives towards the motorway and I rest my head against the seat, closing my eyes. A tear slips out and I quickly wipe it away. I'm not going to be the girl who cries over something a guy she likes did. I stare out the window and watch the lights of the oncoming traffic.

Jessica takes our exit and turns onto the highway, making the next left to head towards Karen's house. We pull up in her driveway, and Jessica kills the engine.

Karen unbuckles her seatbelt and leans forward between the front seats. "You gonna be okay?"

I roll my head to the side and look at my friends. "Aren't I always?"

"Call me if you need me." Karen kisses me on the top of the head, then gets out of the car.

Jessica and I watch her until she's inside, then we reverse out of the driveway and head for home. She pulls up to the kerb outside my house, and I open my door and get out.

"Thanks, Jess," I say through the open door.

"Don't worry about what they all think," she says. "You know the truth. That's all that matters."

I sigh and sit back on the edge of the car seat. "I'm so mad at him, but it's weird, because I'm also excited about what he said. He basically told everyone he thinks I'm pretty. That's good, right?" I look at Jessica.

She reaches over and takes my hand. "You and Levi … it would be awesome. I always used to think you'd end up together. But just … be careful. The way they play truth or dare isn't always fun."

I press my lips together. "Yeah."

Jessica squeezes my hand and I get out of the car again, closing the door. She gives me a wave and drives the few houses down the street to her place. I watch until she turns into her driveway, and then I walk down mine to the front door.

Mum and Dad are on the couch watching a movie.

"Katie," Mum says. "Everything okay? We weren't expecting you home yet."

"Yeah, I'm fine. Tired." I close the front door. "I'm going to bed."

Dad frowns. "Sure you're all right?"

"All good." I kick my boots off and go upstairs.

When I close my door, I suck in a deep breath and throw my purse on my desk. I'm not sure what to do with myself, or how to feel, so I stand in the middle of my room for a minute and close my eyes. How did I get here? What did I ever do to deserve people treating me the way they do?

I'm not a bad person. I've never intentionally hurt anyone. And I'm so sick of not being good enough. I can't wait for this year to be over so I can be rid of that stupid private school and all its ugliness.

I take my cardigan off and hang it back in my wardrobe,

then I change into my flannelette PJs and flop onto my bed.

My phone buzzes with a message.

Karen: U OK?

Me: Will liv

Karen: Call me 2morrow

Me: xxx

I toss my phone back onto my desk and fall onto my pillow. I don't want to go to bed yet. I'm not actually tired, but what else am I supposed to do? Exams finished today so the last thing I need to do is study. I can have at least one day off.

I grab my journal and bunny and take them over to the window seat. After settling onto the cushion, I drape my crochet blanket over my knees and open my journal to the next blank page.

Tonight was a disaster. What the hell was I thinking, getting involved with Veronica and her friends? I should never have truth or dared Levi. I should've picked Karen. Looking at it now, why didn't I take that easy choice? She would've done anything I asked her to, or answered any question, and made everyone laugh in the process.

I'm an idiot.

All I've done is given everyone something to talk about. And I'm so angry at Levi for the way he answered my question. But I also love that he called me pretty. It's so confusing. Why do boys always have to show off like that to their friends? Making everyone think I slept with him. I wanted to slap him, and I hate that he brings out these feelings in me.

Why can't it be easier?

A few hours later, a car rumbling outside pulls me from my thoughts and I close my journal. I part the curtains and stare down at Levi's driveway. The lights of his BMW flick off and the driver's side door opens, but Levi doesn't get out. Instead, Josephine steps onto the concrete.

Levi must have had too much to drink—again.

Josephine closes her door and goes around the front of the car to the passenger side. She almost gets hit in the face when Levi throws his door open. He stumbles out and she tries to catch him, but they fall onto the grass together. Josephine giggles and leans in close to whisper something in Levi's ear.

He glances up at my window, and I quickly close the curtains.

I hear the car door slam. Josephine giggles again, and I can only imagine what they're doing. The last thing I should do is look. What if I see something I don't want to see? But I can't help it, and I part the curtains again.

Josephine hangs off Levi's arm, and they walk to the street where they stop at the kerb. She stands on her tiptoes and slowly presses her mouth over his. I yank the curtains closed. What is going on? Why is he letting her kiss him when I thought he liked me? If this is part of Veronica's game to get to me, then it's worked.

I part the curtains again. Levi stands on the kerb, watching Josephine as she walks along our street. He runs his hand through his hair, and my heart breaks a little more.

I let go of the curtains and get up, tossing my journal onto my desk. *Don't let it get to you.* I pace my room, angry because Levi made everyone think we'd been together when we hadn't, and he also told me I'm pretty, but then he went and flirted with Josephine. *I can't figure him out.*

I flick my hands as I pace, trying to get rid of the horrible feeling inside me. This all started at the beginning of term, when Levi decided to climb in my window drunk. I want to go back to that night so I can tell him I never want to see him or speak to him again, and then none of this would have happened. There would be nothing happening between us, instead of something that I have no control over, something I don't completely understand.

But is that what I actually want?

A part of me has always hoped Levi and I would have something one day.

A sound outside pulls me from my thoughts. The curtains part, and Levi sticks his head through the window. He pulls his knee up and climbs in, falling onto the window seat.

I stare at him, not sure if I want to yell or cry.

"My parents are home," I whisper.

Levi stares at me. His eyes have that glassy drunk look. "Then we better be quiet."

"How drunk are you?"

"I'm fine. Nothing like …"

"The time you climbed in here after face-planting the ground?"

"Nothing like that."

I climb into bed and pull the covers up to my waist, propping my pillow against the bedhead and leaning back.

"You looked pretty drunk when Josephine helped you out of the car."

"You saw that?" Levi stares at his feet.

"She kissed you."

"I pushed her away."

The silence hangs between us for a moment.

"Really?" I finally ask.

"You didn't see me push her away?"

I shake my head.

Levi sighs, then looks at me. "I'm sorry, Katie."

"You know, after tonight, I don't really want to talk to you."

Levi moves to sit on the end of the bed and stares at his hands. His hair flops over his eyes, and I want to reach out and push it away, but I don't.

"I'm *really* sorry. Veronica, she ... I don't know." He sighs again.

"She's a bitch is what she is." My voice is almost a whisper.

Levi pushes his hair away from his eyes and sits up straighter. "She can be, but—"

"No!" I look directly at him. I'm not going to let him do this. "Don't you dare stick up for her. Don't make excuses for the way she treats me. Or the way *you* treat me."

"What ...?" Levi stares at me, his mouth slightly open.

I clutch the edge of my blankets. "You ... what you did tonight."

"I know. I realise how much of an arse I've been."

"Tonight? Or for like, forever?"

Levi shrugs. "Both. I shouldn't have let everyone think that we ... in the treehouse. I'm not proud of what I've done to you. What I've let others do to you. You were my best friend, and I threw you away like a piece of garbage."

I scoff. "Yeah, you did."

Levi moves up the bed so he's sitting closer to me. He reaches out and takes my glasses off, carefully closing the arms before laying them on my desk. I let my hair fall across my face. Not having my glasses on makes me feel exposed. They're like my security blanket.

"Don't." Levi puts his finger under my chin and raises my head. "I meant what I said tonight. I think you're pretty. You're beautiful, actually. Someone needs to tell you that more often."

I shake my head. "Me? No, I'm not … I'm nothing."

"That's not true." Levi studies me for a moment. "You're something, Katie. You're smart, and funny, and kind. You're the most beautiful person I know."

"Then why did you do what you did?" I tuck my hair behind my ear and pull away from him, looking at my hands. "Why did you … leave me?"

"I thought we'd worked this part out," he says, a joking tone in his voice. "I'm a jerk."

"I'm serious, Levi," I whisper. "Why?"

My eyes burn with hot tears, and I force myself to hold them back. I will not cry in front of Levi.

"Because … you're not like the other girls. You're not like any of my friends. You don't fit with them, and … I was ashamed to know you."

I squeeze my eyes closed and suppress a sob, but the tears still manage to find their way out and tumble down my cheeks. I blink them away. "I'm not rich like the rest of you, so you're ashamed of me?"

"I'm so sorry." Levi reaches out and wipes a tear from under my eye with his thumb. His hands are rough but somehow comforting. Still, I pull away. I swipe at my face, then grab my glasses from the desk and put them back on.

We sit in silence. I'm too afraid to speak because I don't think my voice will work properly. After a few minutes, Levi stands and goes to the window.

"Are you leaving?" I ask.

"You need some sleep. Can I see you tomorrow?"

I shrug. "I don't know."

"I want to see you."

"Well, I don't know what I want." And I don't. I'm so confused about everything. "I'm not sure I can trust you."

Levi comes back to the bed and leans down, kissing me on the forehead. "I hope you can again someday, because I've been an idiot, and I will do anything to make it up to you. I've been too blind to see that the one thing I've needed the most has been right in front of me all along."

He climbs out the window, and I stare at the curtain as it falls back into place.

9

Why is it so hard in the first place?

Saturday, I don't go anywhere. I'm not really in a house-leaving kind of mood, so I stay in my room listening to music and writing in my journal. I fill ten pages, but stop after that because all I'm writing about is Levi and how I feel about everything that's happened. His apology hangs over me, and as much as I want to believe he was being genuine, I'm not sure if I should trust his words or prepare for the worst again.

Now, it's Sunday morning. Karen pulls into my driveway, and I race to the front door.

"Katie?" Mum calls. "Remember what I said."

"I know, Mum," I yell over my shoulder. *Spend the money wisely.*

I pull the passenger-side door open and climb into Karen's mum's car, shoving my tote and cardigan on the floor at my feet.

"Ready to rock?" Karen asks.

"Yep. Let's hit the road."

Karen reverses out of the driveway and I glance over at Levi's house. He's standing on the front veranda leaning against the stair railing. He raises his hand and gives me a wave. I offer him a small smile, then look straight ahead. Even after pouring everything into my journal, I'm still not sure how I feel about our last conversation, and I'm not going to let anything ruin today, so thinking about Levi is off limits.

Karen and I head to the shops to look for our formal dresses, and this time we have to come home with something because graduation is only a month away. We wanted Jessica and Stacey to come, too, but they had other plans. I'm not that excited about going to the formal, but I'm looking forward to spending time with Karen, and using the small amount of money Mum and Dad gave me wisely.

After parking the car and grabbing a quick hot chocolate, we hit the shops.

"You would look hot in that dress," Karen says, stopping at a shop window and pointing to a sleek, black pencil number.

"Yeah, if I worked in an office and was ten years older. What is it with you and pencil dresses? Come on, Karen, it's not a formal dress."

"But you'd still look great in it. We should get you a few other things today." Karen grins and claps her hands. "Oh, this will be fun. We can give you a whole new look."

"What's wrong with my look?" I stop and stare at her.

Karen tilts her head to the side and studies me. "Let's

at least get your hair trimmed. We can talk about your glasses later." Karen grabs my hand and pulls me to the closest hair salon.

"I don't usually have my hair done here," I say.

"Which is why we're going to go here. Relax." Karen leads me through the door.

"I thought we were shopping."

"We have all day." Karen waves her hand at me. "This won't take too long."

"I don't want anything off the length." Despite the many things I don't like about myself, my hair isn't one of them.

"Trimmed, I said *trimmed*." Karen turns to the girl behind the counter. "And maybe some foils."

The girl has heavy eye makeup, and black hair with a purple streak. She takes me through the salon and seats me at the only free station. At least there are other people in here, so hopefully I won't end up looking like an apprentice's mistake. I don't like the thought of having someone other than my normal hairdresser touching my hair.

The girl walks away, and I whisper to Karen, "Please don't let her dye my hair black." I like my brown waves, even if brown is boring.

"Foils," Karen says. "Golden ones."

She has a discussion with the hairdresser as if I'm not here. They look at the colour book, and Karen shakes her head a few times. When they finally agree the girl shows me the little swatch of hair, which is a nice golden blonde. I'm nervous, though. I've never put any colour through my hair. What if it turns out to be a disaster?

Karen smiles, and I decide to trust her, so I sit back and let the girl work her hairdressing magic. She divides my hair into sections, putting in foils until my head is covered with little folded bits of silver.

"I'll leave you for thirty minutes to process." She smiles at me in the mirror. "Then we'll wash your hair and give it a tidy up." She goes to the front counter to process some other customers' payments, and then busies herself cleaning up.

I glance around at the other people in the salon. Everyone seems happy, and no one has walked out looking hideous.

"See?" Karen says. "You need to do something different once in a while."

"She hasn't washed it out yet," I say. "Don't speak too soon."

When I'm finally finished an hour and a half later, I can't believe what I see in the mirror. The hairdresser has woven beautiful golden highlights through my previously flat brown locks, and layered it slightly so it falls nicely around my face and over my shoulders.

I almost don't believe it's me staring out of the mirror.

"All done," the girl says. "Come to the counter when you're ready."

Karen grins as I run my fingers through my new hairstyle. Then something occurs to me.

"Um, how am I going to pay for this?" I look at Karen in the mirror. "Mum and Dad only gave me money for a dress."

"This one's on me." Karen walks to the front of the store, and I follow. She takes out two fifties and lays them on the counter. She gets a dollar change.

"I can't let you do that," I say.

"Yes, you can. Come on, it's time to shop." Karen grabs my hand and pulls me out of the salon and into the shopping centre.

"You planned this, didn't you?" I ask as we walk, looking in shop windows.

"You're welcome." Karen slips her arm through mine.

We spend the next hour checking out the department stores. They don't have much in the way of formal dresses, but I end up buying a couple of cheap singlet tops and a nice sheer top to wear over them. I'm a little hesitant at first, but Karen talks me into it. The top is green with a paisley pattern and little cap sleeves. It flows nicely around my waist and will go perfectly with my favourite pair of jeans.

Karen plays with my hair at the checkout. "Wait till Levi sees you."

I take a deep breath. "He climbed in my window again after the party."

"What? And you're only telling me now?"

"It's not a big deal. He just wanted to apologise. I'm not sure how I feel about everything though. It's all so … hard."

"Love isn't meant to be easy." Karen squeezes my arm.

"Can we not talk about this now?"

Karen smiles. "Whatever you want."

We leave the store and head back into the main shopping centre. There are a few small dress shops we can look in, so we start with the closest one. I have trouble finding anything I like enough to try on, so for the next hour I sit in the change room vestibule while Karen tries on dress after dress.

She finally narrows it down to two, and stares at me impatiently as I look back and forth between the dresses she's holding up.

"I think we should try another store," I say.

"You don't like these?" She clutches the hangers to her chest.

"It's not that. Just ... maybe there are nicer ones in another store. And red ... it's a bit much.

"It's the formal. We're supposed to stand out."

"I don't want to stand out."

"Maybe red is a bit much." Karen goes back into the change room.

"Try the blue one on again," I say. "I like it better than the red. The fabric is really nice."

"Okay." She rustles around in the change room, then opens the door.

I nod. "Yep. I like it. More now that I've seen it on you again."

Karen walks into the vestibule and twirls, looking in the full-length mirror.

The sales lady comes in. "Slip your feet into these." She grabs a pair of black heels from the floor and hands them to Karen. "You can get a better idea of what it will look like with shoes."

"Thanks." Karen slips them on.

"I take it you have a formal coming up?" the sales lady says.

We both nod.

"I think I'll take this one." Karen runs her palms over the fabric covering her stomach.

The dress is really beautiful. It's ice blue and has a strapless sweetheart bodice with beading all over it. Then it gathers under the bust and falls in soft waves of chiffon to the floor. Karen looks at herself in the mirror for a few moments more, then gets changed. She pays for her dress, a smile plastered to her face.

We wander through the shops a bit, and every dress shop Karen suggests we go into I make an excuse not to enter. I'm just not a fancy-dress kind of girl, and I know what I'm looking for, but at the same time I don't. It's the kind of thing I have to see … and then I'll know.

We stop outside a small bohemian shop, and I grab Karen's arm. "I want to look in here."

"In the hippie shop?" Karen asks. "I don't think you'll find a formal dress in there."

"Can we just look?" I grab her hand and pull her into the store.

I do a lap of the shop, taking everything in first, then I search through a couple of racks up the front. One particular dress catches my eye. It's the kind of dress that's begging to be bought, even if I had nowhere to wear it, and I want it because it's so unusual. It's like someone took my personality and made it into a piece of clothing.

I take it from the rack and hold it up to get a better look. Biting my lip, I drape it in front of me and gaze down at the dress.

"That's gorgeous," Karen says.

"I know." I beam at her.

"You have to try it on."

"I know!" I almost squeal.

"The end change room is free," the sales lady says.

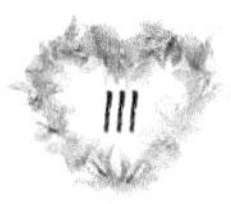

"It's a very lovely dress."

I smile and follow her to the small cubicles at the back of the store. Inside, I shimmy out of my jeans and top, then put the dress on. For a moment, all I can do is stare at my reflection. I'm pretty sure no one at the formal will have the same dress as me. None of those snobs would be seen dead wearing anything that's not covered with diamantes and made of silk or velvet, or whatever expensive fabric they think is on trend.

The dress is perfectly bohemian, and soft and feminine at the same time. It's strapless with a sweetheart neckline and ruched multi-coloured fabric in purples, pinks, blues, and a little yellow. A wide embroidered band encircles my waist. The skirt flows in layers of fuchsia and dark purple which are shorter at the front and longer at the back. A large flower print runs randomly along the hem to complete the look.

Wearing this dress makes me feel amazing.

I step out of the change room and Karen's mouth drops open.

"Oh. My. God!" She jumps up and down and squeals. "That is … wow. You look … I think I'm tearing up." She mock-wipes her eyes and I laugh.

"Isn't it beautiful?" I twirl and Karen squeals again.

I change back into my regular clothes, and pay for the dress. As we leave the store, I smile so much it hurts because not only do I have an awesome dress, but I have enough money left over to find some matching shoes.

We jump on the travelator to head to the ground floor and the shoe shop.

"Well, look who's had her hair done." Veronica stands

at the bottom of the travelator with Rachel.

Britney comes out of the chemist. "You guys, I found the most amazing nail polish." She stops beside Veronica and looks up at Karen and me.

I want to turn and run back up the travelator.

The smart thing to do would be to get to the bottom and walk past all of them. But I guess I'm still mad after Friday night. I step off and walk right into Veronica because she's in the way.

She stumbles backwards. "What are you doing, skank?"

"You're in my way." I face her. "Did you expect me not to get off the travelator?"

"Don't think for one second anything real will happen between you and Levi." Veronica folds her arms and stands taller. "I've seen how you look at him. But he's way out of your league."

As much as I agree with her, I'm done with trying to be nice all the time, and I'm not going to let her talk to me like this anymore.

"Get lost, Veronica," I say. "You're nothing but a jealous bitch."

"Who do you think you are?" Rachel flicks her hair over her shoulder. "You can't talk to her like that."

Britney stays quiet.

"I can do whatever I want." I glare at the three of them.

Karen grabs my arm. "Come on, Katie. They're not worth the time."

We walk away, and I'm itching to look over my shoulder, or give Veronica the finger, but I don't want to give her the satisfaction. I ball my hands and cross my arms tightly over my chest, wishing Veronica didn't get under my skin so easily.

Karen and I head towards the shoe shop, even though more shopping is the last thing I feel like doing now. Karen must sense my mood plummet and she squeezes my arm.

"Shoes, and then we're gone. Okay?"

I nod. "Sounds like a plan."

"You won't need many accessories with that dress. It speaks for itself."

I smile and we enter the shop, confronted by rows and rows of shoes. I walk down the aisle where the size sevens are, and browse what's on offer. There isn't much to choose from and I drag Karen back out of the shop five minutes later.

"Let's go up to the department store. They might have something on sale," I say.

We make our way upstairs again, this time using the steps instead of the travelator, and wander through the department store to the shoe section. Karen goes straight for the glitzy heels lining the wall, while I take a look at the sale tables. My hopes of finding something aren't great, but I spot one shoe from an unusual pair of wedges tucked under a hot pink flat.

The shoe has a decent platform, which will be great to give me some height, but it's the black lace that I love. They're peep-toes, with a T that goes up the front of the foot to a wide ankle band and a zipper at the back. I check the size. Seven and a half. I groan. They probably won't fit. I want to try them anyway, so I take the shoe over to the counter to ask the sales lady for the other one.

"Oh, they're really cool," Karen says. "Beautiful but

not flashy, so they won't take away from the dress."

"Let's hope they fit," I say. "I'm a seven and I think they're the last pair."

"I'll check if we have your size," the sales lady says, going through a doorway into the store room. She comes back a few minutes later with a box and the other shoe to the pair. "All I have left are the seven and a half, and a size nine."

"May as well try it," Karen says with a shrug.

"These are a smaller make, so you might find they'll fit." The sales lady smiles.

I sit in one of the courtesy chairs and kick off my Converse. The sales lady undoes the zipper and hands me the first shoe. *Please fit.* I've never wanted shoes to fit so badly before. *What is wrong with me?* I slip one on, then the other, and stand, the zippers still undone.

"They look awesome," Karen says.

"I think they'll be okay." I look down at my feet encased in the black lace wedges, and my mood lifts. Karen's right, shopping does fix everything.

Karen crouches and does the back zippers up. "Go for a walk."

The shoes are higher than anything I would usually wear, but they feel pretty sturdy on my feet. I think I'll be able to walk in them. I take a few steps, then stride the length of the shelving along the wall, turning at the end and walking back to the chair.

"You have to get them," Karen says. She has the box in her hands, staring at the price.

I smile so big my cheeks hurt, then sit and take the shoes off.

"I'll ring them up for you," the sales lady says.

After paying for the shoes, we decide we don't want to go home yet, so Karen and I grab a late lunch. Then we spend another few hours hanging out, looking at jewellery and window shopping. By five o'clock we've both had enough so we make our way back to the car.

Karen presses the button on her key ring and the door locks on the Swift pop open. I fall into the passenger seat, tossing my shopping bags at my feet.

"That was an awesome day." Karen starts the engine, then swings the car out of the car space and drives towards the exit. "Shopping, and standing up to Veronica."

"She'll pay me back on Monday." I rest my head against the seat.

"Don't worry. I've got your back." Karen turns onto the highway towards home.

We don't talk much during the twenty-minute drive, and when she pulls into my driveway I turn to her, trying to find the right words to thank her for everything, but I don't know what to say.

"I … you …" I tighten my grip on the handles of my shopping bags. "You're the—"

"Sweetie, you don't have to tell me." Karen smiles. "I know I'm awesome."

Laughter bubbles out of my mouth. "Yes, you are. And I love you so much for it."

"I'll always be here for you, no matter what."

What can I say to that? I hug her, then get out of the car and close the door. "Thanks," I say through the open window.

"No problem. And you know what?" Karen leans over

to look at me. "I think you need to ditch the glasses. It will totally complete the makeover. You have such pretty eyes."

"I don't know if I can do that."

"Sure you can."

"I've tried contacts before, and I hate sticking my finger in my eye."

"Promise me you'll try?" Karen grips the steering wheel, staring at me. "At least so you don't have to wear glasses to the formal."

"Okay." I nod.

"That's my girl."

I watch Karen drive away before turning towards the house.

Raised voices come from Levi's place and I stop to listen, but the words are muffled, and I can't make them out. I take a step and Levi bursts out the front door, his brow knitted and his face dark with anger.

"Get your arse back in here," Levi's dad yells from the open front door.

"Screw you." Levi stumbles towards me, blood trickling from a cut on his lip.

Mark glares at his son from the veranda before retreating inside and slamming the door.

"Levi, what happened?" I ask.

"Nothing I can't handle." He walks towards my front steps. When he reaches them, he sits down heavily and rests his head against the post.

I follow him. "Are you drunk? It's five thirty in the afternoon."

"I've been at Jarred's. Lunchtime party with the boys."

Like that explains everything.

I dump my shopping bags on the veranda and sit beside him. "Your lip is bleeding."

Levi faces me. "It's nothing."

"Do you want me to get a washcloth?"

He wipes his mouth with the back of his hand and looks at the red smudge on his skin. "Nah, it's fine."

"I'm going to get Mum." I stand, but Levi grabs my hand and pulls me back to the step.

"You've done something to your hair. It looks pretty."

Heat creeps into my cheeks, making them tingle, and I look away. "Karen took me shopping today … It's nothing special."

"Don't do that, Katie." Levi lifts my chin with his finger. "The colour is really nice."

I push my glasses up my nose, and I wish I didn't have them on. Maybe Karen is right. Maybe I need to ditch them.

I reach up and touch Levi's lip. It looks like someone hit him. "What happened? Who … Who hurt you? Is this why you drink?"

"Dad … Mason … Everything is easier to deal with through the haze."

Did his dad hit him? "It shouldn't be this way."

"A lot of things shouldn't be the way they are," Levi says.

"Will you be okay to go home?" I ask.

Levi licks his lips and nods. "I'll be fine."

"I'm really sorry. What can I do to help?"

"Nothing, Katie. I'll be fine."

The door behind us opens and Mum steps onto the veranda. "I thought I heard voices out here."

I grab my shopping bags and get to my feet. "We were

just talking."

Levi stands and jumps the steps to the path. "I'll see you tomorrow, Katie. Bye Sonja." He stuffs his hands into his pockets and walks back towards his house, stumbling once on the way.

"Come on, honey. Dinner's almost ready." Mum opens the door and we go inside. "Your hair looks great."

I smile and stop at the bottom of the stairs. "Thanks, Mum." I stare at her.

"Something up?" She raises her eyebrows.

"I'm worried about Levi. I think … he's having trouble at home."

I think his dad hit him.

"Did Levi tell you that?"

"Not exactly, but he came out of the house with Mark yelling at him. He had blood on his lip."

She purses her lips and squeezes my shoulder. "I'm sure they'll work it out."

I nod and go up to my room, hanging my dress on the wardrobe doorknob and setting the rest of my shopping bags on the bed. Maybe I'm wrong and Levi's dad didn't hit him. Maybe Levi got into a fight with one of his mates, or he walked into a door.

Who am I kidding? I decide to ask him the next time I see him.

I go to the bathroom, and while I'm washing my hands I study my new hair colour. I'm really happy with the result. I take my glasses off and splash some water on my face. After drying off, I go to put my glasses back on but stop. Karen said I should get rid of them, and Levi told me my eyes shouldn't be covered up.

I've tried contacts before, but I could never get used to sticking my finger in my eye. I have sensitive eyes so if I wore them I'd need to take them out every day. It seems like more hassle than it's worth, but maybe I should try again. And if I want to wear them to the formal, I need to get used to them now.

There are some disposables in the top drawer where I left them when I gave up the first time. I check the packet and they're still in date, so I decide that since I have new hair, I'll give them another go tomorrow.

Back in my room, I stand and stare at my new dress.

Daniel walks past, then stops and rests his hand against the doorjamb.

"You bought a dress."

I nod. "You make it sound like a crime."

"No, it's just … you. Bought a dress." He scratches his head. "I didn't think you wanted to go to the formal."

"I don't really." I sit on the edge of my bed and press my hands between my knees. "Karen convinced me. And I saw this …" I shrug.

"It's nice," Daniel says. "Very you." He comes into the room and sits next to me. "Everything okay?"

"You don't have to do the concerned big brother thing," I say. "I'm fine."

"How're things with Levi?"

I chew the side of my thumb and stare at the carpet. "There is no *thing* with Levi."

Daniel sighs and drapes his arm around my shoulders. "It gets easier."

"Why is it so hard in the first place?"

10

The fairy-tale ending I've always wanted

Going to school today is not at the top of my want-to-do list, especially after the party at Veronica's on Friday night, and running into her on the weekend. But I guess I have to get back into the swing of things. Now that trials are over, the HSC exams are a little more than a month away.

I'm hoping my new hair will draw attention away from what happened at the party.

Who am I kidding? A cut and colour aren't going to save me.

It takes me half an hour to get the contacts in my eyes. I lean over the basin in the bathroom as a wave of nausea crashes over me. The main reason I gave up the first time hits me right in the guts. Still, I'm determined to get used to them. No four-eyes photos for me at the formal.

As I walk into the kitchen, Dad looks up from his morning paper "Your hair is lovely. Did you use the money we gave you?"

I shake my head and sit across from him at the table. "Karen gifted it to me. I couldn't say no. She practically dragged me into the salon and tied me to the chair."

"Well, it really suits you." Mum grabs a piece of toast that's popped from the toaster.

"Where are your glasses?" Dad asks.

"Contacts," I say.

"She spent half an hour getting them in." Mum sets a cup of coffee in front of Dad.

Dad readjusts his paper. "Who are we impressing at school today?"

I say "no one" at the same time Daniel comes into the kitchen and says "Levi".

"Karen said I needed a change." I scowl at my brother.

"It's a nice change." Mum hands me a plate with honey toast on it.

"Need a lift today?" Daniel asks.

I grab my toast and put the plate in the sink. "Nah. I'll bus it with Jess. I've left her on her own a few times lately and I should probably make up for it."

Daniel and I say goodbye to Mum and Dad, and we both head out the door. He jumps in his car, and I start walking to the road.

Levi is in his driveway. "Katie, want a lift?"

What is it with everyone wanting to give me lifts?

"I'm fine. But thanks," I call over my shoulder.

I keep walking quickly with my head down, feeling a bit naked without my glasses on.

Jessica is at the bus stop before me, and she smiles as I approach. "No glasses?"

"I'm giving the contacts another go," I say.

"Cool. You look really pretty today. Your hair is nice."

"Karen made me," I say, and we both laugh.

"You okay after Friday?" Jessica raises her eyebrows.

I sigh. "Yeah. It was … intense. But I'm alive."

"You survived Veronica."

"Yeah." I laugh again, but I'm not sure it's all that funny.

"How'd you and Karen go dress shopping?" Jessica asks as the bus pulls up. We climb on and take our usual seats.

"I found the perfect dress." I dump my bag on the floor and pull out my phone. "Look."

Jessica takes the phone and stares at the photo. "Oh my God. It's totally you."

"I know." My stomach fills with happy feelings.

"And so not what any of those snobs would wear."

"I know!" I can't contain my excitement and I squeal.

"Mum's taking Josie and me shopping this Thursday." Jessica scrunches her nose up. "I'd rather poke hot sticks in my eyes."

"Want me to come?"

"Nah. Mum wants to do the mother–daughter thing. Stacey is so disappointed."

We plug our headphones in and listen to music on the way to the station, where we meet up with Karen. I'm glad to be catching the train, because it means I have a little more time before any potential fallout from the weekend.

School is buzzing with activity when we arrive, and

after we swipe in, Jessica and I say goodbye to Karen and head towards art class. Marking for our major works is next week, and I have a few final touches I want to put on mine.

Veronica is in our class, and she glares at me when she walks in. I do my best to ignore her, but I'm on edge, waiting for her to use her whip-like tongue. Mrs Moran's presence seems to be enough to keep Veronica at bay though, and the room is quiet as everyone works on their art.

When planning my work, I decided to combine my love for reading with something I don't particularly like—fashion. Mrs Moran wanted us to challenge ourselves, so I designed a dress made entirely from old books. I'm really happy with how the gown has turned out, and I'll find out after marking if my work will make it into the Art Express exhibition at the National Art Gallery.

"She's itching to say something to you," Jessica whispers.

I glance up and she nods towards Veronica.

"Yeah, I bet she is." I turn back to my work. "But what's she going to say that she hasn't already?"

I push Veronica and the weekend from my mind and spend the first two periods checking all my paper folds, making sure the glue has set properly in the most important places. Then I add a paper rose, coated in broken gold-leaf, to the waist. I want to do well because even though Mum and Dad are expecting me to get a degree in law or medicine, what I really want to do is fine art. I haven't told them I want to apply for the Sydney College of Fine Arts. I'll cross that bridge when I come to it.

The bell goes, and I'm starting to think this project

will never feel finished. But I have another art class later this week, so I can fix anything then if I need to.

Math class is more revision and discussion, and when recess starts I'm glad to get back outside. It's short-lived though, and we're inside again for English then History. I haven't seen Veronica since Art, and when I walk into History I cringe.

She's sitting in her usual seat with Levi beside her. I pay no attention to either of them and drop into my chair next to Karen. Until now, no one besides Karen and Jessica has commented on my hair, or the fact I'm not wearing glasses.

"Look who's had a makeover," Veronica says.

A few snickers move around the room, but I stay facing forward and ignore them.

"I wonder how she could afford to do that," Rachel says.

"She probably begged for handouts." Veronica laughs.

I close my eyes and take a deep breath. She's almost right, except for the begging part.

"Ignore them," Karen whispers. "You look hot."

I open my eyes and smile at her, then I look over my shoulder and my gaze connects with Levi's. He's slouched in his chair, a pen in one hand, and his elbow on the desk.

"I like it," he says. "Looks nice." He smiles, and I can't help smiling back.

Mr Jenkins walks in and I turn to the front again, Levi's compliment warming my insides. I look down at the book on my desk, my smile falling away. *Concentrate, Katie.* I can't afford distractions now. Final exams are getting closer. I'll know in a couple of weeks if I made dux, but I still have to get the best mark I can in my final exams to get into university. *Stop getting distracted by boys. Or one particular boy.*

The rest of class feels like it goes on for an eternity, but at least I don't get any more comments from Veronica. Mr Jenkins talks too much for that to happen.

When the lunch bell rings, Karen and I are out of there as quickly as we can. We meet up with Jessica and Stacey, and I flop onto the grass, wishing the day would end so I could go home.

"I heard you had a rough weekend." Stacey bites into her sandwich.

"It wasn't so bad," I say. "It could've been worse."

Karen snorts. "Levi was a royal arse."

I don't disagree with her. "We found formal dresses though."

"Yes, we did." Karen smiles. "And Katie is going to knock everyone right out of their fancy high heels."

I blush and stare at the sandwich in my hand. "The only thing missing is a date."

"None of us have dates. You can be mine," Karen says.

Jessica clears her throat. "Um … I might have someone."

Karen's eyes go wide. "What?"

"Who?" I ask.

"When did this happen?" Stacey stares at Jessica with wide eyes.

She shrugs. "Matthew O'Conner may have asked me."

"I can't believe you didn't tell me this morning." I smack her on the arm.

"Not bad." Karen smiles. "He's an okay guy."

Jessica blushes, and we tease her some more. Matthew

really is nice. I see him around school all the time, but we've never had a conversation. He keeps to himself a lot, even though he's in the rich league. I guess it just doesn't go to some people's heads.

"I think you should go with Levi." Karen looks at me.

"What the hell for?" I say, even though I want to. "He's been nothing but *wonderful* to me for the past few years. Why would I want to go with him?"

"Because you're in love with him," Stacey says.

I tear chunks of grass from the ground and throw them at her. "I'm not in love with him."

Jessica snorts. "Are you serious? You've been in love with him since kindergarten."

I take a deep breath because she's right, only I don't want to admit it to my friends. I'm not sure why I don't want to—I just don't. Maybe if I admit to being in love with Levi, it will make the whole situation seem worse. Can I trust him? I don't know if he's just a charmer, or if he's being genuine.

"Hey, Katie?" Veronica's voice travels across the oval, hitting my eardrums like a pick to ice.

I turn in her direction. "What?"

"Come and join us."

Veronica and her group are sitting where they usually do, on the edge of the oval in the best part of the yard. It's the best, because it's the hardest place for the on-duty teacher to see while doing rounds. And because it gets a nice mix of sun and shade.

I have no intention of getting up. "No thanks." I turn back to my small and safe group of friends.

"Oh no, here she comes," Stacey says.

When I reluctantly look over my shoulder again, Veronica is striding towards us, her nose in the air and her bitch-face on.

"You're acting like I was giving you a choice," she says when she reaches us.

I get to my feet and face her. Right now, she's my least favourite person. Ever. And I want to give it to her so badly, but I also don't want to stoop to her level. Despite the other day at the shops, I think I usually do a pretty good job of being nice, so I'm not going to let her change me into someone I'm not.

I take another deep breath. "Why do you want me to join you?"

"We're playing again. Thought you'd be up for the challenge."

"I'm a bit tired of your games, Veronica. Think I'll pass."

She stares at me and I can have a pretty good guess at what she's thinking. Someone like me shouldn't talk like this to someone like her. God forbid I should say no, or even think about standing up for myself.

"Well, it's back to me again, and I choose you," Veronica says.

Karen gets to her feet, and I'm surprised she even waited this long. She squares her shoulders, and Veronica raises her chin.

"If the words truth or dare come out of your mouth, I swear to God I will punch you in the face." Karen steps towards the queen bitch.

Veronica smirks, then she opens her mouth.

Oh God, Karen is going to hit her.

"Veronica," Levi says.

I look over her shoulder at him. He's sitting on the grass with his legs stretched out in front of him, leaning back on his hands.

When Veronica doesn't answer, he calls her name again.

"Your leader is calling you," Karen says.

"He's not my leader." Veronica scowls.

"Ronnie, don't waste your breath," Jarred calls.

She still doesn't move.

"I'm not playing," I say. "You can do whatever you want to me, but you know what? I don't care. Because nothing you do to me rates on my importance scale. You can embarrass me, call me a bitch, whatever—but I'll still be better than you, because I don't use my money to buy my friends."

"That's because you haven't got any." Veronica puts her hands on her hips. "Money, or friends." She turns and stalks back towards her group.

"You do so have friends," Jessica says in her small voice.

"She's a total air waster," Karen says. "Ignore her."

We sit back down, but this time I angle myself so I don't have my back to Veronica and her group. I want to be able to see what's going on. I may have told her I don't care, but that's a big call. She could still jeopardise my chance at dux. *Please, leave me alone.*

"He's looking at you," Karen says.

She's sitting across from me, pulling bits of grass from the ground and rolling them between her fingers.

"He is not." I sneak a look at Levi from under my lashes.

"He totally is," Stacey says.

"Yeah." Jessica smiles at me. "We've both known Levi

a long time, and I reckon he's got the hots for you."

"Levi and me … not going to happen," I say.

Karen sits up straighter. "What is going on now?"

A shadow falls over my legs, and I look up to see Geoff staring down at me.

I freeze.

"Knick off," Karen says. "You're blocking our sun."

He doesn't listen. Instead, he sits on the grass beside me.

"How are you, Katie?" he asks.

Someone who hasn't said a nice word to me ever has just asked how I am. What am I supposed to say?

"I'm fine." I draw my legs up and cross them.

"What do you want?" Karen asks.

"Gee, defensive much?" Geoff says.

"Do you blame us?" Stacey asks. "Your group doesn't exactly talk to ours, unless you're daring us to do something stupid."

"He mustn't be feeling well," Jessica says.

"I'm amazed at how different you and Josie are." Geoff stretches his legs out in front of him and leans back on his hands.

"Yeah, Jess is nice. Josie … isn't," Karen says.

Geoff raises his eyebrows. "I've come to ask a question, actually."

The four of us stare at him, waiting for him to say whatever it is he came over to say. He smirks.

"Is this some kind of dare?" Stacey asks.

Karen glares at Geoff. "The answer is no."

"I haven't even asked the question yet," he says.

"You don't have to."

I brace myself. I want to sink into the ground and disappear. Almost everyone around us is watching. I don't like being the centre of attention.

I go to open my mouth when Levi grabs Geoff by the collar.

"Get up." Levi pulls Geoff to his feet.

Geoff scowls and Levi shoves him away from us. They move out of earshot and have an animated discussion. Jarred joins them. Levi clenches his fists a few times, and I think maybe he wants to hit Geoff.

"What is that all about?" Karen asks.

I pick at the grass. "I don't want to know."

"Sure you do," Stacey says. "Levi looks angry."

"He's not the only one," I say.

"You okay?" Karen asks.

"First Veronica, now Geoff. Why can't they just leave me alone? Surely they have something better to do. Why do you guys even hang out with me, anyway?" I ask, looking around at my friends. "All of you could be one of the popular girls if you didn't pity me so much."

"We do not pity you!" Karen throws a handful of grass at me.

"She's right," Stacey says. "We don't. We know how awesome you are."

"You don't compare to them," Jessica says. "Don't even try to justify why they're bitches. They just are."

"And here we go again," Karen says.

Levi walks over to us, his hands stuffed in his pockets. Geoff and Jarred go back to their group at the end of the oval. Geoff glances over his shoulder a few times on his way.

"Either move or go away." Karen flicks her hand at Levi. "Preferably go away."

When I look up, my gaze meets Levi's and he smiles. I love and hate that smile all at the same time. I love it because it reminds me of how we used to be such good friends, but I hate it because now, after everything that's happened, I don't trust it. I can't tell if his smile is the old him or the new one.

"Katie?" he says.

"Yes?"

He runs a hand through his hair and my heart flutters. "Want to go for a walk?"

"With you?"

He looks around and chuckles. "Um … yeah. With me."

"Is this another dare?" I ask.

He frowns. "Really? That's what you think?"

"Do you blame her?" Karen gets to her feet.

"No, it's fine." I get up, too. "Let's walk."

Levi moves towards the middle of the oval. I fold my arms over my chest and follow. When Levi reaches the cricket pitch, he stops. He's taken me right out in the open where everyone can see the two of us standing together. I imagine every set of eyes in the entire school staring at me and laughing. If I thought everyone looking when Geoff was sitting with us was bad, this is a million times worse.

"What's this all about?" I ask.

"You look really pretty today." Levi stares at his feet.

I scoff. "Seriously? And how can you tell? You're not even looking at me."

Levi raises his head. His brow creases but a small

smile plays at his lips. "I mean it, Katie. Your hair is really nice. And I can see your eyes better without your glasses."

I lick my lips. "You brought me to the middle of the oval to compliment me on my hair and eyes?"

Levi takes one hand from his pocket and rubs his forehead. I want him to run it through his hair, and then I want to run my fingers through his hair, but I clutch my sides with my hands and frown at him instead.

"I want to ask you something," he says.

"Funny, Geoff said the same thing."

"Geoff was being an arse."

"And you're being …?" I roll one hand through the air.

"Can I take you out this weekend? Saturday night?"

For a moment, it feels like everyone around us heard Levi's question and they stop talking. There's a vacuum of silence in my ears before the roar of noise rushes back in a second later.

"You want to take me out?" I ask.

"Yes."

"On a date?"

Levi smiles. "We can call it that if you like."

I bite my lip. He seems to want to make up for how he's treated me, so maybe I should let him. "Okay."

"Okay?"

"Yeah," I say. "If you promise not to be a jerk."

Levi chuckles. "I promise."

My stomach flip-flops. I feel like I'm getting in way over my head, but my heart—it's hoping for the fairy-tale ending I've always wanted.

11

What will I be getting myself into?

Getting through the rest of the week was torture. Four days felt like four months, and now that it's Saturday night, I'm a nervous wreck.

I'm nervous, because Levi is taking me out on a date. Which Daniel has been reminding me of for the past two hours.

"The day has finally come." My brother stands in my doorway, a grin on his face.

"What day is that?" I fling my Converse back into my wardrobe.

"The day my little nerdy sister is going on a date."

"It's not a date."

Daniel laughs. "You really have no clue."

"I have enough of a clue. I'm just in denial."

I dig around the bottom of my wardrobe for my strappy

brown sandals. Levi told me to wear something nice, but as to the level of niceness, I'm not sure how nice I should go. I have no idea where he's taking me, or what he has planned, so I've dressed in my usual jeans, with the new paisley top I bought with Karen. I find the sandals and sit on my bed to put them on.

"Have fun." Daniel goes to his room.

The doorbell rings a few minutes later. I glance at the clock above my desk. The hour hand ticks over to seven pm. He's right on time.

I fish my favourite amethyst ring from the little dish on my desk, slipping it onto my finger, then grab my phone and purse, and race down the stairs to find Mum already answering the door.

Levi steps over the threshold. "You look really nice, Katie."

"Thanks." Heat prickles my cheeks.

"Remember your curfew," Dad says from the lounge room.

"Yes," I mumble. "Bye, Mum." I give her a kiss on the cheek.

Levi and I walk across to his place and down the driveway to where his BMW is parked on the street.

"That's a pretty top," he says. "It brings out the green bits in your eyes."

My cheeks grow hotter, and my hands go clammy. Why am I so nervous? It's Levi. The guy I've known my whole life. The guy who used to be my best friend. The guy who shut me out because I have no money. The guy who is now the captain of the most prestigious high school in the shire.

Yep, that's why I'm nervous.

I stop at the car and frown.

Levi opens the door, but I don't get in.

"What's the matter, Katie?"

"I ..." I bite my lip. "Are you sure you want to take me out?"

"I wouldn't have asked you if I didn't want to." Levi smiles. "But we can stay home if you like?"

I shake my head. When I get in the car, the most amazing spicy smell hits my nose. It's coming from the back seat, and I turn to see what it is.

Levi climbs in behind the wheel. "Dinner. You like Thai, don't you?"

I nod and settle into the leather seat. Levi starts the car and we drive towards the highway.

"Where are you taking me?" I ask.

"You'll see." And he doesn't offer any more information than that.

We drive for ten minutes then Levi makes a right-hand turn into a side street. He pulls over and parks at the kerb. There's a park on the corner. I remember coming here when we were kids, but I haven't been for years. We drive past it every time we go to the shops, but it always goes unnoticed. I'm curious what Levi is up to.

"You have to promise me you won't look," Levi says.

"Are we having a picnic?"

"Just ... don't look, okay?"

"Sure. I won't."

"Great. Wait here."

Levi gets out and opens the back door, grabbing the food from the seat. He also opens the boot, and I pull my phone out to distract myself so I'm not tempted to watch him. After about ten minutes I wonder when he's going to come and get me. I glance up and he's walking towards my side of the car. Levi opens my door and looks down at me.

"You have to close your eyes for this part," he says.

I clutch my phone and my purse, and get out of the car. My legs are a little shaky because not only am I nervous, but I'm scared, too. I keep having visions of Veronica jumping from behind the bushes and yelling 'truth or dare'. Then I giggle, because, really?

"What's the joke?" Levi asks.

I smile. "Nothing. Closing my eyes now." I hug my purse and phone to my chest.

Levi takes my elbow and I move a few steps, hear the car door close, then take a couple more steps.

"Foot up," Levi says, pressing one hand into the small of my back and holding my arm with the other. "That's it. Hang on. I have to open a gate."

Metal squeals.

I shuffle my feet. "Are we almost there?"

"Just another couple of steps." Levi stops and gently turns my shoulders. "Okay, open your eyes."

At first, I'm not sure what I'm looking at. I blink a few times, and draw in a deep breath. We're standing in the middle of the park under a huge gum tree. The playground is to our left and the grassed area is on our right. On the ground is a picnic rug surrounded by tea-light candles. They flicker orange. Levi has set out our Thai dinner with plates and cutlery, and there are pink flowers scattered across the rug and around the candles.

I take a few steps closer, amazed that he has done something like this for me.

"Bougainvillea flowers," I say.

The biggest grin splits his face. "Do you like it?"

How do I answer that? I bite my lip and grip my purse before wrapping my arms around my waist. Tears prick the backs of my eyes.

Levi comes up behind me and puts his hands on my shoulders, pressing his lips to the back of my head.

"I'm so sorry for … everything," he says.

I shudder with the effort of holding back the tears. "No one has ever done anything like this for me before," I whisper. "Thank you."

"You can thank me by helping me eat all this food." Levi takes my hand, and we sit on the rug.

For an hour, I forget about everything. Veronica and her stupid games. Who and what has hurt me in the past. None of it matters right now. All that matters is Levi and me, enjoying each other's company with no one else around to ruin it.

I don't want to ask Levi why he decided to do this for me. I don't want to think about anything other than spending time with him, because maybe there is something between us. Maybe I just need to let it happen and see where it goes.

The food is delicious, and I feel like I've eaten enough for three people. I pick up some of the bougainvillea flowers and twirl them between my fingers. I smile, so happy in this moment, sitting in a kid's park with the boy I've loved since I was a kid.

"Remember I said I shut you out because you don't fit

with my friends?" Levi looks at me with intense eyes.

I frown. "Why do you want to talk about this now?" Anger sparks in my chest, because he's ruining the moment.

"Just, listen." Levi runs his hand through his hair in that way I love so much. "I was wrong. *They* don't fit with you. I realise now I made the wrong choice."

"Yeah, you did. You broke my heart." I drop the flowers and stare at my hands, picking at my fingernails. The moment is totally gone.

"I was an idiot, that's all. Too wrapped up in trying to be the perfect … whatever. Can you forgive me?"

I stare at the flowers on the rug in front of me. Tears well in my eyes again, and the pink outlines of the flowers blur until they're nothing but splotches.

"That depends." I look up and our eyes meet. "Can you forgive yourself?"

"You know what the hardest part was?" Levi stares at me for a few heartbeats, then looks away. "I went through a pretty rough time after Mason died. I'm still going through it. And I wanted to talk to you, but I didn't know how to fix things between us. I didn't know if you would ever speak to me again."

I adjust my position and draw my legs up to my chest, resting my chin on my knees. "I was worried about you. I wanted to talk to you at the funeral, but I figured you didn't want me to be there for you. I would've been though."

"There's no excuse for the way I've treated you."

I hug my knees tighter, and stare at Levi. "The past is the past. It is what it is. We can't change it."

Levi reaches out and takes my hand, giving it a gentle squeeze. "How can you be so forgiving? You must hate me."

"I don't *hate* anyone. What's the point in holding a grudge? It only makes you unhappy." I stare at our hands, Levi's fingers entwined in mine. "I hate what you did, but I don't hate you. I could never …" I let my unfinished words hang between us, listening to the occasional car passing on the road beside the park.

"I don't deserve your forgiveness," Levi finally says. "You're really something, you know that, Katherine Sullivan?" Levi lets go of my hand and starts packing up the food. "We should go. We have a movie to see. Unless you want to stay here?"

"A movie sounds perfect." I smile.

Levi pulls me to my feet, and we pack everything back into the car. Part of me wants to be happy that he's trying so hard to fix things between us, but there's another part of me that can't help doubting his motivations. What if he breaks my heart again? Especially now he's holding so much of it?

I stood up to Veronica.

I'm brave—much braver than I'd ever thought I could be.

Maybe it's time I trust myself to trust Levi. I'm strong enough for this—and he's lucky to have me in his life. I decide to start trusting him and see where it gets me.

Levi parks on the middle level of the car park and we walk out past the restaurants then upstairs to the cinema.

"Action, romance, or drama?" Levi asks.

I look up at the titles rolling across the board above the ticket sales counter. I don't mind what we see. I just want to sit alone with Levi for a while and forget about the rest of the world.

"You choose," I say. "And don't pick romance because it's what you think I want to watch."

"Action then?" Levi laughs.

He gets the biggest box of popcorn he can, and pays for our tickets, holding my hand as we walk to cinema five. We sit in the back row, and when the lights go down my heartrate quickens.

I'm nervous all over again.

Levi lifts the armrest between us and I stiffen.

"Relax," he whispers in my ear.

I settle into the crook of his arm and stare at the screen, but if someone were to ask me what the movie was about, I wouldn't be able to tell them. I'm too preoccupied with savouring the feeling of Levi's arm around me, and the way his body moves in response to the movie.

Disappointment settles into my stomach when the movie finishes, because it means it's time to go and I won't have Levi's arm around me anymore. Reluctantly, I move out of his embrace and we leave the cinema.

"We still have a couple of hours before your curfew," Levi says. "What do you want to do?"

I glance around the foyer of the cinema at all the people leaving. Most of them are couples like Levi and me. What troubles have they been through? I hope theirs haven't been as hard as ours. Seeing how happy they are makes me smile.

"Hot chocolate?" I say. "The café should still be open."

"Chocolate café it is then."

Levi puts his arm around my shoulders and pulls me close. We walk out into the mall.

He stops us at the clock fountain in the centre and pulls

a twenty-cent piece from his pocket, handing it to me.

"Make a wish," he whispers in my ear.

I'm not sure I believe in making wishes, so I think about what would make me happy instead. I feel the weight of the coin in my palm before I toss it in. It makes a little splash as it hits the water. When it sinks to the bottom and settles with the other coins, I stare at it for a moment. The coins glisten under the mall lighting like a star-filled sky.

I wish Levi and I will become something special.

We continue on to the café and I order my favourite. A white hot chocolate with two marshmallows on the side. Levi orders a dark hot chocolate, and we find a quiet table at the back of the café, away from the other patrons.

Levi takes a sip of his drink and smirks. "You have a froth moustache. It's cute."

I lick my lips and return his smile.

We spend an hour talking about our childhoods, and reminiscing about the stupid stuff we used to get up to.

We had such a good time together back then. Before high school, and Veronica, and Mason's death …

Mason.

Is he the reason Levi fights with his dad?

I don't know exactly what's going on, but something isn't right between them. I stare at the dark scab on the corner of Levi's lip. He's had drunken injuries before—maybe this is just another one.

I don't want to ruin the night by asking questions I probably shouldn't, so I focus on Levi's intense eyes and warm smile, as we remind each other of what we used to have.

By the time we're ready to leave, we're both laughing. It feels good.

Our drive home is quiet. I don't want to talk too much because I don't want to say anything that will break the spell that seems to have fallen over us. The night has been pretty perfect, and I don't want to spoil it. I stare out the window and watch the lights pass as we make our way off the highway and towards home.

Levi parks in his driveway and walks me to my front door. It's fifteen minutes before curfew, and I'm not ready for the night to end. I face Levi and chew my lip, still not wanting to say anything that's going to ruin tonight.

We didn't watch a romance, but I've seen plenty of romantic movies, and this is the part when the goodnight kiss is supposed to happen. My heart beats faster, and my palms get sweaty. I hug myself and stare at my feet. I'm not sure I want to go there just yet. Kissing Levi is definitely on my to-do list, but now that he's standing in front of me, staring at me, all I want to do is run away and hide. The anticipation, the look in his eyes—they're making me nervous.

"I should go inside." I fumble my keys from my purse.

"Katie." Levi puts his hand over mine. "I won't kiss you if you don't want me to."

"Oh … you were going to …" I stare at our hands, heat rising into my cheeks.

I want to say something else, but no words come to mind. What am I supposed to say? Yes, kiss me? This is what I've been afraid of—ruining everything. And it looks like I'm going to do it by keeping my mouth shut this time.

"I don't want to ruin the night," I finally say.

Levi steps closer and puts a hand on my cheek, brushing my skin with his thumb. "That's not even possible."

He leans in, and my heart beats so fast I think I might go into cardiac arrest. Gently, he brushes my lips with his. He doesn't open his mouth, or use any force, and the feeling of his lips on mine sends tingles down my spine and all the way to my toes.

He pulls away, his thumb still caressing my cheek, and I stare at him with no words to describe the way he makes me feel. He moves his hand around to the back of my neck and twists his fingers into my hair, pressing his forehead to mine.

"Can I ask you something?" Levi says.

I close my eyes. "Sure."

"Will you ...?" He shuffles his feet. "Do you want to go to the formal with me?"

I pull away, and Levi untangles his hand from my hair. He raises his eyebrows and smiles.

I'm not sure what to say. "I ..."

The front door opens and Mum peers out at us. "Katie? I thought I heard voices."

"Sorry, Mum. I was just coming in."

"Don't be too long. Good night, Levi."

She leaves the door open, and I watch through the screen as she goes back upstairs.

"Thanks for a really nice night." I open the screen door and step inside. "I'll see you at school?"

Levi nods, his smile faltering. "Okay. See you Monday. Want a lift?"

"I'll go with Karen and Jess. Night."

I close the door before he walks away, unsure why I

didn't give him an answer to his question. He seems genuine, but maybe it's safer if I go to the formal without a date. I've pretty much already resigned myself to the fact that that's how it's going to be anyway.

I don't want to say no, but if I say yes, what will I be getting myself into?

12

Who I am

For the next couple of weeks everyone is in full-on study and revision mode. Levi asks about the formal again, but I make it clear I can't think about anything other than exams. I want to say yes, but it all seems too good to be true. What if I agree to go with him and then everything comes crashing down around me?

I travel to school with Jessica and Karen, even though Levi offers to drive me every morning. It makes it easier to avoid giving him an answer, and I don't want to completely abandon my friends.

Today, when I get to school the halls are buzzing with talk of the formal, which is a little over a week away. Discussions about dresses, corsages, and cars are coming out of the mouths of every year twelve student I pass. I don't get why it's such a big deal, today of all days.

Today is Year Twelve Awards day.

Today is the day we're on show to the entire school and our families.

Today is the day I find out if I made dux or not.

"Today is the day my life could potentially be over," I say to Karen as we make our way to the hall where the entire school is assembling for a big morning of presentations, awards, and performances.

"Stop worrying. You'll romp it in," Karen says. "No one here is smarter than you. Besides, there are more important things to discuss."

"Like what?" I stare at her blankly.

"Jess doesn't have shoes to go with her dress yet," she says. "Apparently, she couldn't find any when her mum took her and her witch sister shopping."

"You're talking about shoes at a time like this?" I glare at her.

"Calm down. I told you, you've got this." Karen grabs my hand and we make our way to the front of the hall to our assigned seats. The back section of the hall has seating set out for the parents and family members who are able to attend a ceremony during the day—which is a lot of them, since they're all so rich and can afford the time off work. Mum is here, but Dad had to go to a service call at a building in the city. Something about a burst water pipe that flooded the main electrical board.

Everyone is settled by ten am. We sit through the headmistress's boring speech and a host of awards for various things from sport to citizenship.

Then the academic awards begin. They start with individual subject awards, and Veronica receives an award for academic excellence in Biology. I don't take Biology, so I'm not too concerned. I lean forward. What award will be announced next? Will I get first in any subjects?

"Would you stop it?" Karen whispers. "Sit back."

I try to relax into my chair, but I'm eagerly awaiting the next announcement.

My name is called for academic excellence in Visual Arts, History, and Advanced English. My face hurts from smiling as I walk on stage to shake the headmistress's hand and take my certificates. I spot Mum clapping and smiling as I return to my seat.

There are a few more announcements, then Mrs Pritchard adjusts the microphone.

"Now, the moment everyone has been eagerly awaiting," she says. The hall falls silent. "The student I'm about to announce has been a pleasure to have amongst us for the past two years. She has gone above and beyond to ensure her academic achievements have been of the highest standard."

I tense in my chair. It has to be me. *Just spit it out.*

"This school prides itself on accepting only the best," she continues. "Each year we offer one place to an exceptional student who undergoes rigorous screening for our scholarship program, and this year that student has earned the award of dux. Please put your hands together for Katherine Sullivan."

The hall erupts into applause.

Karen slaps me on the arm. "Get up there."

I stand, and my legs wobble as I walk to the stage. Mrs Pritchard shakes my hand again and congratulates me, then leads me to the lectern.

I've tried not to think about this part too much.

I've been so caught up in everything that's been happening, with study, and Levi, and the formal, it seems like I wrote my speech years ago.

I put my certificate on the surface in front of me, then take the piece of paper from my pocket and unfold it. When I look out into the crowd I see a lot of faces I don't know, some I do, and some I don't like very much. Veronica is sitting with her arms folded, and a scowl on her face. Levi is at the head of the first row of year twelves, waiting to give his captain's speech after me.

Our gazes lock, and he smiles. I take a deep breath.

"Mrs Pritchard, teachers, fellow students, parents." I pause, and Levi gives me a nod. "I'm humbled and grateful to receive this award, but I want you all to know that getting here has not been easy. It took a lot of hard work, but most of all, it took determination. It's not easy being the one who is at a disadvantage, where every obstacle thrown your way is bigger than the last." A few students shift in their seats. "If this school and its students have taught me one thing, it's that no matter who we are, where we come from, or what our position in life is, there is nothing we can't do. We can and will achieve great things with determination, and the belief that no one but ourselves can stop us. Thank you."

More applause sounds around the hall, and Mum stands, clapping furiously. I step away from the lectern and a flash goes off, sending spots across my vision, but I can't help grinning. The photographer clicks away a couple more times before letting me leave the stage. By the time I return to my seat my cheeks ache from smiling so wide.

"Way to go," Karen says, nudging me. "You really gave it to them."

I guess I did. I'm not sure if I'll get any backlash for implying that I didn't have a fair playing field, but I'm not sure I even care. What's the worst they can do? Take the award away from me?

Mrs Pritchard calls Levi to the stage to give his captain's speech. After addressing the crowd, Levi locks his gaze on me, and he doesn't break it until he's finished. "Since our early days as year seven students, we've come so far, and achieved so much. We've laughed together, cried together, and grown together. I'm proud to be captain of such an outstanding group of young adults ready to take on the world. Because now, we are ready. And as Katie said, there is nothing we can't do. Congratulations to all our award receivers. Thank you."

Levi returns to his seat to another deafening round of applause. Mrs Pritchard declares the awards ceremony over, and we all file out of the hall to have lunch with our parents and friends.

Mum hugs me. "Congratulations, honey. You should have no trouble getting into university." She holds me at arm's length. "You'll make a great lawyer or doctor."

I smile and hug her again, but my stomach knots at the thought of telling her I don't really want to study law or medicine. Now is not the time to bring it up though.

Mum hangs around for a while, along with everyone else, and I'm grateful when people start to leave. It quietens down a bit and I can go and sit with my friends.

I lie back on the grass and stare up at the clear spring sky.

"Has he asked you yet?" Karen says. She's sitting behind me, running her fingers through my hair.

I shade my eyes and stare at a solitary cloud drifting across the sky. It looks like a heart, if I tilt my head sideways.

"He has," I say.

"What? And you didn't tell me? When? What did you say?" Karen stops playing with my hair and stares down at me.

"She hasn't given me an answer yet." Levi stands over us, blocking the sun. "She's left me hanging."

I sigh and sit up, crossing my legs. Levi plonks his backpack on the grass and sits beside me.

"You should answer him," Stacey says. "I want to know what you'll say."

"She's going to say yes," Karen says.

"I'm right here." I glare at her.

"Me too." Levi smiles.

Jessica laughs. "Leave them alone."

"Why?" Karen asks. "They obviously need help with this."

Levi throws a twig at her and it lands in her hair. She screws her nose up as she picks it out and throws it back at him.

I dip my head and let my fringe fall around my face. I don't want to make a big deal out of this. No one has ever asked me to a dance before, I've always gone on my own, and I don't want the fuss. I also don't know if I should say yes to Levi. I've been avoiding answering him, because what if it's the wrong decision? I'm so scared that none of this is real.

Levi reaches over and tucks my hair behind my ear. My cheeks grow hot and I want to hide again.

He leans over and whispers in my ear, "Want to take a walk?"

I glance at him and nod. Levi jumps up and offers me his hand. I take it and he pulls me to my feet, putting one arm around my shoulders and tucking me in to his side. I don't look to see if anyone is watching us, but they probably are.

"Where are we going?" I ask.

"You'll see."

Levi leads me to the far side of the oval. Being over here isn't breaking the rules, but not many students bother to come this far away from the comfort of the shaded seats. There's nothing here anyway, and I wonder where he's taking me.

We reach the fence and Levi looks around before jumping over. "Come on." He motions for me to follow.

"Um … we're not supposed to jump the fence, Levi."

"Don't make me throw you over it." He smiles. "Seriously, it's fine. I come here all the time. And the on-duty teacher just walked around the main building, so hurry up before she comes back."

I pivot and hoist myself onto the metal fence. "Turn around. I don't want to flash you."

Levi laughs, but he does as I ask. I put one leg over and then the other, dropping the short distance to the ground on the other side. Levi takes my hand and we follow the fence for a few metres before taking a worn path that leads into the trees behind the admin block. The tall gums enclose a small clearing with a shaded patch of grass. Levi goes to one of the trees which has a hole in the trunk, the perfect size for a possum to live in, and pulls out a rolled up picnic rug.

"You brought me to the make-out room?" I ask.

"It's not what you think." Levi flicks the rug and lays it on the grass.

"Then tell me, what should I think?" I cross my arms and glare at him.

Levi sits and pats the rug next to him.

I don't move.

"Katie, I'm not—"

"I'm not making out with you."

"Why not? Making out is fun." He grins.

"I'm serious. Not here."

He grabs my hand and gently pulls until I'm kneeling and facing him. He runs circles over the back of my hand with his thumb, and I stare at our hands. His touch is so gentle.

"I just want to be with you," he says. "Without everyone staring at us. We don't have to do anything but sit."

I move so I'm sitting with my legs tucked beside me. Levi leans in and presses his forehead to mine. My breath catches in my throat. He closes his eyes, and I stare at the tip of his nose and his eyelashes. His face is so close to mine. His lips part, and his breath tickles my mouth.

I want him. But wanting him scares me.

I touch his lips with my thumb and press my palm to his cheek. "I'm scared," I whisper.

"Of what?" Levi asks. "You don't need to be scared."

"I don't know if I can control myself when I'm with you."

"I have the same problem." He keeps his eyes closed, but circles his arm around my waist and pulls my body closer to his.

"If I let myself … if I get too attached to you … I don't really have you yet, and I'm already scared of losing you."

Levi opens his eyes and pulls away to look at me. "You've always had me, Katie."

He uncrosses his legs and pulls me into his lap, hugging me with both arms. I've never been hugged like this by him, and it makes me feel safe. I lay my head on his shoulder and a hand on his chest, feeling the beat of his heart.

We sit like this until the next bell rings. We don't talk, or do anything, we just sit. And it's comforting.

"We should go," I say.

We untangle ourselves and get to our feet. Levi rolls up the blanket and puts it back in the tree. Then he takes my hand and pulls me close for another hug. When he releases me, he has a smile on his face, and he raises his eyebrows.

"I'm only going to ask this once more. Katherine Sullivan, will you go to the formal with me?"

I mirror his smile. "Since you said you won't ask again, I guess I have to say yes."

"You could say no." He kisses the tip of my nose.

"But I thought you wanted a yes."

"What do you want?" he asks.

"I want … you."

Levi studies me. His mouth curls up on one side and he chuckles. "Thank you."

"What for?" I ask.

Levi leads me back along the path to the oval. "Being you."

My smile grows, and my belly fills with little flutters. For the first time in a while, I'm happy to be who I am.

So heartbreaking

Levi hardly leaves my side for the rest of the week, and Veronica backs off enough for me to think that maybe he has said something to her. I knuckle down and do as much study as I can, helping Levi as well, and before I know it the day of the formal is here.

Karen sets the hair curler on my desk and spins me to face her. She digs through the huge cosmetics bag she brought with her and pulls out a compact and a brush.

"Hair is gorgeous. Now for the makeup." She smiles.

"Not too much," I say. "I want to look like me."

"I promise, you'll look amazing."

She sets to work. I sit patiently in my desk chair while Karen brushes and smudges, and makes me pucker and blot my lips. No doubt Veronica and the other girls will be going to professional hairdressers and makeup artists to get ready. I'm so lucky I have Karen, and her makeup expertise.

After about half an hour, she says, "All done. Have a look."

I stare at myself in the full-length mirror on my wardrobe door. I'm not sure who the girl is looking back at me. It's me, but it isn't. I don't wear makeup, and it feels weird, but I like what Karen has done. It's not too heavy or too dark. There's just a hint of colour on my lips, and some rosiness in my cheeks. I smile at my reflection, twisting a finger into one of the curls Karen has set with the curler. They fall loosely around my shoulders.

"Thank you," I say. "It's perfect."

Karen smiles and busies herself working on her own makeup. I'm not much help in that department, so I lay out our dresses on the bed. When she's done, Karen helps me slip into my dress, and I help her with hers. She puts on a silver choker with a topaz teardrop that hangs from the centre. I don't have much jewellery, and I don't like too much bling, so Karen helps me fasten a silver chain around my neck. The pendant is a small heart with three diamonds in it, a gift from my parents a couple of years ago. Then I slip my favourite silver amethyst ring onto my right hand.

There's a light knock at the door, and Mum pokes her head in.

"Oh, Katie. You look wonderful," she says, tears glistening in her eyes. She comes into the room and hugs me. "You, too, Karen. Your gown is beautiful. You're both so grown-up."

"I guess you scrub up okay," Daniel says from the doorway.

"Gee, thanks." I poke my tongue out at him.

"What's going on in here?" Dad asks. "Well. It seems you have a dance to get to." He smiles and his eyes crinkle. "There's someone at the door waiting for you, Katie."

Karen and I make our way down the stairs with everyone else in tow. Karen's parents come out of the lounge room and look up the stairs at us, huge smiles on their faces.

Levi is standing at the front door, dressed in a traditional black cocktail suit. His tie is a deep purple, which complements my dress perfectly. I look at Karen, and she smiles.

"Someone had to coordinate you. I knew you'd forget," she says.

I stop at the bottom of the stairs and Levi takes the few steps to my side. He kisses me on the cheek and whispers in my ear, "You look beautiful."

"Thanks," I manage to say before Mum announces she wants photos.

"A couple on the stairs first," she says, shuffling Levi and I into position.

Mum snaps away, then she swaps Levi with Karen, and the two of us beam at the camera. I wish Jessica and Stacey could be here, too, but they're leaving from Jessica and Josephine's house. Hopefully our two cars will time it well enough to arrive at the formal at the same time.

Mum herds us out to the front yard for more photos. Levi tugs me gently towards the bougainvillea. The side of the house is a mass of pink blooms, and Levi wanting to have our photo taken in front of it makes my heart flutter with happiness. Dad frowns, but I beam back at him. I'm not going to let anything ruin this moment.

I feel bad for Karen though. She doesn't have a date, but if she's upset about it she's not showing it. She fixes a wide smile to her face, and it doesn't budge as we go next door to Levi's place.

"Hi, Yvonne," Mum says to Levi's mum as we enter the foyer. "Will Mark be joining the fun?"

"I'm afraid he has to work late," she says. "But I promised him photos, so come on, kids."

"Hold on, Mum." Levi grabs a small clear box off the hallstand and hands it to me. "This is for you."

Inside is a small wrist corsage. It's so simple, and it's beautiful—a cluster of three bougainvillea flowers surrounded by greenery and attached to a purple band.

I don't know what to say. Thank you doesn't seem enough, because he hasn't bought just any corsage—he's actually thought about it. I slip it onto my wrist and stand on my tiptoes to give Levi a kiss on the cheek. I don't care that our parents are watching.

Yvonne leads us through to the open-plan family room. Veronica and Jarred are waiting on the lounge, along with Geoff who is going solo. Veronica gives me a smug smile, and I'm not exactly sure how to read it. She stares down her nose, scrutinising me from head to toe before standing up.

Veronica's dress is nothing short of amazing. The cerise cocktail dress stops above her knees, showing off her long legs. The skirt is a mass of ruffles. Silver diamantes and beading cover the bodice, making her look as if she's dripping in diamonds. The spaghetti straps are also a row of sparkling gems. And I hate to admit it, but her silver stilettoes are perfect for the dress.

"You look really nice." I smile. No need to be a bitch when it's true.

"Thanks," she says. "Your dress is ... different. It's pretty."

"Thank you," I say, unsure if she's just being polite.

Levi's mum pulls the camera out again, getting us all to pose in front of the big windows, on the couch, and in every other place she can think of. Geoff and Karen end up standing together and looking like a couple, much to Karen's disgust.

"Everyone, please have a drink." Yvonne gestures to the kitchen counter where a line of champagne flutes sit, filled to the top with bubbly orange juice. Each glass has a strawberry on the rim. "There's more orange juice than champagne, so don't worry." She smiles.

Levi grabs two glasses, bringing one over to me. I sip my drink and watch everyone sipping theirs, nibbling at the finger food, dip, and crackers.

Mum comes over to me. "No more after this."

"Mum, relax," Daniel says. "It's Katie."

"What's that supposed to mean?" I ask.

Daniel shrugs and goes to get a glass and eat the food. Veronica sniggers.

The adults move into the lounge room and the rest of us hover around the food.

"We should toast," Karen says.

"To getting drunk." Geoff raises his glass.

Levi laughs.

"You're an idiot," Karen says.

"To a good night." Levi takes a sip of his champagne.

"Don't drink yet." Karen grabs his arm. "To the future … and to not knowing where any of us will end up."

"Sounds good enough." Jarred raises his glass.

We all chink them together. Veronica even chinks me, but she smirks. I get the feeling she knows something I don't, and my stomach fills with dread. I realise that I'm nervous, only I don't have butterflies—I have bogon moths.

I smile at Levi and take a sip of my drink. The bubbles tickle my nose and I giggle. Levi downs his glass in one mouthful, and I catch his mum frowning from the other side of the room.

"You should pace yourself," Daniel says, sipping his drink. "Don't want to be drunk before you get there."

"I'm good." Levi eats the strawberry, then grabs the bottle from the bench and fills his glass. No orange juice this time.

"Champagne has a habit of going to your head."

"Don't be such a party pooper, Daniel," Veronica says.

Levi drinks this glass more slowly, but it still worries me.

Mum and Dad glance over a few times, and I smile at them, trying not to let on how uncomfortable I am around these people. It would be nice to go outside again.

Levi puts his lips to my ear. "I've got a bottle for the car. We can have more later."

The drunkest I've ever been was at Veronica's party, and I don't plan to get drunk again any time soon, especially after seeing how Levi is when he's had too many.

"The car is here," Yvonne says from the front window of the family room.

Levi grabs a bottle of champagne from the fridge, downs the rest of his drink, and sets the glass on the bench. The others do the same and start towards the foyer. I still have half a glass, and I don't like the idea of drinking it all at once, even if it is mostly orange juice.

Veronica glances over her shoulder and laughs.

I take one more sip of the bubbly drink, then set the glass on the bench before following the others.

Daniel grabs my elbow, and we stop in the foyer as everyone else goes outside. "You okay?"

"I wish you'd stop asking me that. I'm fine."

"Just … be careful tonight. Please. Don't drink too much."

"Daniel—"

"Katie, you're my little sister. I worry about you."

"Well, don't." I grab his hand and pull him out the door towards the others.

"I could talk to him. You know … warn him if he hurts you …"

I stop on the path and glare at my brother. "Don't you dare."

He bursts out laughing, and that's when I realise he's joking. I smack him on the arm and join the group standing next to the black stretch Hummer.

Jarred opens the door and helps Veronica in. Geoff does the same for Karen, and I have to hide my look of shock. I've never seen him act so … gentlemanly. Is it because he wants to be nice, or because the adults are watching us?

"After you." Levi rests his hand on the top of the door.

I kiss Mum and Dad.

"Have fun sweetie," Mum says.

"No more drinking," Dad says.

Levi smiles. "I'll look after her."

I climb into the limo next to Karen. She's sitting across from Geoff, which means I'm directly facing Veronica. The fifty-minute trip to Sydney is going to be great. I quickly type a message to Jessica to tell them we're leaving.

The Hummer pulls out of the driveway and into the street, and Levi pops the bottle of champagne before we even reach the highway. He pours everyone a glass, then sets the empty bottle upside down in the cooler.

"Cheers," he says.

"To a great night," Geoff says.

Jarred smirks. "To truth."

I bite my lip, wondering what he means by that.

Levi takes my hand and gives it a squeeze, but I don't miss the glare he gives Jarred. Something is going on, and I have no idea what. *Why are they giving each other funny looks?*

The bogon moths return.

"To getting drunk." Veronica takes a big mouthful of champagne.

Karen snorts. "To getting out of the hellhole that is our school."

"To new beginnings," I say, clinking my glass against Levi's and taking a sip. "Maybe all of us could do with one of those."

He squeezes my hand again, and we settle back for the ride into the city. The conversation is light, and I listen or join in when I'm not staring out the window. Before I know it, we're crossing the bridge over the harbour.

I crane my neck to look up at the huge steel structure as we pass under it, and the prettiness of the lights makes me smile. The limo takes us through the tight and busy city streets, stopping at the base of Sydney Tower.

The boys get out and help the three of us from the car. Several limos arrive carrying other students from school, and all the girls look amazing. There's so much bling. I fiddle with my necklace as I glance around at the array of dresses.

We make our way into the foyer of the building, and the volume rises with the chatter of excited formal-goers. I don't want to talk to any of them. I'm overwhelmed, and I glance over my shoulder at the entry doors, looking for an exit.

Jessica and Stacey walk through as I'm planning my escape, and I take a deep breath. Now they're here, I have my three girls. Maybe I can get through this in one piece.

Jessica looks incredible in a floor-length royal blue gown. Exquisite pearl beading covers her décolletage and waist. Stacey wears a pale pink mermaid dress with a sheer back and sleeves. Delicate beading covers her shoulders and arms.

All my friends are stunning, and seeing them brings a tear to my eye.

The crowd begins to move, and we pile into the lifts to make the journey to the top of the tower. The theme for the formal is regal, and the thought actually makes me laugh. It's pretty fitting, because every rich kid here thinks they're royalty. The restaurant is decorated with rich purple, red, and gold. The tablecloths alternate in purple and red, with gold sequins and coloured gemstones scattered down the middle. Golden bows adorn the white chair covers. There's even a stage with two thrones for the crowning of the formal king and queen.

Many of the girls fit the royal theme with their full-length gowns. My dress doesn't look like something a queen would wear, with its long and short hemline, but I still feel like a princess, and I'm determined to have a good night.

As we walk through, we're directed to line up for photos before finding our seats. Levi takes my hand and we step in front of the deep purple velvet wall. A curtain of sparkling gold sequins hangs in front of it, giving it a magical touch.

"That's it," the photographer says. "Give her a hug."

Levi pulls me close and presses a kiss to my temple while the photographer snaps away. I stare up at him and smile, lost in his eyes.

"Okay, next," the photographer calls.

"Let's find our seats." Levi tugs my hand and leads me through the rows of tables.

We find our places near the dance floor and to the right of the stage. I'm pleased to see we're sitting with Karen, Jessica and her date, Matthew, and Stacey, but we also have Veronica, Jarred, Josephine, and Geoff. I guess it won't be too bad. I've survived Veronica and her friends for this long—another night isn't going to make a difference.

I scan the room and absorb it all. The people filing in. The teachers bustling about.

"We should do the photo booth later," I say to Levi, pointing to the back corner of the large room.

"Sure." Levi pulls his chair out and sits. "That'll be fun."

We chat amongst our table while we wait for everyone to be seated. Mrs Pritchard addresses us, not saying anything that hasn't already been said at awards day or graduation, and we groan at the parts we're supposed to and laugh at the other ones.

Once dinner is over the music starts pumping, and half the year hit the dance floor. I'm not much of a dancer, so I'm not that eager to get out there. Karen, Stacey, and I sit at the table for a while and watch the commotion around us. Levi is off talking to his mates on the far side of the room, and I'm actually in a good place, happy to sit back and watch life go by for a while, and not have to actively take part in it.

"How was your limo ride?" Stacey asks over the music.

"Not too bad," I say. "Veronica contained herself, if that's what you mean."

We all chuckle, then I slap Karen's arm and point towards the dance floor. Jessica is dancing with her date, Matthew, and her face is plastered with a huge smile. He tries to get close to her every chance he can, and seeing Jessica so happy makes me happy, too.

The music throbs through the floor and vibrates into my feet. It settles in the pit of my stomach, and the feeling isn't something I've experienced before. I'm happy at a school function. No one is being mean to me. Everyone is having a good time. I'm just another person in the crowd, and it feels great.

I jump up and grab Karen's hand, pulling her until

she's on her feet. Stacey follows, and we go to the floor-to-ceiling windows and look out over the city. The lights streak through the darkness, creating a rainbow of movement. We're up so high in the tower, as if we're on top of the world. It's magical, and surreal, and amazing.

The music changes, and I feel someone's presence behind me.

"Would you like to dance?" Levi asks. He tucks his chin into my neck from behind.

I turn into his embrace. "With you? Yes."

Levi slips his hand into mine and leads me to the dance floor. He walks backwards, never taking his eyes off me. His gaze makes me feel as if I'm the only person he sees in the room. We reach the dance floor, and he pulls me close, wrapping his arms around me. I link my fingers together behind his neck, feeling safe in his embrace. We sway to the slow beat of the music, and I rest my head on his shoulder. His scent is like a warm summer's day, and I relax into him, like I would while lazing on the grass in the sun.

"Katie," Levi whispers in my ear.

I raise my head and stare into his eyes. He leans down and presses his lips to mine. I tense and my heart races, thumping against my ribcage, but when he doesn't pull away, I relax. He gently parts my lips with his tongue, and I grip the hair at the base of his neck. He deepens our kiss and I twist my fingers into his hair like I've always wanted to do, gripping the strands as passion courses through me.

Levi breaks away, and I take a deep breath.

"Wow," I say.

"Yeah." He smiles and kisses the tip of my nose. The music speeds up, and Levi leans down to put his mouth to my ear. "I'll be back in a minute."

I nod and look around for Karen. She's at our table with Jessica. When our gazes meet, Karen jumps up and drags Jessica with her over to where I am on the dance floor. Stacey joins us, and we smile and laugh at each other, dancing in our small group. We're having so much fun it's not until my feet start aching that I think it's time to sit down.

I tap Karen's arm and point towards our table, then move off the dance floor. The music pumps around us. I fall into my seat, a bead of sweat trickling down my back. I take my shoes off and dig my toes into the carpet.

"This is so much fun," Karen shouts over the music.

I smile wide because I don't disagree with her.

Jessica and Stacey drop into seats beside us and take their shoes off, too.

I lean towards Karen and yell, "Did you see where Levi went?" I search for him around the restaurant.

She shakes her head. "I think a few of the guys are out in the foyer near the lifts."

I scan the room again, but I can't see him anywhere.

"Back in a minute." I slip my shoes on.

I make my way around the room, looking for Levi, edging along the wall towards the archway that leads to the foyer section in front of the lifts. When I reach the arch, the music isn't as loud, and I hear voices. I stop before going through. I probably shouldn't listen in on someone else's conversation, but it's Geoff's voice, and I'm curious.

"Katie really has no clue?" Geoff asks.

What are they talking about? Maybe Levi has something romantic planned for me. I smile and bite my lip, my stomach filling with little flutters.

"No," Levi says. "And she's never going to find out."

"You know it's not over yet." Jarred sounds as if he's smiling.

"You haven't completed the dare," Geoff says.

My breath hitches. My hands shake, and I flex my fingers to stop the trembling from spreading to the rest of my body.

"Taking Katie to the formal was only half the deal," Jarred says.

"I know." Levi's voice has an angry edge to it.

A laugh bubbles into my throat, but I suppress it, and I want to kick myself for being so stupid. Of course it was too good to be true.

As if Levi would ever have asked me to the formal of his own accord.

Talking to me again. Being nice. Taking me on a romantic date.

It's all been part of their stupid game.

Truth or dare has never been so heartbreaking.

Nothing

All the Things: part two

Veronica was wrong

For a moment I stand there, frozen. I can't believe what I've just heard.

Levi White asked me to the formal on a *dare*.

I twist my fingers together in an angry knot. I should confront him. Part of me wants to, but the other part wants to get the hell out of here. Levi and his mates have something else in store for me, and I have no idea what it is.

"Don't forget about the money," Jarred says.

Money? My back stiffens, and I wrap my arms around myself. Money for what?

"You'll get it," Levi says.

Geoff sniggers. "Hopefully Katie puts out for you. Might make it worth it."

Put out for him?

Cold washes through me, and I break out in a sweat. I grip my stomach as it fills with a sick feeling. I don't know whether to be upset or angry. Why would he agree to do something like this?

I need to get out of here.

But I'm at the top of the tallest tower in Sydney, and I can't move.

Levi comes around the corner and stops under the arch. Our gazes meet, and I'm trying so hard to hold it together. My eyes are hot, and I don't want to cry, but tears spill onto my cheeks anyway. I blink and squeeze my eyes shut, hoping that when I open them, Levi won't be standing there.

He is.

"Katie." He takes a step towards me, his hand out to touch my arm.

I back away and shake my head. "Don't." My lip trembles and I suck it between my teeth.

"What's wrong?" He frowns and drops his arm.

"Really? You're asking me what's wrong?"

Geoff and Jarred come into view behind Levi, and I want to punch both of them in their faces.

"Hey, Katie. Having a good night?" Geoff asks.

I puff out a breath, unable to breathe properly because I'm so mad.

I clench my teeth and stare at Levi. "Truth or dare?"

He raises his eyebrows. "You want to play now?"

"Isn't that how it works?" I ask. "Doesn't your stupid game go everywhere with you and your bunch of ... jerks?"

"How about we save it for the after-party?" Levi runs a hand through his hair and instead of getting butterflies,

I want to rip it off his head.

"What? You don't want to play now? Okay then. How about you, Geoff? Truth or dare?"

"Truth," he says without hesitating.

I take a deep breath. "Did someone dare Levi to ask me to the formal?"

Geoff's smile turns into a smirk. "Yes."

"And did they also bet that he'd get me to sleep with him?"

"You only get one question," Jarred says. "Now it's Geoff's turn."

"Fuck you." I glare at Levi but aim my words at all of them.

"That was the point," Geoff says, grinning.

I turn and run.

I flee across the dance floor, pushing my way past the moving bodies until I break through the other side. Bypassing the main bathrooms, I hug the curved wall of the restaurant and head for the second set, where it's quieter. The door slams open as I enter. A girl I've never really spoken to stands at the sink, touching up her lipstick. She takes one look at me and leaves.

I stop in the middle of the room, staring at my reflection in the large mirror. My eyes are red and puffy, and mascara has run onto my cheeks. I try to hold in the sobs, but I can't. My shoulders heave as I suck in breaths, and my throat goes dry. My brain is telling me to calm down, but my heart and body have other ideas.

Why did Levi have to be such an idiot?

There are three stalls. The first has an *out of order* sign stuck to the door. I push it open and go in, locking myself inside. I sit on the closed toilet lid and cry harder than I ever have before. It's like the pieces of my heart are pouring out with every breath, and falling onto the bathroom floor. I thought Levi and I were working towards something really special, but what we have is nothing.

The bathroom door squeals as someone opens it, and I hold my breath. I don't want anyone to see me like this. To know I'm this upset. I can't let them think they've gotten to me.

A girl giggles. "Shouldn't we check if anyone's in here?"

I recognise Veronica's voice, and I lift my legs to hug my knees to my chest, hoping she and whoever she's with won't discover me.

"Is there anyone in here?" Geoff's voice echoes off the tiles.

What is Veronica doing with Geoff?

I hold my breath.

"Check the stalls," Veronica says.

A door bangs against the stall wall beside me. Another bang. I imagine Geoff looking in the cubicles, and I'm glad there's the *out of order* sign on the door to my hiding place.

"Don't worry. No one's here," Geoff says. "We won't be long."

Veronica giggles again. They both make noises I don't want to hear. *They're making out in the girls' bathroom.* Could they have picked a more disgusting place? I press my palms to my ears, and put my forehead on my knees, waiting for it all to end.

Geoff groans. Feet shuffle along the floor.

"Ouch!" Veronica says.

I take my hands away from my ears.

"Come on," Geoff says.

"Cut it out. You're hurting me."

What is he doing to her?

"You want it."

"No. I don't. Geoff, stop it."

"You do. You want it bad."

They don't talk for about ten seconds but it feels like ten hours.

"Stop, please." Veronica's voice is quieter now. She sniffles. "Please."

I get off the toilet as quietly as I can and put my eye to the crack at the edge of the stall door.

Geoff has Veronica pressed against the tiled wall. He's gripping her small wrists with one hand and has them pinned above her head. His other hand is under her dress. She struggles, then turns her head to the side away from the mirror, and closes her eyes.

I step away from the crack in the door and stand still, my hand on the lock.

What a dick.

As much as I don't like Veronica, I can't stay in here and let this happen. I would hope if I were ever in a situation like this that someone would help me.

Veronica sniffles again.

"Don't cry," Geoff says. "You love putting out."

I'm going to kill him.

Exactly what I'm going to do I'm not sure; I can't think that far ahead. Maybe my presence will be enough to stop what's happening. I look around the stall. There's a plastic toilet brush behind the bowl next to the sanitary bin. I lean over and grab it. It's not much of a weapon, but I'm going for surprise not grunt.

I turn the lock slowly with my other hand. The door creaks as I open it and I stop, my breath catching in my throat. I peek through and my gaze locks with Veronica's. I put a finger to my lips. Her eyes are glassy. She closes them and whimpers.

I creep out of the stall, my fingers curled tightly around the handle of the toilet brush, making them ache. I edge my way towards Geoff. Veronica struggles, as if my presence has given her another burst of strength over submission. He grips her hands tighter and slams her against the wall, making her cry out.

I'm paralysed. All I need to do is say something and this will stop, but I'm frozen.

Come on, Katie. Do something.

"Get off her," I say.

Geoff stops and looks over his shoulder. I raise the toilet brush.

"What are you going to do with that?" Geoff laughs. *He's drunk.*

He's moved away from Veronica enough for her to put her legs together. In a quick motion, she brings her knee up into his groin as I whack him over the head with the brush. He lets out a strangled cry, but it's not from being hit with my inadequate weapon.

Geoff lets go of Veronica's wrists and clutches himself, squeezing his eyes closed. She shoves him away and he stumbles across the floor.

I circle around Geoff so I can get between him and Veronica.

"Get out," I say.

"Or what?"

I shake my head. "Did someone dare you to do this? Is it part of your sick and twisted game?"

"You should back off, Katie. You'll pay for this," Geoff says.

"Don't threaten me." I stand as tall as I can. "I don't have anything to lose. You, on the other hand ..."

Geoff straightens and backs towards the door, glaring at us. I raise the toilet brush, and my eyebrows, and give him the meanest look I can.

"Truth or dare, Katie." Geoff opens the door, and the noise of the music wafts into the bathroom as he leaves.

When he's gone, Veronica lets out a shrill laugh. "I can't believe you hit him with a toilet brush."

I stare at the plastic makeshift weapon in my hand. "It didn't work very well. Your knee was more effective."

Veronica laughs again, then slides down the wall until she's sitting on the floor. The laughter turns to sobs, and she puts a hand over her mouth as she cries. I push the stall door open, tossing the brush into the corner, and sit next to her, not caring if the floor will dirty my dress. I don't like her, and we're definitely not friends, but she needs someone right now, and if that someone has to be me, then so be it. Compared to what Veronica just went through, my problems are insignificant. Yes, Levi has hurt me—more than once—but he's never forced himself on me.

Veronica said stop. Geoff ignored that, and that's not okay.

Veronica wipes her nose with the back of her hand. I

get up to grab some tissues from the box on the vanity and offer them to her. I sit beside her again, wondering what to do next. I can't leave her, and I certainly don't want to go back out to the formal.

"Why are you being nice to me?" Veronica wipes her eyes.

"No one deserves something like this happening to them," I say. "Are you … did he …?" I can't say the words.

She shakes her head. "It could've been worse. You stopped him."

"You need to report him."

"I need to forget this ever happened."

"Have you ever … you know … done … it?"

"You mean sex?" Veronica asks. "Have I had sex?"

"Have you?"

"Jarred has told everyone we have. Geoff will tell everyone we did. It's all part of the game."

"Isn't it supposed to be about truth?"

Veronica laughs, but it's not a happy sound. "It hasn't been about truth for a long time. Now it's all about doing the most damage."

"That's … It's a stupid game."

Veronica gets up and goes to the vanity, leaning over one of the basins that line the wall. She wets a tissue and gets to work cleaning the mascara and eyeliner that has run under her eyes.

I stay on the floor, the emotion of the night overwhelming me. I squeeze my eyes closed and let the tears fall, feeling relief wash over me as I stop fighting. I came in here to grieve my own loss, and instead I have had to be the strong one. I'm tired of being strong. Years of hurt and pain gush out of me, and I don't care that Veronica is here to see it.

Veronica sits next to me again, and this time it's her turn to offer me a tissue.

"Why are *you* crying?" she asks. "Isn't your life perfect now with Levi?"

"It would be if he actually wanted to be with me," I say.

"Trust me, he does."

"Enough to ask me to the formal on a dare?" I look at Veronica, and her mouth opens then closes again. *Guilty.* "Yeah, I found out about that."

Veronica shakes her head and smiles. "Are you this stupid all the time?"

"I think I should be offended."

"Why do you think Levi has never had a girlfriend?"

"Yes, he has."

"Not really," she says. "Sure, he's made out with people, but he's never had a serious relationship. It's always been you, Katie."

"So, he took a dare that forced him to ask me to the formal, and said he had to sleep with me. Oh, and there's money involved with that second part." I laugh. "That's got love written all over it."

"He *is* in love with you. He just never wanted to admit it."

"Can't half guess why." I stare at my hands and wrap the skirt of my dress around my finger. The urge to rip it to shreds washes over me. Maybe I'll burn it when I get home.

"You need to ask him why he agreed to do the dare in the first place."

"I don't want to talk to him ever again."

We go quiet for a few seconds, then Veronica laughs.

"What's so funny?"

"This." Veronica motions between us. "Us ... talking. Never thought I'd see the day." She stares at me, and then her smile falls away. "Thank you."

"For what? Hitting Geoff with a toilet brush?"

She chuckles. "I'm serious, Katie. If you weren't here ..."

"Report him."

Veronica gets to her feet. "It won't make a difference."

"Does Jarred know?"

"Stop trying to fix my problems."

The door bursts open, and Karen spills into the bathroom. She stops dead, and stares at Veronica and me. We must be a sight: both of us with red, puffy faces, and panda eyes. Veronica's dress has a rip in the skirt. She grabs one of the straps that's fallen off her shoulder and puts it back in place.

"What happened? What did you do to her?" Karen comes towards Veronica.

I jump up and stand between them. "Don't, Karen. She didn't do anything. Geoff attacked her."

"She probably asked for it."

"You'd think that, wouldn't you?" Veronica says.

"If the shoe fits." Karen folds her arms and glares.

"Karen, don't be a bitch," I say.

She turns her glare on me. "Okay, one: what did you just call me? And two: you're defending her?"

I wrap my arms around my stomach to stop myself falling apart again. "Geoff tried to ... he assaulted her. And I stopped him."

"Would you shut up, Katie," Veronica says. "It was nothing."

Karen looks Veronica up and down, her gaze travelling over her torn dress. "Are you okay?" she finally asks.

"What do you care?" Veronica pushes past us to the basin and finishes fixing her makeup.

"I'm sorry. I thought you were hurting Katie."

Veronica puts her compact down and leans on the edge of the sink. She drops her head, and her shoulders shake. "Please don't tell anyone about this."

"We won't." I put a hand on her shoulder.

She stands up straight and blinks rapidly. "Thanks."

Veronica goes to the door and Karen takes a few steps with her. "You want us to come out with you?"

Veronica shakes her head and opens the door. "You need to stay with Katie. She has her own problems to deal with."

Karen and I watch the door close, and I wish Veronica was wrong.

My heart, again

I fill Karen in on everything that's happened since I left her to find Levi. She listens without interrupting until I'm finished. Then she goes into attack mode.

"I'm going to kill him. And Geoff, for good measure."

"Please, don't do anything," I say. "I don't want to talk to Levi. I don't even want to look at him."

"Doesn't mean I can't give him what for."

I stare at Karen and suck my bottom lip between my teeth. "Just … keep him away from me for the rest of the night."

She sighs. "Okay, but I can't promise I won't do anything after we get out of here."

We leave the bathroom and go back to the main room. As we pass the dance floor, Stacey grabs my hand and pulls me into the throng. We move to the centre of the crowd, masked by the mass of bodies moving around us. Maybe more dancing is exactly what I need. It's time to really let my hair down.

I glance at Karen and she smiles, moving her hips to the beat. Stacey and Jessica complete our little circle, and everywhere I look people are having fun. Everyone on the dance floor has taken their inhibitions and thrown them in the air. I raise my arms above my head and let loose.

"You, me, dancing. Every weekend from now on," Karen yells in my ear.

The music slows, and so do we, swaying to the beat. I tilt my head back and close my eyes, trying to immerse myself in this moment, and think about nothing else.

A hand slips around my waist. "I've been looking for you." Levi's breath tickles my ear. He smells like sweaty aftershave and alcohol.

How dare he touch me? I turn to face him, and shove his arms away at the same time.

I slap him.

Levi presses a hand to his cheek, but I don't stick around to hear what he has to say. I storm off the dance floor, pushing my way through the crowd. But where am I going to go? We can't leave the tower until the night is officially over. I'm stuck up here, looking out over the city lights. An immense feeling of claustrophobia engulfs me.

"Katie, wait," Levi says, but I don't stop.

When I reach the arch leading into the foyer he grabs my arm, and I spin to face him. "Don't touch me."

"Please, let me explain."

"What is there to explain, Levi? You asked me to the

formal on a dare."

"It's not what you think—"

"Oh, really? So what's the money for? Did they dare you to sleep with me, too? You really are a jerk."

"Come on. Don't be angry," he says.

I take a step towards him. He smiles a lopsided, goofy grin, and I smell the booze on his breath. He probably thinks he looks sexy. I think he looks like a drunken idiot.

"Never, in a million years, will I let you touch me again."

Levi frowns and sways on his feet. "It's not—"

"Oh please. Tell me what I *should* think, because I'm dying to hear your lame excuse."

"I was protecting you."

"From what?" I yell. "The only thing I need protection from is you."

"I can explain."

I shake my head and laugh. "No, Levi, you can't charm yourself out of this one. Tell me, how much is sex with me actually worth?"

Levi opens and closes his mouth a few times before clamping it shut.

I turn to go back into the restaurant and freeze. We have an audience. A small group of formal goers have come over to see what's happening. Karen stands at the front, Jessica and Stacey on either side of her. Veronica is scowling, which isn't surprising. She turns and goes back towards the tables. I'm not the only one having a crappy night.

"You're such a dick, Levi," Karen says. "And your friends are, too."

"Katie, I'm sorry," Levi says.

"It's a bit late for sorry." I find Geoff and Jarred's faces in the small crowd.

I shake my head and turn my back on Levi, moving through the people to go to our table. I slide into the chair beside Veronica and stare at the lights with her. Karen, Jessica, and Stacey sit with us. None of us talk. No one seems in the mood.

After a while, Veronica looks around as if she's just noticed us sitting with her. For once, she doesn't make a snide or bitchy remark. Instead, she smiles, and the five of us watch the lights, waiting until we can get out of here.

The music stops, and I look around the room. Britney Owens, our vice-captain, takes the stage and grabs the microphone.

"It's time," she says in a sing-song voice. "Everyone has voted and we've tallied the results. Gather around to celebrate the crowning of your king and queen."

Karen rolls her eyes, and I laugh at her expression. We pretty much know Veronica will win queen. She has so many supporters. And those who don't like her are too afraid not to vote for her.

Everyone moves towards the stage except us. We're all over tonight, and I, for one, do not care who gets crowned.

"Are you ready?" Britney asks. A few people shout out and wolf whistle. "Please put your hands together for this year's queen, Veronica Porter."

The room erupts into applause, but Veronica doesn't look overly excited about winning. She stands from her seat, and makes her way to the stage using slow steps.

Britney places the crown on Veronica's head, and she adjusts it before taking the microphone.

"I'm honoured, of course," Veronica says, putting on her sweet voice. "And we can celebrate at the after-party." She puts one hand in the air and gives a loud whoop.

Everyone follows suit, and starts clapping and whistling.

"Okay, settle down everyone," Britney says. "Now it's time to announce our king, who is none other than our very own school captain, Levi White."

The room erupts again. I'm not surprised he was voted in. I even voted for him. I spot Levi over the other side of the room, walking around the edge of the crowd towards the stage. Veronica's line of sight follows him as he approaches. Then she laughs, and more laughter bursts from the front, but I can't see what's going on because I'm sitting.

"I'm okay," Levi says when he's up on the stage. He sways a bit.

Whispers move through the students, and I put my face in my hands.

"He's drunk," I say. "This should be good."

"Is everyone having a good time?" Levi asks. More whoops and whistles. "Thank you for voting for me. I'd like to say I'm happy to be standing here beside Ronnie ..." He puts an arm around her and pulls her close. "... but I'm not. I should be standing here with Katie."

"Oh no," I say, peeking through my fingers. "He isn't ..."

Karen jumps up and races over to the music station, whispering in the DJ's ear.

Levi stumbles forward. "Katie, I'm sorry ..."

Everyone in the room stops talking.

I sit back in my chair and let my eyes go blurry. This isn't happening.

Seconds later, music blares from the speakers once again. Britney grabs the microphone from Levi, and pushes him and Veronica onto the dance floor for the king and queen's dance.

I take a deep breath, willing the last hour of the formal to go as fast as possible.

As soon as we can, Karen, Jessica, Stacey, and I get the hell out of there. We're the first ones in the lift. We have no plans of going to the after-party, and we grab the first taxi we can find. It takes us all the way to my place, and none of us talk much on the way home. Jessica and Stacey walk the few houses down to Jessica's place before Karen and I go inside. I put on my bravest face, giving Mum, Dad, and Daniel a quick rundown of the night and how *great* it was.

"How was the food?" Daniel asks.

I shrug. "Okay, I guess." I didn't eat much.

"And the dancing?" Mum asks.

"Yeah, we did some of that." Karen smiles.

I think back to how good it felt to move in time with the music, but the feeling of happiness is crushed by the memories of what happened with Levi and Veronica.

"The best part was the view," I say, pretending there's nothing wrong.

"I'm glad you had a good time," Mum says.

Dad sits at the kitchen table and sips a cup of coffee. "I hope the boys behaved."

"Um ... yeah. They were fine." I fake a yawn. "We

should go and get all this stuff off."

"Yes," Karen says. "Can't sleep in our makeup."

"I'm going to bed, too," Daniel says. "Waiting up for you two is tiring work."

Everyone heads up the stairs and goes their separate ways. The hall echoes with 'good night' as we close our doors.

Once Karen and I are in my room, everything changes, and my mood comes crashing down again. I've managed to mostly hold it together, but I can't contain it anymore.

I flop onto my bed and push my face into my pillow, sobbing. All my heartache pours out, soaking the pillowcase and filling it with sorrow. Karen's weight dips the bed as she sits beside me. She rubs my back, but doesn't speak, and I'm so grateful for her presence and her silence.

"Come on. Let's get you out of this dress," she says when my sobs subside.

She helps me up and unzips me. I stand in the middle of my room, numb. All my emotion is gone, and in its place is nothing. I'm an empty shell, and I want to stay like this, not feeling, because emptiness is better than pain.

Karen helps me into my PJs. She brushes my hair and cleans the makeup off my face with some cleansing wipes.

I stare at my dress pooled on the floor. It's such a pretty dress, but now I hate it. I pull it onto my lap and run my hand over the bodice, brushing my fingertips over the embroidery on the waistband.

"Why did he do this to me?" I whisper.

Karen squeezes my arm. "Because he's an idiot."

My fingers find the loops in the embroidery and I dig them in. Then I pull as hard as I can. The fabric rips, and I tear at it until the dress is a mess of fabric on my knees. Karen doesn't try to stop me. Hot tears sting my eyes. I throw the dress across the room.

Karen wraps her arms around me and I sob into her shoulder. "It isn't fair."

"Shhh, I know." She strokes my hair.

I get under the covers and bury my face in my pillow. Karen pulls the trundle out from under my bed, and busies herself with making up the mattress with the sheets Mum has left on my desk. I lie and watch as she works in silence. She takes her own dress off and changes into her PJs before slipping out the door to go to the bathroom.

I must fall asleep because the next thing I hear is tapping on my window. Karen is snoring softly on the trundle beside me. She has her head under her pillow and I smile. She's always slept like that. She never could sleep with it around the right way. Light from the street shines through the gap in the curtains.

The tapping sounds again.

I get out of bed, careful not to step on Karen, and go to the window seat. When I part the curtains Levi is staring at me, and I hope he can see the hurt in my eyes. I hope he can see it down to my soul.

What he's done has broken me.

I want to open the window and let him climb in like he has so many times before. But there is no room for him in my life anymore. He has reduced us to nothing.

Before I can stop myself I push the bottom sash of the

window up.

"Can we talk?" Levi asks. His breath smells like bourbon.

"There's nothing to talk about."

"Come on, Katie. Please let me explain."

"You're drunk. Again. That's explanation enough."

"You need to hear the truth."

I grit my teeth. "The truth is that you never wanted to be with me in the first place. You asked me out because one of your stupid friends dared you to, and there's money involved. I think all of that is pretty self-explanatory."

He shakes his head. "It's not like that." His foot slips on the roof, and he grabs the windowsill.

I kneel on the window seat and wait for him to adjust his footing. Then I lean in close. He smiles, and I bet he thinks I'm going to kiss him.

In a harsh whisper I say, "If you don't get off my roof right now, so help me God, Levi, I will push you off."

"Katie—"

"No. You're drunk. Get. Down. I never want to see you again."

He presses his lips together and moves away from the window. I pull the sash closed, turn the lock, and draw the curtains. I step over Karen who has slept through our entire encounter, her head still under her pillow.

I climb back under my covers and pull them to my chin, vowing never to let Levi into my room, or my heart, again.

13

Sorry won't fix anything

Attendance at school after the formal is optional, and I opt not to go. I lie in bed and stare at the ceiling, trying not to remember what happened. At least I have a two week break now, and I don't have to leave the house for days if I don't want to. I'll be able to study for HSC exams, which start in three weeks.

Who am I kidding? All I can think about is Levi.

He's broken my heart in the worst way possible, and now I'm lost. I got my hopes up about a future together. Not a get-married-and-have-kids kind of future, but one where we both went off to uni, maybe the same one, and hung out for a while.

I don't know what uni I'll be attending yet. I won't find out until final results are released in December, and acceptance letters start to arrive. If I get my first choice,

Mum and Dad aren't going to be happy. I haven't even told them I applied for a fine arts degree. As I stare at my ceiling, counting the faded glow-in-the-dark stars, I realise that right now I don't care anyway. I'm as dull as the stars have become over the years, blending in with the white paint. An endless expanse of nothingness. And the longer I stare, the bigger it gets.

I roll onto my side and stare down at Karen. She stretches on the trundle and blinks the sleep from her eyes.

"Hey," I say.

"Hey. New day. Has to be better than the last."

I force a smile.

We get up and take turns in the shower before heading downstairs for some breakfast. Daniel is at the stove, flipping pancakes.

"Where's my brother, and what have you done to him?" I ask.

He smiles. "Good morning, sleepyheads. I felt like pancakes. Want some?"

"Why aren't you at work?" I ask.

"First Friday off in ages." Daniel slides a pancake onto a plate, and pours the next lot of batter into the pan. "Grab some plates and cutlery, would you?"

Mum races down the stairs, dressed for work. She kisses me on the cheek. "Morning, girls."

"It's nine-thirty. Why are you still here?" I ask, taking three plates from the cupboard and setting them on the kitchen bench.

"Late meeting." Mum pours herself a coffee and takes a quick sip. "Will you be home for dinner? Dad thought we could order Thai."

"Sure," I say, but my heart sinks at the mention of Thai food.

The last time I ate it was with Levi at the park. It's a nice memory, but thinking about him makes me think about what he's done, especially since that's the night he asked me to go to the formal with him. I've successfully not thought about him for at least ten minutes. Now I can't stop thinking about him, again.

"I'll be home around five. Stay out of trouble," Mum says before putting her mostly untouched cup in the sink and heading for the door.

"Never," Daniel says. "But we promise not to burn the house down."

I grab some cutlery then Karen and I sit at the counter, and Daniel puts a plate between us. Steam rises from the stack of pancakes, and we take one each. I smother mine in maple syrup and dive in. Daniel turns the stove off and puts the pan in the sink.

He leans on the bench and stares at me. "Okay, spill. What's the matter?"

"Nothing." I take a big bite so I don't have to talk.

"You can't fool me, Katie. Something's up. What happened last night?"

"How do you do that?" I ask.

"Do what?" Daniel shrugs.

"Know me so well." I stab my pancake with my fork.

"You're my little sister. It's my job."

"Levi was dared to have sex with Katie," Karen blurts.

"What?" Daniel asks.

I drop my fork onto my plate and glare at Karen. "Why did you tell him that?"

"It's Daniel." She shrugs. "Maybe he can beat him up."

I glare at my brother. "You are not going to beat him up."

"I am *so* going to beat him up."

"I didn't *actually* have sex with him," I say. "And the original dare was to take me to the formal."

Daniel stomps out of the kitchen towards the front door. I roll my eyes at Karen and chase after him. He's already on the front lawn before I make it outside. Daniel pounds on Levi's front door with a closed fist. I hope he won't hit Levi as hard as he's hitting the wood. Or hit him at all. As mad as I am, I've already slapped him once, and it didn't make me feel any better.

As I reach the steps to Levi's house, Yvonne opens the door, surprise masking her face.

"Where is he?" Daniel says before she can open her mouth.

"Sorry," I say, puffing. "Daniel's looking for Levi. Is he home?"

"No. I'm afraid I haven't seen him yet." She frowns. "I thought he'd come home with you, so I'm not sure where he is."

"His car is here," Daniel says. "He must be home."

"Daniel, calm down." I put a hand on his arm.

"What's this about? Is everything okay?" Yvonne looks between the both of us. "Did something happen, Katie?"

My brother opens and closes his fists a few times. "I want to talk to him about something."

"Everything's fine. We can talk to Levi later." I tug Daniel's arm. "We should go."

Daniel presses his lips together, then nods and turns

to walk down the steps. I go to follow, but Yvonne reaches out and touches my shoulder.

"Are you sure everything's okay, sweetie?" she asks.

"You coming, Katie?" Daniel calls over his shoulder.

"In a minute," I reply. Yvonne and I watch my brother walk across our yards and go inside. I take a deep breath and turn back to Levi's mum. "I'm sure everything will be fine."

"Okay." She rubs my arm. "I'll tell Levi you were looking for him?"

"Oh no, it's fine. Don't worry about it." I offer her a smile before descending the steps and walking towards home.

The door to Levi's house clicks closed, and I glance back at the empty veranda. I stop on the boundary of our two properties and look at Levi's car parked on the street. He put it there last night so the stretch Hummer could use the driveway.

I squint against the morning sun, and notice the car windows are partly down. Not just one, but all four. Slowly, I walk towards the BMW, and when I reach the passenger side, I bend to look in through the open part of the window.

Levi is asleep on the back seat.

His head rests at a funny angle on the armrest in the door. He has one leg bent at the knee leaning against the back of the seat, while the other hangs over the edge into the footwell. On the floor is a silver hip flask. My guess is it's empty.

I straighten and back away from the car.

"Katie?" Levi asks.

I stop and stare at him as he moves to a sitting position. He peers at me through the partially open window while the rest of his face is shielded by the tinted glass. Why did I come over here? I don't want to see him or talk to him.

I turn away. I get halfway to my front door before I hear the car door open and close, but I don't turn around.

"Katie," Levi says again.

I keep walking and reach the stairs. The soft thud of footsteps follows me.

"Katie, please." He grabs my arm and I yank it away, turning to face him.

"I should never have come out here."

"Why did you?"

"Daniel wants to punch you. Hard," I say. "I was going to stop him."

Levi clenches his jaw. "What did you tell him?

"You mean besides the fact you're a jerk, dickhead, and an arsehole who ripped my heart out, threw it on the floor, and then stomped on it?"

Levi winces.

"You better get out of here," Karen says through the screen door. "If Daniel sees you …"

"I'm not leaving until Katie hears me out," Levi says.

"You don't deserve to have her listen to you." Karen opens the door.

I move up the steps then stop. "Why were you in your car?"

"Why do you care?"

I scoff and shake my head. "I don't."

We stare at each other, and the longer we stand there the more the anger boils inside me. My eyes burn, but I don't feel like I'll cry. I cried enough tears last night to last me three lifetimes.

"I didn't want to go in and face Dad. Okay?" Levi says.

"Because you were drunk?"

He drops his gaze and stuffs his hands in his pockets. He's still wearing his suit pants and once white shirt.

"Dad … he's not—"

"I can't do this right now," I say. "To be honest, I don't care what you're going through. I don't care if you want to drown your sorrows in a bottle of booze. All I care about is forgetting you even exist. You made me fall in love with you, and now … we have nothing, Levi. You made me feel like I was nothing but a piece in your stupid game."

Karen is still holding the screen door open and I grip the handle, pulling it closed as I go inside.

"You're in love with me?" Levi asks.

I look back at him through the screen. "Not anymore." Then I slam the wooden door as hard as I can.

"Daniel?" I call out, moving past Karen.

"Kitchen," he says.

"Can you help me with something?" I sit at the kitchen counter.

He wipes the frypan over with a tea towel and sets it on the bench. "What would this something be?"

"I want to rip the trellis down."

"You want to what?" Karen asks. "Won't your parents be pissed?"

"I'm hoping they won't notice." I shrug.

"What? You think they're not going to miss the massive pink and green plant stuck to their house?" She puts her hands on her hips.

"I'm not sure, Katie," Daniel says. "Karen is right."

"Then I'll call Dad." I run upstairs and grab my phone from my desk before either of them can protest. I'm already talking to Dad before I make it back to the kitchen. "I think we need a change."

"But you love that bougainvillea," Dad says.

"Change is as good as a holiday." I slide onto a stool at the kitchen counter.

"Did something happen with Levi?" Dad asks.

I hesitate and look at Karen, even though she didn't hear the question. "What makes you think that?"

"Well, last time we pruned it because he was climbing in your window. Now you want it gone ... I'm thinking it might have something to do with you *not* wanting him to climb in your window."

"He doesn't do that anymore. And we pruned it because it scratches the house, remember?"

"Katie," Dad says in his best fatherly voice. "I wasn't born yesterday."

"And you didn't come down in the last shower either." I laugh, but it's bitter.

Dad is silent for a few heartbeats, then he asks, "Are you sure everything is okay?"

I wish people wouldn't ask that question. *No, I'm not sure if everything is okay. I'm not sure about anything.* "I'm fine, Dad," I eventually say.

"All right. If I come home and the bougainvillea isn't there, I won't be angry."

"Great."

"But I will be angry if something's happened and you're not okay."

"Really, I'm fine. We just ... had a fight. It happens." I look at Karen and Daniel, and they both shake their heads.

"Boys, huh?" Dad laughs.

"Yeah. Bye, Dad." I end the call and set my phone on the counter. "Who's up for some bougainvillea butchering?"

"I guess we'll need the ladder, and a couple of butchering devices." Daniel smiles, puts the frypan in the cupboard, and heads for the back door. "I'll grab some tools and meet you girls out the front."

Karen looks at me and bursts out laughing.

"What's so funny?" I ask.

"This is not how I pictured us spending the first day of our break."

I follow her to the front door. "We don't exactly get a break. Remember those things called exams?"

"Yeah, whatever. You already made dux. Don't sweat it." Karen opens the door. "And we have your birthday to celebrate next week as well."

I groan. "You know I hate doing stuff for my birthday. And this year is worse because it's right before exams."

"You're turning eighteen! I'm making you do something."

I close the door, and we walk down the steps and around to the side of the house. Daniel is there and has set up a ladder. He's also laid two pairs of pruning shears and a garden saw on the ground.

"Looks like hard work." I pick up the garden saw.

"This was your idea." Daniel grabs a pair of shears and walks up the ladder a few steps. "Not mine."

"Daniel, tell her she has to do something for her eighteenth." Karen stands with one hand on her hip, looking up at my brother and shading her eyes with her other hand.

"Katie hates parties," Daniel says. He leans over and snips a branch off near the top of the bougainvillea.

I nod. "He's right. I do."

Karen sighs. "Fine. But we're going to talk about this later." She picks up the other pair of garden shears.

The three of us set to work, cutting and sawing at the branches of the bougainvillea. Some of them have really entwined themselves into the lattice, and it's hard work cutting them loose.

"Maybe we need the chainsaw," Daniel says.

Karen laughs. "Do you even know how to use one?"

"If it's too hard just cut all the branches that have flowers," I say.

"But there's so much pink." Karen snips another branch then stands back and stares at the pile we've made on the ground.

Daniel steps down a rung on the ladder. "Pass me the saw, Katie."

I hand it up to him and take the shears, attacking a lower branch while Daniel works on a higher one.

The lattice is attached to the house from around a metre off the ground. There are two panels side by side that reach up to the second storey, but it's the one on the right that gives access to the small section of roof outside my bedroom window. The main trunk of the plant grows up in front of the left panel, so I concentrate on untangling the limbs and leaves from the right one.

"Maybe we only have to cut half of it down," I say. "I want to get the right lattice panel off the wall."

"Are you making this up as you go along?" Daniel asks.

"Pretty much." I smile at him. "I don't want Levi climbing up to my room … ever again."

"That's nice to know," Levi says.

I spin around.

He's standing on his driveway, glaring at me.

Anger rises into my chest. Is *he* mad at *me*?

Daniel climbs down the ladder. "Get lost, Levi."

"I'd listen to him if I were you," Karen says. "He has a potential murder weapon in his hand."

"You're cutting down the bougainvillea?" Levi ignores Daniel and Karen.

I take a step towards Levi and adjust my grip on the garden shears. "Yes, we're cutting it down."

"Why? If you don't want me to climb it, I won't."

"You say when you're sober." I glare at him.

He folds his arms over his chest, and looks at the pile of cut branches on the ground then back at me. "Katie, can we please talk?"

"Oh, did you hear that?" Karen says. "He said please."

I shake my head. "No. I told you I don't want to talk to you."

Levi laughs, and I grit my teeth.

"Why are you laughing?" Karen asks. "Nothing about this is funny."

Levi rubs his face, and has one last chuckle into his hand before stopping. "It kinda is." He turns his stare on me again. "Katie, I'm trying to apologise, and I at least deserve to be able to give you an explanation."

I take a deep breath and say, "No. What you deserve

is to be treated the same way you've treated me. You ruined everything, and I will never forgive you."

"Cutting down the bougainvillea won't change anything," Levi says.

I clench my fingers around the handle of the garden shears. "And you think telling me you're sorry will? Sorry won't fix anything."

4

Second chance

Mum and Dad didn't say much about the bougainvillea. After Mum saw it, she gave me one of those 'I understand' kinds of looks. The ones only mums know how to give.

For the past few days I've thrown myself into study. It's the first week of the break, and if I was in any other year at school, I'd be off having fun with my friends and doing whatever. Just chilling out. But I have HSC exams starting the second week of term four, so even though I've officially finished school classes for like forever, I haven't finished school.

But, as much as I want to study today, and hide in my room away from the world, Karen won't let me.

She's taking me out for my birthday.

Yay.

I have never liked celebrating my birthday. Not because I'm a party pooper or anything, but because I don't see the point. We never had enough money for Daniel and me to receive presents that we didn't need or that weren't practical, so it took the fun out of it. Now, if Mum and Dad spend money on me it makes me feel guilty, not happy.

Okay, maybe I am a party pooper.

"We're hitting the shops," Karen says from the other end of the phone. "I have a surprise for you, and then I'm taking you out for hot chocolate."

"Great," I say. "I love surprises." *Not.*

"I'm picking you up in fifteen minutes, so be ready." Karen hangs up.

I stare at my screen. A surprise? This can't be good.

It's warm today, so I change into my favourite denim skirt and a pale blue singlet top with wide straps. I slip my feet into a pair of sandals, grab my phone and tote bag, and head downstairs, dumping my stuff at the front door.

"Happy birthday," Mum says when I come into the kitchen. There's a small present sitting on the bench.

Mum is busy making coffee and breakfast. I give her a kiss, grateful that she's going about her morning routine, and not making a fuss.

"Happy birthday, kiddo." Daniel kisses me on the cheek on his way through from the lounge.

"Neither of you working today?" I ask.

"I took the day off." Mum flicks the kettle on. "Thought I'd make your favourite breakfast for you."

"Toast and tea?" I raise my eyebrows. "I can do that."

"Nonsense. I've got this." Mum smiles and puts two pieces of bread in the toaster. I laugh, and her smile is infectious.

"I'm not rostered on today," Daniel says. "Open your present."

"Are you scheming with Karen? She said she has a surprise for me." I slide onto one of the stools at the kitchen bench and pick up the small box.

"She may know what's going on." Daniel laughs. "You'll love it."

"God help me," I mumble.

"This is the first part." My brother sits on the stool beside me, pointing to the box in my hand. "Open it."

I take a deep breath and turn the small present over in my hands a few times. It's wrapped in pretty purple paper with a white ribbon. I have no idea what's inside.

"Dad left early?" I ask, already knowing the answer.

"He looked in on you but you were sound asleep," Mum says. "He didn't want to wake you."

"I shouldn't open this until he gets home," I say.

"He won't mind," Daniel says. "Open the present!"

I raise my eyebrows but don't say anything else. I pull the end of the ribbon to undo the bow. Daniel leans on the bench, his eyes wide and a smile on his face. I take extra care not to rip the paper as I peel the sticky tape off, knowing that it's driving my brother crazy. Still, he doesn't say anything. But he leans closer when I remove the paper.

Underneath is a purple box with a lid. I take the lid off and there's white tissue paper inside.

"Oh, come on, you're killing me," Daniel says. "Hurry up."

I laugh, and take the tissue paper out. Something

metal falls onto the bench.

It's a key.

And I'm pretty sure it's the kind that starts a car.

I pick the key up and stare at the Toyota logo imprinted on the bow, running my thumb over it. The button that opens the locks hangs off a small keychain loop.

"Did you buy me a car?"

Daniel laughs. "You'll have to go and see."

"But … we can't afford for you to buy me a car." I look at Mum.

"It's okay, sweetie. We haven't bought you a car," she says.

Now I laugh. "Damn." But I smile as well. I look at the key again. "Is this your car key, Mum?"

She grins.

"Would you just …" Daniel shoves his fingers into his hair. "Go and look in the car!"

I get off the stool and go out the front door to the driveway. Mum's Toyota Camry is parked where it always is. The car doesn't look any different, and I wonder what on Earth my family has in store for me. I lean down and peer through the front driver's side window. There's another package on the front seat.

"Seriously, do you need help unlocking the car?" Daniel asks.

Mum laughs behind me.

A horn blares before I can answer, and I straighten to see Karen pulling up to the kerb. She turns her mum's car off and jumps out.

"Did you open it?" Karen asks. "Has she opened it?" She looks to Daniel and Mum.

"She's taking her sweet time," Daniel says.

I poke my tongue out at him and press the button on the keyring. The door locks pop up. Daniel grabs the handle and pulls the door open. He looks more excited than I feel. Right now, I'm just confused.

Daniel pushes me into the car and I swipe the parcel off the front seat before sitting on it. The package isn't very big, about the size of a DL envelope, wrapped in the same pretty paper as the box. Daniel leans on the open car door while Mum and Karen peer at me through the window.

"Hurry up," Karen says. "This is torture!"

I smirk then unwrap the parcel, quickly this time. There's a card and an envelope. When I open the card I see straight away it's from Mum, Dad, and Daniel. Karen's eyes are wide and she's waving her hands around.

"Dear Katie," I read. "We can't believe our little girl is all grown up ..." Mum smiles when I glance at her. "You've worked so hard to get this far, and we wanted to reward you with something you'll hopefully never forget. Your surprise is in the envelope. We hope you love it."

I put the card on my lap and pick up the envelope, turning it over so I can tear it open. I pull out the contents. There's a folded piece of A4 paper, and another envelope that has *Love Daniel* written on the front. I rip it open and find one hundred and fifty dollars inside.

"It's not much," Daniel says. "But I saved it so you could have some spending money."

My mouth hangs open. "Spending money? For what?"

"Unfold the paper," Mum says, grinning.

I slip the money back into the smaller envelope and open the piece of paper. Printed on it are reservation details for two people at a hotel in Surfers Paradise. Seven nights in an ocean-view room, breakfast included. Written at the bottom in my father's sprawling handwriting are the words, *Love Mum and Dad.*

"Two weeks after exams, we're going on a road trip," Karen squeals.

I stare at the paper and my smile falters. How can they afford this? Staying anywhere on the Gold Coast during schoolies week isn't cheap. I fold the paper again and put everything back into the envelope, then get out of the car. Daniel steps back and I close the door.

"Before you say anything," Mum says, "don't worry about the cost. You work so hard, Katie. Your father and I want you to have this. Okay?"

I force a smile. "Sure, Mum. It's going to be great."

"I haven't given you my present yet," Karen says, handing me a small package.

I lean against Mum's car and open the card taped to the top of the carefully wrapped present, also in purple paper. It's from Karen and her parents. When I rip the paper off, I find a fuel card, a pen, and a beautiful leather-covered journal.

"Mum and Dad are paying for our fuel. We can take Mum's car," Karen says. "And I know you love to write in your journal, so I figured you'd want a special one for this trip."

"This is all really … great," I say.

"Well, don't get too excited." Daniel frowns.

"I'm sorry. I am. I just …"

Mum gives me a big hug. "I know, honey. But all I want you to focus on is having an amazing time."

I bury my face in her hair and nod.

A door opens and Mum pulls away. I look over to Levi's place where he's coming down the front steps of his veranda. He stops on the path and our gazes meet. I do *not* want to see him today.

He presses his lips together. "Happy birthday, Katie."

I push off the car and don't reply, heading straight for my front door and not looking at him.

"Sorry, Levi," I hear Mum say. "I didn't raise her to be so rude."

Seconds later Mum, Daniel, and Karen are all in the foyer with me.

"You could've said thank you," Mum says.

"No," Karen says.

"Nope," Daniel agrees. "He deserves everything he gets."

"What's going on?" Mum folds her arms. "Dad told me you and Levi are fighting. Is it so bad between you two that you've lost your manners?"

"I don't want to talk about it," I say.

Mum purses her lips. "Well, just don't forget who you are."

"Okay ..." Karen says. "I think it's time for birthday activities, part B."

"There's a part B?" I stare at her.

"You, me, hot chocolate." Karen grabs my wrist. "Come on."

She plucks my birthday presents from my hands and gives them to Mum, then shoves my tote bag at me and pulls me out the door.

"Have fun," Mum calls after us.

Levi is still outside, and I concentrate on getting to

the car so I'm not tempted to look at him. I don't care what Mum said about me being rude. When I reach the car parked at the kerb I yank the door open and climb in, slamming it closed once I'm in the seat.

"Easy," Karen says from the driver's seat. "The car never did anything to you."

"Just … drive," I say.

We pull onto the road and head towards the highway. Karen chatters non-stop on the way to the shops. I stare out the window and try not to think about how everything has become so messed up.

"Are you excited?" Karen asks.

I roll my head across the headrest and stare at her. "About what?"

Karen grips the steering wheel. "Oh my God, Katie. Schoolies!"

I smile. "Oh, that. Yeah. We'll have a blast."

"Are you kidding? It's going to rock."

"Are Jess and Stacey coming?"

Karen grins. "Of course. They have a room booked at our hotel, too."

We pull into the car park. Karen stops at the boom gate to take her ticket, then we circle the car park looking for a space. We eventually find one. My phone buzzes in my bag as I get out of the car. I glance at the screen but don't recognise the number, so I ignore it.

Karen and I walk through the busy shops and outside to the mall, passing the clock fountain on our way to the chocolate café. I remember stopping there with Levi and making a wish that we'd become something special. Seems like that's not going to come true.

At the café I order my usual white hot chocolate, and Karen gets a dark. We sit in the back corner and sip our drinks.

"So … how does it feel to join the eighteen club?" Karen asks.

I raise my eyebrows. "I don't feel any different."

"Come on." She sets her hot chocolate down. "You're practically a free agent now. We can go anywhere and do anything we like."

"Not quite." I laugh and take a sip of my drink. It warms my insides.

Karen smiles. "What do you want to do after this?"

"I don't know," I say. "I'm not in the greatest mood, sorry. I've been a bit of a bitch, haven't I?"

"I still love you." Karen squeezes my hand. "But seriously, you're eighteen today. We could hit the RSL."

"In the middle of the day?" I sit back in my chair.

"Don't you want your first alcoholic drink as an adult?"

"I don't want any drink, other than this delicious hot chocolate." I take another sip from my mug. "And I can have a drink at schoolies."

"Now we're talking," Karen says.

"But I'm not getting drunk. I might be eighteen today, but I'm not stupid."

"It's your birthday?" someone asks.

I look up, and Veronica is standing a few metres away from our table.

"Oh … hey." *What is she doing here?* I force a smile. "Yeah. I'm officially an adult."

"Katie hates her birthday," Karen says. "It's the only day of the year when she's truly unhappy."

Veronica laughs, but it seems forced. "Can I sit?"

I take my tote off the seat beside me. "Um … sure. How did you know we'd be here?"

Karen stares at Veronica. I adjust my position on my chair, because the way they're looking at each other is making me uncomfortable.

Veronica slides into the seat. "Levi gave me your numbers. I tried calling you, but you didn't answer. Then I called your house. Your mum said you were here."

I'm not sure what to make of any of this. I open my mouth, but then I close it again. *Levi gave her my number?*

Karen leans on the table. "What's making you slum it today?"

Veronica leans forward to match Karen's pose. "I wanted to make sure Katie was okay."

"If this is another one of your stupid games, you can leave now."

"It's not." Veronica clenches her teeth.

"I'm fine," I say. "To be honest, I'm more worried about you. Have you reported him yet?"

Veronica rolls her eyes. "Katie, I'm okay. He didn't do anything."

"But you told him to stop, and he didn't."

Karen wrinkles her nose. "Geoff is a dick."

"You haven't told anyone, have you?" Veronica looks down at the table.

Karen sighs. "We said we wouldn't."

I let out a breath, glad that the bitchy tone has left my best friend's voice.

Veronica looks from me to Karen then back again. "For the record, I think Levi and his mates are all dicks, too."

I press my lips together. "But you're a part of this whole dare thing."

"Yes, but after … maybe it was a bit too mean …"

Karen raises her eyebrows. "Are you trying to apologise?"

Veronica scowls. "You should hear Levi out," she says, ignoring Karen.

"What did he say to you?" I ask.

Veronica shrugs. "Just that you won't let him explain."

"That idiot asked her to the formal on a dare," Karen says. "Katie doesn't need an explanation."

Veronica gets to her feet and adjusts the strap of her purse. "There's more to the story."

"There always is," I mumble.

"Did he send you here to do his dirty work?" Karen stands, too.

"He loves you, Katie." Veronica looks down at me, and there's something in her eyes that makes me believe what she's saying.

Or maybe I just *want* to believe it.

"He has a funny way of showing it." I look away, and stare into my mug of hot chocolate.

Veronica shrugs again. "Suit yourself. See you at exams."

I stare at her back as she walks out of the café. Karen sits again and sips her drink.

"You don't believe her, do you?" she asks.

I take a deep breath. "I don't know what to believe anymore."

And I don't, because I've been burnt too often.

I'm not sure if I should give him a second chance.

5

With you

HSC exams started in the second week of term, and for the past four weeks I've been alternating between studying and taking exams. I'm confident I did well on most of them. Pretty much the only time I've left the house has been to go to school, and I've lain low enough to stay away from Levi. We only have a few subjects together anyway, so our time tables haven't crossed paths much.

I finish reading over my essay then stare at the clock on the hall wall, thinking about schoolies coming up in a couple of weeks. Jessica and Stacey are flying up, but because Karen and I are driving, we'll be leaving a day earlier and spending a night in Coffs Harbour along the way.

"Pens down," the exam supervisor says. "Please close your exam booklets and leave them on your desks. The row on my right may leave first, followed by the next, and so on."

Papers rustle, and students stand to put pens and pencil cases back in their bags. I wait until it's my row's turn, and then I file out of the hall and into the afternoon sunshine.

Jessica is waiting for me. "I have to run. Josie sent me a message. She's picking me up."

"No probs," I say. "I can train it."

She smiles and runs off towards the main entrance to the school. I make my way from the hall towards the back gate to catch the train home. Art was my last exam. Relief washes over me, and I turn my face to the sky to feel the sun's warmth.

No more exams. No more school. I can finally relax for a while.

"How do you think you went?" Veronica asks, falling into step beside me.

I shrug. "However I went."

"Have you spoken to Levi yet?"

I stop and face her. "No. What's he said now?"

"I'm getting a lift home with him. Why don't you come ask him yourself?"

I tilt my head to the side and stare at Veronica. I still can't work her out. Since the formal she's been really nice, and the last time someone was nice to me unexpectedly it turned out to be a dare. Veronica acting like this makes me uncomfortable. I'm not used to it. It's like wearing a really scratchy sweater.

"I'm not sure I'm ready to talk to him."

"Katie, it's been ages." Veronica sounds like a whiny

child. "If I have to listen to him anymore, I think I'll kill him."

"I'm okay to catch the train," I say.

"Come on." She shakes her head and grabs my arm, pulling me away from the direction of the train station and across the street.

Levi's BMW is parked up the road. Veronica shoves me at the front passenger side then gets into the back seat.

Great.

I pull the door open and get in, looking anywhere but at Levi.

"Katie," he says.

I turn to him. "Don't …"

He takes a deep breath and starts the car, pulling away from the kerb. I wind my window down a bit and let the air blow on my face.

Levi didn't have an exam today because none of his subjects were scheduled, and I wonder what the hell he's doing here. Surely Veronica didn't ask him to pick her up. But then I think that's exactly the sort of thing Veronica would do.

"You didn't have an exam today," I say.

"Ronnie wanted a lift."

"And you're her personal chauffeur?"

Veronica snickers from the back seat. "Now you don't have to study, what're you doing tonight, Katie?"

"Sleeping," I say.

"You should come celebrate with us."

I turn in my seat so I can look into the back at her. "Let me guess: you're having a party."

"You should come." She smirks.

"Yeah, because the last time I did that it went *so* well."

"If it helps, I'll promise not to talk to you." Levi stares straight ahead.

What he should be promising is not to take any dares involving me, or not to play the stupid game in the first place.

"I think schoolies will be a good enough party for me," I say.

Levi doesn't respond. He just drives, gripping the steering wheel with one hand and resting the other on the gear stick.

"I'm not taking no for an answer," Veronica says.

I pretend I'm thinking about it. Then I actually think about it. Maybe a party would be fun. Maybe getting out of the house I've been cooped up in would be good for me.

Who am I kidding? Going to Veronica's is the worst idea ever. I'll be opening myself up for more torture and ridicule.

"If I come, can I bring Karen?" I ask, and then I regret it because there's no way I'm going to this party.

"Yes," Veronica and Levi say at the same time.

"You promised not to talk to me." I glare at Levi.

His lips curl a little, as if he's about to smile, then he stops and presses them together.

I want to look away from him, but I can't. It's been so long since I've had the opportunity to look at Levi, and I miss him. I miss his smile, and his voice, and having him climb in my window.

I miss being around him.

But I haven't only missed him for the past couple of months. I've been missing him for years.

A lump rises in my throat, and I finally turn away, staring out the side window and watching the houses go past as we turn into Veronica's street. Levi pulls over.

"I'll see you two tonight," Veronica says, getting out of the car.

We sit and watch her go inside before Levi pulls back onto the street again.

I can't look at him.

I can't let my emotions take over.

Suddenly, I feel trapped inside the car. Unable to get away from him so I don't have to face what I'm feeling. I'm stuck with nowhere to go.

My breaths come short and fast, and I squeeze my eyes closed to try and get some kind of control.

"Katie, are you okay?" Levi asks.

Am I okay?

I want to scream, *no!* But instead, I laugh. The sound is bitter. Then it starts to hurt, and a sob rises into my chest, forcing its way out of my mouth with so much force I feel like my ribs will crack. With that sob comes a cry, and my laughter turns to tears.

I put my face in my hands and cry. *Really* cry.

"Katie—?"

"No, Levi!" I yell. "I am *not* okay."

My chest rises and falls as I heave breaths in and out of my mouth. I want out of the car, but we're travelling at one hundred and ten kilometres an hour on the motorway. There's nowhere to pull over. And where would I run to anyway? I grip the door handle. We'll be home soon.

Levi moves across to the left lane and takes the next exit. It's not our exit. It's too early. At the top of the ramp he turns left then right into the first side street, and pulls over, killing the engine and tugging the handbrake on.

I want out.

I need to get out of the car.

My fingers grapple with the handle, and I cry harder because I can't get it to work. Then the door opens and I spill onto the grass. I stumble to my feet and run, but I don't get far before I trip and collapse on the ground—a blubbery, snotty mess. I draw my knees to my chest and put my head on them, sucking in deep breaths.

Levi sits beside me. He doesn't say anything. He just sits there. I concentrate on slowing my breathing, because what else can I do? I can't get up and walk home, and it's obvious Levi isn't going anywhere.

"Katie," he finally says.

I squeeze my eyes closed. "What?"

"Let's get you home."

I nod, and he helps me to my feet. I should be embarrassed at having a complete breakdown in front of the one person I've loved my entire life. The person who caused the breakdown to begin with. But I'm not embarrassed. I've known Levi for so long, and I'm glad he's had the chance to finally see what his actions have done to me.

He reaches out and puts his arms around me. Instead of fighting him, I fall into his embrace and press my face into his neck. It brings back the memory of how we were dancing before our first real kiss. That memory makes my heart smile when smiling is the last thing I feel like doing.

"I want to explain everything to you," Levi says.

I pull away. "I'm not sure an explanation will make

any difference."

Levi rubs my back in circles, and for a moment I let him, then I step away. I'm not going to allow him to do this now. Not while I'm weak and emotional, and not thinking straight. I take another step back, and he drops his hand to his side.

"Let's go home." He walks to the car and I follow.

We don't speak for the rest of the drive. I turn the radio on to drown out my thoughts, but it's not that effective. I wish I could go home and not have Levi there, right next door, in my face all the time. Maybe if we had some distance everything would work out in its own time. Right now, I feel smothered, with nowhere to run.

Levi pulls into his driveway, and I get out of the car as soon as he kills the engine. I shoulder my bag, and cross over to my yard.

"Will I see you tonight?" Levi asks.

I turn and face him. "Maybe."

He nods and I go inside. No one is home yet. I'm grateful, because I can go straight to my room and get rid of any of the breakdown episode evidence. I dump my stuff and go to the bathroom, washing my face and taking my contacts out.

I stare at my reflection and push my glasses onto my nose. There was a time when they were a big part of me. Now, they're only a side thought. Nothing important. Like I was a side thought to Levi. Not important enough for him to consider my feelings instead of his reputation.

Another tear slips down my cheek and I swipe at it, turning away from the mirror.

I'm not going to this party.

All I want to do is curl up in bed with my headphones in and write in my journal.

Back in my room my phone rings. I fumble around in the bottom of my tote bag, pulling it out. Karen's name flashes on the screen and I swipe it to answer.

"Hey." I flop onto my bed.

"How'd you go?"

"Fine. It was fine. Can we not talk about exams ever again?"

Karen laughs. "Done. Did you talk to Jess?"

"She had to go meet her mum after, so not really. Why?"

Karen pauses and I listen to her breathing.

"There's a party tonight," she finally says.

I roll onto my side and put my phone between my ear and my pillow, then grab my bunny and play with its ears.

"I know."

"At Veronica's," Karen says.

"Yep."

"We should go."

I sigh. "You should go. I should stay home."

"Come on, Katie. Jess is going. We'll have safety in numbers. Everything is different now. School is over. Exams are finished. We need to celebrate. And those bitches don't rule us anymore. This is our chance to show them that nothing from the past matters from today onwards." Karen goes quiet again.

I take my glasses off, close my eyes, and hug my bunny to my chest. Nothing from the past matters? Everything from my past matters. It's shaped me to be the person I am, and my past is what has put me in the position I'm in. "If it weren't for my past, I wouldn't be—"

"Stop it," Karen says. "This is exactly what I mean. *Nothing* matters. We have our future in front of us. Screw them. And screw Levi for what he's done. Tonight you can either stay home and choose to let them beat you, or you can walk in there and party like you've never partied before."

"I'm not sure I want to face him after what happened this afternoon," I say.

"Oh my God, what now?" Karen asks.

I take a deep breath. "I may have had a breakdown in front of him." I pause. "He drove me home and on the way I ... cried a lot."

"Oh, Katie. Are you okay?"

I laugh, so hard it brings tears to my eyes. And I can hear the frown in Karen's voice when she says, "What's so funny?"

My laughter subsides. I get control of myself and wipe my eyes. "That's exactly what Levi asked me, and it set me off."

"Well, at least he knows how much of a jerk he's been. Hopefully you dug his cold heart out of his chest and warmed it up a bit."

"I still don't want to face him."

"You can, and you will," Karen says.

"You're not going to take no for an answer, are you?" I ask.

"I've already told Jess to pick us up at eight. I'll be there in half an hour, and we can plot your revenge."

I laugh. "I don't want revenge ... I want Levi."

"Stop talking nonsense. See you in a bit."

Karen hangs up, and I roll onto my back, staring at my phone. It rings again while I'm holding it, and this time 'Mum' flashes on the screen.

"Hey, Mum."

"Katie, honey. How was your last exam?"

"Fine. Like all the others."

"How are you feeling?" Mum asks.

I stop myself before I say 'fine' again. "I'm good. Got home not long ago."

"Great. Can you fix yourself something tonight?" Mum asks. "Your Dad is taking me to a movie."

"Sure. What about Daniel?"

"He's a big boy. He'll probably be out."

"Actually, I'll be out as well," I say. "Veronica's having another party. You know, to celebrate our transition into the real world."

Mum chuckles. "Okay. You know your curfew. I'll see you in the morning."

"Bye, Mum." I end the call and toss my phone on the bed.

I close my eyes, and try to clear my head of everything, but thinking about nothing is pretty much impossible. No matter how hard I try, my thoughts keep going back to Levi. What if he does have a good explanation for what he did? What if all I need to do is listen? But then what if I do, and we work at building our relationship again, but then it all gets stripped away like it has before? Do I really want to take that chance?

Can I put myself out there again?

Hot tears sting my eyes, and I shove the heels of my hands into them.

No. It's better to keep my distance and not get involved with him again. With anyone.

I'll go to this party, but I'll stay away from Levi.

The doorbell rings, and I wipe my eyes then get up to go downstairs. When I open the door, Karen is standing on the step with a big smile on her face, and a backpack slung over her shoulder.

"Why so happy?" I ask.

Karen pushes past me and into the foyer. "We have work to do."

"What are you talking about?" I close the front door.

"Makeover." She walks up the stairs. At the top, she looks down at me. "We can do our nails and hair. You're going to rock this party, and we're going to make Levi rue the day he *ever* decided to fuck with you."

6

Good one

Karen sits on my bed and pulls all sorts of items from her backpack, spreading them over my quilt.

"Go and put your contacts in," she says.

"But I only took them out when I got home."

"I don't care." She stares at me. "You're not wearing your glasses to this party."

Reluctantly, I go to the bathroom and put my lenses in. Back in my room I sit in my desk chair. Karen sweeps a makeup wipe over my face, followed by a loaded powder brush.

"Close your eyes," she says.

I do as she asks. "I want to look natural. Not like a hooker."

"Stop worrying. You will not look cheap."

I sit for another ten minutes as Karen works on my

face, but I've pretty much had enough. Two minutes of this is too long. "Are you finished?"

"Gloss your lips," she says. "Then you're done."

I jump up and rummage around in my tote bag to find my favourite lip gloss, then stand in front of the full-length mirror on my wardrobe door. A smile spreads across my face when I look at my reflection. I definitely don't look like a hooker, and Karen has done an amazing job of making my skin glow. She's put the slightest hint of pink into my cheeks, filled out my lashes, and added sparkle to the lids of my eyes. I swipe my gloss over my lips to complete the soft look.

"Now … clothes," Karen says. "You have to look hot."

"Jeans and a top will be fine." I open my wardrobe and pull out my favourite pair of jeans.

Karen digs into her bag again. "Nope. Put those away. You're wearing these."

She holds up a pair of dark skinny jeans—the kind I would never be able to afford. They have a really fine silver sparkle in the fabric. She hands them to me and I take them, feeling the thickness of the good-quality denim. So much nicer than my old thin pair.

"I can't wear these," I say. "Everyone will know I can't afford them."

"Don't be an idiot. I just gave them to you, so they're yours. You can say they were a birthday present if anyone asks."

I bite my lip, and look down at the jeans in my hands. They're so nice, and I've never owned a pair from anywhere other than a cheap department store.

"Thank you." I hug Karen, and she pats my back.

We both shimmy into our jeans. Karen's are light blue and have fashionable rips in the legs, and they hug her in all the right places. She looks amazing. I sift through my wardrobe, searching for a top to wear, but I don't have anything good enough to complement the jeans. Karen tries to give me her black top that also has sparkles embedded into the slinky fabric, but I don't let her.

"I want to go simple," I say. "You know I'm not a fancy kinda girl."

I pull out a plain white singlet top, one with wide straps, and put it on over my nicest bra.

"Good choice," Karen says. "It shows off your boobs."

"Stop looking at my boobs." I grab my favourite black ankle boots from the bottom of the wardrobe, and sit on the edge of the bed to put them on.

Karen shrugs. "You have nice boobs."

She grins, and puts on a tight black sleeveless top that zips up at the front. Then she slips her feet into a cute pair of strappy black heels. Karen sits beside me on the bed, digs into her bag, and pulls out a few bottles of nail polish. She chooses a shimmery aqua and gives it a shake before setting to work on her toenails.

"No point me doing mine." I look down at my shoes.

"Do your nails." Karen glances at the clock above my desk. "We're not meeting Jess out the front for another twenty minutes."

I search through the bottles lying on the bed between us and go for a bright purple. I coat my fingernails as carefully as I can, blowing on them to get them to dry faster. Karen coats her fingernails as well, then we head downstairs. I opt not to take my purse or a bag this time, so I slip my driver's licence into my phone cover along with a twenty. We lock the front door with the hidden spare key, and walk to the road to wait for Jessica.

"Josie is driving," Karen says. "Jess said she'd drive us home."

"Like Josie would give her any other choice." I tuck my hair behind my ear and check my phone.

A crash comes from Levi's house, like a plate smashing or something hitting the tiled floor inside. Someone yells. Then more yelling. I recognise Levi's voice but I can't make out his words.

"What's going on?" Karen looks towards Levi's place.

The front door flies open, banging onto the outside wall of the house. Levi tumbles onto the veranda, but it's not until his dad is standing in the doorway that I realise Levi didn't fall. Mark pushed him.

Yvonne clings to Mark's arm, trying to pull him back inside. Levi gets to his feet and his gaze meets mine before he quickly looks away. I'm aware that my mouth is open, but I don't close it. I stand frozen with my phone in my hands, gaping at my neighbours who are obviously arguing about something. Only Levi's dad hasn't seen us yet.

Mark steps towards Levi. "You will show some respect—"

"Or what, Dad?" Levi yells. "You'll make me? I'm not scared of you."

"You should be."

I step forward. "Levi, is everything okay?"

Mark turns in my direction, his eyes widening. Then his brow narrows into a frown. He says something to Levi that I can't hear before going inside with Yvonne and slamming the door behind them.

"I'm not Mason," Levi screams. He stands on the veranda, staring at the door, his shoulders heaving, his fists clenched at his sides.

A car sounds behind us, and I glance over my shoulder as Josephine pulls up to the kerb. She winds her window down. "Get in, bitches."

"Charming." Karen opens the back passenger door.

I glance at Levi. He's sitting on the steps of his veranda with his head in his hands.

"Hang on." I walk towards Levi.

"Katie, what are you doing?" Karen asks.

I wave her away and keep walking until I reach the veranda. Asking him if he's okay is a stupid thing to do because he obviously isn't. And I hate it when people ask me that question.

"Are you coming to the party?" I ask instead.

Levi raises his head, then sits up straighter. "You look really nice, Katie."

I shift on my feet and fidget with my phone. "Thanks."

"I have no car," Levi says. "Dad took my keys."

"Come on, Katie," Josephine yells.

I glance back at her, then look at Levi. "Come with us."

Levi gets to his feet. "That would involve you and me being in the car together."

"I've gotten pretty good at ignoring you." I offer him a small smile.

Levi drops his gaze to the ground. I grab his hand and pull so he'll follow.

Heat.

Warmth.

Levi.

It hits me all at once.

I let go of his hand before I want to hold it forever. It feels too good.

Levi stands at Josephine's window. "Room for me?"

She nods. "Get in."

Levi opens the passenger side back door and I climb in, scooting across to the middle so I'm sandwiched between Levi and Karen.

It's impossible to talk on the drive to Veronica's because Josephine cranks the music and winds her window down. I don't mind. It's not like I have much to say to Levi anyway.

Every now and then I catch Karen glaring at him, but he's not looking at her. Whenever I chance a look at him he's staring at me, and I press my knees together to try and make myself as small as possible in the middle of the back seat.

Levi's leg and shoulder rest against mine, making me warm, and I sit rigid because I don't want to relax and make him think I'm comfortable. I concentrate on staring ahead through the front windscreen, and I let my hair fall over my face like a curtain.

We pull into Veronica's street, and something touches my hair. I flinch and realise it's Levi, holding his hand out. It hovers in front of my face, then he tucks my hair behind my ear.

Josephine parks on the street and turns the car off, the music dying with it. I stare at Levi who still has his hand in my hair. He smiles, his lips curling slightly, and

I get lost in his eyes. The way he's looking at me turns my stomach to mush, and I want to throw myself at him and slap him at the same time.

I'm not prepared for the way he's making me feel, sitting so close to him in such a confined space. I'm supposed to be angry with him. After what he did, I never wanted to see him again, and yet here we are.

Slowly, I reach up and wrap my fingers around his wrist then pull so his hand comes away from my face.

"Please, don't," I say.

We're close enough that I could lean forward and kiss him. My heart wants to, but my head stops me. I want him, but I don't, all at the same time. How can I want someone so badly who has hurt me the way Levi has?

One of the car doors slams, and then another.

"Come on, lovebirds," Josephine says from the footpath. Through the window, I see her standing with Jessica.

"Katie?" Karen is still in the seat beside me.

"I'm good," I say. "I'll get out Levi's side."

Karen's door closes a few seconds later and I'm alone in the car with Levi, my hand still gripping his wrist.

"I'm not going to give up on you," he says.

I let go of him. "Can we get out now, please?"

He shakes his head. "I love you."

"What?" I breathe.

But he doesn't answer. Levi throws his door open and gets out. I stare at his back as he walks towards Veronica's front door. There's no one out on the porch tonight like there was at the last party. Levi doesn't turn around, and it's not until Karen bends down and fills my line of sight that I move to get out of the car.

"What did he say to you?" she asks.

"Nothing." I'm not going to tell anyone what he said, because repeating it won't make it true.

Josephine locks the car, and we follow Levi's path to the house. Inside, Rachel, Jarred, and Geoff are in the lounge room, along with a few others from school. The sight of Geoff makes me sick, and I cringe when he looks at me. I can't believe Veronica has let him in her house after what he did to her. The coffee table has several bottles of booze on it, and a few bottles of water.

Veronica comes out of the kitchen with plastic cups, a bottle of Coke, and a bottle of orange juice, followed by Levi who has three cans of beer in his hands. Our eyes meet, and I want to ask him not to drink, but I'm not the boss of him. I make a note to talk to him later and find out what's really going on with his dad.

He sets two of the cans on the coffee table.

Veronica pours herself a bourbon and Coke. "You made it." She smiles, and I'm surprised at how genuine she seems.

"Hey." I smile back.

"Pick your poison." She points to the table, taking a sip from her cup.

"Don't mind if I do." Karen fixes herself a vodka and orange.

"I'll have a beer." I grab one of the cans. I figure beer is less lethal.

Jessica takes a bottle of water.

Josephine joins Rachel on one of the big lounges. I set my phone on the coffee table and sit on the lounge opposite them with Karen and Jessica. Jarred makes a big display of going over to Josephine and kissing her in front of everyone. My eyes widen and I look to Jessica, who shrugs.

"What did I miss?" I ask.

"Apparently a lot," Karen says, settling back into her seat. "But so did I."

Veronica comes over and drops onto the arm of the lounge beside me. "Jarred and I haven't been together since the formal. I much prefer being single." She glares at him, then she glares at Geoff.

Levi takes a seat in an armchair near the open fireplace and sips his beer.

"Where is everyone?" I look at the cold can in my hand. I haven't taken a sip yet.

"Small party tonight." Veronica looks down at me. "Mum and Dad got a bit funny after the last one."

Josephine gets up so Jarred can sit down. "Who's going first?" Jarred says as he pulls her onto his lap.

I raise my eyebrows. "First for what?"

"Come on, Katie," Rachel says. "You should be a pro at truth or dare by now."

I grit my teeth and frown. "What makes you think I want to play?"

"Come on guys," Veronica says. "Do we have to?"

"We always do," Geoff says.

"Doesn't mean we should now." I look at each person in the room.

Veronica sighs. "Okay. No one has to do anything they don't want to. Only solid rule is you can't truth or dare the person who just truth or dared you. I thought maybe we could have some harmless fun this time."

"Harmless?" I stand. "You think this game is harmless?"

Levi looks up at me from his seat, and takes another sip of his beer.

"This game is stupid," Karen says.

"No, hang on." I sit again and take a big gulp from my can. "You want to play, I'll play. Let's have some *fun*." I stare at Levi. "Truth or dare?"

He sits forward and puts his beer on the coffee table. "Truth."

"Why did you accept the dare to ask me to the formal?" Looks like I do want to know the truth, as much as I've tried to deny it.

Levi's stare bores into mine. "Because I wanted to take you."

"You couldn't have asked me anyway?"

"That's two questions," Rachel says. "You only get one. Levi's turn."

Everyone waits.

Levi picks up his beer and takes a deep drink. "Josie, truth or dare?"

"Truth," she says.

Levi sits back. "Have you and Jess ever twin-swapped where it involved you being with your sister's boyfriend?" He raises his eyebrows, and a chuckle makes its way around the room.

Josephine hesitates and glances at Jessica. "Yes."

"Oh my God, who?" Karen sits forward.

"I don't have to answer that," Josephine says. "My turn … Karen, truth or dare?"

"Dare," she says. "Might as well make this interesting."

Josephine sits forward on Jarred's knees and grins.

"Choose one boy in the room then stand with your back to the rest of us and flash him."

Karen jumps up. "Okay, Jarred, let's go. Behind the lounge." She walks around our seat and leans against the back of it.

Josephine's smile drops away. Jarred moves Josephine off his lap so he can follow Karen, and Geoff and the others whoop and catcall. Josephine crosses her arms over her chest and stands with her hip cocked. Her frown is so deep she has shadows from the lines between her eyes.

"You asked for it," Levi says, popping another can of beer.

"You ready?" Karen asks.

Jarred's eyes go wide as Karen lifts her top. More hollers fill the room. Then Geoff reaches out and grabs Karen's boob as she's pulling her top down. She spins around and lashes out, catching the edge of Geoff's jaw with her fingertips.

"Ouch!" Geoff cries.

"Really?" I jump to my feet and shove him. He falls onto the screen around the fireplace. "You deserve more than that."

"I was just having *fun*," he says.

Levi gets up and grabs Geoff by the collar, pushing him towards the other lounge. "Go and sit down, you idiot."

I look at Karen as she finishes adjusting her top, and mouth *you okay?*

She nods, and comes to sit back down, taking up Veronica's old position on the arm of the lounge with her feet on the seat cushion. Veronica is quiet and stares at her hands, and I get the feeling she's remembering what Geoff did to her at the formal. Why anyone is friends with him is beyond me.

"Geoff," Karen says. "Truth or dare?"

"Dare." He smiles. "You're not getting anything from me."

Karen bites her lip. If I were her, I'd be thinking of making him do something that would embarrass the shit out of him. Maybe bring him down a few pegs and put him in his place. But then again, not much fazes guys like Geoff.

"I dare you to kiss Jarred … on the mouth. Open. With tongue," she says.

Geoff sniggers and sits back. "No way. We don't have to do anything we don't want to. Ronnie's rules."

"What, you scared?" I ask. "It's just a kiss."

"I don't do guys." He looks at Veronica and licks his lips.

I cringe. He is such a sleaze.

"Then you forfeit your turn," Karen says. "Pick someone to go next."

"Rachel. You can go." Geoff takes a big swallow of his bourbon.

"Katie, truth or dare," she says.

I should have known she'd pick me. Everyone stares at me, waiting for my answer.

"Dare," I say.

Jarred raises his eyebrows. "Wow, I wasn't expecting that."

"Make it good," Geoff says.

Rachel claps her hands and squeals. "Oh, this is fun. Ten minutes in the closet with one guy in this room. No lights."

I raise my eyebrows. "That's it?"

I'm trying to act cool when really I'm freaking out.

"Pick Levi," Karen whispers in my ear. "But if he touches you I'll kill him."

I turn my nose up. There is not one boy in this room who I want to spend ten minutes in the dark with right now, Levi included. I'm not sure I'm ready to be alone with him.

"Come on, say it." Rachel smirks. "We know who you want."

"Katie, you don't have to," Karen says.

"You didn't have to flash anyone either," I say.

She smiles, and I love her because she knows that just like her, I'm not going to back down from a dare.

I get up from my seat and walk to the door set into the side of the huge staircase that leads to the upper floor. I stop and face everyone, shoving my fingertips into the front pockets of my jeans.

"Levi," I say, and the room erupts with whistles and whoops. I'm surrounded by a bunch of immature, hormonal idiots.

I don't miss the smile on Levi's face before he looks at his feet and stands. He sets his beer on the coffee table and walks slowly towards me. He probably thinks we're going to make out, but that's the last thing I want to do with him right now. No, I'm going to tell him that I'm finally ready to listen to him and hear what he has to say.

His excuse for what he did to me better be a good one.

7

Forgive yourself

When Levi reaches me, he takes one of my hands and gives it a squeeze.

"You don't have to do this," he says.

"I know." I smile with my lips closed.

I open the door, and pull him into the closet. The door clicks closed behind us, and I freeze in the darkness. I feel disoriented because I can't see anything. The only thing anchoring me is the fact I'm still holding Levi's hand.

There's a murmur of voices outside, and someone wolf whistles again. If the lights were on I'm sure Levi would notice the blush creeping up my neck. The heat prickles my skin. I wasn't embarrassed out there, but now we're alone, it's different.

"I don't want to make out with you," I say.

"I know." Levi's breath is hot on my ear, and it startles

me. He's breathing in short breaths, and my heart races.

"We have ten minutes," I say.

"Probably nine now." I hear a smile in his voice.

"This isn't funny," I say around a smile. "I want the truth."

I stand in the dark and wait. Heaviness surrounds me as Levi lets go of my hand. For a second, I panic, not knowing what's in front of me or behind me.

"What's wrong?" Levi asks. "Your breathing's changed."

"I … It's dark." I clasp my hands together and stand still.

His hands find my waist and he pulls me close. His warm breath is beside my ear again.

"The truth?" he asks.

"All of it." I swallow. "Why did you ask me to the formal?"

"Because I wanted to." His grip tightens on my waist. "And before you say anything, that *is* the truth. And if I didn't ask you, then Geoff would have. Veronica dared him to first."

I scoff. "That bitch! But there's no way I would have said yes to him." I shudder, and Levi laughs.

"I was trying to protect you, Katie."

"Seriously, that's it? That's your excuse?" I ask. "I'm a big girl, Levi. I can look after myself."

"You don't know Geoff like I do."

"I have a pretty good idea of what he's like. But I'm guessing he didn't tell you about the toilet brush incident."

"The what?"

"I promised Veronica I wouldn't say anything."

"You can trust me, Katie."

Now it's my turn to laugh. "Can I?"

"We all know Geoff has trouble keeping his hands to himself."

"Yeah, well. Veronica found out the hard way." I pause. "He was getting a bit hot and heavy with her in the girls' bathroom at the formal. She said no. He didn't listen. I whacked him with a toilet brush."

"He said he and Ronnie got it on, which is why Jarred broke up with her, but Geoff did *not* tell me that. I should've guessed."

"I told Veronica to report him, but she wouldn't."

Levi adjusts his hold on me. His fingers splay across my lower back. "Can you see now that I was trying to protect you from him?"

"That doesn't explain the money—"

"Geoff accepted the dare to ask you to the formal, but Jarred wanted to make it a bit more interesting. He dared Geoff to sleep with you as well."

"They're both jerks," I say.

"Yeah. That's when I said I'd give them a hundred bucks each to leave you alone. But they only agreed after I said I'd take on the dares myself."

"So you *were* dared to take me to the formal?"

"Only because I wanted to. I wasn't going to let Geoff near you."

I chew my lip. "And did you pay them?"

Levi's breath tickles my cheek. "Yes, but not once did I ever consider forcing you to sleep with me. I would never have done that. Can you forgive me for all of this?"

I take a deep breath, and let it out slowly. "That depends."

"On what?"

"You can't say all this and expect me to be okay with any of it. I have big trust issues with you now."

Levi pulls me close again and presses his hands firmly into the small of my back. It's so dark I'm scared what will happen if I try to pull away. I'll probably end up tripping over something, and falling on the floor. But I'm scared what will happen if I don't pull away either.

I stiffen, holding my arms between us and clasping my hands together. I'm not sure where else to put them. Levi presses his forehead to mine.

"How can I get you to trust me again?" His breath tickles my lips.

"Trust is earned, Levi. I—"

He crushes his lips to mine, and I press my hands to his chest.

I didn't want him to kiss me.

I'm not ready for this … am I?

Light pours over us, and Levi pulls away.

I blink at the glare.

"Time's up," Veronica says. "Looks like you two have been having fun."

I stare at Levi, and run for the front door.

"Katie," Levi yells. "Katie, stop."

Levi's kisses are amazing, but this was a mistake. I can't trust him. I can't trust anyone. I reach the street and look around. The street lamps cast pools of light on the footpath. I spot Josephine's car. She drove us here. How am I going to get home?

I turn in the direction of the train station, déjà vu washing over me. I've been here before, and Levi was the one making me run last time as well. Why do I keep letting this happen? What is it about him that I can't stay away from? Every time I go back, every time I think we might have something worth fighting for, he reduces it to nothing again.

He keeps hurting me over and over.

"Leave her alone," Karen yells, and I stop to look back at Veronica's house. Karen grabs Levi's arm so he faces her. She shoves him in the chest, and he takes a step back. "You have been a dick to her too many times. I'm not going to let you hurt her again."

Levi steps towards Karen. "You don't even know what happened in there."

"She's running, so I can take a pretty good guess." Karen's voice is loud, and I glance around to see if anyone else has come out of the house.

I twist my fingers together. *What do I do?* Getting out of here and away from Levi is my number-one priority, but then I look at my hands and remember that I left my phone on the coffee table in the house.

I have to go back.

"When are you going to realise she would do anything for you?" Karen says, her voice sounding louder again as I walk towards them.

"I would do anything for her." Levi is yelling as well.

"You have a funny way of showing it." Karen folds her arms over her chest.

"Can you guys stop, please?" I say when I reach them.

Karen and Levi look at me. Levi runs a hand through his hair, and I close my eyes for a second, hating the effect he has on me.

Karen comes to my side. "You okay?"

"I really wish people would stop asking me that," I say. "I'm going to get my phone."

Inside, the others are sitting around the coffee table, laughing about God knows what. Me, probably. But I'm beyond caring. I'm tired, and I want to go home.

Jessica stands up. "Katie, are you—"

"I'm. Fine." I grab my phone from the coffee table. "Any chance we could go?"

Jessica looks from me to Josephine.

"Go." Josephine waves a hand at her sister. "Jarred can bring me home later."

I don't wait for another response from Jessica, heading to the front door and back outside into the warm summer night air. Karen and Levi are down on the footpath at the end of the driveway. Their discussion looks heated, but at least they've stopped yelling.

I walk past both of them to Josephine's car. The hazard lights flash and the locks pop. Jessica must have pushed the button on the keyring. I grab the front passenger door handle and rip the door open, ready to be done with tonight. After I slide into the seat I take a deep breath to calm myself, and rest my head against the headrest.

For a moment, I wonder why I'm so angry. Levi kissed me when I'd told him I didn't want that, but I still liked it. Am I overreacting? He didn't keep going like Geoff did with Veronica. Levi backed off as soon as I pushed him away, so am I angry that he kissed me, or am I angry because being angry with him is easier than letting him in?

I cover my face with my hands and close my eyes. There are voices outside the car but they're muffled, and

I don't try to make out the words they're saying. A moment later, Jessica climbs into the driver's seat, and Karen gets in the back.

There's a tap on my window. I wait for Jessica to start the car before taking my hands away from my face. Levi is at the window making a circular motion with his hand for me to wind the window down. I press the button on the door and let it down halfway.

"Can I get a lift home, too?" he asks.

I shrug and look out the front windscreen. "Not my car."

Jessica sighs. "What are we going to do with you two? Just … get in."

"Great," Karen says.

Levi goes around to the driver's side and gets in the back. I close my eyes again, and wait for Jessica to start driving. I keep my eyes closed for most of the trip.

No one speaks.

When we reach Karen's place, she squeezes my shoulder, and whispers in my ear, "Call you tomorrow."

I nod but I don't reply. I like the quiet right now.

Jessica continues on to our street, dropping Levi and I outside our houses. She offers me a small smile. I thank her for the lift, then get out of the car and watch her until she turns into her driveway up the road.

I don't look at Levi or talk to him as I make my way to my front door. I feel his presence behind me though, and when I reach my steps I turn around to face him.

He stands with his hands stuffed into his pockets. "I'm sorry. I shouldn't have kissed you when you said you didn't want me to."

I press my lips together. "No. You shouldn't have."

We stand and look at each other for what feels like forever. There are so many thoughts running through my head, and so many feelings pounding at my heart. I don't know which way is up, down, left, or right. I feel as if I've been torn apart and then put back together again a million times over, and it hurts.

I wish I could explain all of this to him so he'd understand.

"You can't kiss me and think everything will be okay." I clutch my phone with both hands. "And you can't kiss me after I've told you not to."

Levi runs a hand down his face, and rubs the back of his neck. "How else do I apologise? I've already said I'm sorry, and tried to explain what I did."

"That was an apology?" I ask. "You kissed me to apologise?"

"No … yes. No. I kissed you because I wanted to." Levi shakes his head and stares at his feet before looking up again and locking his gaze on mine. "Can we start again?"

I close my eyes and take a breath. "Ask me in the morning," I say, opening my eyes again. "Everything always looks better in the morning."

Levi smiles and nods. "Okay."

"Okay."

"Good night, Katie."

I wait until he's back on his side of the lawn before I unlock the door as quietly as I can, and go up to my room. I'm pretty sure no one is home because our driveway is empty. I hope Mum and Dad are having a good time.

When I get to my room I toss my phone on the bed, and pull my PJs from under my pillow. I change quickly, then go to my window seat and pick up my journal. I sit and tuck my legs beneath me.

Tonight totally sucked. I should never have gone to that party. I think I said that last time, so I obviously didn't learn my lesson.

Veronica was being okay for once. She wanted to play nicely. But Levi … what am I going to do? I don't know anything anymore.

I don't know what to think about everything he told me. Can I really believe he asked me to the formal to protect me?

He ripped my heart out and stomped on it, but every time I look at him, he melts me.

Is it possible to love someone and hate them all at the same time?

I stop writing, and bite the end of my pen. Out of habit, I glance over to Levi's place. He's sitting on the bottom step leading up to his veranda, his face in his hands. There's something at his feet, and it's not until he picks it up that I realise it's a bourbon bottle.

He's drinking again.

Where did he get it from? I didn't notice him having anything when he got in the car, but then again, I didn't look at him during the ride home.

Why is he doing this to himself?

The front door to Levi's house opens, and his dad steps out. Levi looks over his shoulder then gets to his feet, the bottle in one hand. I don't have to hear what Mark says to know he's angry. It's written all over his face. He clenches his fists, and takes a step towards Levi.

I kneel up on my window seat, and push the bottom part of the window open, then press my palms to the windowsill. I shouldn't be watching or listening, but I want to know what's going on. Obviously, Levi's dad isn't happy about Levi's drinking. I guess if my other son had died because of alcohol, I wouldn't like it either.

Levi's dad rushes at him and rips the bottle from his hand, pouring the contents onto the front lawn. Levi tries to grab for the bottle but Mark shoves him away. Levi falls hard onto the path, his hands flying out to break his fall. He gets to a sitting position and stares at his palms. I can't see if they're bloody, but I'm guessing they are.

"This has to stop," Mark yells, standing over Levi.

Levi's shoulders shake as if he's crying. "Why?" he yells. "You don't understand."

"No, *you* don't understand. You'll end up where your brother is." Mark goes back up the steps and inside, slamming the front door.

"Maybe that's where I belong," Levi yells after him, then he falls onto the path and covers his face with his hands.

My heart breaks a little bit more.

Levi rolls onto his side, and I catch his gaze as he looks up to my window. Now I regret pulling the lattice off the side of the house, because if it was still there I would ask him to climb it.

I've been so selfish, focusing on myself when Levi has been hurting like this after the death of his brother. Maybe Levi is more broken than I realised.

I jump off the window seat and go to my door, stopping

on the threshold to the hallway. Do I want to go out there? I'm the only one around to help. But can I do that, or will I make it worse? Can I put aside my hurt and anger to help him with his?

What have I got to lose? He needs someone.

I take the stairs two at a time and burst out the front door. By the time I make it onto my front lawn, Levi is sitting with his knees bent and his arms resting on them. I stop at our boundary and take a deep breath.

"What do you want, Katie?" he asks.

"To help … if I can."

Levi shakes his head. "No one can help me. I'm too messed up."

"That's not true." I walk over and sit on the grass near him.

"Yeah it is. I screwed everything up with us, and I'm just … following in my brother's footsteps."

"You are *not* Mason." I play with the grass in front of me, tugging at the spiky leaves and breaking some off.

"What I am is a disappointment."

"That's not true either," I say. "You were our school captain. You had so many people looking up to you, and being proud of you."

Levi scoffs. "Yeah, because of who my parents are, and how much money we have. I've been nothing but an embarrassment. Not like you." He moves to the grass and lies down. "You got to where you are because you worked for it."

"And you think that's been easy?" I lie beside him and look up at the stars.

"Would you rather have had it handed to you?" Levi

rolls his head to the side, but I don't move to look at him.

"No. I don't want anything handed to me. If I can't achieve something myself then it's not worth it."

"Exactly." Levi sighs. "Mason was a hard worker. He got everything he wanted because he earned it. Then because of me he made one mistake, and he lost his life. *I* lost him. He was my motivation, my support, my everything. Without him, I'm nothing."

This time, I roll my head to the side to look at Levi. He keeps staring at the night sky. He blinks, and a tear rolls from the corner of his eye.

I slip my hand into his. "I know how you feel, but you need to stop blaming yourself."

"How could you possibly know?" This time he does look at me. His eyes glisten in the moonlight.

"You may not be dead," I say. "But I lost you for a long time."

Levi squeezes his eyes closed, and more tears find their way onto his cheeks.

I roll onto my side, and put my other hand on his chest over his heart. It beats softly under my fingertips. "Mason's accident wasn't your fault."

"I gave him back his keys," Levi says. "I promised Dad I wouldn't, but I did it anyway, because I could never say no to Mason."

"Mason made the choice to drive that night, not you," I say. "You are *not* responsible for someone else's actions. Only for your own."

"And I've made some amazing choices, haven't I?"

I give his hand another squeeze. Levi may not have made the best decisions about a lot of things, but I probably haven't either.

I smile. "We're here now. We're alive, and the past is in the past. We all make mistakes, Levi; we can't change them. And maybe it's not just me who has to forgive you for the things you've done. Maybe you need to find a way to forgive yourself."

Start living again

It's been two weeks since I laid on the front lawn with Levi, staring at the stars. We haven't spoken much since then, and I think he's keeping his distance to give me some space, but now I'm leaving with Karen to head north for schoolies, and I wish Levi and I had made the time to resolve things a bit more.

Karen pulls into my driveway, and I roll my suitcase to the car.

"Don't do anything stupid," Daniel says, following me.

I smirk. "Me? As if."

Daniel shrugs. "Dad told me to say that."

"He couldn't say it himself?" I glance over my shoulder as Mum and Dad come through the front door.

Karen jumps out of the car and pops the boot. Daniel lifts my case in and wedges it beside Karen's. I swear she's packed for a month away, not nine nights.

"Seriously, Katie." Daniel slams the boot closed. "Have fun, but look after each other."

Karen punches Daniel on the arm. "You can cut the 'concerned big brother' act now."

"Bring my sister back in one piece." Daniel punches her back, but not as hard.

"She's in the best hands." Karen winks, and grins at my brother.

Mum and Dad come over, and they both hold me tight. You'd think I was going away for a year.

"Make sure you call us when you reach Coffs Harbour," Mum says.

"And drive safely." Dad looks from Karen to me, and back again.

"Don't worry, Bill. We'll be extra careful." Karen beams at my parents.

Mum and Dad go back to the veranda, and Daniel hugs me before following them.

"Spend that money wisely," he calls over his shoulder.

I laugh then look at Karen. We both squeal, and I run around to the passenger side of the car. As I open it, I hear the screen door squeak over at Levi's house. I lean on the top of the car door and watch him walk down his front steps. Karen starts the car and Levi quickens his pace.

"Will I see you up at Surfers?" Levi asks when he reaches me.

I smile. "I guess. Maybe ... hopefully." My cheeks burn, and I bite my lip.

He shoves his hands into his pockets and rocks on his heels. "We're bound to run into each other somewhere."

"Probably," I say. "But, you know … you can go and have fun with your mates. Don't worry about me."

"I always worry about you." Levi stares at me, and I wish we didn't have the car door between us, because I want to hug him.

"Maybe a holiday is what we both need. Time away from home might help us figure everything out," I say, even though I know all I want is Levi. All I've ever wanted is him; he's just made it really hard.

I move to get in the car.

"Katie?" Levi says.

I straighten again. "Yes?"

He reaches out and tucks a lock of my hair behind my ear. "Look after yourself." Then he leans in and gives me a kiss on the forehead.

I smile and nod, then drop into the passenger seat of Karen's mum's car. Levi gently closes the door, and when I go to press the button to wind the window all the way down, Karen is already doing it.

Levi leans on the window opening, and bends down to look in. "Can I call you?"

"Sure," I say. "That would be nice."

"Have a safe flight tomorrow," Karen says.

"I'll do my best." Levi smiles. "Probably see you some time on the weekend." He pushes off the car, and takes a couple of steps back.

Karen puts the car in reverse and backs onto the street.

"Let's do this," she says.

I smile. "Bring it!"

We crank the music, and head to the highway, turning

north when we reach the traffic lights. Karen merges onto the motorway, and I settle into my seat, so ready to take a break from everything and have some fun. The drive to Surfers Paradise is more than eight hundred kilometres, and around nine hours non-stop driving time, so we're aiming for Coffs Harbour today, which is roughly halfway.

The drive is pretty non-eventful. We spend the hours chatting about the year, what we've been through, how we think we went on exams, what uni we'd like to go to, and all the usual boring stuff.

"Have you told your parents yet?" Karen asks.

"You mean about doing a fine arts degree?" I shake my head. "No. Mum will freak. She keeps telling me how I'm so smart I can do anything. I'm not sure 'artist' is on her list."

"What about Bill? He's always been pretty supportive of anything you've wanted to do."

"Yeah, but I reckon he'll take Mum's side."

We both go quiet. For a while we don't talk, and sing along to the music at the top of our lungs instead. I love Karen for not pressing me about anything to do with Levi. And I love her even more for knowing me well enough to be able to tell that I don't want to talk about him.

"So … What do you want to do this week?" Karen asks.

"Lie on the beach," I say. "With my journal and a good book."

"We should go shopping, too," Karen says. "And eat as much ice cream as we can."

"I'm sure Jess and Stacey will want to go out to dinner."

"Of course." Karen glances at me and smiles. "And we

can also stay in and have a girlie night."

"Or two." I smile back.

"Or three ... if you want."

Karen knows that's exactly what I'd prefer over going to dinner or out to a nightclub. I was the last of us to turn eighteen, so now we're all legal, I'm pretty sure there will be one or two nights where the four of us will go dancing. I think I'm looking forward to it, but I'm also looking forward to chilling out.

We stop at Taree for a quick lunch, and to switch drivers. Karen uses the fuel card her parents gave us to fill up the car, and we get back on the road. Around three hours later we arrive in Coffs, and Karen uses Google Maps for directions to the caravan park where Mum and Dad booked us a cabin.

It isn't much, but it's a bed. After a quick call to our parents, we grab dinner from a Chinese takeaway across the street, and have a picnic on the floor in the cabin. There's not much on TV, so Karen logs on to Netflix on her phone, and we huddle together on the lounge.

I rest my head on her shoulder, and stare at the phone screen, but don't really see what's playing on it.

"Do you think things will ever work themselves out?" I ask.

Karen rests her head on top of mine. "You mean with Levi?" She takes a deep breath. "I think you've known each other far too long to give up now. Yes, the guy can be a dick, but I do believe he cares about you."

I sigh. "Sometimes he has a funny way of showing it."

"Guys are idiots."

I laugh. "Yeah."

We watch the screen for a while until the show stops. I yawn and sit up to stretch, then yawn again.

"We should go to bed," Karen says, standing. "More driving tomorrow."

I nod, but there's something I want to get off my chest first. "You know, Levi's drinking has been getting worse."

Karen stops and faces me. "I thought he only drank at parties."

I shake my head. "The fight we saw him have with his dad the other night … I've seen it more than once. Levi blames himself for Mason's death, and I think maybe his parents do, too."

Karen sits beside me. "That's a big call."

"I know, but I just … I want to help him."

"Well, I guess you have to try and be there for him if he needs you." She stands again. "Come on. Bedtime. Everything will look better in the morning."

I smile, because I told Levi exactly the same thing.

We go to bed, and I lie there for a while, taking slow and even breaths. We've only just left on this trip away and I'm already homesick. I want to be in my room, staring up at the glow-in-the-dark stars on my ceiling. I want to know that Levi is right next door. Instead, he's probably out drinking with his mates.

The thought of him drinking scares me, and I squeeze my eyes closed. How am I supposed to help him? For all I know it could be nothing to worry about, but my instincts are telling me otherwise.

I must fall asleep, because the next thing I know, Karen is tapping me on the shoulder, and the sun is shining through the window.

"Let's get this party started," Karen says.

I look at her through bleary eyes. "Are you showered and dressed already?"

She grins. "In four hours we'll be soaking up the sun, sand, and surf."

"Make that five. I need to get ready." I push myself up, and swing my legs over the bed. "What time is it?"

"Seven-thirty. Now, come on." Karen grabs my arm and pulls me to my feet.

After I have a quick shower and get dressed, we throw our stuff in the car, check out, and hit the road. We pump the music and sing along at the top of our voices, and I try to enjoy the ride, but I can't help my thoughts drifting back to Levi.

I lean down and grab my phone from my bag sitting at my feet. There are no missed calls from him, or anyone. Should I call him? Maybe I should leave him alone. But now that I'm away from him, I'm not sure I want to be.

Levi will be getting on a plane soon, and he'll probably reach Surfers before us. Knowing we're both going in the same direction is comforting.

"Want me to turn the music down?" Karen yells.

"What? No." I shake my head and smile. "I'm good."

She turns it down anyway. "You going to call someone?"

I sigh. "Levi hasn't called yet." I run my finger over my phone screen, and it lights up.

"Give him a chance," Karen says. "He'll probably call tonight or tomorrow once he knows you're actually at Surfers."

"Maybe I'll call him when we get there."

"Which will be in about half an hour," Karen says.

"We just crossed the border."

"Oh. I missed the sign."

Karen smiles. "I always miss the sign."

I wind my window down to get some air on my face, and soon we're pulling into the driveway of our hotel. The concierge loads our bags onto a trolley, and Karen and I check in while the valet parks the car.

"Five-star service," I say. "Nice."

"I'll call Jess." Karen pulls her phone out, grinning. She dials Jessica's number and puts the phone to her ear. Her eyes light up. "We're here."

I can hear Jessica and Stacey squealing at the other end of the phone.

Karen hangs up, and we jump in the lift and take it to the twelfth floor where our rooms are booked. Karen squeals as she opens the door, bounding into the room, throwing her backpack and handbag onto one of the twin beds, and making a beeline for the balcony. We have an unobstructed view of the beach and the ocean, with glimpses of the streets of Surfers Paradise below. Karen's enthusiasm is infectious, and I can't help smiling.

Jessica and Stacey tumble into the room in a wave of laughter and more squealing. My cheeks hurt from smiling so much at my friends and how excited everyone is.

We ask the concierge to dump our suitcases in the wardrobe, then the four of us head downstairs and out to the strip. We have the rest of the afternoon to get our bearings before our first night begins.

Karen drags us through the shopping mall before we grab an ice cream and head for the beach. I dig my toes into the sand and stare out at the ocean. As I eat my ice cream, I think about Levi again, and I wonder for the millionth time whether he's worth all the pain. I'm like a yo-yo going up and down between loving him and hating him, and now I'm so confused.

I don't want to be angry with him anymore. I just want him. I haven't even been here a day and all I want to do is go home and spend time with him. I take a deep breath and close my eyes for a second, listening to the waves crashing on the shore, and the chatter of my friends' voices. I push Levi from my mind, and look around at my girls. I need to be in this moment with them, not thinking about a boy who has made the past few years of my life a misery.

"Earth to Katie." Karen throws a handful of sand on my legs.

"What? Did you ask me something?" I lick my ice cream to stop it running onto my hand.

"What do you want to do tonight?" she asks.

"Sitting right here sounds pretty good," Jessica says.

"We could go dancing," Stacey says. "I feel like letting loose."

I laugh. "Surfers better watch out."

Stacey also throws a handful of sand at me, a huge smile plastered on her face. "I like dancing."

"So do I," I say. "But it's our first night. Maybe we can just chill out. You know, hang out at the markets. Go for walks and feel the sand between our toes."

"Oh no. This can't be good." Karen looks past me along the beach.

I turn to see what she's looking at. Jarred and Geoff are walking along the water's edge, and I immediately look for Levi. I scan the shoreline and the sand, but I can't see him anywhere. I'm not in the mood to talk to Levi's friends, Geoff especially.

"I think I'll head back to the room for a bit." I get up and brush the sand from my shorts.

"Want us to come?" Karen asks.

"No, it's fine. I'll go call Mum and unpack a few things. Meet you when the markets start?"

"Sure." She smiles up at me, shading her eyes from the afternoon sun.

"We'll make sure the beach doesn't go anywhere," Jessica says.

I walk up the sand towards the steps leading to the strip. Jarred and Geoff look in my direction, but I keep walking. As I make my way back to the hotel, I keep an eye out for Levi, hoping to run into him, but I don't.

When I get to our room, I fuss around for a bit, unpacking some clothes and setting my toiletries up in the bathroom, making sure there's enough space for Karen as well. I wash my face to freshen up, then I go and open the sliding door and sit on the balcony.

A crisp breeze blows off the ocean, and I rub my arms, even though it's been warm today. I stare at the water, and loneliness settles into my stomach.

"Snap out of it, Katie," I mumble to myself.

I pull my phone from my pocket and call home.

Mum answers on the first ring. "Sweetie, how are you?"

"Great, Mum. The room is amazing ... thank you."

"No problems getting there?"

"No," I say. "Everything is fine."

I put my feet up on the railing, and lean my forehead on my knees. Nothing is fine. I'm not fine. I want to go home, but fine is what you say when you're eight hundred and fifty kilometres from home, and you're supposed to be having fun.

"Okay, well, stay safe," Mum says. "Give me a call in a couple of days."

I hit End, sit back in the chair, and rub my face, then look at my phone to see what time it is. Karen, Jessica, and Stacey are expecting me to show up back at the beach in a little more than half an hour. The Friday night markets start at four o'clock, and I really want to wander through them, but now I don't feel like leaving the room.

I stare at the ocean, and try to decide what to do.

My phone buzzes in my lap with a message.

Daniel: How r u?

I sigh and write a reply.

Me: Need new word 4 fine

Daniel: Want 2 talk?

Me: No. But WYWH

Daniel: Call me later?

Me: OK

As I hit send, Levi's name flashes on the screen, and my phone buzzes out its ring tone. I blink and stare at it for a few heartbeats.

I swipe my finger across the screen. "Hey."

"Hey," Levi replies. "You get here okay?"

"Yeah. You?"

"All good. No hassles."

"Our room is really nice. You should see it."

"Maybe you can show me later." I hear the smile in

his voice, and I smile as well.

I pick at the edge of the chair handle and stare down at the beach, wondering if Levi is walking along it. The sun will be setting soon, and the reflection through the clouds has set the sky ablaze.

"Where are you?" I ask. "Can you see the water?"

"No. I'm at the pub. The boys and I are having a beer."

"Oh." I go quiet for a moment. "Well, the ocean looks beautiful. And the sky is amazing." I stare at the red and pink tones seeping into the clouds. "Even though the sun doesn't set over the water, it looks like the show will be good."

"Want to sit on the beach at sunset tomorrow night?"

My breath catches, and I open my mouth then close it again. "I'd love to, but I'm not sure what the girls want to do."

Levi is quiet on the other end of the phone. Then he says, "I miss you, Katie."

What am I supposed to tell him? I miss him, too, but I feel like I can't breathe. Still, this might be my opportunity to move forward. Is it time to let Levi do the breathing for me?

"I'll be down at the markets soon," I say. "Maybe we'll run into each other."

"Yeah, okay. I'll look for you." Levi says, his voice sounding happier. "I'll see you later?"

"Bye."

The phone goes dead, and I smile, staring at the screen until it blinks off. The sun is lower, and I check the time. I'm surprised Karen hasn't called to see where I am. I quickly text her to let her know I'm on my way. My phone buzzes a few seconds after I hit send.

Karen: Meet U at mall entrance

Me: OK

I grab my cardigan and purse, lock the room on my way out, and head for the lift. I stare at my reflection in the mirror as the lift takes me to the lobby, and I smile again.

Maybe for the next few days I can pretend I don't have any problems, or baggage. I'm not the poor girl. I'm not the girl everyone goes out of their way to embarrass. And I'm not the girl who has had her heart broken by the boy next door more than once.

I'm the girl who's ready to open her eyes, and start living again.

9

What I'm looking for

When I get back to the foreshore, I walk through the markets and glance around quickly as I make my way towards the pedestrian lights across from the entrance to the mall. All sorts of items are on display, from brightly coloured artworks, to knitted hats, and tie-dyed sarongs. I snort. There's even a stall where you can get your fortune read.

I find Karen, Jessica, and Stacey near the lights.

"Did you see the fortune teller?" Karen says, grabbing my arm.

"Yes." I raise my eyebrows. "Why?"

"You should totally get a reading."

I bite my bottom lip. "No way."

"It could be fun." Stacey shrugs.

"You could ask about Levi," Jessica says.

"Yes, yes, yes." Karen jumps up and down, still clutching me. "You could find out what's going to happen between you two."

I laugh. "You don't seriously believe that stuff, do you?"

"Come on, Katie," Karen says. "Lighten up. We're here to have fun."

"Then why don't you get your fortune told?" I ask.

"Me? I'm boring. I have no love life." She pulls me back into the markets and towards the fortune-teller stall. "You're far more interesting."

We stop outside the small tent. There's an A-frame sign on the right advertising 'Fortune Telling by Madame Leora'. The marquee is draped in purple fabric on all sides, with the panels at the front pulled aside and fixed to the poles like curtains. Attached to the fabric around the door is a variety of dried flowers, and herbs. Trinkets, beads, and crystals hang in strings in the open space.

"Looks cute." Stacey touches the fabric.

"And creepy," Jessica says.

Karen pushes me towards the threshold of the stall, and I part the beaded curtain to gaze around at the inside. The floor is covered with a Persian-look rug. Paper lanterns hang from the fabric ceiling. There's a small table in the centre with flickering candles on it, and a tarot deck set to one side.

A woman dressed in a black lace dress, purple headscarf, and with heavy eye make-up stares at me from one of the two seats at the table. She leans forward and rests her hands on the wood in front of her. Her bangles and the several rings on her fingers clink with her movement.

"Welcome," she says in a low, husky voice. "I am Madame Leora. What is it you wish to know?"

I stare at her, then whisper to Karen, "I don't think this is a good idea."

"Come on." Karen nudges me towards the empty chair. "Katie would like her fortune told. How much?"

No beating around the bush then.

"Twenty-five dollars per reading," Madame Leora says. "Forty for two."

"Here." Karen hands over the money.

I glance at Jessica then Stacey, and they both shrug. With a sigh, I pull the chair out and sit at the table. I make a note to buy Karen something this week. I don't want to waste her money, but who knows? I might find out something interesting.

"Only the subject can be in here," Madame Leora says.

Karen folds her arms. "Why?"

"We can't have any outside influences. If you want to stay, it's another fifteen dollars, and I will read the cards for you, too."

"Okay. We'll come back in half an hour." Karen ushers Jessica and Stacey out of the stall.

I watch the beads and crystals fall back into place, then turn to face Madame Leora.

"I've never done this before." I twist my fingers together in my lap.

"Relax," she says. "It will help us get a more accurate reading. Are you ready?"

I take a deep breath and let it out slowly, shake my hands, and put them on the table, then nod. "How does this work?"

Madame Leora picks up the tarot deck. "First, we need to clear the deck to remove all the energy from the last reading, and attune the cards to you." She hands me the deck. "Shuffle them. Then hold them with both hands, and close your eyes. Visualise a bright white light extending from your fingers and into the cards."

Okay then.

I do as I'm told, sitting up straight and shuffling the cards, flipping them clumsily between my hands. Then I clutch them tightly. With my eyes closed, I try and picture whiteness surrounding me. I feel like an idiot, but I'm strangely calm.

Madame Leora says, "Open your eyes. Now you need to ask your question."

"How do I do that?" I stare at her, my fingers gripping the cards.

"Ask your question in your mind." She nods at me. "Go on."

I adjust my hold around the deck of cards, and stare at them. What am I going to ask? What do I *really* want to know? I can't ask if Levi loves me, because I already know he does, although he has a weird way of showing it. I want to know if we have a future together, but I also want to know if that future will work out. Will everything be okay between us? Will we be happy? Or will all our problems get in the way? I don't want a future with him if that future is bleak.

Then I think of a question that seems almost too perfect, and exactly what I want to find an answer for.

Will Levi and I be able to find forgiveness?

It seems forgiveness is the one thing both of us are

seeking, whether it's from each other, or from ourselves. And I'm hoping that with forgiveness will come happiness.

"Okay, I have my question." I look up.

"Good." Madame Leora places her hands over mine and leans forward. "Now, channel that question into the cards."

I stare down at my hands again, and take a deep breath. *This isn't going to work, surely.* Fortune telling is ridiculous. But I want an answer to my question more than anything.

Madame Leora takes the deck from my grasp and places it on the table. "Split the cards with your left hand."

My fingers shake as I reach for the cards, taking half the deck and placing it to the left side of the pile. "Now what?"

Madame Leora puts the two piles of cards back together. "Now we see what the cards have to say." She places the first three cards face down in a line on the table in front of me. "Turn each card over, starting from my left. The first card represents your past. The middle is where you are now, and the third is what your future may give you."

I hold my breath, my hand hovering over the first card, eager to find out what the cards will say, but completely scared at the same time. I pinch the edge of the card and turn it over. A knight in silver armour, sitting on a white horse and holding a black and white flag, stares up at me.

"Death," Madame Leora says.

"That doesn't sound good," I mumble.

"You have had a sudden change in your past. Someone close to you instigated this change, but you must not dwell. Because where one door closes, another opens."

I stare at Madame Leora and crinkle my nose. Really? She's using that old cliché? But then I think about it for a second. Levi was close to me, and he instigated a big change in my life. He ended our friendship. Killed it. Maybe the death card is pretty spot on.

With a deep breath, I grab the middle card and turn it over. A man, looking like the pope and holding a sceptre, stares at me.

"The Hierophant," Madame Leora says.

"The what?" This is so bogus. Why am I even here?

"Recently, you have come to terms with doing what is expected of you, even when you have not wanted to." Madame Leora's voice is becoming huskier. The flames from the candles on the table flicker in her eyes. "You have been wise in conforming. It has led you to great achievements."

I bite my lip. Does she mean becoming dux? I can't think of any other great achievements in my life, and I was pretty much forced to do what everyone expected the day I won my scholarship. Now, I want to pursue a career in the arts. That's not exactly conforming to my parents' wishes.

I pick up the third card. My fingers slip, and another card drops to the table, landing face down. Were they stuck together?

Madame Leora presses her fingertips together. I still have the third card in my hand.

"What? What does this mean?" I ask, my fingers trembling.

"Put the card on the table." She lays her hands in front of her and spreads her fingers. "We will worry about the fourth card in a minute."

I put the third card down beside the middle one. A man in a black cloak stands with five cups at his feet. Three of them have been knocked over.

"What's this one?" I ask.

"The five of cups." Madame Leora looks at me. "You are feeling disappointed, and you're having trouble letting go of your past." She points to the death card. "You need to find forgiveness, whether it be for someone else or yourself. It is not until you can learn to forgive that you will find happiness."

My mouth drops open. Then I snap it shut. Did she know my question? How has she been able to read the cards to mirror exactly what has happened to me, and what I've been thinking?

It has to be a generic response to whatever card gets turned. *What a load of crap.* It's a coincidence this card has come up and this weirdo has said what she's said. I stare down at the cards in disbelief, and a wave of cold rushes through me.

This is totally creeping me out.

"Turn the fourth card," Madame Leora says.

I don't want to. But I slip my fingernail under it anyway and turn it over, placing it beside the five of cups. A tower sits on top of a mountain. Lightning strikes the tip of it, and flames billow from the windows.

"This doesn't look good either," I say. It would take an idiot not to see that.

"The tower," Madame Leora says. "You will face great turmoil. Something unexpected and tragic lies ahead. You will be tested in your ability to forgive. You need to be prepared." The psychic sits back, and regards me for a moment. She doesn't say anything else.

"That's it?" I ask. "My future holds something tragic and unexpected? Could you be more vague?"

"I just read the cards," she says. "Now, you need to close the reading. Pick them up and place them back in the pack, please."

I stare at her with my mouth agape before scoffing and sweeping the cards together. "Okay, then." I get up from the chair and go to the curtained door, then turn to face Madame Leora. "How much of this should I believe?"

Madame Leora stacks the cards on the table near the candles. "As much as your heart can manage." She stares at me, and I turn away, parting the beads and stepping out into the markets. "I hope you find what you're looking for," she calls after me.

I hesitate for a second, hugging my purse to my chest. Nothing she said could possibly be true. It's all a hoax. A pre-written script designed to apply to pretty much every person ever. But so much of what Madame Leora said is close to … everything. A shiver runs down my spine, partly because of the outcome of my fortune telling, and partly because Levi is standing across from me.

Maybe I've already found what I'm looking for.

10

Still standing

I stare at Levi as a trickle of people walk between us. He has his hands shoved into his jeans pockets, and is wearing a nice shirt, as if he's ready to go out on the town. Of course he is. He's probably going to hit the nightclubs later with his mates.

I'm still wearing the shorts and singlet top I threw on this morning when Karen and I left Coffs Harbour. Was that really this morning? It feels like a million years ago, and I stifle a yawn.

Levi comes towards me, dodging a few people to cross the main thoroughfare of the markets. I glance around to see if I can find Karen and the others, but they're nowhere in sight. I look back to Levi and smile.

"Fortune telling?" he asks when he reaches me.

"Yeah. It was … totally a waste of money." I chew on

my bottom lip, and look around again.

"What's wrong?" Levi shifts on his feet.

"Sorry … I'm just looking for Karen."

"Call her." Levi shrugs. "She's probably checking out the stalls."

I open my purse and take my phone out to text Karen instead.

Me: Finished. Will look at stalls then B on beach

Karen is quick to reply.

Karen: Jess getting a tatt

What? I stare at the screen with my mouth open, then another message comes through.

Karen: Don't panic not real

Karen: Henna

I smile then laugh, because for a second, I did panic. Besides, if any of my friends are going to get a tattoo, I want to be there.

"What's so funny?" Levi asks.

I put my phone away. "Jess is getting henna. Karen was trying to freak me out, that's all."

Levi smiles and pulls his hands from his pockets, running one of them through his hair. My insides flip, and I smile wider because he still has this effect on me.

"What did the fortune teller say?" Levi asks.

I shake my head and look up at him. "Nothing important. Or true."

I clutch my purse, and fiddle with the zipper pull, not sure what else to say or what to talk about.

"Hey, Levi," someone yells.

Levi turns towards the voice. I look around him to see who it is. Jarred and Geoff are walking towards us.

"Come on," Jarred says. "We want another beer."

"Or two, or three." Geoff grins.

I scrunch my nose up. I can't believe Levi is friends with him. I'm not about to tell him who he can and can't be friends with though.

Levi faces me again. "What are you doing tonight?"

I look up and down the stalls. "Shopping, and I'll probably sit on the beach for a bit."

"What about tomorrow? Want to have lunch with me?"

Geoff snickers. "Dude. Beer. Let's go."

I glare at him, then make eye contact with Levi. "You should go be with your friends."

"Yeah, but I'd really like to spend some time with you."

"Can I call you? I'll check what the girls are up to. I don't want to ditch them."

Levi backs away a few steps, nodding. "Okay." He turns and walks with his two mates into the crowd.

I let out a long breath. Is it ever going to be easy to be around Levi? To talk to him normally again like I used to when we were younger? I don't know why I'm finding it so hard now. Actually, I do.

It's a trust thing.

And a forgiveness thing.

Like Madame Leora said. I need to find forgiveness.

I shiver again, and move away from the fortune-telling stall without looking back. I should never have gone in there. Not that I *really* believe any of it, but a horrible feeling has settled into my stomach since I left that tent. To try and shake it, I walk the stalls for a bit, stopping at a stand where a pretty girl with a nose ring is selling her artworks. They are all beautiful black ink drawings with splashes of colour. A unicorn catches my eye. Its mane and tail are painted in a rainbow. I love the magical feel to it, so I pay the artist, tuck the small artwork into my purse, and move on to the next stall.

The hum of voices around me is soothing, and I get lost in the crowd for a while. I don't buy anything else, but I enjoy looking at everything and forcing myself not to think about anything other than exactly what I'm doing right now.

Eventually, I end up on the beach where I'd told Karen I was going. I pull my phone out and send her a message

Me: On beach now

Karen: C U soon

I walk towards the ocean, sitting and kicking my shoes off so I can sink my toes into the cool sand. I move them back and forth, concentrating on the feeling of the grains running over my skin.

I prop my elbows on my knees, and listen to the waves pounding against the shore. The noise from the markets hums behind me, and I breathe in a deep breath, holding it for a few heartbeats before slowly letting it out. I close my eyes, and my thoughts immediately go to Levi. Forgiveness is hard to find, but I want it so badly.

"There you are." Karen drops onto the sand beside me. "How did the reading go?"

Jessica and Stacey flop onto the sand as well, their faces all smiles.

"Yes! Tell us," Stacey says.

I look at Jessica's hand. "Show me your tatt first."

She giggles, but holds out her arm. "It's henna. Not permanent."

"It's beautiful." I look closely at the swirls and dots marking her skin in a light brown ink.

Jessica drops her arm. "You should get one."

"Maybe later," I say.

"We could all get one done," Stacey says.

Voices drift to us along the beach, broken by the sound of the waves crashing on the shore. I spot a group of people sitting in the sand at the base of the steps leading up to the markets, about a hundred metres away.

"So, the reading?" Karen asks.

"It was totally bogus." I stare in the direction of the other voices. "I reckon they work to a script and tell everyone the same thing, depending on which cards get turned over."

"It must have been more exciting than that," Stacey says.

I laugh. "It wasn't."

"Should we go back to the room?" Jessica says. "We could curl up and eat chocolate and watch TV."

"It's our first night," Stacey says. "We should go and have some fun."

"We should get some sleep," Jessica says. "We have plenty of time. And I think Katie and Karen are pretty tired after driving for two days to get here."

"I'm good with chocolate and TV," Karen says.

I smile at her. "You guys go ahead. I want to sit and listen to the ocean. I'll come back in an hour."

Jessica gets up and brushes the sand from her shorts. "You'll be okay by yourself?"

"Sure." I nod. "It's a five-minute walk to the hotel."

Stacey sighs and gets to her feet as well. "You guys

promise we can go dancing tomorrow night?" She reaches down and pulls Karen up.

"Let's just see what happens," I say.

"That's a yes." Stacey jumps up and down and claps her hands. The rest of us giggle at how silly she looks.

"That's a maybe." I smile at my friends.

Jessica and Stacey make their way back towards the strip.

Karen looks down at me. "You won't be long?"

"No." I shake my head, loving that she knows exactly when not to push me, or ask if I'm okay. I'm pretty sick of that question.

"See you back at the room." She walks backwards a few steps in the sand. "An hour … then I'm coming to look for you."

"I'll text you when I'm on my way." I smile.

Karen turns and joins our other two friends, and I watch them until they're up on the footpath and walking towards the hotel. The voices up the beach drift to me again, and I face their direction, digging my toes deeper into the sand. They sound so happy. I could use some happiness right now, but I don't move.

I need this time to think. I don't want to talk to anyone. I just want to listen to the water, and stare at the huge vastness of the ocean. Be swallowed by the nothingness, and maybe find a single moment of peace.

Sand flicks into the air and lands on my legs as someone sits down beside me.

"Nice night, isn't it?"

I look at the guy. He's cute and has nice eyes. He stretches his legs out in front of him and grins, then leans back on one hand and sifts sand through his fingers with the other.

"Yes." I hug my knees to my chest and stare at the water. "It is."

"Where you from?"

I look at him again. "Sydney. You?"

The guy flicks his head to shake his blond hair from his eyes. "Same. I'm from the Shire."

I chuckle. "Sydney is a big place. I live on the North Shore."

"Cool," the guy says. He stares at me. "What's your name?"

I hesitate before saying, "Katie."

"Well, pleased to meet you, Katie. I'm Scott." He sits up and sifts more sand through his fingers. "We're having a party up the beach if you want to join us."

"Yes, I can hear the noise," I say. "Maybe later." I don't really want to move from my quiet spot.

Scott gets to his feet and brushes the sand from his hands. "No problem. Hope to see you again." He gives me a wink.

I'm not used to this sort of attention from guys, so I'm not sure how to respond. I opt for a smile and a wave as he walks away. Levi is the only one who has ever offered me any sort of romantic attention. Scott is cute, and he seems nice enough, but he's not Levi.

I watch Scott's back as he makes his way along the beach towards the small but noisy group of people, and I can't help wondering how long it will be until the cops come and break up their little party.

I wriggle my toes in the sand. I should go back to the

hotel and find my girls, and I stand to do just that when I hear someone call my name. I search the faces I can make out and find Veronica waving at me. She's standing a little way away from the edge of the main party group.

"Katie, come over," she says.

I glance towards the direction of the hotel, and then at Veronica again. I guess I could talk to her for a few minutes. I lean down to scoop my thongs and purse up before making my way towards her and the party.

"Hey," I say when I reach her, glancing around at all the unfamiliar faces. "Good party?"

"Nothing like the ones we have back home." She laughs.

I press my lips together, then laugh with her. "So you haven't truth or dared anyone yet?"

She shrugs. "All they're interested in is drinking."

"And you don't want to?"

"I'm not stupid. Especially after …"

Veronica's unfinished words hang between us, and I get the feeling she's thinking about what Geoff tried to do to her.

She toes the sand. "But we don't need to talk about that."

"Is the rest of your group here?" I ask to change the subject.

"Geoff is around somewhere. Rachel is sitting on the steps." She points, and I follow her hand to halfway up the stairs. "Levi, Jarred, and Josie are I-have-no-idea-where. We left them at the pub."

Veronica moves, and I see Scott behind her. Our eyes connect.

"Katie, you came over," he says, walking towards us.

"Want a drink?"

"Um … no thanks, I'm good," I say.

"Come and meet my friends then." Scott backs away before turning and walking to the far left of the steps.

"I'll catch up with you later," Veronica says, looking at Scott, then back to me and smiling.

"Sure," I say, my thongs dangling from my fingers.

Veronica joins Rachel on the steps. I should go back to the hotel, but I'm here now. I guess meeting some new people won't hurt. I'm here to have fun, and apart from Veronica, and Rachel, I can't see anyone I know. The thought comforts me. It's the perfect opportunity to be whoever I want to be.

Scott introduces me to a few people, and their names blur together. There's no way I'm going to remember them, so I don't even try. I take a quick look around. Veronica said Geoff was here, but I haven't seen him yet.

I settle into the sand, planning to stay for ten minutes, but time gets on as I fall into a conversation with a nice girl named Mia. Scott inches closer to me with every beer he has, and I think it's time for me to leave.

I get to my feet, and wipe my sandy palms on my shorts.

"Are you going to uni?" Scott asks, jumping up to stand beside me.

"I'd like to." I don't elaborate. I want to get away and go back to the hotel.

"What do you want to do?" Mia asks.

I want to be an artist, but that probably won't happen.

"I have no idea." I don't want to get into it with these strangers, so I reach down to grab my purse and thongs. "I'm going to call it a night. It was nice meeting you.

Maybe I'll run into you guys later."

Before any of them can protest, I head up the beach, planning to walk the sand until the last set of stairs. After sitting amongst the loud chatter, I want some quiet.

"Katie, wait," Scott says from behind me. "Don't go yet."

"I'm tired." I turn and take a couple of backwards steps before continuing.

I quicken my pace, aware Scott is following me. This end of the beach is almost deserted. Fear rises into my belly, being so far away from other people with a guy I don't know. I turn and head for the closest set of stairs that will take me onto the road and towards people and traffic.

Scott grabs my arm. "Come on. I thought we could have some fun tonight."

"Let go of me." I yank my arm free and walk a few more steps.

Scott jogs past me, then stands in my path. "What is it with you girls? We're at schoolies."

I glare at him. "And you think that means someone you just met is going to put out?"

Scott steps towards me. He stands so close his breath brushes my face. It smells like stale beer, and it makes me want to gag.

"You only live once. I say you have to grab every opportunity with both hands."

I take a step backwards and stumble. Scott locks his hands around my upper arms and stops me falling. He yanks me towards him, and holds me tightly against his chest with one arm. Bile rises into my throat. He caresses my cheek with his free hand, then runs his fingertips down to my collarbone before wrapping his hand around my throat.

My purse and thongs fall to the sand as I reach up and try to free his grip.

"Get off me!" I shove him as hard as I can, but it makes no difference.

"Come on, Katie." He holds me tighter, his thumb pressing into my windpipe.

"Please," I manage to force out as I wriggle in his grasp. "Let go."

I struggle for a few more heartbeats, then I settle. It's obvious I'm not going to get out of this with pure strength. I relax in Scott's arms, and stare into his eyes. They're glassy, and I'm pretty sure he's drunker than I've ever seen Levi.

"That's better." He relaxes his grip, then leans in.

I turn my head to the side as he tries to kiss me, suddenly very aware of how Veronica must have felt.

"Please," I say again. "I have a boyfriend."

Scott laughs. "Where is he then? What he doesn't know won't hurt him."

How do I get out of this? I need to distract him.

"You're right," I say, turning to look into Scott's eyes. "He's not here, so I guess there's no harm in fooling around."

Scott smiles, and he moves his hand onto my shoulder. I have to stop myself gulping air, taking an even breath instead. I smile back at him, and wait for him to loosen his hold a little more. Finally, he does, leaning in to kiss me again, and I take the opportunity to pull my leg back.

Then I knee him in the balls.

Scott lets go of me and doubles over. "You bitch," he chokes out.

I push him away and try to go back towards the party, but he grabs my arm. We're too far away from anyone to hear me if I yell. I glance up the beach and spot a group of people walking towards us, but it's too dark to make out any of their faces. If they come close enough maybe Scott will leave me alone. I fight to pull my arm free, and the image of Veronica fighting Geoff enters my head. I remember standing there with the toilet brush, and I laugh.

"What's so funny?" Scott asks.

"You're a drunk idiot." I try to pull away again, but he grabs me around the waist and yanks me to his chest. "Get off me! I'll kick you again."

From the corner of my eye I see someone running towards us.

"Hey!" he yells. "Leave her alone."

I twist in Scott's arms and break free.

The guy grabs Scott and rips him away from me. The two boys tumble to the sand and roll over each other.

My mouth drops open when I see it's Geoff who has tackled Scott. Geoff pulls his arm back and slogs Scott in the face.

I look around, and Veronica is here with Rachel.

"Katie?" Veronica says. "Are you all right?"

I open and close my mouth a few times, staring at the people I thought I hated the most, but who have come to my rescue. Scott gets to his feet, and Geoff shoves him before he's fully upright. He lands heavily in the sand.

"Who's this guy?" Geoff asks.

"He was at the party over there." I point to where we'd been on the beach.

Geoff kicks sand at Scott. "Get lost, before I make you."

"She was asking for it." Scott scrambles to his feet and staggers along the beach, back towards his friends.

Veronica puts her hand on my arm. "Did he do anything to you?"

I shake my head and rub my neck. "Just grabbed me."

Rachel doesn't say anything. I'm grateful, because I will probably burst into tears if she does.

I look at Veronica. "Thanks, for ... you know ...?"

"I know." She hugs me, and at first, I'm not sure what to do. Then I lift my arms and hug her back. "I figure I owe you," she says softly.

"Come on, guys," Rachel says. "Katie's fine. Let's go."

Veronica pulls away from me.

I retrieve my purse and thongs from where I dropped them. "I'm heading back to the hotel now anyway."

"Want me to walk with you?" Veronica asks.

"I can walk her," Geoff says.

I frown at him. "I'm good."

"We'll catch up later then?" Veronica and Rachel link arms and head off together.

I nod then walk to the steps, because continuing up the dark beach alone is not a good idea after what just happened. When I reach the top stair I stop, slip my thongs on, and turn to look back at the waves. Veronica and Rachel are walking along the sand, but Geoff is standing at the bottom of the stairs looking up at me.

He takes the steps two at a time until he's a couple down from me. "You should let me walk you."

I laugh, even though it's not funny. "I'm a big girl. I can look after myself."

"Really? What would you have done if we hadn't shown

up tonight?"

"What would Veronica have done if I hadn't been there at the formal?"

He frowns, then glances at his feet before meeting my eyes again. "For what it's worth, I know I'm a dick. Especially when I'm drunk."

"Yeah, you can say that again." I press my lips together. "It's no excuse."

He nods. "You're right. What I did to Ronnie was … unforgiveable. And I'm glad you stopped me. I would've hated myself in the morning."

"Veronica would've hated you more."

Geoff walks up the remaining stairs and stands beside me. "Come on, Katie. Levi would kill me if I let anything happen to you."

I frown, and stare at him for a moment. "Let's go then."

I don't completely trust Geoff, but we fall into step beside each other.

"Why did you help me?" I ask as we walk. "I'm the last person you'd want to be seen with."

Geoff scratches his head and shoves one hand in his pocket. "I guess it's my way of apologising for … you know … everything. You said it yourself. We could all use a new beginning."

I chew the side of my thumb, not sure what to say. One thing I do know is that I'm tired of people saying sorry to me. Don't do something in the first place that requires an apology, and everyone will be so much happier.

"I'm not sure I can give you that. I don't trust you, or like you very much."

"That's okay. If I were you, I wouldn't like me either."

We stop outside the hotel. "This is me. Thanks."

"No problem. Maybe I'll see you around this week," Geoff says.

"Maybe." I walk into the hotel and don't look back.

Inside, I suck in a deep breath and take my phone out of my purse. I have five missed calls from Karen. When I get to our room, Karen, Stacey, and Jessica are all waiting.

"Where have you been?" Karen pounces on me. "You didn't text me. I was about to come find you."

I look at my phone screen. The door clicks shut behind me. "I'm ten minutes late. I met some people on the beach. Lost track of time."

I'm not about to tell them what really happened. I'd rather forget the whole night, what with the creepy tarot reading, getting assaulted, and then Geoff helping me. I should have come back with my friends.

Or kneed Scott in the balls harder.

"Everything all right?" Jessica asks.

"Yeah." I nod. "I'm tired though. Think I'll call it a night."

"We could probably all use a good night's sleep," Karen says.

Jessica and Stacey hug me before going next door to their room. Karen gives me a hug, too, and I go into the bathroom to wash my face. I stare at the mirror, and I smile at myself, because despite everything I've been through, I'm still standing.

You have to choose

We all sleep in the next morning, and it's nice not having to get up for anything in particular, or be anywhere special. The four of us spend the day lazing by the pool at the hotel, soaking up some sun. We have a light lunch on the beach, and I enjoy walking along the sand.

I told Levi I would call him, but I've been putting it off because spending time with my friends right now is exactly what I need. I text him to say maybe we can do lunch another time. He doesn't reply, and it's not until my phone rings late in the afternoon that I feel a little guilty for not calling him instead. Still, I stare at Levi's name flashing on the screen and let it ring out. After last night and what happened with Scott, maybe I should swear off boys forever. I'm yet to meet one who hasn't hurt me, not including Daniel and Dad of course. But then, Levi isn't Scott.

"You don't want to talk to him?" Karen asks, linking her arm through mine as we walk up the beach.

"I don't know what I want," I say. "And I have no idea what to do."

"Maybe now is when you need to give him a second chance."

I squeeze Karen's arm. "Maybe. But not today." I slip my phone into my back pocket. "Today I want to be with you."

We spend the rest of the afternoon and night at the hotel. Jessica and Stacey go out dancing for a couple of hours, but they're home and on the couch with Karen and me by ten pm. My friends must sense I'm not in the mood to party, and I'm grateful to have their company.

The next two days go pretty much the same. Jessica and Stacey do their own thing for a few hours at night, and Karen keeps me company either on the beach, or back in our room. We gaze at the stars together, and talk about life and what we want to do when we grow up.

Levi calls every day.

But I don't answer.

Now it's six-thirty pm, and I'm looking at another night on the couch because I don't feel like going anywhere. I hear my phone ring, and when I come out of the bathroom, Karen is staring at me. She has my phone in her hand.

"What?" I ask. "Why are you looking at me like that?"

"This has gone on long enough," she says. "We've been here for five days, and all you've done is mope in our hotel room, and walk on the beach."

"That's not true." I twist my finger into the hem of my top. "I had my fortune told."

"Yeah, which you haven't given me any details about. Come on, Katie." Karen stands. "Tomorrow we should go and get some henna done. Or have a drink in one of the bars tonight."

"I don't want to drink."

She drops her hands to her sides. "I spoke to Levi. He wants to see you."

"What happened to you hating him for what he did to me?"

Karen walks towards me and wraps me up in a hug. "I do hate him for what he did. But I know you, and I know you're trying to figure out a way to forgive him. Because he's Levi." She pulls back and smiles.

Tears sting my eyes, and then they're spilling onto my cheeks faster than I can wipe them away. "I'm so confused," I say between sobs. "What if I forgive him and he hurts me again? What if—"

"You won't know unless you try." Karen strokes my hair. "You don't want to spend the rest of your life wondering 'what if', do you?"

I look at my best friend, and take a deep breath, shaking my head. "I'm scared."

"Not knowing what will happen is part of the fun." She smiles.

I laugh, because so far none of this has been 'fun'.

"What did he say to you?" I ask.

Karen hands me my phone. "He wants to take you to dinner. We have a few days left before we have to go home. Just ... go and see him."

I take my phone and look down at it. "Okay."

Karen goes into the bathroom, and I sit on the edge

of the couch, squeezing my knees together. My fingers hover over the screen of my phone, then I key in my passcode. Levi is at the top of my most recent calls list. It looks like he spoke to Karen for a few minutes.

After a moment of hesitation, I hit Levi's name and hold the phone to my ear.

He answers on the second ring.

"Katie, hi."

"Hey," I say. "Karen said you called."

I wince at my stupid words, since I've been ignoring his calls for the past few days.

"So she convinced you to call me back?"

Silence hangs between us, and I bite my lip. This is harder than it should be. "Yeah."

"Did she also tell you she said she'd rip my balls off if I hurt you again?" He laughs.

I cough and stand. "She said what?"

Levi's laugh intensifies.

Karen comes out of the bathroom, and our gazes meet. "Did you threaten to rip Levi's balls off?"

Karen raises her eyebrows and smiles. "I sure did."

I shake my head and walk onto the balcony, leaning on the railing. There's still some light left in the sky even though the sun has gone down. The stars twinkle above, and I watch them blink in the hazy darkness.

"What've you been doing?" I finally ask.

"The usual." Levi pauses. "Hanging out. You?"

"Same. Pool. Beach. Chocolate in front of the TV." I close my eyes and shake my head. *I'm so lame.*

"Want to grab something to eat tonight?" Levi asks.

"Um ... Okay. What time?" I ask.

"Now," Levi says.

"You'll have to give me a chance to get ready."

"You're beautiful exactly how you are." I hear the smile in his voice. "Look down, Katie."

My chest warms at him telling me I'm beautiful. I drag my gaze away from the sky and look to the street. Levi is standing on the other side of the road, his face tilted up towards me.

"How did you know …?" I adjust the phone at my ear.

"Karen told me which hotel you're staying at. I just spotted you."

I press my lips together. "Give me ten minutes." Then I end the call.

Levi pulls his phone from his ear before I go back inside. Karen is standing in the middle of the room holding up a summer dress. My one pair of nice sandals hang from her fingers.

"Better change quickly," she says.

"Not that dress," I say. "It looks amazing on you. Me … not so much."

I dig around in my case until I find my three-quarter jeans and paisley top. Karen sighs, but doesn't say anything as I tug off my shorts and change. I set my glasses on the coffee table while I run a comb through my hair.

"Don't you want to put your contacts in?" Karen asks.

"No time," I say. "And if he likes me, he has to like everything about me. Glasses included."

"You're testing him."

"I guess." I shrug. "But you know how long it takes me to put those things in. I really don't have time."

Karen hands me my purse, and I slip my phone inside

after quickly coating my lips with gloss. I grab one of the room keys on the way to the door. As I step into the hall, Jessica and Stacey's door opens.

Stacey looks me up and down, smiling. "Where you going?"

"She has a date with Levi," Karen says.

"Finally." Jessica comes out to the hallway.

"Call me if you need us," Karen says. "I'll text you and let you know where we end up."

I smile and back away before turning to head towards the lifts. My hand shakes as I reach out to press the button. Why am I so nervous? I've known Levi my whole life, and there's pretty much nothing he doesn't know about me. I get into the lift and press the button for the ground floor.

When I step out into the lobby, Levi is waiting. A smile spreads across his face, and I can't help smiling back. I clutch my purse to my chest like a shield, and walk over to him.

"You look great, Katie," he says.

"Thanks." Heat prickles my cheeks, and I resist the urge to touch my glasses, gripping my purse tighter instead.

"What do you feel like eating?" he asks, walking towards the front doors of the hotel.

I fall into step beside him. "Anything. I don't mind."

"Let's hit the mall and see what we can find."

We step out into the balmy night air, and walk down to the foreshore. It gets busier as we get nearer to the mall, and the hum of activity wafts along the street. We walk in silence for a bit, and I listen to the crashing of the waves on the beach. It's dark enough now that I can't see the water from the strip, but I turn my face in that direction anyway.

"Can we go down to the beach later?" I ask. "I like listening to the waves."

"Anything you want," Levi says.

I smile at him.

We keep walking, and I people watch. Couples out like us. Larger groups of friends. People on pushbikes and skateboards. There's activity everywhere.

We stop at the lights to cross the road into the mall. When the little man turns green, Levi takes my hand. I look up at him and smile. He leads me through the mall to the pub, and while I said I don't mind what we eat, I'm not sure I want to eat here. Still, I go with it, and a few minutes later we're seated together in a booth up the back.

It's noisy, with groups of people filling most of the seats, and every stool at the bar is taken. A waitress in a short black skirt and tight white button blouse sashays over to us, a notepad in her hand.

"What can I get yas?" she says, her bright red lips turning up into a wide smile.

I pick up the menu from the table and quickly scan it.

"I'll have the steak burger," Levi says, without looking at what's on offer.

I bite my lip and flip the menu over, then back again. The meals look big, and I'm not very hungry.

"Wedges, thanks." I look up at the waitress, but she's ogling Levi.

"Drinks?" Miss Flirty asks.

I frown, and glance at the drinks menu that's sitting on the table.

"Water, please," I say.

The waitress raises her eyebrows and makes a note on her pad.

"I'm assuming you'll have your usual?" Miss Flirty winks at Levi.

"Yes, please." Levi smiles.

The waitress saunters away, and I can't help watching her path to the bar.

When I look back at Levi my mouth is hanging open. "She was flirting with you."

"No she wasn't." He leans back, and puts his arm along the top of the booth.

I scoff, and clench my fingers under the table. "You're blind then."

Levi sits forward and leans his forearms on the table. "She's doing her job."

I glance in the direction of the bar, and see Miss Flirty doing exactly what she did with Levi to another customer. My shoulders loosen. I don't feel so uptight about it now. When I look at Levi again, he's staring at me. Heat creeps into my cheeks.

I realise how this must look to him. I'm jealous of another girl looking at him. Is that what this feeling is? Jealousy? I wasn't prepared for the way her flirting has made me feel, but at least it seems like she does it with all the male customers. Knowing Levi probably isn't special to her makes me feel better. Still, Miss Flirty ogles him again when she brings our drinks.

"She checked you out again," I say.

"Katie, would you relax?" He picks up his beer and takes a sip. "Can we just have some fun?"

I lean forward and take a sip of my water. "Sure. I can do fun."

Our meals arrive, and I'm grateful this time that Levi doesn't take his eyes from mine.

We chat over our dinner. Levi tells me about this great nightclub they've been going to, and I describe the resort pool at the hotel. Levi orders another beer, and I take a deep breath to stop myself from saying anything. I'm not his mum, so I can't, and shouldn't, tell him what to do.

After that, he orders another, and another. I stick to water, and listen as his words start to slur. He's full of energy though, and he looks so happy. When he goes to the bathroom I take my phone out to check the time. Ten pm. The pub is pretty much full, and the noise level has risen to above comfortable. I want to leave, but I can't do that until Levi comes back.

"Katie. How are you?" Geoff slides into the booth beside me.

By the time I look at him, Jarred and Josephine are seated across from me, a beer in each of their hands. Veronica stands at the end of the table.

"I'm great, thanks," I say.

I don't want to spend the rest of the night with them around, and I crane my neck to see if Levi is coming back from the bathroom.

"Where's Levi?" Veronica asks.

"Here," he says, nudging her shoulder with his.

He has another drink in his hand.

"Nice dinner?" Jarred looks from me to Levi.

"Yeah, great," I say, turning to Geoff. "Could you move, please?"

He stands, and I shuffle along the seat to get out of the booth.

"Where are you going?" Levi asks.

"Thank you for dinner," I say. "But I'm going to head back."

"Is something wrong?"

I press my lips together. "I'm tired is all. I'll catch up with you later."

"Let me walk you." He sets his drink on the table.

"No, it's fine." I turn and make my way through the crowded pub as quickly as I can, hoping Levi doesn't follow me.

I'm not in the mood to spend time with his friends when I thought I was spending time with him. And I also don't want to be having a conversation with him when he might not remember it tomorrow.

Why does he have to drink? Why can't he just have dinner with me?

I step out into the fresh night air and take a deep breath. It was really claustrophobic inside the pub.

A hand touches my shoulder, and I stop.

"Katie," Levi says. "Why are you going?"

I shrug away from his touch and face him. "I told you, I'm tired. I'll see you later."

But when I try to leave, Levi darts around in front of me, so I stop again. We're in the middle of the mall with the noise from the pub behind me.

"Please stay," Levi says.

"Why? So I can watch you drink yourself stupid?" I snap.

The surprise on his face makes me regret my words.

Levi takes a step back. "I've only had a few."

I close my eyes for a second and collect myself so I don't say anything else too mean. "We should talk tomorrow. When you're sober."

"We can talk now." Levi crosses his arms over his chest, and I'm surprised he's so coordinated after the number of beers he's had.

"No, really," I say. "We'll talk about it tomorrow."

"Well, I want to talk now."

"Please move." I look up at Levi, but when I go to step around him he steps in my path again. Anger fills the pit of my stomach and rises into my chest. "Get out of my way, Levi."

"No. I want to talk. Something is bothering you."

I glare at him. The middle of a busy mall is not where I want to be discussing this.

"Fine," I say. "I thought you were taking me out to dinner so we could spend some time together, but instead … You're drunk. And then your friends showed up. It's not my idea of a romantic night. So excuse me again, and move."

"I'm not drunk," he says, like that explains everything.

I blink a few times in an attempt to control my anger. "Has drinking become so normal to you that you can't even see what you're doing to yourself?"

"It's just a few beers, Katie."

"A few too many."

"I'm fine."

"I bet Mason thought exactly the same thing." The words are out before I can stop myself.

The way Levi's brow pinches and his mouth puckers tells me I've stepped over the line. But right now, I don't care. Maybe he needs to hear the cold hard truth.

"Don't you dare bring him into it," Levi says, clenching his fists. "This is not the same."

"It's exactly the same!" I yell, tears pricking my eyes. My chest heaves as I try to breathe. "You forget, I was there, too. I went through the pain, and the loss, and the heartache, just like you did. I don't want to go through that again."

He shakes his head. "You don't know ..."

"I do know. I know I couldn't stop crying for a month after Mason died. And I know it opened a hole in my chest so wide I never thought it would close. But the worst part was, you shut me out. I love you, Levi. And I'm so close to forgiving you for everything you've put me through. But what's the point if all you're going to do is drink yourself stupid all the time? One day, you'll end up right where your brother did, wrapped around a telegraph pole." I stop and swipe the tears from my cheeks. "I can't watch you do this."

"Katie ..." Levi reaches for me, but I step back.

"No," I say. "You can't keep doing what you're doing. And if you do, I won't stick around. It's me or the booze. If you want me to stay, you have to choose."

12

The mess I'm in

Karen knew something was wrong the moment I walked into our hotel room. I told her everything. How he's been drinking a lot since he started talking to me again. Or maybe he's been doing it longer than that, and I haven't noticed. How he let me walk away once I delivered my ultimatum. We speculated about a lot of things, and in the end I told her I was tired and wanted to go to bed, because I didn't want to think about it anymore.

Now, it's almost the end of our last day of holidays, and I feel like I haven't had a break from anything.

I dig my toes into the sand, and stare out at the ocean. I came down to the quiet end of the beach, hoping the sound of the waves might calm me, but they haven't.

I'm tired of being on a merry-go-round. I don't know how I should act or feel when I'm around Levi, and it's tearing me apart. One minute everything is perfect, and he's perfect, but then everything changes in an instant.

Is it me?

Am I the one to blame?

Am I asking too much of him?

Or am I overthinking everything?

Last night was the most we've talked about Mason ever, and I accused Levi of being exactly like his brother.

I'm so scared that he'll do something stupid as well.

Today has been hard, because I want Levi to call me so badly, but it's late afternoon and he hasn't. I want to call him, but that would be like saying he doesn't need to be responsible for his actions. If I call and apologise for what I said, where will that leave us?

Right back where we started.

I want to hear his voice, but I also want him to realise he can't keep drinking like he does.

It will destroy him.

It will destroy me.

"Hey." Karen flops onto the sand beside me.

I pull my knees to my chest and hug them. "Hey."

"Feeling any better?"

"I'm ... I don't know."

Karen tucks my hair behind my ear. "Why don't we go out tonight? It's our last night. We can go dancing. You know how much Stacey loves dancing."

I shrug. "Okay."

"We can go to the nightclub Jess and Stacey told us about," Karen says, getting to her feet. "I can't believe you're eighteen, and we haven't gone to a club together yet."

I look up at her. "Sounds noisy."

"Come on, Katie." She grabs my hand and pulls me up. "You need to let your hair down. Let's go get ready." She tugs me up the beach towards the road.

We walk the five minutes back to the hotel. Jessica and Stacey are already getting ready for one more night out before going home. While Karen does her makeup, I put on the clothes she suggests, slipping into skinny jeans and a black halter top. Then I go through the trauma of putting my contacts in. Even after all the months I've been wearing them, I still can't seem to do it easily. Still, I like the way I look without my glasses. I don't wear a lot of makeup though, so I just use my usual gloss on my lips, and run a brush through my hair.

"Ready," I say, slipping my feet into my sandals.

Karen grins and grabs her room key from the table. "Let's go have some fun."

"Who said fun?" Stacey asks from the hallway.

"I said fun." Karen pulls our room door closed behind us.

Jessica smiles, but doesn't show as much excitement as the other two. We head downstairs and onto the street.

"It's early," Stacey says, turning her face to the darkening sky. "Dinner first?" She looks at us over her shoulder as we walk.

"Sounds perfect," Karen says. "We can go to the pancake place in the mall."

"For dinner?" I ask. We stop at the lights and wait for them to change.

"I think pancakes for dinner sounds awesome," Jessica says.

We laugh and cross the road, walking towards the

mall with a steady stream of other people. I look around at my friends and feel a moment of gratitude towards them. I'm so lucky to have these three girls in my life. I'm not sure I'd be able to get through any day, let alone every day, if I didn't have them. I want to hug them all.

I settle for slipping my arm through Karen's and giving it a squeeze. Jessica and Stacey walk ahead.

"Everything good?" Karen asks, glancing at me sideways.

I lean my head towards her. "Yeah. I have you."

"Always." She smiles.

When we reach the pancake place it's already pretty full, but they squeeze the four of us onto the end of a long table. It's informal dining, and none of us mind. The atmosphere is full of happy energy. Maybe it has something to do with the sugar everyone is eating.

We each order something different so we can try as much of the menu as possible. Traditional pancakes with maple syrup, pancakes with berries and ice cream, waffles with chocolate and strawberries, and a banana crepe, plus milkshakes all round.

I enjoy a couple of hours with my friends, eating, laughing, and talking about what we plan to do when we get home.

"I would love to take a year off," Jessica says. "Maybe do some travel with Josie? She's pretty excited about it actually. We just have to convince Mum and Dad."

"I think everyone wants a gap year." Karen takes a sip of her milkshake.

"We don't always get what we want," I say.

"I don't think they're a good idea," Stacey says. "You end up a year behind. I think I'd rather get my degree out of the way, then have a year off while I decide if I want to use it or not."

I sip my milkshake. "Why wouldn't you use it?"

Stacey shrugs. "Right now, I want to go into vet science. But in four years' time I might hate animals."

"There's no way you'd ever hate animals," Jessica says.

"Anything can happen."

I look around at my friends. Yes, anything can happen. We don't know what the future holds, but that's what makes it so scary, and, according to Karen, fun at the same time.

I'm suddenly aware of how much time I've wasted this week moping about when I should have been making the most of every second I have with my friends. Who knows where we'll end up next year? What if I've ignored the most important time of our lives together?

"We should go," I say. "There's a dance floor waiting for us."

Karen jumps up. "I think you're right."

Jessica and Stacey get to their feet, and I smile at everyone's enthusiasm. This is what I want. To see my friends happy, and to share that happiness with them. I've been so wrapped up in Levi that I forgot how good I have it. How lucky I am to have these girls in my life.

We pay for our meals at the counter on the way out and head up the mall towards the nightclub. The entrance is via a flight of steps leading to an upper level. We all get carded on the way in.

As soon as we pass through the doors the noise level rises. Lights strobe around the club in blue, pink, and green. A smoky haze floats above the large room. We move farther in towards the bar. Music pumps, and the bass vibrates through my feet. People move violently around the dance floor. The dancing here is nothing like it was at the formal. Stacey's face lights up, and she cranes her neck to get a better look at the dance floor. Karen pulls herself up onto a stool at the bar, and I take the one next to her.

"Come on." Stacey tugs Jessica's hand and leads her through the crowd towards the dance floor.

Karen and I laugh, and watch with smiles on our faces.

"Drink?" she yells in my ear.

I nod. Karen picks up the cocktail list and raises her eyebrows. I hesitate, but then nod again. I'll only have one. I'm not going to drink to get drunk. I just want to enjoy a night with my girlfriends.

Karen orders two Pina Coladas, and the bartender asks us for ID, even though we were asked at the door. I don't mind, and I smile when I hand him my licence. He winks at me before making our drinks.

I sip my cocktail and scan the crowd, watching Stacey and Jessica on the dance floor, and checking out what some of the girls are wearing. Their outfits make my jeans and halter top look like rags.

Karen and I sit like that for another two rounds. Every now and then, she points and I smile or laugh. Or the other way around. I'm surprised at how easily the cocktails go down, and a nice buzz courses through me. I feel happy.

Someone sits on the bar stool beside me, but I don't pay them any attention.

The person leans over and yells in my ear, "You can't stay away from me, can you?"

I turn to see Scott, the guy I met on the beach who tried to force himself on me. Seems like my knee to his crotch wasn't obvious enough. I stiffen, smile with my lips closed, and then angle my body away from him and towards Karen, taking another sip of my cocktail. We're in a crowded nightclub and Karen is right next to me. Surely Scott won't touch me here.

Scott moves to stand in front of us. "Would you ladies like a drink?"

I hold up my glass and raise my eyebrows. "Already have one." But I don't know if he can hear me.

"Who is this guy?" Karen yells at me over the music.

I crinkle my nose, and lean close to her ear. "Met him on the beach. He's a creep."

I never told Karen what happened that night. If she knew, she'd be kneeing him in the balls right now, harder than I did.

Karen looks him up and down. "Yeah, I'll have a drink."

I glare at her and hope she gets my 'What the hell are you doing?' vibe.

Scott grins, and I turn away, cringing. I finish my cocktail, but I don't think accepting a drink from him is a good idea. Still, I go with the flow, keeping an eye on Scott and the glasses to make sure he doesn't spike them with something. Scott hands us a vodka and orange each. I sip the sweet drink through the straw, not sure if I like the taste of it after three Pina Coladas. I take another few sips, then set my glass on the bar.

I lean over and put my lips to Karen's ear. "Let's dance."

She sucks half her drink through the straw, then jumps down from the bar stool. I link my fingers through hers, and follow her through the crowd to the pulsating mass of bodies on the dance floor. It takes us a few moments, but we spot Stacey and Jessica a few people in, swinging their hips, and waving their hands like everyone else.

Karen and I join them, and it takes five minutes of dancing for me to be grateful I wore flat shoes. The lights strobe around us, and I lose myself in the rhythm of the music, moving to the beat and concentrating on nothing but how it makes me feel. I'm buzzing from head to toe, and I figure it's the alcohol, but I don't care. The power of the bass beats through my body, and I forget about everything that's happened.

It feels good.

Hands touch my waist, and someone presses up against my back. I turn to see Scott behind me, and my happy moment is ruined. In my frantic attempt to get away from him, I stumble into the people beside me, and a girl falls to the ground.

"I'm so sorry," I yell, but my voice is drowned out.

I reach down to help her to her feet, aware that someone's hand is on my arse. Once the girl is up, I turn again and confront Scott. I want to scream at him but there's no point. He won't be able to hear me, so I'd be wasting my breath. He grins at me.

I push my way off the dance floor.

I can't breathe. It's too stuffy in here.

I make it as far as the bar, and my head spins. I grab a stool to steady myself. The barman smirks then pours a glass of water and pushes it towards me. I sit on the stool and take the glass, downing the cool liquid in three gulps.

"What the hell happened?" Stacey yells in my ear.

"Are you all right?" Jessica grabs my arm.

Karen pulls me to my feet. "Let's get out of here. You need some air."

My friends surround me, and we shuffle towards the exit. I stumble going down the stairs and into the mall. The cool night air hits my face, and I break out in a sweat. A sick feeling creeps into my stomach. I'm not sure if it's from the alcohol or having Scott's grubby hands on me again. It's probably a combination of both.

I concentrate on the sound of the waves crashing on the beach across the road—anything to take my mind off the way that creep looked at me. The way he touched me, tonight and the other night on the beach … My hand goes to my throat.

"Let's sit down," Karen says. She leads us to the pedestrian crossing, and we make our way over to the beach side of the strip. The four of us head to the steps and sit on the top few. I stare out at the dark ocean and take slow breaths, trying to get the sick feeling in my stomach to settle down.

"What did that guy do to you?" Stacey asks.

I grimace and turn my face towards her. "He grabbed me."

"Looked like he wanted to dance with you." Jessica tucks her hair behind her ear.

"He bought us a drink while you guys were on the dance floor," Karen says. "I think he wanted more than a dance."

"You're right." I take a deep breath and stare at my hands. "Our first night here, when I stayed on the beach—"

"When you were late, and I was about to come look for you?" Karen asks.

I nod, my stomach rolling. I swallow before continuing. "That guy ... Scott. He came over and talked to me. He asked me to come to this party they were having near the steps that lead to the sand. I said no, but then I saw Veronica and she called me over." I shrug. "I went to talk to her, then Scott saw me and introduced me to his friends. After I left to come back to the hotel, he followed me. The beach was dark. He ... grabbed me."

"That bastard," Stacey says.

I offer her a small smile. "I gave him a good knee in the balls."

"Go you," Karen says.

My friends laugh, and I do, too, but it's not funny, and I still feel sick.

"I'm not sure I would've gotten away from him if it wasn't for Geoff," I say.

"Geoff?" Karen asks. "Geoff Wilcox?"

"It's ironic really." I look at her. "Geoff is ..."

"Yeah. He's a dick. What he did to Veronica ..." Karen stops. Her eyes go wide, and her hand flies to her mouth.

"What did he do to Veronica?" Stacey stands up.

I shake my head. "We promised her we wouldn't tell." I glare at Karen.

"No, you can't do that. You can't say something then not tell us," Stacey says.

"I know about it." Jessica stares out at the beach.

"What?" Karen and Stacey say at the same time.

I put my face in my hands. I'm not surprised. Josephine and Veronica are friends. Josephine probably told Jessica at some stage.

"She asked us not to tell anyone, okay?" I say. "Just … let it go. And to Geoff's credit, if he didn't turn up, who knows what Scott would've done to me."

"You should report him," Karen says.

I shrug. "I told Veronica the same thing."

"And did she?"

"I don't think so." I look at Karen. "There's no point. I'll never see him again, and he didn't … I got away."

We all go quiet. Stacey frowns, then walks down a few steps and leans against the stair railing, crossing her arms over her chest. Karen bites her lip and stares at her feet. Jessica puts her arm around my shoulders and gives me a gentle hug. I concentrate on not throwing up, swallowing a few times to suppress the urge. My head spins, and I think now it's definitely the alcohol.

There are a few people about, walking into and out of the mall, and hanging out on the beach. Murmuring voices float on the air, mingling with the crashing waves. Cars pass on the road. The traffic lights behind us tick as they change.

"There she is," someone says.

Feet shuffle behind us. I look over my shoulder towards the voice. Scott stops a few metres away from the steps, and he's brought friends. My head pounds, but I recognise the other boys from the beach earlier in the week.

I get to my feet, swaying a little, and face the three boys. Jessica gets up as well, and she and Stacey move to my side.

Karen steps forward. "You touch her again and I'll hurt you."

Scott laughs. "Wow, Katie. Your friend is feisty." He stares at me, and it makes my skin crawl. "We just want to buy you a few more drinks."

"Yeah." One of the boys grins. "Why don't you come back to the club and show us a good time?"

"Because you putting your hands where they're not wanted isn't our idea of a good time," Karen says. "Go find someone else to have *fun* with." She makes quote marks in the air with her fingers. "Or I'll call the cops."

"You do that." Scott raises his chin.

The three boys come towards us. Karen stands her ground, but Stacey and Jessica pull me down the stairs until we're standing on the halfway platform. My knees are weak, and it's getting harder to stop myself from being sick.

Scott puts his hands up. "I'm sorry about that, really. Can we start over?" He smiles at me, and my stomach rolls.

Jessica and Stacey are still beside me, so close I can hear them breathing.

"He looks like a creep," Stacey whispers in my ear.

Scott shoulders past Karen and comes down the stairs. His two mates stay at the top.

Karen looks up and down the street before following. "Get away from them."

"I want to talk to Katie." Scott stops in front of me. "I really like you. I'm sorry if I went about it the wrong way. The other night ... I was a drunken idiot. Can we take a walk and maybe chat?" He angles his head down and stares at me through his lashes, giving me a look I'm pretty sure he thinks is going to win me over.

"I don't want to talk to you," I say, swaying. I have to

blink a few times to see him properly. "Didn't you get the message when I kneed you in the balls?"

He comes closer, still smiling, and then I vomit all over him.

"You bitch," Scott yells.

I'm off the ground and over his shoulder.

Stacey cries out and stumbles on the steps.

"Katie!" Karen yells.

Bitterness fills my mouth. The taste makes me gag. I kick my legs and pummel Scott's back with my fists, but he doesn't let go. When his feet hit the sand he stumbles, his shoulder digging into my stomach. Karen, Jessica, and Stacey yell but I can't see them. Their voices blur into one frantic sound. Scott's shoulder digs into my stomach as he runs, and more bile rises into my throat. A siren wails on the strip, and I catch a glimpse of red and blue lights.

The waves crashing on the shore get louder. Scott stops and drops me. I hit the water and the cold envelopes me, filling my mouth and my nose. When I come up I cough and splutter, flopping around in the shallows as I try to get to my feet. Then I'm plunged under again, a hand forcing my head down. *Scott's hand?* His fingers curl into my hair and yank me up. I cough again, my arms flailing as I try to grab onto something.

"Hey, what are you doing?" I hear Levi's voice.

The hand releases my hair, and I fall to my knees in the shallows. I try to turn towards Levi, but pain shoots into my head and the world spins.

"None of your business," I hear Scott say. I don't know where he's gone.

Then he grabs my arm. His fingers dig into my skin.

"Get off her," Levi yells.

Where is he?

More voices shout around me, but I can't make out the words.

I scramble on the sand on my hands and knees. The water rushes over my legs as the tide comes in. I look up as Levi's fist connects with Scott's face. I vomit again, then fall onto the sand and roll until I'm looking at the sky. The twinkling stars remind me of the stickers on my bedroom ceiling, and I wonder how the hell I got myself into the mess I'm in.

13

The chance to begin

I open my eyes. Sunlight sears my retinas, so I squeeze them shut again. There's a dull ache in my head, and when I lift it, a sharp pain pierces my temple. I wince as I try to sit up, but everything hurts, so I resort to rolling onto my side.

"Hey, sleepyhead," Levi says.

I open my eyes to slits. He's sitting on the floor beside my bed, leaning against the wall with his knees pulled up. There's a bucket between us with a face washer draped over the lip.

"What are you doing here?" I groan. "What happened?"

"You got drunk."

"I tried to make him leave." Karen leans out of the bathroom doorway. "But he wouldn't go away. He's been here all night."

Levi chuckles. "I take it you're not feeling so good."

"Like someone has scooped my brain out with a spoon." I groan again, and cover my eyes with my hand.

"Do you still feel sick?" Karen asks.

I peek at her through my fingers. "I don't think so. But I haven't stood up yet. How many times did I ... was I sick?"

"Before or after you upchucked all over Scott?" Karen raises her eyebrows and grins.

I move my hand to my mouth. "Oh ... that happened, didn't it?"

Last night comes back to me in a huge tidal wave. Drinking cocktails. The vodka Scott bought us. Dancing. Scott grabbing me. He and his friends following us. Me vomiting all over him. Then him trying to drown me in the ocean. Levi clocking him one in the jaw. The police showed up after that. Apparently, they'd been looking for Scott, and I wasn't the first girl he'd assaulted. They questioned all of us. I refused to go anywhere but back to the hotel, so they told Karen to get me to bed.

"He deserved it," Karen yells from the bathroom.

"He also deserved my fist in his face." Levi says.

Karen sticks her head out the bathroom door. "It was fun watching the police take him away in the paddy wagon. I'm going to take some stuff to the car."

"Okay."

She grabs her suitcase and rolls it out to the hall. We're going home today, but the last thing I feel like doing is sitting in a car for hours. I wish we could fly home, so I could be in my own bed tonight.

The door clicks closed.

Levi clears his throat. "My flight's in a couple of hours. I should go soon."

I hang my arm over the side of the bed and study him. Levi seeing me like this is really embarrassing, but I don't want him to go.

"Did you have a good break?" I ask.

Levi moves the bucket and gets on his knees, coming to the side of the bed. I move so he can rest his elbows on it, and he's close enough to kiss me. I press my lips together and hope my morning breath isn't too stinky.

"It was okay," he says. Then he frowns. "Katie, I … I'm really sorry for the way I've behaved." He stares at me. "What you said the other night … about me having to choose. I choose you."

I smile, but I don't say anything, because I'm not sure if I completely believe him. Is he saying this in a last-ditch effort to win me back? Or does he *really* mean it?

"How can I be sure you mean it?" I ask. "What if we get home, and nothing changes?"

Levi adjusts his position and takes my hand. "After seeing you drunk … everything has changed. Do I look like that to you?"

My eyes widen. "Oh my God, what did I do?"

Levi chuckles. "You didn't *do* anything, Katie, but you were a bit … messy." Levi wrinkles his nose. "Am I like that?"

"Mostly you're cocky and obnoxious." Despite the pounding in my head, I prop myself up on my elbow and smile.

"Really?" He laughs again.

"But you're like that when you're sober, too." My smile

widens, and I hope he knows I'm teasing him.

Levi leans forward and presses his forehead to mine. "Katie." He takes a deep breath.

I put my finger on his lips. "Don't. Please don't apologise again. You don't need to. I need to thank you … If you weren't there last night …"

"That guy is a right royal dick," Levi says.

"Yep, he is." I close my eyes, and concentrate on the feeling of Levi's skin touching mine.

"Last night," Levi says a few moments later, "I saw you in a way I never have before."

"Yeah. Drunk," I say without looking at him.

"Well … yeah." He plays with the ends of my hair. "But jokes aside, seriously … do I look like that? You know … when I've been drinking?"

I open my eyes and pull away so I can take in Levi's face.

"Look like what?" I ask.

He presses his lips together. "Messy. Out of control. You couldn't talk or walk straight."

"You're acting like you've never seen anyone drunk before."

Levi shakes his head. "That's not it. Seeing you like that, then thinking about how I must look to you … it made me feel ashamed. I understand now why you get so upset when I'm drunk, and why you don't like it."

I sigh and link my fingers through Levi's. "I *don't* like it. I just wish you'd talk to me instead of trying to hide from everything. But I can't tell you what to do. I can only tell you how your actions make me feel." I move, and wince at the pain in my head. "How do you cope with a hangover? It's horrible." I flop back onto the bed.

Levi gets up on his knees and leans over me. "Katie, you're too good for me."

I stare up at him. "You know I think the same thing about you?"

"When we get home, can we start over?" Levi squeezes my hand. "Can we put everything behind us and … try again?"

He's asking me for a second chance, and I want to give it to him. But how do I know everything is going to be okay? Am I about to set myself up for another fall? But then how amazing would it be if everything worked out?

Pretty amazing.

Maybe I need to take the chance.

"Starting over would be nice," I say.

Levi's lips curl into a smile. I hold my breath, because in a perfect world now would be when he kissed me, and my breath probably stinks.

I want him to kiss me though.

Levi leans down, and brushes my lips with his, then the door bursts open and his touch is gone just as quickly.

"You're still in bed?" Karen asks.

I glare at her. "We were talking."

"Your bags won't pack themselves. Come on. I'll be next door." Karen goes back out to the hall.

Levi and I look at each other, then burst out laughing. I push myself up, and Levi gets to his feet. He holds out his hand and helps me out of bed.

"I need a shower," I say. "Can you wait?"

Levi checks his phone. "Sure. I've got time."

"Great." I tuck my hair behind my ear, and search

through my case for a clean top, shorts, and underwear. "Be right back."

The shower helps to relieve the horrible heavy feeling in my body. I vow never to touch alcohol again. I hope Levi meant it when he said he wanted to start over. We both could use a new beginning, and going home seems like the best place to start.

I smile at my reflection in the mirror, at the thought of spending time with him when we get back. After towelling dry, dressing, and brushing my teeth, I don't bother with my contacts since Karen and I will be in the car half the day. When I come out of the bathroom, Levi is sitting on the bed.

He stands and comes over to me. He takes the wet towel from my hands and throws it on the bed. Then he brushes my cheek with his fingertips. I blink behind my glasses, and stare up at him. He leans down, and I part my lips.

The door to the room opens again.

"Oh my God, you two have the worst timing," Karen says.

I glare at her for the second time this morning. "We have bad timing?"

Karen looks from me to Levi. "Just kiss her already."

I clear my throat. Karen shakes her head, and goes into the bathroom.

When I turn back to Levi, he's staring down at me with a small lopsided smile. "Can I kiss you now?"

I nod, but I don't speak, because if I do my voice will crack.

Levi pulls me close, and I put my arms around his

neck. I bite my lip as he closes the gap between us, and then his lips are on mine, firm but soft. In that kiss I forget about all the fights we've had, and all the stuff that's happened between us. I forget how hard it is to love him sometimes, because right now loving him is the easiest thing in the world. For a few heartbeats, it's just me and Levi. Nothing else.

Levi breaks our kiss. "I should go. Don't want to miss my flight."

"Okay." I'm not sure how I get the word out, because he's taken my breath away.

"You and me … tomorrow," he says.

"I'll come see you when I get home."

"I'm looking forward to climbing in your window."

"You'll need a ladder." I laugh. "I ripped the lattice down, remember?"

"Shouldn't be a problem." He kisses the tip of my nose.

Levi walks to the door, and I want so badly to pull him back and hug him, but I twist my fingers together and offer him a small smile instead. There will be plenty of time for hugs when we get home.

The door clicks closed with Levi on one side and me on the other, and I let out a long breath. I move around the room to collect all the things that have made their way into various places since we've been away.

"Is it safe to come out?" Karen calls from the bathroom.

I laugh. "Yes, he's gone."

The door opens and Karen smiles. "You almost ready?"

"Yep." I throw the last of my clothes into my suitcase and zip it closed.

We go next door and say goodbye to Jessica and Stacey

before checking out and heading to the hotel car park. Karen and I pack the last of our things into the boot of her mum's car. It's been a long break with so much happening, and I'm glad we're finally heading home. After last night, and my talk this morning with Levi, I think I'm finally ready to forgive him for what he did. Because even after all the things he's done that have hurt me, I know there is nothing he wouldn't do for me if I asked him.

Maybe that's been my problem all along. Maybe all I have to do is tell him exactly how I feel about him, and *ask* him if he feels the same. Maybe I need to stop living in the past and look to the future.

"Ready?" Karen asks, closing the boot of the car.

"Yeah. Let's go home."

We get in and drive out of the hotel car park to navigate the streets of Surfers Paradise. We hit the motorway heading south, and before long we cross the border back into more familiar territory. I wish we could be home tonight, but we have a cabin booked in Coffs Harbour, and I'm looking forward to spending the time with Karen. It will be nice to debrief on the week, especially since I didn't make it all that great for her.

After a quick lunch stop we keep driving, and we make it to Coffs with plenty of time to grab some fish and chips for dinner, and hit the beach at sunset. Even though the sun isn't setting over the water, the sky is still lit with beautiful shades of pink, peach, and gold.

I dig my toes into the sand, and pick at the food sitting on the brown paper between us.

My phone buzzes so I pull it from my pocket. "It's Jess.

She and Stacey got home okay."

Seconds later, Karen's phone trills with a text message. She holds it up so I can see the screen.

"Same message," we both say at the same time, then we laugh.

Karen stares out at the water, and I sigh, happy that my friends are safe, and that I get to be here with my best friend in this moment.

"I'm sorry," I say, stuffing another chip in my mouth.

Karen turns to me. "What the hell for?"

I shrug. "You know … ruining your week."

"You did not." She throws a chip at me. "Don't be stupid."

"Come on. We both know it could've been better."

"Maybe. But it doesn't matter." Karen smiles. "You and Levi made up."

A grin spreads across my face. "Yeah. We did."

"So …" Karen pops a chip in her mouth. "What next?"

"I guess we see what happens. Go with the flow."

It's the best answer I can give her, because I'm not entirely sure about the future. I don't know exactly where I'm heading. But I do know I want Levi, and when I get home that's the first thing I'm going to tell him. I want him, and this time, nothing is going to come between us.

"You've forgiven him then?" Karen asks.

"Forgiveness is an ongoing thing." I dust the salt from my fingers and lean back in the sand. "I'm not sure I'm completely there, but I'm close. And we have to start somewhere."

"Well, I'm here for you whenever you need me."

I smile at my best friend, so grateful that I have her in

my life. We roll up what's left of our dinner and put the parcel in the bin on the way back to our cabin. We're both pretty tired and have another day of driving tomorrow, so we turn in early. I have trouble getting to sleep though, and I lie awake for a while, wishing I was at home staring at the stars on my ceiling.

I lie here and think about the first thing I'm going to say to Levi when I get home. I close my eyes, and when I open them again, it's morning and sunlight is streaming through the window. Karen is making breakfast in the little kitchenette. I roll over and watch her through the door of the tiny bedroom.

"Tea?" she asks, smiling.

"That would be great."

My head doesn't ache this morning like it did yesterday, and getting up isn't as hard. A warm shower wakes me up even more, and I feel pretty great when I get out. I sit at the little table with Karen and towel-dry my hair before downing my tea as quickly as I can.

"In a hurry?" Karen asks.

I bite my lip and get up to put my cup in the sink. "Is it that obvious?"

"It's okay." She laughs. "Summer is officially here, and I want to get home, too."

"Let's go then."

We quickly clean up and pack our stuff into the car. We don't talk much on the drive, and I like that I don't have to fill uncomfortable silences with Karen. We crank the music, so talking is a bit hard anyway. I roll my window down, lean back in my seat, and close my eyes, letting the wind brush my face.

It's mid-afternoon by the time we pull off the motorway, and in less than ten minutes I'll be able to go and see Levi. My hairs prickle on my skin, and a shot of excitement runs through me. We're not in school anymore. I don't have to see all the people who have made my life hell for so long every day of the week. I can spend time with Levi without anyone judging us.

We have our whole future ahead of us.

Karen pulls the car up to the kerb outside my house and kills the engine.

"Home sweet home," she says.

I smile. I think we're both happy that schoolies is over and we can resume our normal programming. Karen flings her door open and gets out. I grab my purse and follow, meeting her at the boot of the car.

"Thanks for a great week," I say. "Even if I wasn't so great at times. It was … an experience."

Karen laughs. "It sure was. And I wouldn't have wanted to spend it with anyone else."

She pops the boot and I grab my bags, hoisting my backpack over one shoulder and grabbing the handle of my suitcase.

"Are you going to go see Levi?" Karen nods in the direction of his house.

I shrug and look over to his empty driveway. "Yeah. I guess. Doesn't look like he's home though."

"If he's not, call him. Then call me tomorrow?" Karen gives me a hug, slams the boot, then gets back in the car. "We can go get hot chocolate," she calls through the open window.

"Sounds great." I wave as she drives away, then make

my way to the front door. "I'm home," I say as I push the door open. "Hello?"

Mum and Dad come through from the kitchen.

"Katie, honey. I'm so sorry." Mum wraps me in a hug, and I drop my bags to hug her back.

I pull away. "Sorry about what?"

"We thought you might have heard already."

"Heard what?" I ask with a bit more force.

Mum presses her lips together and glances at Dad. Her eyes sparkle with tears.

"I'm sorry," she says again. "There's been an accident."

I stare at her. "What do you mean? What's happened?"

"Maybe you should sit down." Dad takes me by the elbow.

I pull away from his grasp and step back, my heart racing. "I don't want to sit down. Tell me what's going on."

Mum and Dad exchange another glance.

"It's Levi," Mum says. "He's in the hospital."

"It doesn't look good." Dad steps towards me.

Mum presses her lips into a thin line. "It's too early to tell if he'll make it."

I move away from them again, and my back hits the front door. My fingers tighten on the purse in my hand. Blood rushes to my ears and my heart pounds. *Hospital? Accident? What kind of accident? What do they mean, if he'll make it?* I want to ask my parents these questions, and so many more, but when I open my mouth, no sound comes out.

I shake my head. My hands go numb. This can't be happening.

"No," I whisper.

Levi is in the hospital?

He can't be. I'm ready to tell him I forgive him. Starting from now, we're supposed to have our entire future ahead of us, but what if he doesn't make it?

I can't lose him.

I love him.

My heart breaks at the thought that I may not be able to tell him.

Are we over before we've had the chance to begin?

Everything

All the Things: part three

A little bit more

What do I do?

How do I deal with this?

How do I deal when I've just been told the boy I love has had a life-threatening accident and is in the hospital?

I stare at my parents, clutching my purse to my chest. My phone inside vibrates through the fabric. I look at my hands and frown. A text message.

Maybe it's Levi.

But he's been in an accident.

Accident?

What kind of accident? Did he fall over?

I turn and fumble with the handle on the front door.

"Katie," Dad says. "Honey."

But I have the door open. I race down the steps and run to Levi's house, stepping through the garden bed that borders our two properties.

Where is his car?

He told me he'd be home.

Was he driving? Was he drinking?

No. He said he wouldn't do that anymore.

What the hell is happening?

"Katie," Mum calls.

I reach the steps to Levi's veranda and take them in two bounds. I pound on the front door. My purse vibrates again and I fumble with the zipper as I try to get it open. My fingers shake and I can't get them to do what I want them to.

Finally, I get my phone out.

Karen: have u heard?

Karen: Katie? Call me!!!

Karen: Coming over now

The door to Levi's house opens before I can type a reply.

"What happened to Levi?" I blurt.

Yvonne presses her lips together, then looks over my shoulder. I glance behind me as Mum puts her foot on the bottom step.

"I'm sorry. Katie didn't give me a chance to tell her the details," Mum says.

"What details?" I look back at Yvonne.

She wrings her hands together. "Levi was in an accident."

"I know!" I shout.

"Katie." Mum puts her hand on my arm.

A tear slips down Yvonne's cheek. "I came home to get some things. I'm going back to the hospital soon. Maybe—"

"Tell me what happened, please." My palms go sweaty.

This can't be happening. "Is he okay? He told me he'd be here when I got home." Panic rises into my chest and I feel sick, like I'm about to vomit.

"Levi …" Yvonne presses her lips together again, and folds her arms around herself. "He's … in a coma. The doctors say he should recover."

I draw in a sharp breath. "Coma? *Should* recover?" I turn to Mum. "What …?"

"Honey, you need to come home." She takes my hand and pulls me away. "I'm sorry, Yvonne. I'll tell her everything when we get inside."

I fight to free myself from Mum's grasp. "Tell me what?"

Karen pulls up at the kerb, and she's out of the car faster than I've ever seen her move. Her face is streaked with tears.

"Jess," she yells, stumbling across the lawn. "We have to go and see Jess."

Dad intercepts Karen in the driveway. He grabs her arms gently and tries to hug her. Karen struggles at first, but then she lets him hold her. I stop struggling as well, and let Mum guide me back down from Levi's veranda onto the path.

Levi is in the hospital.

Is Jessica as well?

Tears sting my eyes. I don't really know what's going on, but it's obviously bad. The fortune teller told me I needed to be prepared for something tragic. Well, I'm not prepared, and that stuff is all a bunch of bull. It's not supposed to be true. But an accident is a tragedy, and from the way all the adults look, it isn't good.

The front door to Levi's house clicks closed behind

me. Karen's parents pull into our driveway and get out of their car.

"I'm sorry," Karen's mum, Rebecca, calls. "Karen took off, and we assumed she'd come here."

"I think we should get the girls inside." Mums leads me over to our yard.

Dad nods, and passes Karen over to Rebecca. I walk numbly towards our front door. Karen buries her face into her mum's neck and sobs as she walks. I have no idea why she's so upset, but the sound makes me want to cry, too. I take a breath and hold back the tears.

Mum opens our front door and ushers everyone in. Rebecca is still hugging Karen, a grim expression marring her usually beautiful features. Karen's dad, Oliver, wraps both his girls in his big arms. Dad gently guides me until I'm sitting on the lounge. I drop my phone and purse onto the cushion.

"We're really sorry, honey," he says. "Levi is in the hospital, like we said, and he's in a pretty bad way, but there's more." He pauses, and exchanges a quick glance with Mum.

She continues, "Josephine was in the accident as well."

I let out a long breath. "But Jess is okay?" I glance at Karen.

"Not exactly," Mum says. "Josephine ... she didn't make it."

I suck in a sharp gasp. "What? What do you ... She died?" I shake my head. "No!"

I thought Josephine was a bitch, but I never wanted her to die. *Jessica.* Oh no, she must be crushed. She loves her sister, even if they fight more than they get along.

"No!" I say again, my voice too loud in my ears.

The room is quiet except for Karen's sniffles. I close my eyes, and put my face in my hands. A tear squeezes its way onto my cheek. This isn't happening. Yesterday, everything was perfect.

My heart strains at the thought of Levi lying in a hospital bed. *In a coma.* Can he hear anyone? Would he know me if I went to see him? I want to go and see him.

But Josephine.

Jessica.

Her sister is dead.

She'll need her friends.

"Jess … can we go see her?" I ask through my splayed fingers.

Karen pulls away from her parents' embrace and rubs her eyes.

"Yes, of course. Daniel is already over there," Mum says.

I look up. "When did this happen? *What* happened?" I squeeze my eyes closed again. What was Levi doing with Josephine?

"Last night," Dad says. "Josie … the police don't know exactly what happened yet. Levi can't … They can only go by the evidence at the accident scene. Levi's car hit Josie's directly on the driver's side. She … He's very lucky to be alive."

"They were in separate cars?" I ask. "Was there anyone else …?" I stare at Dad.

"No one else was involved," Mum says.

"Jess." I jump up from the lounge. "I need to see her."

Mum and Dad exchange a glance.

"Don't be too long," Mum says. "Jess will probably be tired. Bridget said she's been quite distraught."

Karen sniffles, and stares at me with wide eyes. Her face blurs through my tears, and I blink them away then go to the front door. Karen follows, and as we reach the bottom of my front steps, she slips her hand into mine. We walk down the street to Jessica's house in silence. I don't look back, but I get the feeling all of our parents are standing on the veranda watching us.

When we reach Jessica's front door, I raise my hand to knock and Karen releases her grip on me, hugging herself. After one of the longest minutes of my life, I go to knock again, but the door opens and Jessica's mum, Bridget, peers out. Her eyes are red and puffy, and she looks much older than her almost fifty years. She doesn't really look at us. It's as if she's looking through us.

"Come in, girls." Bridget turns away from the open door, and we follow her into the house. "Jess is in her room," she adds.

Karen and I exchange a glance

"I'm really sorry," I say, because what else do you say to someone who has lost their daughter?

Bridget nods before walking through to the kitchen.

Karen sets her foot on the top step and walks down the stairs. I follow her to Jessica's bedroom where we find her lying on her bed facing the wall. My brother sits in a chair at Jessica's desk, leaning forward with his elbows resting on his thighs.

What is he doing here? Jessica had a crush on him years ago, but I didn't think they were friends. I frown, and he stands. Karen and I hover in the doorway.

Daniel comes over to us and whispers, "I think she's sleeping."

Karen moves to sit on the end of the bed, and stares at our friend. I want to hug them, and Daniel. I want to hug all of them, and tell them how much I love them, because they could be gone at any moment. Like Josephine.

It's as if Daniel reads my mind. He puts his arms out and I step into them, pressing my face into his chest. He wraps me up in a brotherly hug, and rests his chin on the top of my head.

"How's she doing?" I ask, my voice muffled in Daniel's chest.

"Not so good," he says.

"What are you …?" I take a breath. "You and …?" I pull away and look up at my brother.

He shrugs. "You weren't here. She needed someone."

I frown, and look from my brother to my sleeping friend. Karen has her hand resting on Jessica's arm. "Is there …?"

"Katie, I'm just trying to help."

"Why didn't you call me?"

Daniel takes a deep breath. "We wanted you and Karen to get home safely. We didn't want you both worrying, and rushing to get back here."

I want to ask if he's seen Levi, but why would he have? He probably hasn't had time to go to the hospital. And Jessica might hear me. I'm still not sure exactly what happened. I don't want to upset her. She may not want to hear Levi's name.

"We can talk more when you get home," Daniel says, and I love that he knows me so well and can guess what

I'm thinking. He gives me another hug.

"See you soon," I say when he pulls away and moves towards the door.

Daniel gives me a closed-lipped smile. "I'll take you to the hospital later if you like."

"Maybe tomorrow," I say. If Levi is in a coma, his family might want to spend time with him first.

And right now, Jessica needs me.

Daniel gently closes the door on his way out.

Karen sniffles, and I take a few steps towards the bed and my friends. Hot tears prick my eyes, but I hold them in. I don't want to cry in front of Jessica.

When I reach the bed, Karen shuffles along a bit and I lie down beside Jessica. She stirs, and when I drape my arm over her and find her hand, she squeezes it tightly.

"I'm so sorry," I whisper.

Karen leans over and wraps her arms around both of us. Her fringe tickles my cheek. I prop myself up on my elbow and stroke Jessica's hair. She blinks, then closes her eyes so tight they crease at the corners. A tear slips out and rolls down onto her nose. Her body shakes under my embrace, and I grip her tighter. Karen tightens her hug as well. I know in that moment that we're holding Jessica together.

The door creaks as someone opens it, but none of us move.

The bed dips and Stacey crawls up it so she can lie between Jessica and the wall. She faces her, and her lips curl into a small smile.

"Hey you," Stacey says.

Karen and I stay how we are, me hugging Jessica,

and Karen hugging both of us.

Jessica swipes at her cheek with her free hand. "Hey," she whispers.

Stacey plays with the ends of Jessica's blonde strands, twisting them around her finger. She glances up at me and presses her lips together. What are we supposed to do now? How can we help Jessica? There's nothing we can do.

I feel helpless.

But that's nothing compared to how Jessica must feel.

My heart breaks for her, and I squeeze my eyes closed. Karen takes a deep breath behind me, and Stacey puts her hand over mine, the one that's holding Jessica's.

The four of us lie here on Jessica's bed, a bundle of messed up emotions with no idea how to fix what's broken.

"It's all my fault," Jessica whispers, and I raise my head a little, looking at Stacey with my mouth open.

"Oh no, Jess. It's not your fault," Stacey says, raising her eyebrows at me.

"Yes, it is." Jessica buries her face in the mattress.

"It was an accident." I stroke her hair again. "Just an accident."

"All my fault," Jessica says, her words muffled by the sheets on the bed.

She screams into the mattress, her body going rigid beside me.

Stacey's eyes widen. Karen lets go of us, and I prop myself up, putting my hand on Jessica's arm.

She screams again, balling the sheets in her fists.

"It's okay," Stacey says. "Everything will be okay."

"Nooooooo," Jessica wails. "Nothing is okay. I did this.

It's my fault. I did this, Josie. Oh my God, Josie!"

I jump up, my hands shaking. A mix of fear, pain, and heartache course through me, making my insides go cold. Stacey tries to hold Jessica, but she kicks and lashes out. Not really at Stacey, it seems, but at the world. Stacey gets off the bed, and the three of us stand and stare at our friend.

"It's not your fault, Jess." Tears burn tracks down my cheeks because I can't hold them in anymore.

"I killed her," Jessica yells. "It's my fault … all my fault."

"What do we do?" Karen whispers.

Stacey kneels beside the bed and murmurs to Jessica, her voice so low I can't make out her words.

Jessica calms a little, then rolls onto her stomach, and presses her face into her pillow. "Josie," she whispers. "Josie, Josie, Josie."

I take a step towards the bed and kneel down beside Stacey, laying my cheek on the mattress so my face is close to Jessica's. She's still whispering her sister's name.

"We're here for you," I whisper back. "Always."

Jessica angles her head until she's facing me. I offer her a small smile, and brush her matted hair away from her eyes.

"Where's Josie?" Jessica asks.

Oh, Jess.

"Shhh." I tuck her hair behind her ear.

"Josie," Jessica says again.

"It's all right," I say. "Close your eyes."

"Can I see Josie?" Jessica blinks, and teardrops bead on the ends of her eyelashes.

Karen kneels on the other side of Stacey. Stacey rubs Jessica's arm, and Karen strokes her back.

"I'm sure you can see her any time you like," I say. "All you have to do is close your eyes."

Jessica calls her sister's name another five times, and with each one of my friend's breaths, my heart breaks a little bit more.

My everything

Jessica fell asleep after her outburst, so Karen and I left Stacey with her. Karen's parents took her home, and Mum and Dad wanted to 'talk' but talking was the last thing on my mind. I went to bed early, and had a restless sleep because all I could think about was Josephine, and the fact that Levi is lying in a hospital bed, in a coma, and won't be climbing in my window.

Now, it's mid-morning and I'm sitting at the kitchen counter, picking at a piece of toast, because not only did I not sleep very well, but I have no appetite.

"Visiting hours for ICU start soon," Mum says. "Want me to drive you?"

"Daniel said he'd take me."

"You don't want your dad and me to come?" Mum sets her cup of coffee on the bench.

I shake my head. "No. It's okay."

Mum comes to my side of the counter and slides onto the stool beside me. She puts an arm around my shoulders, pulling me close. "You should try and prepare yourself, okay? I won't lie. It's not nice. But when I saw Levi, he'd just been brought in. Mark was at work, so I drove Yvonne to the hospital not long after it happened. She was … distraught." Mum pushes my hair away from my face. "Today will be different though. I'm sure they're taking good care of him."

I rest my head on Mum's shoulder and stare at my hands, picking my fingernails. "I'm scared," I whisper.

"I know." Mum kisses my temple. "Sure you don't want us to come?"

"I'm sure."

"Okay." She gets up and takes her coffee cup to the sink. "I'll call Yvonne and let her know you're coming. She'll need to clear it with the hospital."

I nod, then put my forehead on the counter and stare at the little flecks in the laminate surface. I let my eyes relax, and it looks as if I'm surrounded by black stars in a daytime galaxy.

"Katie," Daniel says a few minutes later.

I roll my head to the side to look in the direction of his voice. He has his cheek resting on the counter and is staring at me.

"What?" I ask.

"You ready to go to the hospital?"

"What if I say no? What if I say I'm sitting here waiting to wake up from this nightmare?"

"I'd tell you visiting hours start at eleven-thirty, and

your ride is leaving in five minutes." He smiles.

"I'm not dreaming?" I close my eyes.

Daniel doesn't answer, and I don't open my eyes. I feel him move beside me. He covers my hand with his and squeezes. "Come on."

I sigh and get up from the stool, go to my room, and quickly brush my hair. I don't bother with my contacts today. Levi won't see me anyway. I grab my purse and phone, and go outside. My brother is already waiting in the car.

He turns the key in the ignition as I slide into the front passenger seat. I grip my purse in my lap to stop my fingers trembling, and chew my bottom lip.

Daniel pulls onto the street, and we head towards the highway. He turns the music up, and I'm grateful he doesn't try to talk to me.

I think about Levi as we drive. What will he look like? Will he have tubes coming out of him? Are his injuries bad? They must be if he's in a coma. But maybe it's a precaution. I've heard of doctors putting people in comas on purpose.

"Did you hear me?" Daniel says.

"Huh?" I turn towards my brother.

He glances at me before making a left-hand turn into the street the hospital is on. "Do you want me to come in with you?" He finds a park on the street and pulls over.

I bite my lip again. Yes, I want him to come with me. I'm not sure I can walk in there on my own.

"Do you ... want to come in?" I ask.

"I want to make sure you're okay."

"Then yes," I say. "Please come with me."

"Okay." Daniel nods. "Let's do this." He opens his door and gets out.

I hesitate, fiddling with the zipper on my purse. I'm not sure I can get out of the car. I can't do this. I don't want to face what's inside the hospital.

My door opens, and Daniel looks down at me. He doesn't say anything. He just reaches out and takes my hand, gently pulling me from the car.

"I can't do this," I whisper.

"Yes, you can." He closes my door and leads me across the street.

I hesitate at the front doors to the hospital. Daniel gives my hand a gentle tug, and I follow him through to the cool interior of the reception area.

"We're here to see Levi White," Daniel says to the nurse behind the desk.

"One minute." She turns to her computer and taps at the keyboard. "He's in ICU. Are you family?"

I press my lips together and shake my head, blinking to hold back my tears.

"We're neighbours," Daniel says.

"I'm sorry, family members only." The nurse smiles with her lips closed.

I tuck my purse under my arm and wring my hands together. My breath hitches. Daniel puts an arm around my shoulders, and I lean into him.

"Our mum was calling Yvonne White to let her know we were coming," Daniel says. "Can you call the ward and ask if we can go in? Please? We're Daniel and Katie Sullivan."

The nurse frowns, but she picks up the phone anyway.

I close my eyes and wait, listening to the beat of Daniel's heart.

"Yes, this is front desk," the nurse says. "I have some people here to see Levi White. Is there approval for non-family members?"

I open my eyes and stand up straighter.

The nurse nods. "Yes. Daniel and Katie … okay." She places the phone receiver back in the cradle and smiles at us. "You may go in. Along the hall to the end, then turn right. Use the phone on the left wall to request access, then make sure you wash your hands before you go in."

"Thank you," I say.

Daniel guides me away, and we follow the nurse's directions to the ICU.

He lifts the phone receiver. "Hi, we're here to see Levi White."

I don't hear what's said on the other end, but my brother nods and hangs up the phone. We scrub our hands with warm soapy water in the small sink on the wall, then wait.

The automatic doors open, and another nurse greets us with a smile. "Daniel and Katie? Levi is in room seven."

We follow her into the ward, and past another reception desk. I can't help looking into the rooms. There are so many machines and tubes. Lots of beeping. My chest tightens because I have no idea what to expect, or how Levi will look.

The nurse stops outside room seven. The curtains are drawn most of the way across the large glass window in the wall. She taps lightly on the door before opening it wide enough to put her head through.

"Daniel and Katie are here," she says.

I step up to the window and look through the gap in the curtains. Yvonne gets to her feet from a chair beside Levi's bed. I fix my gaze on her, because I'm not sure I can cope with looking at anything else. The other details of the room become a fuzzy blur.

Yvonne takes the few steps to the door, and I blink, readjusting my focus as I finally look at Levi. My breath hitches, and a tear splashes onto my cheek.

There's a big tube coming out of his mouth, leading to a machine beside the head of the bed. His face is covered in an angry red graze. A bandage comes out from under his hospital gown and over his left shoulder. Wires extend from the creases of his elbows and the backs of his hands, draping over the sides of the bed where they're hooked up to several more beeping machines.

I step back from the window. Panic makes my blood cold, and I shake. Daniel puts his hands on my shoulders from behind. "Calm down," he whispers in my ear.

"Katie," Yvonne says. The nurse holds the door open for her as she comes out of the room. "Do you and Daniel want to go in?"

I tear my gaze away from the window and stare at her. Her eyes are redder than they were when I saw her yesterday. I rub my arms to try and ward off the cold feeling inside me. Then I nod.

"Only two visitors at a time," the nurse says when Daniel and I reach the door.

"I'll go and get a coffee," Yvonne says.

Before I can protest and tell her she can go back in

with Daniel, she's already walking down the hall. Daniel nudges me gently into the room. He sits in a chair against the wall, leaving the one beside the bed empty. I stop a couple of metres away from Levi. I can't sit near him yet. I need more time to process everything.

The nurse quickly checks something on one of the machines, and makes a note on the chart hanging from the end of the bed.

"Can he hear us?" I ask, clutching my purse tightly.

"We don't really know," the nurse says. "He's in an induced coma."

"How … how long for?" I ask.

The nurse comes over and puts a hand on my arm. "Levi has a broken collarbone, three broken ribs, and a punctured lung … as well as other internal injuries. He had surgery following his accident, and his pain would have been excessive, so he needed help to heal. There's no way to know exactly how long he'll be under, but the doctors will monitor him and decide when to bring him out."

I take a step towards the bed. "Can I … hold his hand?"

"Of course," the nurse says. "Just pretend I'm not here. I'll be in and out on a regular basis, but if I'm not here and you need anything, press the green button on the wall beside the bed." She smiles and busies herself checking Levi's drip line.

I glance at Daniel, unsure what to do, then I look back at Levi. I have so many things to say to him, but can he even hear me? What if it all falls on deaf ears? Am I better off just going home? What good am I to him anyway?

"I reckon he can hear us," Daniel says, as if he can read my mind. He props his elbow on the armrest of the chair. "I'll go find us a drink while you have a chat." He gets up and gives me a quick kiss on the forehead on his way to the door. "Back soon."

I wait for what feels like a full minute after Daniel leaves, then I sit in the chair beside the bed, setting my purse and phone in my lap. The railing is up, and I drag the chair a little closer. I'm not sure how to hold his hand. There are so many wires and tubes, and he has a pulse monitor on his index finger. I don't want to bump anything, or hurt him, so I sit and stare at him for a few heartbeats.

If I didn't know it was Levi lying in this bed, then I'm not sure I would recognise him. The tube used to intubate him is thick, and strapped to his head. The air being pushed in and out of his lungs makes a haunting sound. His face is red, and I guess that it's from the airbag in the car, but I really don't know. The rest of his body is covered by a white hospital gown, and going by the scratches and bruises on his arms, it's probably a good thing.

I reach through the bars and rest my elbows on the side of the bed. Carefully, I touch the back of his hand with my fingertips. His skin is cool. Tears well in my eyes, and I lean my forehead against the metal bedrail.

"Hey, Levi. It's me. Katie." I swallow, but it's hard because my mouth is dry. "I want you to know I'm mad at you again. You said you'd be there when I got home." I press my palm to the back of his hand and curl my fingers around it. "You weren't there." The tears come faster, and I choke back a sob. "You said you'd be there."

I blink, but more tears fall, wetting my cheeks and making my eyes burn. I slip my other fingers under Levi's so I'm cupping his hand with both of mine. The machines beep around us in time with my heartbeats, and I count to fifty before I'm able to talk again.

"But I also want to tell you … I forgive you." I take a deep breath, sit up straight in the chair, and stare at Levi's face. If only I could will him to open his eyes and see me. "You hurt me, more than once, and I can't pretend to understand why you did everything you did, but I can understand what my heart feels. I forgive you for everything. I love you. I have always loved you, and we've been through too much for either of us to give up now." My voice shakes, and I have to stop as more tears come. "You're going to get better."

The door opens behind me, and Daniel comes to my side. He puts a hand on my shoulder. "I brought you a cup of tea."

I reluctantly let go of Levi's hand and take the steaming cup from Daniel. "Thanks." I offer my brother a half-smile. "I wish I could go back to the last time I saw him." I take a sip of my tea. "Telling him I love him now doesn't seem to count."

"I think it does," Daniel says.

I smile and hope Daniel is right.

We're quiet for a few minutes, sipping our drinks and listening to the ventilator and the beeping machines. My phone buzzes in my lap, and I look down at the lit up screen.

Karen: How ru 2day?

I pick up the phone and unlock it, pressing the message icon.

Me: At hospital

Karen: How's Levi?

Me: Alive

I put my phone away, sit back in the chair, and glance towards the door. Yvonne is at the window, looking into the room through the gap in the curtains. She smiles at me, but it doesn't reach her eyes.

A knock sounds at the door and the nurse comes in. She fusses about, checking some readings on the monitors. Then she opens the curtains on the window.

Mark stands beside Yvonne, towering over her, a frown furrowing his brow. She has one arm wrapped around herself, and her other hand covers her mouth. Her eyes glisten under the hospital lighting.

"Maybe we should go," I say, turning back to look at Levi.

"You don't want to stay longer?" Daniel asks.

"I think they want to spend time with him." I nod towards the window behind my brother.

He glances over his shoulder. "Okay. Time to say goodbye."

"Goodbye is too final," I say, getting up from my seat beside the bed.

I lean over the bedrail and concentrate on Levi's face. His eyelids are purple, and I want them to open so badly so I can look at him, but all I get is the tiny ripple of his eyes moving underneath. I hope he's dreaming about me. About us.

His hand is still cool when I slip my fingers around it and squeeze gently. "I'll see you soon," I whisper.

I take a couple of steps towards the door. When I reach it, I can't help looking back, and a wave of emotion hits me all over again. It crashes into my heart, drowning it in sorrow, and pain. My breath catches in my throat. I'm somehow shocked even more now at the sight of Levi lying broken in his hospital bed than I was when I first entered the room.

How do I fix him?

How do I put his pieces back together again? I have to, because Levi is *my* missing piece. He's all the things that make me whole.

He's my everything.

So broken

My phone rings, buzzing against the surface of my desk, for what seems like the millionth time. I lie on my bed, staring at it, waiting for it to shut up. It stops, and I close my eyes.

The buzzing starts again.

I blink a few times, then reach out and snatch my phone up.

Karen's name flashes on the screen.

I don't want to answer it, because she'll ask me about Levi, and I'm not sure I'll be able to talk about him without bursting into tears.

The phone stops again, and I roll onto my back to stare at my ceiling. It's mid-morning, so my glow-in-the-dark stars are dormant.

My phone rings again.

I lift my arm and stare at the screen. Karen is persistent.

I sigh, and press the answer icon. "Hello."

"Oh my God, why won't you pick up your phone?" Karen asks.

"I answered it," I say. "I'm talking to you now."

"Come on, Katie. You've been moping in your room for three days. I'm coming to pick you up."

"No," I say, but she's already hung up.

And I haven't been in my room *all* that time.

I've been to see Jessica a couple of times—as hard as it was.

I've also been to the hospital to see Levi every day.

The first time I saw him was traumatic. He had so many tubes and wires sticking out of him. It was scary, and unreal, and emotionally draining. But I know what to expect now, so it's getting a little easier.

Ten minutes later, a car pulls up outside, and I take a deep breath. Karen will be in my room any second, trying to cheer me up. I love her, and that she wants to do that, but I'm not sure I have the energy today.

"Katie," Daniel calls from downstairs. "Karen's here."

"In my room," I say.

A few moments later, Karen pushes my door open and comes to sit on the bed. She looks a lot better than she did the day we got home from Surfers Paradise. I've never seen her so upset before, but today it's as if she's back to her old self. I guess we all cope in our own way, but I hope she's not bottling stuff up.

"You okay?" I ask.

"Today is a new day." She smiles. "We should make the most of it. You never know when your time will be up."

I pinch the bridge of my nose. "Our world fell apart three days ago."

"We need hot chocolate." Karen grabs my hands and pulls me to sitting. "Hot chocolate fixes everything."

"I don't want to go out," I whine.

"Well, I do." She stands, and pulls my arms again, and I give in and get up, too. "Ten minutes and I want you in the car. You can't go out in your PJs."

I stare at Karen's back as she leaves my room. It looks like she's not taking no for an answer, so I pull on a pair of shorts and a clean top. I go to the bathroom and give my face a quick wash, then run my fingers through my hair and put my glasses on. Back in my room, I grab my tote and shove my phone, purse, journal, and a pen inside.

"Daniel? I'm going out," I say on my way down the stairs.

"Have fun." He waves at me from the lounge.

Karen smiles as I hop in the car. She starts the engine, then grips the steering wheel and pulls out into the street.

"Have you been to see Jess?" I ask when we turn onto the highway.

"Not since the other day," Karen says. "You?"

"Yeah." I stare at my hands. "There's no change. If anything she seems … more broken. She has Stacey, so maybe she can help her? I'm not sure me being there has been good for her. I think I'm too close to Levi, and he's probably not her favourite person right now."

"It would be hard. Has she talked about him?" Karen says.

I shrug. "She doesn't talk much."

"Do you blame Levi for what happened?" Karen stares straight ahead.

I study the profile of her face. "We don't know the details. And I haven't heard his side of the story, so how can I?"

We drive for a bit before Karen breaks our silence. "Are you going to see him today?"

I fiddle with the handle of my tote bag. "I've been to see him every day since ..."

Karen turns into the shopping centre car park. "Want me to come with?"

"Do you want to see him? We'll have to get Yvonne to authorise it though. The hospital has said family only. We could go later this afternoon."

Karen swings the car into an empty space and kills the engine. She turns in her seat to face me. "Is it ... hard to, you know. See him?"

If I had been a good friend and answered my phone, then I would have told Karen all this stuff already. But I didn't want to talk about it, and I still don't. I squeeze my eyes closed, but then I open them again because my thoughts immediately fill with images of Levi in his hospital bed.

"He's in a coma, so yeah. It's hard. He's pretty bad."

"Oh, Katie, I'm so sorry." Karen leans over and hugs me.

She presses her hands into my back, and I bury my face in her neck. I don't want to cry. Crying doesn't fix anything. But I can't hold it in. And I don't want to be strong. I want to go home and crawl into bed and forget about the world.

"Come on," Karen says. "Hot chocolate?"

I nod and we get out of the car, walking through the shopping centre and into the mall. We order our usual, but instead of sitting in we decide to wander through the shops while we drink. It feels good to be out walking around, but my heart is heavy, and every time I think my mind has taken a break from picturing Levi fighting for his life, it reminds me what's happened all over again.

Why can't I switch off for a few minutes? I'm going crazy.

"I want to go home," I say to Karen.

She's looking in the window of a jewellery store. "Okay."

She links her arm with mine, and we make our way through the lunch crowd in the shopping centre, back towards the car. We drive home with the windows down and the music up, only I don't sing along like I often do. I lean against the window frame and let the wind blow my hair away from my face, pretending that it's also blowing away the pain.

Karen leans over and turns the music down. "Have you driven past where … you know? It happened?" she asks when we turn off the highway.

I bite my lip. "You mean the accident site?" I shake my head. "No."

Karen grips the steering wheel. "Want to? I hear there's a great tribute going on."

"Sure, I guess." But I'm not sure. Do I want to see the place where the sister of one of my closest friends died? The place where Levi's life was changed in an instant?

Karen turns onto a backstreet we don't usually take. She waits at the stop sign before driving through the intersection and parking at the kerb. The telegraph pole on the corner is an explosion of colour. Karen gets out, and I slowly follow, squinting against the sunlight.

The pole is covered with flowers, pieces of paper, and photos. In the middle of it all is a white cross with a photo of Josephine and her name on it. There are more flowers on the ground surrounding the pole.

Emptiness fills my stomach, because I don't have anything to offer Josephine. I haven't written her a card, or brought her anything. I should have brought her something.

"Can we go?" I turn away and head to the car before Karen can answer.

She doesn't object, and by the time we pull into my driveway, everything hurts more than it did before.

"You've got mail," Karen says before getting out of the car.

I glance over at our letterbox. A few rolled up white envelopes stick out from the front. I take a deep breath and get out of the car, too. My uni letters are probably in there somewhere, they should be arriving soon, but right now I'm not all that interested. How can I think about my future when Josephine doesn't have one, and Levi might not have one either?

We might not have one together.

I go to the mailbox and grab everything that's inside, flipping through the envelopes, pieces of paper, and brochures on the way to the house. Karen holds the bundle while I unlock the front door.

"Hey, you've got uni letters." Karen waves some of the envelopes in the air. "My money says they're all acceptances."

"I don't really care at the moment." I close the door

behind us and walk through to the kitchen.

"But this will take your mind off things." Karen drops the mail onto the bench.

I stare at the envelopes and shake my head. "I'll open them later."

"Open what later?" Mum comes through into the kitchen, dumping her handbag and keys onto the bench.

"Sorry, Sonja. I parked in the driveway," Karen says.

Mum smiles. "Don't be. There's plenty of room on the street."

"You're home early," I say.

"I wanted to check on you." She kisses me on the temple, then goes to boil the kettle.

"I'm fine, Mum. Karen took me for hot chocolate."

"Katie has university letters," Karen says.

I shoot her dagger eyes.

Mum gets her coffee cup down from the cupboard. "Have you opened them?"

"No," I say. "And I'm not going to."

"Why not?" Mum spoons coffee into her cup and pours in the boiling water.

"Because I'm not in the mood." I stare down at the letters, then move them so I can see the university logos. The specific one I'm waiting for isn't there, but another catches my eye.

I pick up the envelope, and look at the front. The Art Express logo is printed in the upper left-hand corner.

Karen peers over my shoulder. "Oh my God, open it!"

A bolt of excitement hits me, and I slip my finger under the edge to rip the paper open. I pull the letter out and unfold it, quickly scanning the words.

"What does it say?" Mum asks.

"What does what say?" Daniel looks over my other shoulder.

"Where did you come from?" I look up at him.

"Through the door." He glances over his shoulder then back at me.

"Katie!" Karen says. "What the hell does it say?"

I scan the words again to find the most important part. "Your artwork, *Wearable Wisdom*, has been selected for the upcoming Art Express exhibition. Another letter will follow shortly with instructions on how to submit your work."

"That's great news," Mum says. "I'm so proud of you." But there's something about her tone that suggests she's only saying that because she has to.

"Congrats, little sis." Daniel play-punches my arm.

Mum picks up the uni letters. "Now you can open these."

I bite my lip and stare at her hand, shaking my head. It's one thing to get accepted into an art exhibition, but it's another to have to look at something that's going to decide the next four years of my life.

"Not yet," I say.

"Katie, I want you to open them." Mum pushes the paper towards me.

"No." I back away.

Mum frowns, picking the letters up. "I can open them for you."

"No!" I say again, lunging forward and snatching them from her grasp.

"Katie! What is wrong with you?" Mum says.

I clutch the envelopes to my chest. "The past few days

have been a nightmare. Sorry if I don't want to look at something that could determine my entire future. Levi might not even have a future, so how can I think about mine?"

Mum's eyes widen, and she stares at me.

I turn and run outside, still holding the letters to my chest. I have to resist the urge to rip them up and throw them straight in the recycling bin. How can she want me to open them now? Can't I have a little while to fully process everything that's happened?

I stand on the lawn and look at the bougainvillea, and a fresh wave of grief hits me.

A door slams, and I look over to Levi's veranda. Yvonne comes out with hurried steps, Mark hot on her heels.

"Come back here," he says.

Levi's mum turns at the top veranda step, her brow furrowed. "I'm going to the hospital, and you can't stop me."

"Don't use that tone with me." Mark grabs her wrist.

She tries to yank it away. "Let go! You're hurting me."

He pulls her closer to him and mumbles something, but I can't make out the words. I can only hear the low, menacing tone in his voice. Why are they fighting?

"Let go." Yvonne grimaces, and fights her husband to free his grip on her arm.

Her gaze flicks to me, and I stand as still as I can, clutching my uni letters. Mark stops pulling her and follows her line of sight. He lets her go, narrows his eyes at me, then goes back inside the house.

Yvonne presses her lips together, walking to her car with her eyes forward and her shoulders back. She starts the engine and pulls away from the kerb.

What is going on?

I never saw Levi's dad act like this when I was a kid. How long has he been treating his wife like this? How long has Levi been dealing with it, and I haven't known?

Karen bumps me with her shoulder, and I snap out of my shock.

"Did you see any of that?" I ask.

"Any of what?"

"Levi's parents. Something's going on, and it doesn't look good."

Karen moves so she's standing in front of me. "Something? What something?"

"He was being … He looked like he wanted to hit her."

"That's pretty heavy." Karen glances over her shoulder at Levi's house.

"Yvonne went to the hospital."

"You want to go now, too?" Karen turns back to me.

I nod. "I'll put these inside."

I run in and dump the uni letters on my desk, grabbing my tote on the way back out. I don't bother telling Mum where I'm going. I'm still upset that she tried to make me open my mail, and I'm sure she'll be able to figure it out.

Karen and I take the motorway to the hospital. I curl my fingers around the shape of my journal inside my tote bag. I've wanted to write in it ever since I found out about Josephine's death, and Levi ending up in hospital. But for some reason I can't. I figure if I take it places with me, the motivation might strike when I least expect it.

I take the small book out and hold it in my lap, running my finger over the smooth cover.

"You going to write in that?" Karen asks, turning into the hospital street.

"I don't know if I can," I say. "The past few days are filled with things I don't want to remember. If I write them down, they'll always be there."

"Everything will always be there no matter what." Karen parks the car on the street. "If you write it down, at least it will be out of your head, and you might be able to make more sense of it all."

"Maybe." I put my journal back in my bag.

We get out and cross the road to the hospital. This time I don't bother with reception, and we walk straight to the door of the ICU.

I pick up the phone on the wall. "Hi, this is Katie Sullivan. I'm here to see Levi White."

"Hi Katie," a nurse says, and I recognise her voice from the other day. "Are you by yourself?"

"I have a friend with me. Karen Mitchell. Can you ask Yvonne if Karen can come through, please?"

"One moment." There's some rustling at the end of the phone line. "Yes, Katie. Yvonne says that's fine."

"Thank you." I hang up the phone.

The automatic doors open as Karen and I finish washing out hands. I lead her to room seven, noticing that she looks into all the rooms as we pass, like I did that first time. At Levi's room, the curtain is fully open this time, so he's on display to the entire ward. I understand why the rooms are like this—it helps with monitoring the patients—but looking at him like he's in a fishbowl makes me sad.

Karen stands at the window. "He doesn't look too bad."

I stand beside her, and rest my hand on the window

frame. "His breathing tube is gone."

"They took it out this morning." Yvonne is on my other side, staring through the glass at her son, a takeaway coffee cup in her hand.

"Oh." I look her up and down quickly. She seems more composed now than when I saw her at home. "That's a good thing, right?"

She turns to me. "It means they're bringing him out of the coma. He's still heavily sedated, but he's breathing on his own, which is good, yes. You girls can go in." She smiles weakly.

Karen moves to the door, and I go to follow but stop and turn back to Levi's mum. "Is everything okay?"

"I'm sure everything will be fine. I'm just trying to focus on getting Levi better."

I press my lips together and nod, then go into the room with Karen.

"Can he ... hear us?" She fidgets with the bangle on her left wrist.

"I asked the same thing the first time I saw him." I drop my tote on the floor and sit in the chair beside the bed. "They said they don't really know, but talking to him can't hurt."

Karen comes closer. "Okay, um, so, Levi. I think you're an arse, and you've done some stupid stuff, but, you know. Don't die, please. Because then I'll have to put up with Katie. So, yeah."

I look up at Karen. She raises her eyebrows, and we both burst out laughing. My shoulders shake, and it feels good to let the emotion out. Tears run down my face and I swipe them away, but they keep coming until my laughter turns to sobs.

"Oh, Katie." Karen stands beside me and puts her arm around my shoulders.

I spurt another short laugh, then sniffle. "I hope he can hear us, because the other day I told him I love him."

Karen rubs my back. "I'll leave you two kids to talk."

I smile up at her and she leaves the room, standing with Yvonne on the other side of the window.

I turn back to Levi. "Hey, you."

He doesn't look as scary, now that the big tube is out of his mouth. His face is still quite bruised and chaffed, but he looks more like himself.

"I brought my journal with me." I reach down and take it and a pen out of my tote bag. "I haven't written in it yet. Not since ... you know." I grip the edge of the small book and hold it in my lap. "It's hard to process everything that's happened. I'm not sure I can write it down in words, because my brain is so full of stuff, and it feels all mixed up." I pause, and slip one hand through the bedrail to hold Levi's. He's a little warmer today. "Karen seems to think if I write everything down, it might help me cope better."

I let go of his hand and open my journal, grasping the pen and pressing the nib to a fresh page. I write the date, then stop.

"But where do I start, Levi?"

I take a breath and write.

The day we left Surfers, Levi told me he would be there when I got home. I was so upset that he wasn't, because I was ready to tell him I forgive him.

Then I found out Levi had been in an accident which put him in intensive care, and killed Josie. Her death is terrible, and Jess is so broken over it, but I'm broken, too.

In a way, I'm also happy. Not because Josephine died, but because Levi lived. And while I don't know all of the details yet, I'm so happy that he's still here. Is that an awful way to think? Am I a bad person, because I'm so glad he lived when the sister of one of my close friends didn't?

I don't know how to deal with all the emotions, or how to put my thoughts in the right order. Levi is in a pretty bad way. They say he'll be fine, but it's hard to believe that when he can't even talk to me.

I stop and lean my forehead against the bedrail. Tears come again, and I close my journal. I can't write anymore. It's too hard, and my heart hurts because right now, even though I'm alive and Levi is fighting to live, we are both so broken.

4

It will come true

The past week has been hard. Daniel has been the best big brother ever, taking me to the hospital whenever I ask, even though staying at home in my bubble would have been the easier thing to do.

Now, it's the day of Josephine's funeral, and I have to face Josephine's family, and Levi and Josephine's friends. Is everyone angry with Levi? Do they think the accident was his fault? I haven't asked Mum and Dad any questions about the accident, and they haven't offered any more information.

I'm not sure I want to know the details.

Because I'm already hurting so bad.

I change slowly into a navy A-line dress with little cap sleeves. It's one of the nicest dresses I own, but I haven't worn it since Mason's funeral, which makes wearing it now even harder. The memories that go with it are painful.

In the bathroom I put my contacts in, and dust some powder over my face before sweeping gloss over my lips. I'm as ready as I'm ever going to be, so I grab my purse and head downstairs.

"Katie, can you take the paper recycling out?" Mum asks as I walk into the kitchen. She's dressed in a sleek black dress that stops at her knees, and is putting in black teardrop earrings.

"Sure." I set my purse down and grab the basket off the counter.

Mum stops and stares at me. "Oh, honey. You look so lovely in that dress."

"Thanks." I stare at the basket of paper in my hands.

"I haven't seen you wear it since—"

"Mason's funeral." I can't look at her or I'll cry, so I head outside to the bins at the side of the house.

With the basket tucked under my arm, I flip the lid of the bin open then rest the basket on the edge to tip it up. I stop halfway and stare at the newspaper sitting on top of all the other recyclable stuff inside. There are photos of Levi and Josephine on the front page. I stand there for a few moments, staring at it. Do I want to read it? Why have I not seen this yet? Are Mum and Dad hiding things like this from me? I set the basket on the ground, fish the newspaper out, and quickly scan the article.

LOCAL GIRL KILLED IN CAR ACCIDENT
Josephine Hart was killed when her Honda Civic was struck by a BMW late Friday night. Levi White, the driver of the BMW, is currently in a

critical but stable condition. Mandatory tests revealed both drivers were not under the influence, and police have ruled out speed as a factor. There were no witnesses. Evidence at the scene suggests Miss Hart failed to stop at the intersection for reasons unknown. Police are hopeful a future statement from Mr White will shed some light on what happened.

At least Levi hadn't been drinking. And everyone would know the intersection the article is referring to. Anyone who runs that stop sign is asking for trouble. I'm not sure why Mum and Dad don't want me to see this, because knowing Levi wasn't drunk has lifted a weight from my shoulders. But that weight crashes back down again, because Josephine is still dead. Me feeling better is not going to change that.

I toss the paper back in the bin, then dump the rest of the recycling on top.

Mum, Dad, and Daniel come out the front door. Dad takes the basket from me and puts it in the foyer.

Mum hands me my purse. "We have to go."

I take a deep breath, and we all pile into the car.

The local church is five minutes away, and when we arrive there's already a crowd of people milling around outside the doors.

"Why is everyone looking at their phone?" Daniel asks.

"HSC results release today," I say.

"Oh, I completely forgot," Mum says. "Katie, do you want to look at yours?"

"No." I glare at her. "Mum, we're at a funeral."

"We're still in the car. I'm sure you can take a couple of minutes."

I shake my head, open my mouth to say something but close it again, then get out. What is wrong with everyone? Josephine can't look at her results. Neither can Levi.

"Katie ..." Dad says when we're all out of the car.

"My results will still be there tomorrow." I glare at my parents before turning towards the church.

"You okay?" Daniel comes to my side.

"No. I'm not." I stomp away from him, towards Karen and Stacey who are standing on the edge of the crowd staring at their phone.

"Did you get your results?" Karen asks when I'm close enough to hear her.

My mouth drops open. "No. Have some respect. Put your phones away."

Karen and Stacey exchange a glance but do it anyway.

Veronica comes over to our little group. "Hey, Katie." She plays with the small black purse in her hands. "How are you?"

I sigh, because this is where I'm supposed to tell her I'm fine, but I'm far from it, and I'm tired of pretending. Then I remember that Josephine was one of Veronica's best friends, and Levi is still her friend, so I say exactly what I'm supposed to. "I'm okay. Thanks for asking. How about you? This must be hard."

Veronica offers me a weak smile. "I haven't been able to see Levi yet. None of us have. His mum won't let us into the ICU. Is he ...?"

"I think he's doing well," I say, surprised that Yvonne

let Daniel, Karen and I in, but not the others. "They brought him out of the coma, but he's on heavy painkillers. He hasn't been awake when I've been to see him."

Veronica nods, then angles her head towards the church. "I'm going in."

Most of the crowd has moved inside already, so Karen, Stacey, and I follow. We take the left-side aisle along the wall, and I notice Yvonne sitting in the very back row by herself. I can't see Levi's dad anywhere.

Karen, Stacey, and I move towards the front to see if we can sit near Jessica. She's in the front row with her parents, and we take the pew two rows back. Mum and Dad are across the aisle from us, but when Daniel spots me he moves to sit beside me. He gives my hand a gentle squeeze, and I think maybe I can get through the next few hours.

The service is emotional, and when Jessica gets up for the eulogy, I cry just as hard as she does. I'm so proud of her though, because she manages to get through it on her own. We stay until the hearse takes the coffin away.

Outside, Daniel hugs me, and I hold onto him as if he's the only thing keeping me on my feet.

"Want to go to the hospital?" he asks.

I nod into his chest.

"I can come with you," Karen says, rubbing my back. "I don't think I can handle the wake."

I pull out of Daniel's embrace. "I'd like to go see Levi by myself today."

"Okay." She tucks my hair behind my ear. "Stacey and I will look after Jess."

"Do you think she'll mind if I'm not there?"

"Why don't you ask her?" Daniel says.

I crane my neck to search for my friend. She's with her mum and dad, doing the rounds. Jessica's eyes are puffy and red. I walk over to her and touch her on the elbow. When she sees me her face crumples, and I take her into my arms and hold her while she cries.

"I'm so sorry." I grip her tightly.

"Are you coming this afternoon?" Jessica pulls away and searches my face.

I press my lips together. "I'd like to go and see Levi. They've taken him out of the coma. He might be awake." I pause, and Jessica stays quiet. "I can come if you'd like though?"

She shakes her head. "No, it's okay. He needs you."

"But you need me, too."

"I have Stacey." She glances at our friend. "And Karen. Levi needs you more than I do."

I hug her again, because no words I have will be able to take away her pain. "I'll call you later."

Daniel and I go home with Mum and Dad. I don't bother to change, but I do run inside to grab my journal. Then my brother and I head for the hospital.

"You right to get home?" Daniel says.

"Yeah. I'll call if I need you." I shut the car door and cross the street, making my way to the ICU.

A nurse lets me in, and I go to Levi's room, knocking gently on the door before going inside.

"There's no change," Yvonne says, getting up from the chair beside the bed. "I'll let you have some privacy."

"Thank you," I say.

Yvonne touches me on the arm on her way past. I

want to say more to her, but I don't know what, so I stay quiet. Once she has left, I sit in the chair and take out my journal.

"It's me again," I say to Levi, squeezing his hand. "They had Josie's funeral today, but your mum probably already told you. Jess did okay. Her eulogy was really beautiful." I go quiet for a minute.

"HSC results came out today as well. I haven't looked at mine. I'm not sure I want to. I don't think it's fair, you know, because you can't look at yours." I pause. "I was hoping we could look at them together." I squeeze his hand again, waiting for some sort of response, but there's nothing. All I can see is the steady rise and fall of Levi's chest as he breathes, and hear the constant beeping of the machines around us.

"I got some uni letters as well. I didn't tell you about those because I haven't opened them yet. Mum wants me to, but ... all of this I want to do with you. I thought I was going to come home from schoolies, and we were going to start a new chapter, one where we had a fresh page, and we could make our story whatever we wanted it to be." I rub circles on the back of Levi's hand with my thumb. "I also don't want to open them because the letter I've been hoping for the most hasn't come. I haven't told anyone but Karen I applied for a fine arts degree. Mum and Dad would freak out if I said I want to do something in the arts. They've always assumed I would do law, or become a doctor, but after seeing you like this, I don't think I could cope with that." I stare at Levi's face, searching for any sign that he can hear me. "I'm scared. If I tell them what I *really* want to do, they'll probably think I've completely wasted my scholarship."

I close my eyes and concentrate on the feeling of Levi's warm hand in mine. I don't want to talk anymore. Pouring all of this out has made me tired, to the point that I don't want to write in my journal either.

The hinges of the door squeak, and Yvonne comes into the room. "I need to go home for a while. Do you want a lift, Katie?"

I sit up straight and angle my body towards her. "That would be lovely, thank you."

Yvonne and I walk out to the car park in silence. I'm nervous because I think the drive home is going to be uncomfortable, but when Yvonne smiles at me, I relax.

"He was excited about you coming home," she says once we're on the motorway. "He couldn't wait to see you."

"I'm sorry, about coming over ... I didn't know how serious it was ..."

"It's okay," Yvonne says. "We just have to pick ourselves up and deal with what life throws at us."

I bite my bottom lip. "Sometimes what it throws us totally sucks."

Yvonne chuckles. "Yes, it does. But on the up side, Levi opened his eyes the other day."

"He did?" I stare at her, wide eyed. "Did he say anything? Did you talk to him?"

Yvonne shakes her head. "The pain medication is keeping him pretty heavily sedated. He fell asleep again quite quickly, but it was nice to see his eyes." She smiles.

I would love to be able to look into Levi's eyes again.

We spend the rest of the trip in silence, and I listen to the noises rushing past us. I miss Levi already, and I wish I had a way to be close to him when I'm not at the hospital. The bougainvillea reminds me so much of Levi, but I can't sit on the trellis.

As we turn onto the highway, I think about all the places where I've been happy with Levi. The park when we had a picnic dinner. The small clearing at school. My bedroom. And the treehouse.

Yvonne pulls into her driveway and turns the car off. "How are you holding up, Katie?"

"Me?" I turn to her, ripped from my thoughts. "I always make it through."

"If you ever want to talk, just come and knock, okay?"

I nod, and we both get out of the car, moving towards our own houses.

"Yvonne?" I spin to face her again. "Can I … go and sit in the treehouse?"

She smiles. "Of course. Any time you like."

I wait until she's inside, then I make my way down the side of Levi's house to the backyard. It feels like an eternity since I've set foot down here, and so many memories come flooding back. It's as if I can see Mason and Levi, and Daniel and me, all chasing each other, our laughter filling the air.

In the back corner of the yard sits the treehouse, built into the branches of a gum tree. As I make my way towards it, I remember the day the four of us started building it. Mason and Daniel thought they knew what they were doing, but after Mason hit himself on the thumb with a hammer, his dad ended up finishing the platform for us. That's how I remember Levi's dad. He always helped if we asked, but I don't remember him smiling much.

I stop at the base of the tree and put my foot on the bottom step. We made them from timber offcuts and nailed them to the trunk. I climb up and crawl onto the floor of the treehouse. It has a roof made from tin sheets, but only two walls, one along the back and one along one side. The back wall has a square cut out of it, and the purple curtains I made so long ago are still here, although they're worn and faded now. I touch them with my fingertips and smile.

In the corner is an old wooden kids table-and-chair set. The seats seem so small now, but I pull one out and sit on it, setting my journal and purse on the scratched table. For a moment I sit and take it all in. The four of us spent so much time up here when we were kids. It feels like home.

I adjust myself in the seat, and my foot bumps something under the table. There's a shoebox shoved into the back corner, and I reach in to pull it out. I've never seen it before. We never had much stuff up here because the four of us took up all the space. I set the box on the table and stare at the lid. It's not very dusty, so it can't have been up here long. Either that, or it gets used a lot.

Maybe I shouldn't open it. It's not mine.

I put my fingers under the lip of the lid and take it off.

The box is filled with envelopes neatly stacked from front to back like a filing cabinet, and the one at the front has my name written on it. I flip it forward, and the next one has my name on it as well. When I riffle through the rest of them, they're all addressed to me, and each one has a date on the back.

I'm pretty sure it's Levi's handwriting.

Has he written me a box of letters?

Why didn't he give them to me?

Am I supposed to read them? Maybe not, if he never actually gave them to me. I look around at the treehouse with its two walls and dirty curtains. How often does he come up here? I take out the first letter. The date on the back is the day Josephine died, which means Levi must have written it before the accident. I take out the last letter, and the date on the back of that one is the day of Mason's death.

Has he been writing to me this whole time? Why would he do that? For so many years I thought he didn't want to have anything to do with me because he wouldn't talk to me, and Levi was writing to me instead.

My eyes blur, and a tear drips from my cheek onto the envelope in my hand.

How can I possibly read these? What if I don't want to know what's in them?

The past should stay where it is. We're supposed to be looking to our future.

"Knock, knock."

I look up as Daniel's head pops over the floor of the treehouse. He climbs the rest of the way and sits on the edge of the platform. I swipe at the tears rolling down my cheeks.

"You didn't need a lift?" Daniel asks.

I'm glad he didn't ask if I'm okay. "Yvonne drove me home."

"I know, I was just talking to her. She said you were up here. What's that?" Daniel points to the box.

"A shoebox."

Daniel laughs. "Really, Katie? What's *in* it?"

I stare down at the envelopes all lined up neatly. "They must be letters, but I haven't opened any yet."

"Who are they addressed to?"

"Me," I say. "I think Levi has been writing to me."

"If they have your name on them, read them."

"There must be a reason why he never gave them to me," I say. "He might not want me to know what's written in them. Like I don't want anyone to read my journal. Reading these without his permission would be invading his privacy."

Daniel shrugs. "Do what you think is right."

I take a deep breath then place the lid back on and crouch down to put the box back where I found it. "Maybe I'll ask him about them when he's awake."

"Come on," Daniel says. "Dinner's ready."

I follow my brother down the rungs of the treehouse and through Levi's backyard. The night is clear, and as I cross the boundary into our front yard, a star blazes in the blackness. I say a prayer for Levi, and then I wish for everything to work out, hoping it will come true.

5

What is the point?

Levi has been off the respirator for a while now, but he hasn't been awake any of the times I've been to see him. His waking moments are few due to the sedation, but I wish he would wake up long enough to know I'm here. It's hard not knowing if he can hear me.

Since finding the letters, I haven't talked about them to Levi, and it's eating away at me. Why did he write them? What did he write in them?

I sit in the chair beside his bed and pull my journal out, tapping my pen against the cover while I stare at the tinsel and Christmas baubles the nurses have put up around the room.

I've managed to form a routine with my visits. I come about an hour after visiting time starts, so Yvonne can be here for a while first, then when I arrive she gives me some time to spend with Levi alone. I always start with writing in my journal, then I sit and talk to him.

The paper rustles as I open the small book to a fresh page. I'm finally able to use the one Karen gave me for my birthday because my other one is full, and remembering the day she gave it to me makes me smile. It seems so long ago.

"I'm going to write for a bit," I say to Levi. "Don't go anywhere, okay?"

I press my pen to the page …

Levi hasn't been awake during my visits. They say he's too heavily sedated to have many periods of consciousness. Yvonne assures me he has been awake, although never for very long, and even she isn't sure if he knows what's going on yet. Apparently he needs to be sedated in order for his body to rest and heal.

I want him to wake up.

I want to tell him I love him, and that I'm so sorry for not trying harder.

I haven't told him I found the letters yet. I'm not sure if I should mention them at all. Maybe they were hidden because he doesn't want me to read them. But why would he have kept them?

I have so many questions for him.

Please, wake up, Levi.

I need you.

Levi groans softly, and I look up from my page. His head moves, and I stand, my journal and pen dropping to the floor. The pen rolls under the bed.

"Levi?" I ask.

He doesn't respond.

I take his hand, and he moves his head again, but he doesn't open his eyes. His lips part and I hold my breath, waiting to see if he'll say something. I squeeze his hand and his fingers move, curling around mine.

"Levi," I say again. "Are you awake?"

He groans again, and his head settles back to the side. His eyes stay closed. I sit back in the chair, still holding his hand. The door opens and the nurse comes in.

"How are you, Katie?" she asks, coming to the foot of the bed and looking at Levi's chart.

"I'm good … I think Levi is waking up."

The nurse looks up and goes around to the other side of the bed. "We've been lowering his dosage slightly each day, so any time from now he can become fully aware. Just keep talking to him." She smiles. "Everything looks good though. His vitals are fine, and his readings are where they should be."

"Thank you," I say.

The nurse leaves, and I turn back to Levi. A tear rolls down my cheek, and I swat it away with my free hand.

"Look at me crying again. You'd think I'd done enough of that." I stare at him, hoping for a response. When I don't get one I continue, "You remember when I told you we had Josie's funeral? I came to see you after, and your mum drove me home." I pause. "I wanted to be close to you, so I went to sit in the treehouse. It hasn't changed much. Although the curtains could do with a wash." I smile. "I sat up there for a while, thinking about a lot of stuff. How happy we were when we were kids. The fun we used to have. I miss that. I miss what we used to have before … anyway. I found something while I was up there." I stop again, and trace circles on the back of Levi's hand with my thumb. "I found a shoebox filled with envelopes with my name on them. And I so desperately want you to wake up, because I want to talk to you about them."

More tears spill onto my cheeks, and I rest my forehead against the bedrail.

"I haven't read any of them yet. Daniel said I should if they're addressed to me. But what if you don't want me to read them?" I look at him again, my eyes hot. "And they're all about the past, right? Do I want to revisit that? Do I want to know what you wrote back then but couldn't for whatever reason tell me? Because the past is in the past, isn't it? And how can we move forward if we keep dwelling on it?"

I try to hold the tears in, but more come and I can't stop them, and within seconds I'm sobbing, my shoulders shaking. *Wake up! Please.*

My vision blurs, and I glance up at the decorations on the walls, the red and gold baubles blobs of colour against the stark hospital walls. Christmas will be here soon. I want to spend it with Levi. How can I spend it without him? How will I get through another day without him?

"It's not fair," I whisper in between gulps of air.

A hand touches my shoulder and I sit back, surprised to see Yvonne. I hadn't even heard her come in.

"The doctors say he'll make a full recovery," she says.

I sniffle and let go of Levi's hand so I can stand. "I know. I just …"

She offers me a small smile. "I know. Me, too."

Yvonne wraps me up in her arms, hugging me like every mother knows how to hug her child. Even though she's not my mum, I'm so grateful to have her here.

I pull away. "Thank you. But I'm the one who should be comforting you."

She tucks my hair behind my ear. "Maybe we can comfort each other. I'm very happy that you're here for Levi."

We sit together for a while, but as the seconds tick by, I don't have anything I want to say to Yvonne, and I don't feel comfortable talking to Levi in front of her.

"I should go," I say, getting to my feet.

Yvonne nods. I gather my things and head towards the door, glancing back at Levi and his mum. She has already taken the seat beside the bed and is holding his hand. I slip quietly out the door and take a deep breath to pull myself together.

On my way through the ICU I pull my phone out to text Daniel. He said he'd come and get me when I was ready. He'd just be hanging around over at the shopping centre. I wait until I'm out of the ward and in the main part of the hospital before I pull up his number and send him a quick message.

Veronica, Jarred, and Geoff come into the hospital foyer. Veronica smiles, and the three of them walk over to me.

"You've been crying?" Veronica frowns.

I push my glasses up my nose and look at my phone. "Um ... yeah."

She doesn't ask me why or if I'm okay, and I let out a breath.

"How is he?" Jarred asks.

"You haven't seen him yet?" I put my phone away and look at him.

Jarred shakes his head, and I sense that he's mad, but I'm not sure if it's directed at me or at the fact he hasn't been able to see his best friend.

His friend who was driving the car that killed his girlfriend.

I blink a few times to settle the heat pricking at my eyes.

"They told us family only," Geoff says. "You're not family."

I bite my lip. "I thought you guys would have been able to see him by now."

"You didn't answer my question," Jarred says.

I fiddle with the ends of my hair. "He's … they say he'll be fine. But it's going to take a while."

The four of us stand there, staring at each other. I don't know what else to tell them. It's hard to explain what Levi looks like. And when I think about him, I want to cry again.

"You should ask Yvonne if you can see him," I say. "They only let two visitors at a time into his room though."

"Is she here?" Veronica asks.

"Yeah." I glance at the reception desk then lower my voice. "Use the phone on the wall at the entrance to the ICU, and ask for her. Hopefully she'll say you can see him."

Geoff walks off without saying anything else. I probably shouldn't expect a thank you from him, but I thought we'd made some progress while we were at Surfers Paradise. His arrogance now makes me dislike him all over again.

"Thanks, Katie," Jarred says, following his friend.

I offer him a small smile, and hope he does get to see Levi. If I hadn't been able to all this time I think I'd be crazy by now.

Veronica hangs back. She purses her lips and adjusts the strap of her bag on her shoulder. Her mouth opens, then she closes it again.

"What's wrong?" I ask. "Is there something you want to say?"

She takes a breath. "I just … I'm having a New Year's party, and I thought maybe you'd like to come? If you're around, that is."

I chew the side of my thumb. "I don't have a very good track record with your parties."

We stare at each other for a second, then both laugh. I'm surprised at how good it feels. I haven't laughed in what seems like ages.

"Dad's booked me a couple of hotel rooms overlooking the harbour." Veronica shifts on her feet. "He said I can ask my friends if I like."

Does she think of me as a friend now?

"Harbour views, on New Year's?" I don't hide my shock very well. "That sounds … expensive."

I drop my gaze because despite the fact we're no longer in school, Veronica and I are very different people. Something she used to like reminding me of on a regular basis.

"Come on, Katie. It'll be fun."

I look up. "Why do you even want me there?"

Veronica folds her arms and squares her shoulders. "You don't *have* to come. I just thought … you know …" She looks away, then at the floor, then back at me. "New year, new opportunities. A fresh start?"

I'm quiet for a few heartbeats, trying to figure out if she's somehow asking me to be friends with her.

"A party sounds great," I eventually say. "We could all use some cheering up."

"Hey, Ronnie," Jarred calls along the hallway. He's standing at the turn that leads to the ICU. "You coming?"

She waves at him then turns back to me. "I better go." She takes a few steps. "Bring Karen. I've already asked Jess and Stacey."

I nod, and watch her walk towards Jarred, before going outside into the warm summer air. Daniel is waiting for me on the street. He smiles as I slide into the passenger seat.

"How is he today?" he asks.

"No change really," I say. "He did groan. The nurse says he has some moments when he's awake and more aware, but they're not often. They're weaning him off the sedatives, so hopefully he'll wake up soon." I look at my brother, fresh tears in my eyes. "I want to hear his voice."

Daniel reaches over and squeezes my hand before pulling the car out onto the street. We head for the motorway, and I wind the window down a bit to get some fresh air on my face. I settle my head back against the headrest.

"You should go see Jess when we get home," Daniel says. "She's not doing so well today."

I roll my head to the side to look at Daniel, studying him for a moment. "You went to see her this morning?"

He nods. "I'm not sure how to help her though."

"Yeah, it's hard." I chew my lip and glance sideways at my brother. "You're really worried, aren't you?"

"Well, yeah." He shrugs. "It's Jess."

"Is there something you're not telling me?"

Daniel glances at me sideways. "Like what?"

I sit up straight in my seat. "Like you … and Jess—"

"Can't I be worried?"

I smile and decide not to push him. "Of course you can. I'll go and see her."

We don't talk for the rest of the trip. Daniel parks the car in our driveway and we get out. He glances at me and smiles, but his eyes don't have their usual sparkle. He makes his way towards the front door. His slumped shoulders tell me he's got something on his mind.

I watch him for a second before calling out, "Hey. Want to come with me?" Daniel turns when he reaches the door. "I'm sure Jess would love to see you again, too."

Daniel comes back to where I'm standing on the grass. "I'd like that."

He doesn't say anything else, and we walk together down the street to Jessica's place. Her mum lets us in. She seems a little better today.

"Jess is in her room," Bridget says.

"How is she?" I ask.

Jessica's mum purses her lips and takes a deep breath. "She's … not coping very well. She won't look in the mirror, and I can't get her out of her room. Maybe …" She stares at me and a tear rolls down her cheek. I hug her because I'm not sure what else to do, and sometimes a hug makes you feel better when words can't.

"We'll just sit with her for a bit," Daniel says.

I pull away from Bridget, and Daniel puts a hand on my shoulder. We go downstairs to Jessica's bedroom where we find her sitting in her desk chair, staring out the window. She doesn't look at us when we come into the room.

Jessica is still in her pyjamas, the bed is unmade, and there's a towel taped to the wardrobe door, covering the mirror. Daniel and I exchange a glance.

I sit on the edge of the bed and face Jessica. "Hey. We thought you might like some company."

Daniel sits beside me. "Maybe we could go for a walk?"

Jessica finally looks at us. "I don't feel up to a walk."

I look out the window at the bush that backs onto the houses on our side of the street. Jessica's house is farther back on the block than Levi's and mine, so there isn't much backyard, but the view down into the valley is pretty.

"We could go upstairs and sit on the balcony," I say. "Look at the trees and listen to the birds."

Jessica smiles with her lips closed. "Can we just sit here?"

"Sure," I say.

Daniel shuffles back on the bed so he's leaning against the wall under the window. I'm not exactly sure what to do, so I stand and tidy the room a bit, arranging the things on Jessica's side table, putting rubbish in her bin, and taking the dirty clothes to the laundry.

When I get back I stop in the doorway, then quickly step into the hall again. Jessica has moved to the bed to sit with Daniel. He has his arm around her, and I have to stop myself from frowning. I peek around the doorjamb at them.

Jessica looks up at my brother and smiles. A weight lifts from my shoulders, because I haven't seen her smile in what feels like forever. Daniel leans down and kisses her softly on the lips, and I step back again. I shouldn't be watching this. It's their private moment, but I peek around the door jamb again because it's so nice to see Jessica happy.

"Katie?" Karen whispers in my ear, and I jump. "What are you doing?"

"Oh my God, you scared me," I whisper back.

Stacey comes down the stairs.

"Thought I should be quiet." Karen keeps her voice low. "Since you're already spying on Jess."

"Why are we whispering?" Stacey looks from Karen to me. "What's going on?"

I point to Jessica's room. "Daniel and Jess … he kissed her."

"What?" Karen says, then claps a hand over her mouth.

I cringe. "Maybe we should leave."

"You don't have to go," Daniel calls. "You think we can't hear you?"

I step into the doorway. "I know you heard Karen."

She laughs, and pushes me into the room. Stacey follows.

"Hi girls," Daniel says.

I sit in the desk chair and glance sideways at my brother. Karen dumps a shopping bag on the floor, and Stacey puts another one beside it.

"I'm glad we're all here," Karen says. "Stacey and I brought supplies."

"We've got chocolate, and lollies, and chips, and tea, and DVDs." Stacey kneels on the floor and unpacks one of the bags.

"All the stuff we need for an afternoon in." Karen plonks down beside Stacey.

I smile at my friends, and wish I had been a part of organising this for Jessica. Instead, I've been wrapped up in going to see Levi. I really want to talk to my friends about him, but I'm scared Jessica won't want to hear his name. I'm not sure how she feels about Levi at the moment. Even if Josephine ran that stop sign, he was still driving the car that killed her.

"I should probably go," Daniel says. "You girls look like you have a busy afternoon ahead of you."

Jessica bites her lip and looks at him. She doesn't say anything, but from the way she's gripping his hand, I don't think she wants him to leave.

"Don't be stupid," Karen says, glancing from Jessica to me. "You can stay."

Karen rips open a family-sized block of chocolate, passing it to me. I break off a few pieces then toss it onto the bed for Jessica and Daniel. For the next half an hour we stuff our faces, and talk about Christmas.

"Anyone going away?" Karen asks.

"Nope, we'll be at home," I say, smiling at Daniel.

Jessica shakes her head. "Staying home, too. Mum cancelled everything."

"We have to go up the coast to Nan's place," Stacey says, crinkling her nose. "It's always noisy."

"Well, I'm being dragged down south to my aunt's," Karen says. "Four nights of sleeping on the floor in my cousin's room."

"You love it," I say, smiling.

"Yeah, the little rug rats are kinda cute."

"What's everyone getting for Christmas?" Stacey asks.

"I want my own car," Karen says, popping a piece of

chocolate in her mouth. "But that's never going to happen. I usually ask for money so I can go shopping at the sales in the new year."

"Socks," Daniel says, smiling. "I need socks."

We all laugh.

"The presents don't matter so much," I say. "I just like being with fam …" I stop before I finish the word, but it's too late.

The room goes quiet.

The smile drops from Jessica's face. She snuggles down into the crook of Daniel's arm, looks at her hands, and takes a deep breath. I'm such an idiot for talking about family. Jessica is missing a piece of hers.

"I'm sorry … Jess, I … I'm sorry," I stutter.

"It's okay." She sniffles, and tucks her hair behind her ear. "Family is really important. And friends are, too." She looks up and stares at me. "How's Levi?"

I open my mouth to reply, but no sound comes out. How do I answer that question? He's lying broken in a hospital bed.

"He's … they say he'll be fine." I drop my gaze and pull my knees to my chest, resting my heels on the edge of the chair. "He's not awake properly yet, so I haven't … he hasn't talked to anyone."

The room falls quiet again.

A kookaburra laughs outside.

We all avoid looking at each other.

"Oh!" Karen says, breaking the silence. "I got two acceptance letters yesterday."

"That's great," Daniel says. "Where to?"

"One for Newcastle, and one for Macquarie."

"I got a letter from Sydney Uni," Stacey says.

"Let me guess." I rest my chin on my knees. "Vet science?"

"Yep." She grins.

"What course were you accepted into, Karen?" I ask.

"Psychology." She opens a packet of chips and stuffs some in her mouth before passing them to Stacey. "Think I'll go to Newcastle."

"I got into Newcastle as well," Jessica says, quietly. "For their communications degree. I think I'd like a career in journalism ... someday."

"What do you mean, someday?" I ask.

Jessica looks at me with sad eyes. "I've always wanted a year off to travel. Josie was going to come with me. Now, I don't know what I want to do. With Josie gone ..." She shrugs, and stares down at the bed. "What's the point? Why go to uni, or travel, or do anything, when I could die tomorrow? Any of us could ..."

Jessica's voice trails off, and the air in the room becomes heavy with sadness.

"Have you opened your letters yet?" Karen breaks the silence and raises her eyebrows at me.

"No, she hasn't." Daniel frowns, taking the chips from Stacey and shoving some in his mouth.

Jessica is still staring at the bed, worrying at the side of her thumb.

My future isn't something I want to think about right now.

I stare at my brother and shrug. "Maybe Jess has the right idea. What *is* the point?"

6

So hard

I open my eyes on Christmas morning and stare at the stars on my ceiling, wondering how I'm going to get through the day. I guess I just have to focus on what I have rather than what I don't. Try and be grateful that my brother is alive, my parents aren't fighting, and that I have a wonderful family who loves me.

But it's going to be hard, because even though I have so much to be thankful for, I still have holes in my heart that need fixing.

I've been visiting Levi as much as I can during the past week. On a couple of occasions I couldn't go in to see him, because the doctors were in with him doing tests or physio or other doctor stuff, and the times I did get to sit with him, he still wasn't conscious enough to talk to me. He's moving his head around a bit though, so hopefully next time I see him he'll be awake.

I can't wait to hear his voice.

I managed to get some last-minute Christmas shopping done, and I've seen Jessica every other day as well. She's been spending more time with Daniel, which is a good thing, but I'm worried about her. She seems to have lost all motivation for anything. I can relate to how she feels, and I want to help her, but I'm not sure how. Today will be a sad day for her and her parents without having Josephine.

"Merry Christmas," Daniel says from the other side of my door.

I stretch and roll onto my side. "You can come in."

The door opens and my brother sticks his head around it, smiling. "Get up. There're presents under the tree."

I fake a yawn. "I want to stay here."

Daniel pushes the door open all the way. "Come on, Katie." His smile widens, and he pulls a Santa hat onto his head.

I laugh and throw my covers back, getting out of bed. "You're such a dork."

I quickly wash my face and follow my brother downstairs. Mum is in the kitchen with the oven already on. It's going to get a workout today. Shortbread cookies are the first thing on the menu, by the looks of it.

"Merry Christmas, you two," Mum says, wrapping both of us in a hug.

"Where's Dad?" I ask.

"He's gone to the bakery to get the bread rolls."

"You mean we have to wait to open presents?" Daniel asks.

"No more waiting." Dad comes into the kitchen and puts a bag full of rolls on the bench. "Let's go. Presents." He rubs his hands together.

We all pile into the lounge room and sit on the floor around the Christmas tree. I'm not excited because I want to find out what I got. I'm excited because I want to see everyone else's faces when they open their presents. We've never done big expensive gifts because we've never been able to, but I always love seeing how happy even the smallest gift can make someone.

"Who wants to be Santa?" Dad asks.

"Daniel's wearing the hat," I say.

"All right then." Daniel jumps up and goes to sit beside the tree.

He hands out the presents until the base of the tree is bare. Then we all start ripping paper. Mum smiles at the pair of silver earrings I bought her, putting them in straight away. I got Dad a book, and he starts reading it as soon as he opens it. Daniel laughs at his metal Slinky, and I grin.

"Open your presents, Katie," Daniel says.

I rip open the parcel from my brother. It's a beautiful pen and a new set of headphones. I pick up my present from Mum and Dad, smiling because I think it's another notebook or journal. It's definitely shaped like one, although it must be in a box. Maybe it's a writing set.

"Have you looked at your results yet?" Mum asks.

I slip my finger under the edge of the wrapping paper. "No, and I told you, I don't want to."

"Well, we think you should," Dad says.

I look up at him and frown. "You looked?"

"We're so proud of you, honey." Mum's grin is so wide she's going to split her cheeks.

"You looked?" I ask again. "When you knew I didn't want to?"

"Katie," Dad says. "You got in the top two percent of the state."

"Open your present," Mum says. "We got you something special for doing so well."

I should be happy that I got such good marks, but does any of it even matter? I look down at the package in my hands, my finger still under the edge of the wrapping paper. What have they bought me? It does feel heavier than a normal notebook. I frown and rip the paper back, letting it fall to the floor.

I stare at the box with a picture of a small laptop on it.

"That's a pretty awesome present," Daniel says.

My mouth drops open. I'm not sure what to say. I've never had my own computer. I'm lucky I have a phone.

"We thought you could use it for uni," Mum says. "You'll need something to do your assignments on."

"Thank you." I don't say anything else, because I don't want to sound ungrateful, but how can they afford this? We already have a computer; I can use that. I turn the box over to look at the details and a folded piece of paper falls into my lap. I pick it up. "What's this?"

"You got into Newcastle and Macquarie Universities." Mum's grin widens.

I stare at the letters. "You opened my mail as well?"

"Honey, you need to make your decision before it's too late."

I set the computer box on the floor and the letters on

top of it, then stand. "You had no right to open my mail."

Dad gets to his feet. "Now, hang on a minute. We've given you space after what happened with Levi and Josephine, but you need to step up, Katherine. We have every right to make sure your future is secure."

"By expecting me to do something I don't want to?" I yell.

"What do you mean?" Mum asks as she gets to her feet as well.

"Law or medicine, Mum." Tears prick my eyes and heat seeps into my cheeks. "I've never been allowed another choice."

"But … that's what you always wanted to do." Mum frowns.

"No." I shake my head. "It's what *you* want me to do."

"If not a lawyer or a doctor, then what?" Dad asks.

Air puffs out of my mouth in short breaths. "You have no idea, do you? You've never actually asked me what I want to do with my life, until now."

"Katie, calm down," Daniel says from his seat on the floor.

"I don't want to be calm," I shout. "All my life I've tried to be better than I really am. I've tried to fit in with what everyone else wants, and be who everyone wants me to be. I'm smart, so I must want to use my brains for a high-profile, highly academic career. What about what *I* want?"

"Tell us, Katie," Dad says. "Tell us what you want."

"Right now, I want Levi to get better." Tears stream down my cheeks, and I clench my fingers. "I want him to wake up, and I want to hear his voice. Until then, I can't think about the future."

Mum takes a step towards me, her face twisted into a teary grimace. "Katie ..."

I turn away from her and run to the front door, yanking it open. I don't stop to put my shoes on, racing across the grass and through the garden bed to Levi's yard. I hurry down the side of his house, the rough ground cutting into my bare feet, but I don't care. I keep going, my vision blurry from my tears, until I reach the treehouse.

At the top of the steps I haul myself onto the platform and crawl to the little table in the corner. I swipe at my eyes to clear them, then pull a chair out and sit. My lungs heave as I take deep breaths to try and calm myself, but I can't. It's all too much.

I look out at the morning sunlight through the branches of the tree. A light breeze tousles the leaves, and shadows dance on the ground below. I stare at the way they move sporadically, and I feel that chaos in the pit of my stomach.

A sob rises into my chest, and I squeeze my eyes closed. I try not to let it free, but I can't help it. My mouth opens, and out comes a sound so heartbreaking it makes me cry harder. My shoulders shake, and I grip the edge of the table. I shove it, releasing a burst of anger, and it bangs against the wall. I pound my fist on the tabletop, and the impact vibrates up my arm. I hit it again, with both fists this time, again, and again, and again, until my hands ache. But still, it's not enough.

The pain is not enough.

I need something else to hurt just as much as my heart.

I kneel on the floor and grab the chair, swinging it so it hits one of the walls. It makes a loud crash, but it doesn't break. I swing again, and again, and the chair cracks. One more swing and a leg catches on the curtains, ripping them down. I crawl along the floor, looping my fingers into any hole I can find in the fabric, and tearing until the curtains are shredded.

Blood drips onto the floor from a cut on my index finger. I sit on the wood, rest my hands in my lap, and stare at them, my shoulders heaving from the effort and the tears. Why is everything so hard? In frustration, I kick out with my legs and knock the table. It topples onto its side.

My breath catches in my throat at the sight of the shoebox in the corner.

Levi's letters.

I stare at the box for a while, waiting for my heartbeat to slow, and my breathing to even out. After a couple of minutes, I wipe my hands on what's left of the curtains. The cut on my finger stings, and I suck on it. The coppery taste of my blood fills my mouth.

"Katie?" Daniel says, and I look over the edge of the platform.

"I don't want to talk right now," I say.

He stares up at me. "I just want to make sure—"

"That I'm okay?" I snort. "No. I'm not."

"Please come back inside." Daniel glances towards our house. "Mum's taken the cookies out of the oven."

I move away from the edge so I don't have to look at my brother. "Maybe later. Please go away."

Daniel doesn't reply. I listen for a few heartbeats then I crawl to the corner and retrieve the shoebox, sitting with my back against the wall with the box in my lap.

"What happened in here?" Daniel comes into the treehouse and sits with his legs hanging over the edge.

"I did a little remodelling," I say.

Daniel smiles but it doesn't reach his eyes, and his sadness radiates from him like the pain must be radiating from me. I rest my hands on top of the shoebox and study my brother. Sisterly intuition tells me he's worried about something other than me.

"You read any of those yet?" He points to the box.

I shake my head. "Daniel … are you … is there something you want to talk about?"

"Are you changing the subject?"

"No." I cross my legs under me and set the box to the side. "I can tell when something's bothering you."

"I'm worried about you, Katie."

I shake my head again. "It's not that. Tell me. You already know everything that's bothering me."

Daniel chuckles. "Yeah."

We stare at each other for a moment.

"Seriously," I say. "You can talk to me."

Daniel takes a deep breath, and adjusts his position on the edge of the platform. "It's Jess. She's … in a really bad place."

"Her sister died," I say. "I think she's allowed to be."

"She won't look in the mirror. She says every time she does, all she sees is Josie. And she's been having, like mini breakdowns. Bursts of violence." Daniel runs a hand down his face.

I look around the treehouse. "I can relate to that."

"This is different. She … she smashed a mirror the other day and cut her hands."

"Oh … I hadn't noticed."

We both go silent.

I've been too caught up in myself and Levi.

I'm a terrible friend.

"Does she talk to you?" Daniel asks. "About Josie? About anything?"

I pull my knees up to my chest and hug my legs. "No. We mostly hang out and listen to music. She's like she was last week when we were all there. She talks, but she hasn't told me anything about … that night. Or about how she's feeling."

"Jess blames herself." Daniel stares at his hands and picks at his fingernails. "She said she and Josie had a big fight over something. Josie wouldn't have gone out otherwise."

"Jess wasn't driving," I say. "She can't blame herself. She can't control other people's actions."

Daniel shrugs. "I've tried to tell her that." He looks up at me and his eyes are red. "I don't know how to help her."

"You really care about Jess?" I press my lips together. "When did this happen? How did I miss it?"

"You've been pretty caught up in your own stuff."

I glance down at the shoebox. "I guess I have."

"Are you coming home now? It's Christmas, and I want to spend it with my sister."

I tuck my hair behind my ear. "Give me fifteen minutes. I need to clean up in here."

Daniel nods and shuffles down onto the treehouse steps. "See you in a bit."

I watch my brother walk across Levi's backyard, then I set to work putting everything back. The chair will need some glue, but I'll worry about that later. I push the table into the corner, tuck the chairs under it, and rehang the curtains. They look worse than they did before. Now they have big tears in them, and some blood stains courtesy of the cut on my finger. The last item to put back is the shoebox.

I stare at the box on the floor of the treehouse. It needs to go under the table again, but I can't help opening it to take another look inside. I pull out the letter at the back of the box. The one with the oldest date on it. The date of Mason's death. I want to read it. It is addressed to me, so I should be allowed to, but will Levi be upset?

Would I be upset if he found and read a box of letters I'd written to him?

Maybe.

What if Levi read my journal? Would I be angry?

I run my finger over my name on the front of the envelope. I'm pretty sure I'd be devastated if Levi read my journal without asking, but even if he did read it, I don't have any dark secrets. I just write to make sense of my life and what's happened to me over the years. Maybe Levi wrote to me to try and do the same.

The envelope isn't sealed. I open the flap and carefully pull out the piece of paper that's inside. Then I settle back against the wall to read.

Dear Katie,

Mason died today.

That's probably not the best way to start a letter, but it's the truth. I've learnt the hard way that the truth really hurts.

Some other things that are true: I regret ignoring you.

I regret thinking I'm better than you. I want to climb in your window. I so badly want to talk to you. I need you. I miss you.

I know it's my fault that we're not friends anymore, and I wish I could change that, but I don't know how. You have every right to never speak to me again. And I haven't tried to fix things because I'm so scared you'll tell me no. That you'll tell me you don't want me in your life. It kills me to see you every day and not be able to talk to you like I used to.

I have so much to tell you.

Like how Mum and Dad fight all the time. And how it's my fault Mason is dead. Dad can't even look me in the eye. He's angry. I don't like being in the house, but now it's worse. I'm worried about Mum.

I so badly want to talk to you. I have no one to tell my secrets to.

I miss the way you used to listen.

I miss how you always knew what to say.

I miss your laugh.

I miss your smile.

I miss everything about you.

When I saw you after Mum told you all that he'd died, I wanted to tell you how beautiful you looked. I wanted to tell you that the look in your eyes at knowing my brother is dead explained exactly what I'm feeling. Because I know you must be hurting as well. I know you love my brother, too, and that losing him hurts more than words can describe.

I wanted to hold you, and cry in your arms, and mourn my brother with you. I wanted to tell you that life is too short to let go of the people we love.

Because I love you.

I love you, Katherine Sullivan.

And I will probably never get to tell you that.

I hope one day I can, because walking away from you is the biggest regret of my life.

I want to tell you everything, but now I'm afraid you won't listen, or you won't know what to say.

Levi.

A tear runs down my cheek and splashes onto the paper, marking it and making the ink run. The L in Levi's name blurs. I quickly fold the letter back in half and slip it into the envelope. Why didn't Levi give me this letter? Why didn't he talk to me? I would have listened to him. If only he had told me what he was going through, maybe finding my way back to Levi wouldn't have been so hard.

That stupid game

The rest of Christmas Day passed in a blur. Mum and Dad stepped around me, pretending nothing had happened, and we had our traditional family meal with ham, prawns, and pavlova for dessert. I fell into bed, exhausted physically and emotionally, and I didn't sleep well thinking about Levi's letters. I didn't read any more. I really want to ask him about them first.

Now it's New Year's Eve, and I'm sitting in the hard plastic chair beside Levi's bed, waiting for him to wake up enough to talk to me. He's improved over the past few days, having more periods of semi-consciousness. They're mostly in the mornings before visiting hours start, so by the time I get here he's already had his medication. He's opened his eyes a couple of times, but never long enough to focus on me.

Karen is back from her aunt's place, and we're going into the city for Veronica's party tonight, but I couldn't go without seeing Levi first. The nurses joke that I've become a permanent fixture in his room, and soon they'll have to start dusting me.

"I have to go soon," I say to Levi, squeezing his hand. "We're going into the city for New Year's. I wish you could come." I go quiet, waiting for a response, but as usual, there isn't one.

I've already told Levi about Christmas, and what happened with Mum and Dad, but I left out the part where I read one of his letters. I feel guilty, as if I've invaded his private thoughts. Which I have.

"I don't think I told you the other day that I went to the treehouse again. On Christmas morning." I chew my lip. "I was so upset at Mum and Dad, and I wanted to be close to you. I didn't know where else to go." Levi's eyelids flutter, and I lean forward. "Can you hear me, Levi?"

I wait again, but he's still.

"I had a ... an outburst. One of the chairs will need fixing, and there're some holes in the curtains ... Anyway, I ... I read one of your letters." I stop again and press my forehead to the bedrail. The metal is cool against my skin. "Please don't be angry with me. But I want you to know, from now on, I will always listen."

A tear rolls down my cheek and splashes onto the bed sheet. I stare at the small wet mark, and take a deep breath before sitting up straight in the chair.

"I have to go, okay? I'll come and see you tomorrow. Next year." I smile and squeeze his hand, then get to my feet.

The door opens and Karen sticks her head in. "You

ready?"

"Ready." I nod, then follow my best friend out of the hospital and to the car.

We haven't had a chance to talk much with her being away, so I haven't told Karen about what happened. I don't get the chance though, because Karen's mouth is going a million miles an hour, telling me about her Christmas.

"Sounds like you had a great time," I say, smiling.

"Have you packed anything for tonight yet?" Karen asks as we merge onto the motorway.

I raise my eyebrows at her. "It's one night. I'm sure I can grab something when we get to my place."

She shakes her head. "What am I going to do with you?"

I chuckle and stare out the window for the rest of the ride home. When we reach my house, Karen and I grab a quick sandwich for lunch before heading to my room. We don't have to be on the train to the city until later, so I sit on the bed and watch Karen pack my carry-on suitcase with a heap of stuff I won't need.

"One night." I stare at Karen. "Which word do you not understand?"

"A girl needs to be prepared." She folds three tops and puts them in the case on top of my jeans.

"I'm sure I'll only need one change of clothes, my pyjamas, and my toothbrush."

Karen tsks at me. "Phone, purse, keys, contacts, makeup."

"All in my tote bag already."

Karen raises her eyebrows. "Lip gloss does not count as makeup."

"Fine, I'll get my powder, but that's it." I push off the bed and go to the door. "We're staying in a hotel overlooking the harbour. I don't think we'll be going anywhere."

"Get your eyeliner as well." Karen smiles.

I roll my eyes and go down the hall to the bathroom, grabbing my small makeup bag. I may as well take the whole thing. That way Karen will leave me alone.

Back in my room I change into my denim skirt and a clean singlet top, then we jump in the car to go to Karen's.

My phone buzzes with a message as she pulls into her driveway. Karen parks in front of the double garage, and we both get out of the car.

"I'll be five minutes," Karen says, popping the boot with the button on the car keys. "Then we can walk up to the train."

"Sure." I wave a hand at her and look at my phone. "Message from Mum."

I haven't spoken to Mum or Dad much since my fight with them on Christmas Day. I'm still upset that Mum opened my mail. I stare at her message.

Mum: Have a nice time 2night

Even though she said exactly the same thing to me this morning before I left the house, her message makes me smile.

Me: Okay

Mum: See you next year :)

I laugh out loud and smile wider, because I not too long ago said the same thing to Levi.

Me: Funny

Mum: Stay safe. Don't drink too much

Me: Stop worrying

Mum: It's my job

Mum: I love you

Me: I know. Luv U2

"Ready?" Karen asks.

"Hang on." I put my phone away and go around to the back of the car to grab my little case before closing the boot. "Let's go."

Karen and I walk the short distance to the train station, our suitcases bumping along the cracks in the footpath. We jump on the first train to the city, and settle into some seats upstairs for the forty-five-minute journey.

"How was your Christmas?" Karen asks.

I stare at her and bite my lip. "I had a fight with Mum and Dad and ran out of the house."

"Ouch. What was it about?"

I sigh. "Uni letters."

"You still haven't opened them?"

I tuck my hair behind my ear and look out the window. "Mum did it for me. I was so angry."

"So you read them? You need to decide which one you want to go to."

I look back at Karen and her raised eyebrows. "Yes, I eventually read them. I've been accepted into law at Newcastle and medicine at Macquarie. But you know I applied at the Sydney College of the Arts for a fine arts degree. They haven't sent me a letter yet."

"Well, maybe you can reapply to do fine arts at Newcastle, and we can go to uni together." Karen smiles.

"There's no way Mum will agree to let me do anything arts-based. She doesn't think my career opportunities will be good enough ... I really want to go to SCA. I didn't tell Mum and Dad I applied." I shrug. "I don't want to do law or medicine and I figured if I got into SCA, I could convince them somehow. But I can't do that without an acceptance letter."

Karen folds her arms and huffs. "You shouldn't have to keep her happy."

"Tell her that. It doesn't matter anyway. If I was going to get in I would've gotten my letter by now."

Karen nudges my shoulder. "It'll work out."

I offer her a small smile, then look out the window for the rest of the trip. I hope everything does work out, but right now it doesn't seem promising. All I want to do is focus on having a good time on the last night of the year.

The train pulls into North Sydney Station and we get off, making our way out to the street. The hotel Veronica has booked is a five-minute walk, so we roll our cases down the hill until we reach the front driveway. I tell the receptionist we're with Veronica Porter and give her our names.

She smiles with her lips closed. "ID please." We both flash our drivers' licenses while she taps on her keyboard. She hands me a room key. "Floor eleven. Enjoy your stay."

"Thank you." I smile back then follow Karen to the lifts.

"She didn't look too impressed," Karen says as we get in.

I press number eleven. "Would you be if you had to work tonight?"

"I guess not."

We get out on the eleventh floor and follow the signs to the room. We stop outside and I glance at Karen.

"Let's get this party started." She smiles.

I have a room key, but I don't want to be rude, so I raise my hand and knock on the door. Shuffling and voices sound from inside. Then the door swings open.

"Hello!" Veronica cries. "Welcome to party central. Only fun allowed."

I chuckle and look Veronica up and down. Her cocktail dress and stilettoes make me feel inadequate in my denim skirt and singlet top. With a deep breath, I grin back at her and step into the hotel suite, holding the door for Karen. It clicks closed behind us and I glance around at the sitting room. There's a table set up with snacks and drinks, and streamers hang from the light fittings.

"Chuck your bags in the second bedroom," Veronica says, pointing to a door behind the small dining nook. "Then come join us on the balcony."

I crane my neck to have a look. Rachel is outside standing at the balcony railing, a glass of champagne in her hand. Stacey and Jessica are sitting at a small table and they jump up when they see us, coming inside. A door in the far corner stands slightly ajar.

"Hey." I smile at my friends.

"Yay, you're finally here," Stacey says.

I point to the internal door. "Is there a third bedroom?"

"We have adjoining suites," Veronica says. "Plenty of beds for everyone, although we have to fight over who gets to sleep with the boys."

Karen crosses her arm. "I don't think we'll be fighting."

"I don't think we'll be sleeping." Veronica laughs.

"Tonight is going to be so much fun," Stacey says, clapping her hands like a little kid.

Veronica grins. "That's the plan."

Stacey's smile is so wide it looks like her cheeks are hurting. Jessica is quiet beside her.

Karen and I put our stuff in the bedroom, then join the others on the balcony. Veronica hands us both a glass of champagne. I accept it, but make a mental note to sip it slowly. I don't want to end up drunk again. It wasn't much fun.

"Don't drink that too fast."

I glance over to the neighbouring balcony where Geoff is leaning against the railing, and Jarred is sitting at the small table. Both of them have beers in their hands.

"I'll make sure I don't," I say.

"Wouldn't want you throwing up on anyone," Geoff teases.

I frown. "How do you ... who told you I did that?" I don't remember anyone being there other than my friends and Levi.

"Word travels," Jarred says.

I glance around at my friends. I'm not angry that someone said something, I just don't want to remember that night. It wasn't a very good one.

"It's not like you've never been drunk and done something stupid before." Karen raises her eyebrows at Geoff.

He chuckles. "Fair enough."

"Can we just have a good time tonight?" Veronica says. "Tomorrow is a new year. We can put all the crap from this one behind us."

"I'll drink to that." Stacey raises her glass and takes a sip.

"We need music," Veronica says. She goes inside and comes back out with her phone and a small speaker.

"What should we listen to?"

"Anything," Rachel says, putting her feet up on the railing. "As long as it's loud."

She glances at me and scoffs before turning back to her drink and the view over the harbour. I know Rachel doesn't like me, but Veronica is making an effort, so why can't she? Maybe I'll have the chance to talk to her later on.

We all take seats on the balcony and get comfortable. The boys stay on their side, both of them looking out towards the harbour, drinking their beers. I wish Levi was here to spend the night not only with me, but with them as well. If it meant he was here, I'd share him, and it makes me sad that we're having fun, or at least trying to, without him.

Veronica brings some food out, and we sit and watch the boats on the harbour. It really is a great view, and despite Levi not being here, I'm actually looking forward to seeing the fireworks tonight. I've never come into the city to see them. Usually I'm home on the lounge watching the nine pm fireworks, then I fall into bed minutes after the second round ends at midnight. I'm actually excited about seeing them up close and in person, and getting to hear them, instead of listening to the bangs filtered through the TV.

Veronica cranks the music, and I'm happy to sit and listen, watching people walk around below, getting ready and finding places to sit for the night.

"Thank you," I say to Veronica. "For ..." I wave my hand, "... all this."

"No worries, bitch." She grins, and I laugh.

For a few hours we sit and talk, listen to music, watch

the harbour, eat food, and drink. I pace myself, but by quarter to nine, some of the others haven't been as careful.

Rachel is a sleepy, giggly drunk, and with fifteen minutes until the first round of fireworks, I figure now is a good time to talk to her. She gets up to go inside for another drink, and I follow. I make myself look busy grabbing some food from the table. Rachel sways on her feet as she pours herself another glass of champagne.

"You want some food as well?" I ask, filling a bowl with a fresh packet of chips.

"Okay." She smiles.

I look at her for a few seconds then open my mouth, but I have no idea what to say. She's so different to me, and I feel inadequate somehow, like I'm not good enough to be standing next to her.

I hold the chips out to her. "Here you go."

"Thanks." She sticks her hand in and stuffs some food in her mouth.

I follow Rachel back to the balcony, shaking my head at myself, and plonk into a seat beside Karen. *That was successful.*

"What's the matter?" Karen asks.

"Huh? Nothing, why?"

"Your face is all screwed up." Karen gestures with her hand.

I flick my gaze towards Rachel then lower my voice. "Just … thought I could talk to her, you know. And … nothing."

"Don't sweat it." Karen pinches a chip from my hand.

"Two minutes," Geoff calls from the boys' balcony.

Those who are sitting get up, and we all try to squish

together along the balcony rail. There's not enough room for six of us. Jessica is beside me so I grab her hand and pull her inside.

"There's more room next door," I say.

She follows me through to the adjoining suite, and we go onto the balcony with the boys. Geoff looks at me sideways, and Jarred frowns, but I'm not sure if it's aimed at me or Jessica.

Soon, the sky is filled with bursts of colour in red, blue, yellow, and white. I grip the railing and tilt my head back, taking it all in. Bangs echo over the harbour. The murmur of traffic and voices drift up from below, drowned out with every new explosion. A light breeze pushes my hair away from my face, and I smile. For a moment I'm lost in the fireworks display. My mind is blank, and I concentrate on the beauty of it all. Then the last sparks fall, and I'm pulled back to reality.

I glance at Jessica beside me. She's staring at the water, her eyes glistening.

Geoff pushes off the railing and sits at the small table. "I hope the midnight show is better than that."

"It always is," Jessica whispers beside me.

Jarred frowns, and looks at Jessica before going to sit with Geoff. Something is going on between them, but I have no idea what. It's as if Jarred is angry at her for something. Why would he be though? Jessica hasn't done anything to anyone.

I lean into her, gently nudging her shoulder. "Midnight will be awesome. You know, I've never seen the New Year's fireworks up close."

"It's been a couple of years since I have," Jessica says.

"The last time was with Josie. Mum and Dad let us come to the city on our own." A tear slips down her cheek and she swipes it away.

"I remember that," I say. "I wanted to come with you, but I wasn't allowed."

Jessica takes a shaky breath, and she puts her head on my shoulder. "I miss her."

"I know." I put my arm around her shoulders

"It's my fault she's dead."

"Don't be silly. It was an accident," I say. "You weren't even there."

"I'm the reason she was out."

Jarred scoffs from the table. When I look at him, he shakes his head, and takes a long draw from his beer. He stares at me over the top of his can.

"It's still not your fault," I say.

Jarred gets up and goes inside.

"The last thing I said to her was ..." Jessica's breathing hitches. "I called her a bitch, Katie." She pulls away from me and grips the railing, turning towards the lights of the bridge so I can't see her face.

"Hey, what're you doing over there?" Karen calls from the other balcony. "Come back. We have more food."

"Hang on," I call. I touch Jessica's elbow. "You didn't mean it. Josie loved you, and she'd hate to see you like this. Let's go eat something. You might feel better with food in your stomach."

She turns back to me and nods. I follow her through the door into the suite. Jarred immediately goes outside to the balcony again. *What is going on?*

I glance at my friend then out to Jarred. "What's up

with him?"

Jessica opens her mouth to speak, then snaps it shut again. She shakes her head and takes a quick look at Jarred. "Nothing. Don't worry about it."

"Okay, but you know you can talk to me, yeah?"

Jessica smiles with pursed lips. "Of course."

We go next door to where the other girls are gathered around the small dining table. It's covered with open pizza boxes, and my stomach rumbles.

"More champagne," Rachel cries, grabbing three slices of pizza and her full glass before going out to the balcony.

Veronica rolls her eyes. "I have a feeling I'll be picking her up off the floor soon." She takes a slice, following Rachel.

Jessica puts a slice of pizza on a napkin. She sits on the couch, squishing herself into the corner and tucking her legs underneath herself.

"Jess okay?" Karen whispers before stuffing her mouth with food.

I shake my head. "She still thinks Josie dying is her fault. And there's something going on with Jarred. He's … acting weird and broody around her."

"Jess said she had a huge fight with Josie the night she died." Stacey glances over at our friend on the couch. "She won't give me any details though."

"Daniel said she told him the same thing, but no details either," I say.

"She'll talk to us when she's ready." Karen picks up her glass. "I'm getting a refill."

Stacey and I do the same, and we spend the next couple of hours sipping our drinks, eating too much food, and watching the world go by out on the harbour. Rachel falls asleep in a chair around a quarter to twelve.

"She's going to miss the fireworks," Stacey says.

"If I hadn't switched to vodka and Coke, I think I'd miss them, too." Karen looks at us with droopy eyes.

"We should draw on her face," Veronica says.

"I'll get a pen." I giggle and jump up from my seat. The balcony moves, and I stumble a step, giggling again.

"You're drunk," Karen says.

I straighten. "Am not." But when I go to walk it's not as easy as it should be.

"Hurry up and come back. The fireworks are on soon. And get Jess out here."

I go inside, the pen forgotten, but Jessica isn't on the lounge where she's been since dinner. I glance around, then shuffle towards the bedroom. Maybe she went to sleep.

"Katie, come on," Stacey calls. "Five minutes."

I open one bedroom door and flick the light on, but Jessica isn't in there. I check the other bedroom, but she's not in there either. Then I hear voices. Someone yells, but I can't make out the words. My head is a little fuzzy from all the champagne, even though I've tried to pace myself, but I feel happy and floaty. I pull the bedroom door closed.

"Katie!" Karen calls. "Hurry up."

Voices sound again.

The door to the adjoining suite is slightly open, and I walk towards it. Maybe Jessica went next door to talk to the boys. The voices get louder, and when I reach the door I can finally make out the words.

"What you did was a low move," Jarred says. "You deserve everything you get."

I suck in a breath. *What did Jessica do?*

"Katie!" Karen yells again. "Countdown is on."

Voices chant in the background. *Seven, six, five …* but I block them out.

I grip the edge of the door and pull it open.

Fireworks explode. Karen and the girls on the balcony behind me cheer. Bursts of colour flash through the sky. The combination of loud voices and banging hurts my head.

"I'm so sorry." Jessica stands in the middle of the sitting room, tears coursing down her cheeks, the fireworks making them glow.

Jarred has his back to me, his fists clenched at his sides. "Tell that to your dead sister."

I quickly glance around the room. Geoff is on the balcony, leaning his forearms on the railing. His head hangs as if he's staring down at the ground.

"I thought you knew it was me," Jessica says.

"I did, eventually, but …" Jarred grips his hair with one hand. "I expected you to stop."

What the hell happened?"

"Then how can you blame me if you knew?" Jessica steps towards Jarred, her face crumpled. I've never heard her raise her voice like this.

"Because you're the one who agreed to the dare," Jarred yells.

Oh no. There was another dare? What was Jessica dared to do? Who dared her? Do I want to know? Whatever it was, Josephine wound up dead because of it.

Fuck! Everything comes back to that stupid game.

8

Thick and fast

I stand in the doorway staring at Jessica and Jarred. Fireworks continue to explode behind them. Neither of them has seen me—they're too fixated on glaring at each other.

"Katie?" Karen says at my side. "You missed the countdown. What's going on?"

Jessica's gaze meets mine, and she swipes the tears from her cheeks. I go into the room, not answering Karen. Jessica's sister died, and Levi ended up in the hospital.

Because of a dare.

"I can't believe you're still playing that game!" I yell. "What happened, Jess?"

She closes her eyes and cries harder. I want to comfort her, because she's my friend and she's hurting, but after what I went through with Levi, why would she have agreed to play?

Geoff comes in from the balcony and stands in the doorway, his face marred with a deep frown.

Jarred turns around and faces me. "Josie should never have been in that car." Then he grabs his keys off the coffee table and heads for the door.

"Jarred, stop," I say.

Has he been drinking? We've all been drinking. He can't drive if he's been drinking. Does he have his car here? Why would he bring his car to the city? So many questions fill my head in seconds, and my mind goes fuzzy.

"What?" he asks.

"Don't drive," I say. "Don't … don't drink and drive."

Jarred picks up a backpack that's sitting beside the dining table. He doesn't respond with anything more than a small nod, then he leaves.

Geoff runs a hand down his face. Then he lashes out at the wall beside him, punching it. He leaves a red smear on the rendered concrete.

"This is so fucked up." He grabs his stuff and follows Jarred.

"What's happening in here?" Stacey asks from the doorway to the other suite.

"I have no idea." Karen throws her hands in the air and sits on the couch.

"Jess?" Stacey walks towards her. "What happened?"

Jessica's shoulders heave, and she shakes her head, looking down at her feet. "Can we go home?" Her voice is barely a whisper. "I can't do this anymore." She drops to her knees, then lies down and curls into a ball.

"How about we get you to bed," Stacey says, kneeling

beside her. "The boys are gone so we can sleep in here. Tomorrow will be better, I promise. And we can go home first thing." Stacey helps Jessica to her feet and they start towards one of the bedrooms. "We'll see you all in the morning." They go in and close the door.

"Well ..." Karen gets to her feet. "I think this party's over. I'm going to bed, too." She raises her eyebrows at me, and I'm pretty sure she wants me to go with her so we can talk about what the hell is going on.

I follow her back into our suite. Rachel is still outside, asleep in the chair. Veronica is sitting at the dining table, picking at the leftover food.

"Sounded intense in there," she says. "I didn't want to interrupt."

"Jarred and Geoff left," I say. "Jarred's pretty pissed at Jess. Something about her doing a dare, and that's why Levi and Josie had their accident. You know anything about that?"

"If you think I had anything to do with it, then you're wrong." Veronica sits up straight in her chair.

"Who did then?" Karen asks. "And what the hell was she dared to do?"

Veronica stares at both of us and sighs. "The day we all came home from Surfers, Josie dared Jess to twin swap with her."

"Why would she do that?" I ask. "And why were you even playing truth or dare in the first place?"

"We weren't. It was more of a spur-of-the-moment thing." Veronica munches on a pizza crust. "None of us knew about it. Josie wanted to see if they could pull it off. If any of us would notice. Apparently, they switched at the airport up there. Then Jess came with us, and Josie went home with Stacey."

"That's crazy," Karen says, dropping into a seat at the table. "Did it work?"

"Mostly … It took me a while, but Josie is … was … one of my closest friends. By the time we landed in Sydney, I knew it was Jess with us." Veronica glances outside at Rachel asleep in the chair. "Rach is too caught up in herself to notice anything. Ever."

I rub my temples, trying to get my thoughts around what Veronica is telling us. Too much champagne has made my head ache. Jessica and Josephine twin swapped? They've done it before, but one of them must have done something bad for them to have had a huge fight after. I sit at the table next to Karen.

"Then what happened?" Karen asks, leaning towards Veronica.

"Josie and Stacey were on a different flight to ours, so Jess went home with Jarred. Josie called me when she got home. She said Stacey was clueless, and she wanted to know if I'd figured it out, but she also asked where Jess was." Veronica shrugs. "I told her she went with Jarred. I don't know what went down after that. The twins obviously fought about something big though, and my money is on Jess and Jarred …" Veronica bites her lip, makes an O with the thumb and finger on her left hand, then moves her right index finger in and out of it.

"No," I say. "Jess would never do that to her sister."

Veronica shrugs again. "I guess we'll never know unless she tells one of us."

I shake my head. "This is so messed up."

"Yeah," Karen says beside me. "I think I need to sleep now. Too much excitement for one night."

Sleep is probably what we all need. Rachel already seems pretty comfortable out on the balcony. Veronica gets up and stumbles out there, shaking Rachel's shoulder until she stirs. She helps her friend inside and they disappear into the first bedroom. I grab my bag and go to the bathroom to wash my face and take my contacts out, then Karen and I crawl under the covers of the double bed in the second bedroom.

"I hope Jess didn't do what Veronica thinks she did," Karen says. She lies on her side, facing me, and tucks her hand under her head.

"I hope so, too." I sigh.

"Happy New Year." Karen blows me a kiss then rolls over.

I lie on my back and stare at the ceiling, wishing I was in my own bed. Within minutes, Karen is snoring softly. I close my eyes and try to sleep, but my mind is racing with too many thoughts, and I open them again.

Why did Josephine want to twin swap with Jessica? Why did Jessica agree? If they hadn't done any of this, would Josephine still be alive? Would Levi never have hit her car?

I squeeze my eyes shut and pinch the bridge of my nose. When did everything become so messed up? At what point did my life, and the lives of my friends, start to fall apart? If one event changed, or didn't happen at all, would we be somewhere else right now?

What if Josephine didn't die?

What if Levi was fine?

What if everything had happened differently?

What if?

My brain goes over the past six months, over and over, each time remembering something different. I'm not sure how long I lie here unable to sleep. I think I drift off a few times, but my thoughts always bring me back.

Light seeps into the sky outside, and Karen stirs beside me. I feel like I've had no sleep, but the only thing I want to do is go home.

I carefully get out of bed, trying not to wake Karen, and use the bathroom before going onto the balcony to watch the sunrise. Jessica is sitting in a seat on the other balcony, slumped down with her feet up on the railing.

"You couldn't sleep either?" I ask, moving a chair so I can sit at the end closest to her.

She shakes her head. "I don't sleep much at all these days."

I let her voice drift out into the morning noise before I reply, "Do you want to talk about anything?"

Jessica looks over at me. Her eyes are rimmed with red. "I'm not sure I can get the words out and make any sense." She pauses, and her eyes go vacant. "None of it makes any sense."

"Maybe you should write it down. I find writing in my journal helps with a lot of stuff."

Jessica looks away again, gazing out towards the bridge. "Maybe."

We sit for a while, listening to the commotion below, and watch as the sun lights up the horizon. Its rays spread across the city, showering diamonds of light onto the harbour. For a moment I feel at peace, watching nature's beautiful display.

"Every day is a fresh start," I say, then I look over at Jessica. She takes a deep breath. "It has to be better than the last, right?"

"Who wants to go home?" Karen asks, coming onto the balcony and stretching.

"I think home sounds fantastic." I get up and put the chair back at the table. "Want to train it with us?" I ask Jessica.

She nods. "I'll have a shower, and see what Stacey's doing."

We're all a bit slow this morning, and by the time we've had our showers, packed our stuff, helped Veronica clean up a bit, and thanked her, the four of us don't make it home until almost lunchtime.

Karen and I say goodbye to Stacey and Jessica at the station, then walk back to Karen's place before jumping in the car to go to mine.

"How was your night?" Mum washes some lettuce in the colander, then wipes her hands on a towel before facing us. Karen and I sit at the kitchen bench.

"All right," I say.

"The fireworks were awesome," Karen adds.

"You didn't get up to too much mischief I hope." Mum smiles, then turns back to the chopping board. "What are your plans for the rest of the day?"

I lean my elbows on the counter, and rest my chin on my hand. "Going to see Levi."

Mum puts down the knife she's been using to cut the tomatoes. "Maybe you should go over your uni letters and decide what you're going to do. You don't have long until final enrolment is due."

I sit up straight in my seat. "Maybe ... I was thinking I could take a year off."

"A year off what?" Dad asks, coming into the kitchen from outside.

"Everything," I say. "Defer for a year."

"In order for you to defer, you have to make a decision about which university you're going to attend," Mum says, putting her hands on her hips. "And the answer is no. You're not taking a year off."

Karen is quiet beside me, and I bet she's wishing she wasn't here.

I stare at my hands, and twist my fingers together. "Jess is going to."

"You're not Jessica," Dad says. "You haven't been through what she has."

No, but my life hasn't been a walk in the park either.

"Katie, you've worked so hard," Mum says. "Don't throw it away now."

"You think all my hard work equals a high profile career as a lawyer or a doctor?" I ask.

"Well, yes." Mum folds her arms over her chest. "And if you take a year off you'll be twelve months behind."

"I don't want to study law. And after what happened with Levi and Josie, there's no way I'm doing medicine." I jump up from my seat.

Dad comes around the counter to stand beside Mum. "Tell us what you want to do, honey."

"I want to do a fine arts degree, and I applied at SCA as my first choice above everything else. But I haven't received a letter from them."

Mum presses her lips into a thin line. She drops her gaze from mine, then walks past me to the sideboard in the dining room. She comes back with an envelope in her hand and passes it to me.

I take it from her, trying to read her expression. When I look down at the envelope, it has the Sydney College of the Arts logo on it.

The letter I've been waiting for.

I turn the letter over. It's been opened. I shake my head and pull the paper out. I've been accepted, but when I read further, I've missed the interview cut-off date.

"Why didn't you give this to me?" I look up at Mum. "It's my life. You had no right!"

I throw the letter onto the bench and storm out, grabbing my tote bag on my way to the front door. I'm tired of trying to live up to everyone's expectations. Why can't I make my own decisions?

The sun is hot on my face as I run across the front yard to the road. I really wish I had my own car—then I could go anywhere I wanted to. But instead I have to rely on everyone else for everything.

"Arrrggghhh!" I scream at the sky and stamp my foot.

Josephine is dead.

One of my closest friends is falling apart.

Levi is still in hospital.

And my parents are trying to control my life.

I just want to run away from everything.

I adjust the strap of my tote bag on my shoulder, hang my toes off the edge of the kerb, and look up the street.

"Want a lift somewhere?" Karen asks.

I turn to my best friend. "Can you take me to the

hospital, if it's not too much trouble?"

Karen comes over and puts an arm around my shoulders. "Nothing for you is ever too much trouble. Get in."

I slide into the front passenger seat and buckle my belt. Mum is standing at the front door as we pull away from the kerb. I'll have to face her and Dad again later, but hopefully I'll have calmed down by then.

"They'll come around," Karen says, turning onto the highway.

"It's not that," I say. "It's too late anyway. I've missed the interview, so I'll have to settle for one of the other unis."

"You shouldn't settle for anything."

I shrug and stare out the window the rest of the trip, not really in the mood to talk about it with Karen. I want to tell Levi what's happened, even if he doesn't talk back.

Karen parks the car on the street outside the hospital. "Want me to come with?"

"Do you want to?"

She smiles. "I know you probably have a lot you want to tell him."

"Yeah, but I like having you around."

"Let's go then."

We get out of the car and take the familiar walk into the hospital and to the ICU. I use the phone at the door, and the nurse at the desk lets us in. When we reach Levi's room, he already has visitors. Jessica is standing next to Levi's bed with Daniel at her side. As far as I know, it's the first time Jessica has come to the hospital.

"Hi girls," Yvonne says, coming over from the water fountain.

"Hi." I turn to her. "Happy New Year. How is he?"

"Since yesterday? Not much change." She looks through the window at her son. "But they say he should be fully conscious any day now."

I look through the window, too. "When did Daniel and Jess get here?"

"Not long ago," Yvonne says. "Maybe ten minutes?"

Daniel wasn't home when we were there, so he must have met up with Jessica and brought her straight here.

"Jess … is she … Are you okay with …" I stop and take a breath, looking at Yvonne. "You don't mind her being here?"

Yvonne smiles. "No, sweetie. Of course not. I hope seeing Levi helps her somehow. I know she's been struggling."

Yeah, she has. I turn back to the window.

Daniel puts an arm around Jessica's shoulders, but she shrugs him free. She turns with the movement, and I can see the profile of her face. She's crying really hard, and her chest heaves. Daniel reaches for her again, but she steps back, shaking her head.

"What's going on in there?" Karen asks. "Jess is pretty upset."

"I'll go and see." Yvonne steps around us and opens the door.

"It's all my fault," Jessica screams, her voice piercing the relative quiet of the ICU.

Yvonne takes a few hurried steps forward. "Jess, honey, calm down."

I catch the door before it closes, stopping at the threshold. The rules are only two visitors at a time in Levi's room. There are already three people in there. Karen and I aren't supposed to go in.

"You don't understand," Jessica yells, tears streaming down her cheeks. "It's my fault. I killed my sister. I killed her." She shoves her hands into her hair and pulls, letting out a strangled cry filled with heartache and pain.

I want to go to her, and hold her, and tell her everything will be all right. Yvonne whispers to Jessica in hushed tones, so low I can't make out the words. With a motherly touch, she manages to untangle Jessica's hands from her hair. Karen presses into my side and we both fill the doorway.

"What's happening?" a nurse asks from behind us, but neither of us turn around.

Daniel reaches out to Jessica and pulls her to his chest. She doesn't resist this time, going to him easily. She sobs into his shirt, and he gently moves her away from the bed.

My gaze follows them, then I look at Levi.

My heart skips.

I try to move, but my feet are like lead bricks.

"Levi!" I cry.

He turns his head slowly, and finally I get to look into his eyes.

"Katie?" he asks. "Mum ...? Where am I?"

Yvonne rushes to his side.

Then I stumble into the room, my tears coming thick and fast.

9

My escape

A nurse shoulders past me, and then a doctor and another nurse come into the room.

"Everyone, out," the female nurse says. "There are too many people in here." She gets between me and Levi, and I want to shove her out of the way.

Daniel pulls Jessica towards me. She's still sobbing and trying to get words out.

"Levi, I'm sorry," she says, struggling in Daniel's arms. "It's my fault. It should've been me … My fault … Josie …" She wails, and Daniel manages to get her out the door.

Karen grabs my arm and pulls me back.

"Levi." I try to shake my best friend off and push forward.

"You can talk to him later," the nurse says, forcing me back towards the door. "Right now we need to check him over and keep him calm. You being here isn't helping."

I stumble out of the room and the door is shut in my face. I run to the window, aware of Karen at my side, but I ignore her, too intent on watching Levi through the glass. I press my palm to the cool surface, and search for his face behind the bodies of the medical staff. The doctor leans over him, and the nurses fuss around the machines.

Yvonne is still in the room. She stands back and to the side, a hand covering her mouth. Jessica sobs behind me, and I look over my shoulder at my brother.

He frowns. "Come on, Jess." He rests his chin on top of her head and stares at me. "I'll take you home." Daniel leads her away, and I turn back to the window.

"He'll be okay," Karen says, rubbing my back.

"I want to talk to him." I press my forehead to the glass. "I *need* to talk to him."

A nurse opens the door and comes out.

"Katie?" Levi calls.

"Levi!" I yell.

His lips move and form my name again. "Katie …" He struggles to sit up in bed, but the doctor puts a firm hand on his shoulder and pushes him back.

One of the nurses goes to the drip beside his bed and inserts a syringe into the line. *What are they doing?* I run back to the door and open it, but I'm quickly stopped by the same nurse who forced me out of the room.

"You can't be in here," she says.

"I want to talk to him." I sniffle and stare at her with wide eyes.

"Not yet. He needs to be calm."

Yvonne comes over, and I step back onto the ward. She closes the door behind her, leaving the nurse on the other side. Leaving Levi on the other side.

"Maybe it's best if you come back tomorrow," Yvonne says. My eyes fill with more tears, and everything blurs. She reaches out and rubs my arm. "The doctors say he's under too much stress now that he's fully awake. Everyone being here has made it worse. He can't make any sudden movements." Yvonne looks at me with sympathetic eyes. "Once he's had time to adjust, and I can explain to him what's happened, I think it's best if no one else is here. I don't know what he remembers. If he remembers anything at all. Okay?"

I nod, and suck in a deep breath, letting it out shakily. "I can see him tomorrow?"

"Yes, I'm sure tomorrow will be fine." Yvonne smiles, but her eyes are sad.

"Come on, Katie." Karen leans gently against my shoulder. "I'll drive you home."

Reluctantly, I follow Karen out of the ICU to where we parked the car on the street. I've been waiting for this day since we got back from schoolies—for Levi to finally wake up. Now that it's happened, I can't even talk to him. I have so much to tell him, and so many lost days to make up for.

I get in the car and dump my tote at my feet, leaning my head back against the car seat and closing my eyes. I hope Karen doesn't want to talk on the way home, because I can't. I'm not sure my voice will work without cracking. How can I wait until tomorrow to see Levi?

Tomorrow may never come.

The thought scares me, and I have to take deep breaths to calm myself down.

"Everything all right?" Karen asks as we turn off the highway towards my place. "You look like you're having a panic attack."

I open my eyes and turn to her. "I want to talk to him, Karen. What if something happens and I never get to do that? Tomorrow is so far away. What if—"

"Stop," she says. "Don't do that. If you go there, you'll go crazy. I know life is short, and we've all learnt that first hand recently, but you can't think like that." She pulls into my driveway and turns the car off. "You have to keep believing that tomorrow will come, and it will be better than today."

I nod, and then the tears come again. My shoulders shake as I try to hold them back, but then I let out a sob that rattles my chest and makes my heart ache.

"Oh, sweetie, come here." Karen reaches over and wraps her arms around me. She rubs my back while I cry, and we sit like that for a couple of minutes before she says, "I should get home. You going to be okay?"

I sniffle and pull away. "Yeah, I'm good."

Mum's car is in the driveway, which means she's home, and I remember our argument this morning about uni, and me running out. I squeeze my eyes closed for a second, then get out of the car and walk to the front door, waving to Karen when I reach the step. I hope Mum's not on the defensive, because I'm not in the mood for another fight. When I get inside, she comes out of the lounge room and meets me at the bottom of the stairs.

"Daniel said Levi's awake." She looks at me and waits. I nod. "Oh, honey, that's great news." She wraps me up in a hug, and it feels better than any hug I've had in the past few weeks, because it's Mum. "I'm sorry about this morning." She strokes my hair.

I pull away. "Can we talk about it later? I'm … My mind is elsewhere. They wouldn't let me talk to Levi. I can't go back until tomorrow."

"Sure, honey. We'll work it out." Mum smiles. "Do you want something to eat?"

"I'd like to go over to the treehouse first," I say. "I want to write in my journal."

Mum presses her lips together. "Don't be too long."

I adjust the strap of my tote on my shoulder and go back outside, cross over to Levi's yard, and walk down the side of the house.

Up in the treehouse, I sit on the floor, take my journal and a pen out, then settle against the wall, feeling comfortable in this space where Levi and I share so many good memories.

Levi woke up today. I guess I couldn't ask for a better New Year's present, except they wouldn't let me in the room, so I couldn't talk to him. My head understands the reasons, but my heart doesn't. I've been waiting to hear his voice for so long, and now I know he's awake, it's torture not being able to be by his side.

Tomorrow.

If tomorrow ever comes.

Karen told me off for thinking like that, but after everything that's happened, I'm scared. I'm scared of losing him again.

I put my pen down, because I'm not sure what else to write. Mum said not to be too long, but I don't want to go back yet. I like the quiet up here. Levi's box of letters is still in the corner, and I want to read another one, but guilt settles into my stomach, making it churn.

I argue with myself for a few minutes before reaching under the table and pulling the box out. I reason again that the letters have my name on them, so it should be okay for me to read them. This time, I decide to read the most recent one. The letter that Levi wrote the day he came home from schoolies. The day Josephine died.

Dear Katie,

I just got back from schoolies, and I can't wait for you to get home tomorrow. I bet if you were to read this you'd be able to imagine the smile in my voice. I'm not sure if you ever will though … read this, that is. Because I've never had enough courage to give you any of the letters I've written you. Maybe I will soon, because I do want you to read them. All of them.

But that's not what I wanted to write down.

I wanted to write down how excited I am about everything! You and me. Our future. Hopefully, we have one together.

I've learnt a lot of stuff about you, and about myself. I've realised what's most important, and it's not money, or possessions, or what other people think … it's all the things that money can't buy.

Sunlight on your hair.

How your mouth is a little lopsided when you smile.

The warmth of your hand in mine.

So many things that matter more than anything else. All the little things that add up to make the big picture so much brighter.

I'm sorry for everything I've put you through. I hope you've forgiven me, because when you get home, I want to hold you and never let you go.

I have so much to tell you about everything. So many things I want to share with you that until now I've been too afraid to say out loud.

Today is the last day of our past.

Tomorrow is the first day of the rest of our lives.

I love you.

Levi x

With a sad smile, I fold the paper again and slip it back into the envelope. The first day of the rest of our lives didn't work out how we expected it to, but now that Levi is awake, maybe we have another chance. I hope he remembers writing this, but what if he doesn't? What if he doesn't remember anything? I've heard of that happening to patients who have been in serious accidents or suffered extensive trauma.

I need to talk to him.

I pull my legs to my chest, and wrap my arms around them, closing my eyes and resting my forehead on my knees. With a few deep breaths, I try to steady the shake creeping into my shoulders. Knowing Levi is awake but not being able to go and see him is torture.

I concentrate on breathing evenly, keeping my eyes closed. I listen to the world outside the treehouse, the birds chirping and the rustle of the summer breeze through the gum trees.

Then a voice breaks the serenity.

I can't understand the words, but they sound angry,

with an abrupt edge.

The voice becomes clearer, and I raise my head, staring out through the gaps in the leaves of the tree.

Mark and Yvonne are standing on the back deck. From where I'm sitting, I can see straight into the top level of the house. If either of them glanced over at the treehouse, they could probably make me out in the shadows. I move to the other wall where the curtains are, and crouch beside the table, hoping that the piece of torn fabric and the dimness of the late afternoon light is enough to hide me from their sight.

"I don't want you there," Yvonne yells.

Mark's fists are clenched. "He's my son."

"I don't care." Yvonne crosses her arms, and looks at her feet. "You've done enough damage to this family already."

"Don't you talk to me like that."

I shouldn't be listening to their conversation. It's none of my business.

"It's about time I stood up to you," Yvonne says.

Mark raises his hand.

I hold my breath.

Yvonne stands her ground, but she leans away, her shoulders hunched to her ears.

Mark slaps Yvonne across the cheek, and her head whips to the side.

My hand flies to my mouth, and I squeeze my eyes shut, but tears still make their way out of the corners.

He hit her!

A door slams.

Slowly, I open my eyes, my vision blurry and my hand still over my mouth.

I blink a few times.

Yvonne is now alone on the back deck, her arms wrapped around herself as she cries.

I've known Levi and his family my entire life. Mark has often seemed angry and unapproachable, and I've been suspicious of him hitting Levi in the past, but I have never *seen* Mark raise a hand to his wife or his kids.

I want to un-see it.

What am I supposed to do?

When I told Mum I was worried about Levi, she just told me to be there for him. How do I do that? How do I help someone who has potentially been abused by his father? I don't know what it's like. And what about Yvonne? I don't know how to deal with this.

Levi shouldn't *have* to deal with this.

Maybe I should have paid more attention. Were there more signs? Should I have been able to tell this was going on? I can't rush in accusing Mark of abuse when I don't know any facts.

I hug my knees and rock back and forth, waiting for Yvonne to go inside so I can get out of here and go home. She stands at the railing of the deck, staring out towards the view of the bush I know is behind me. I hug my knees tighter, and try to make myself as small as possible so she doesn't see me.

A car starts out the front, and Yvonne moves to the back door. I hold my breath. She finally goes inside, the sliding door clicking closed behind her. As quickly and quietly as I can, I climb down the treehouse steps and race across the backyard, making my escape.

10

Together again?

I don't sleep well, worried about what I saw and what I should do about it. It's really none of my business, but what if Yvonne needs help? What if Levi does, too? How can I live with knowing what I know, and not say something to someone?

I'm quiet at breakfast, with so many things rushing through my head. Soon I'll get to talk to Levi for the first time in what feels like forever.

"Katie?" Mum says. "Katie, did you hear me?"

"Huh?" I drop my spoon into my bowl of cereal.

"What's the matter? You're a million miles away."

I shrug. "Just thinking."

"I can see that." Mum stands on the kitchen side of the counter and crosses her arms. "I said, we need to talk about uni tonight when I get home from work."

I look down at my bowl and my half-eaten cereal. "I already told you, I don't want to do law."

"I know, honey. Just ..." She sighs. "We'll talk tonight. I need to get going."

I nod, and she comes around the counter to give me a kiss.

"Mum?" I say as she reaches the door. "If you knew something about someone, and it wasn't very good, like they were hurting someone you loved, would you step in? Would you say something?" I bite my lip and stare at her. "Would you get involved when you know it's none of your business?"

Mum smiles at me, but her eyes are sad. "Sometimes it's best not to get too involved. But if someone I loved was getting hurt, I would do whatever I could to help." She looks at me for another moment, and I get the feeling she's about to ask who I'm talking about, but then she comes over and gives me a hug. "Say hi to Levi for me today, okay?"

I nod and bury my face in her chest, hugging her back. She pulls away then leaves for work, and I'm left in the empty kitchen to think about what to do. Dad left early, and Daniel is sleeping because he worked the late shift, so I have no one else to talk to.

I go upstairs to my room and get ready to go to the hospital. I haven't worn my contacts much lately, but today I want to make the effort. Because it has been a while it takes me a little longer to get them in, and by the time I'm done my eyes are watering and a sick feeling has settled into my stomach.

Or maybe it's because I know I'm eventually going to

have to ask Levi about his dad.

If I don't, I'm a terrible friend.

But if I do, will it make it worse?

I stare at my reflection in the mirror, and take a second to be grateful for my parents and how wonderful they are. I've had it tough in other ways, but Mum and Dad having big dreams for me is a very different kind of torture compared to being physically abused by the people who are supposed to protect us. My parents have always loved each other, and Daniel and me.

I take my time brushing my hair, letting my eyes settle while I do, then I put a little bit of gloss on my lips. I grab my tote, making sure my phone, purse, and journal are in there, then I go out to the front yard to wait for Karen. I turn my face to the summer sun and let it warm my cheeks. I hear a door open, and Yvonne steps onto the front veranda next door. She waves, and I wave back, offering her a smile as well.

Yvonne comes down the steps and onto the path. "I'm going to the hospital, Katie. Would you like to come with me today?"

"Oh, thank you, but I'm waiting for Karen."

Seconds later a car comes over the rise.

"All right. I'll see you both there." She smiles as Karen pulls up to the kerb. "Levi is looking forward to seeing you. He wouldn't stop asking for you yesterday."

I study Yvonne's face for a few heartbeats, trying to see if there's any evidence of Mark's assault yesterday. There doesn't seem to be—on the surface.

"Does he ... is he ..." I tuck my hair behind my ear. "Does he remember what happened?"

Yvonne takes a deep breath. "His memory of before the accident is fine, but he seems to have lost a little bit of time. He doesn't remember the accident, or why he was driving in the first place."

I nod. "Okay, so I can … talk to him about Josie? Does he know …?"

"Yes, sweetie. I told him what happened to Josie."

I nod again. "Okay."

Yvonne heads to her car. "See you soon."

I wait until she's out of the driveway and up the road before getting into the car.

"All set?" Karen asks.

I take a deep, shaky breath. "Yeah, I'm nervous though."

"Don't be. It's Levi. I'll bet he can't wait to see you."

I don't reply, because seeing Levi isn't the only thing I'm nervous about. It's also what I want to talk to him about that's making me shaky. But I'm not going to say anything to Karen until after I talk to Levi. I'm sure he wouldn't want me airing his dirty laundry. I don't know how to even start the conversation with him. *Hey, I was just wondering if your dad hits you and your mum. Want to talk to me about that?* How do I be tactful without sounding … not tactful?

"Earth to Katie," Karen says when we're almost at the hospital.

"Huh?" I turn to her.

"You zoned out."

"Sorry, just … thinking." I tell her what I told Mum when she caught me in my own world at breakfast.

Karen parks the car and gets out. I follow, crossing the street to the front entrance of the hospital. The walk

444

along the corridor feels different this morning, like I'm doing it for the first time, and when we reach the doors to the ICU, my hands are shaking and I can hardly pick up the phone.

Karen rubs my arm. "Calm down. Deep breaths."

After we wash our hands one of the nurses lets us in, and we make our way to Levi's room. Yvonne is with him, and Karen and I stop at the window. I look in, waiting for him to adjust his gaze and see us. When he does, his eyes light up, and a smile spreads across his face. I can't help smiling as well.

Yvonne turns, then gets up from the chair beside the bed, coming to the door. I meet her at the threshold, eager to go in.

"I'll wait out here," Karen says. "Actually, I'll go get us some hot chocolate."

"Thank you," I say.

Yvonne holds the door and I walk into the room. "I'll go with Karen," she says.

I watch the door close, then I turn to Levi. I'm itching to run at him and hug him so tight, but I'm not sure if he's in any pain. It takes all my effort to walk normally to the side of the bed.

"You're a sight for sore eyes," Levi says.

I drop my tote on the floor, then my shoulders start to shake. I can't hold myself together anymore, and the tears course down my cheeks. I'm crying because I'm happy and sad all at the same time.

Levi lifts his hand and holds it out to me. The bed railing is down now, so I don't have to reach through it. I take his hand, and it feels so warm in mine as he gives me a gentle squeeze.

"Welcome back," I say through my tears. "I've been waiting so long to hear your voice."

"Don't cry." He pulls my hand.

I lean forward, then look him up and down. "Can I ... hug you? I don't want to hurt you."

Levi smiles, and pulls my hand again. I reach around him with my other arm and lay my head on his chest, careful not to put too much weight on him. The wires and pads under his hospital gown are hard under my cheek.

For a few moments, I listen to the beating of Levi's heart and count his breaths with the rise and fall of his chest. I squeeze my eyes closed, and breathe in time with him.

"How are you feeling?" I finally ask, pulling away and straightening up.

"I'm sore in places I didn't know I had, but I'm okay." He smiles. "The doctors say I've healed well. My lung and ribs are good, but I'll be tender for a while yet."

"When can you come home?"

"Now that I'm fully awake and handling the pain, they're going to move me to the ward tomorrow. After that, I'm not sure how long. A week or two?"

"It's too long," I say. "I want you to come home. We've already lost so much time."

"We have all the time in the world, Katie."

I shake my head and grip his hand. "No, we don't. We don't know what's going to happen tomorrow. Tomorrow might never come. I can't lose you, not again. I've just gotten you back. We have to ... we have—"

"Shhh." Levi reaches up and cups my cheek with his free hand. "It's okay. I'm here now. I'm not going anywhere."

"We don't know …" I sob and press my face into his warm palm, closing my eyes. "We don't know what the future holds," I whisper.

"My future holds you."

I open my eyes and stare at Levi. "I have so much I want to talk to you about. So many things … I don't know where to start."

Levi smiles. "How about I go first? How's Jess? From what I remember yesterday, she was pretty upset. Is she coping? Is she …?" Levi takes his palm from my cheek and looks at our entwined fingers. "You have to be there for her, Katie. I'm sure she needs her friends."

When he looks up at me again, there's a sadness in his eyes that speaks for every person who has ever lost a loved one. If I ever lost Daniel, I fear my eyes would be just as haunted.

"She's not doing so well," I say. "She blames herself for Josie's death."

Levi half-laughs. "She wasn't driving the car that killed her."

"And it wasn't your fault." I pull the chair as close to the bed as I can and sit, never letting go of Levi's hand. He rolls his head to the side on his pillow, and I continue, "I'm guessing you haven't spoken to Jarred, or Geoff. Or Veronica?"

He shakes his head.

I take a deep breath because it's all so messed up. Everything is messed up. "There was … Josie and Jess … they twin swapped on the way home from Surfers. Jess went home with Jarred. Something must have happened, because Jess and Josie had a big fight. I don't know what about, but Jess is beside herself and thinks it's all her fault. She had an argument with Jarred on New Year's. I ... don't know how to help her."

"Just ... be there, and hopefully that will help enough."

I adjust myself in my seat, trying to think of a way into a conversation with Levi about his dad. "How about you?" I ask instead. "How are you coping with ...?"

"Josie's death?" Levi raises his eyebrows. "I'm trying not to think about it. I can't remember much of that night, so I don't know what happened. Mum said the police will come and talk to me in a few days to get my side of the story, but I have no idea what to tell them. My car smashed into hers, but I don't remember it." Levi shoves his free hand into his hair and closes his eyes. "Since I woke up, I've tried to remember even getting in the car. A small detail. Anything. But I can't. The last thing I remember is going out to the treehouse and ..."

I wait for him to continue, but he doesn't.

"I've been spending some time in the treehouse since you've been in hospital." I twist a lock of hair around my finger and look down at the bed. "I found the box of letters."

I hold my breath and wait for the question I think is coming next, but Levi doesn't ask it.

"I was wondering how long it would take you," he says. "I've been hoping for a long time that you'd go to the treehouse, but you never did."

"Don't you want to know if I've read them?" I look up at him again, guilt stabbing me in the stomach.

"Do you want to read them?"

"Do you want me to?"

Levi goes quiet and holds my gaze. Eventually, he says, "I do, but to be honest, I never intended to give them to you. So ... the decision is yours."

"Why did you write them if you never wanted me to read them?"

"Why do you write in your journal?" He smiles.

I chew my bottom lip. "I write stuff down because it helps me deal with it better."

Levi nods. "Yeah, it does. I so badly wanted to talk to you when I started writing those letters, but I couldn't just come and see you, so I wrote it down instead. You were a pretty good listener."

I lean on the side of the bed with both elbows and adjust my hold on Levi's hand. "I've read two of them so far ... I feel really guilty about it, like I've invaded your privacy."

"It's okay. I don't mind. Which ones have you read?"

"The last one you wrote, after coming back from Surfers, and the first one. The one after Mason died." I go quiet for a moment before continuing. "I would've listened. If you came to me, I would've listened."

"I did come," he says. "But I managed to screw everything up."

I think back to that first night Levi climbed into my bedroom window. Was that his way of trying to talk to me? To tell me what was going on with him? Back then I just thought he was drunk and being an idiot.

"Maybe I didn't listen hard enough."

Levi shakes his head. "No, none of this is your fault." He pauses. "If you do decide to read any more of the letters, read the one from the day of Mason's funeral."

"Okay." I don't say any more on the subject of the letters. "Have you seen your dad?" I ask instead.

Levi hesitates, and a funny look passes over his face. "Not yet. He hasn't come ..."

I bite my lip, and try to think of the best way to word my next question. I open my mouth a couple of times to speak, but then close it again.

"What's wrong, Katie?" Levi asks. "You're doing that thing with your mouth where you look like a fish."

I smile at the memory of Levi telling me I looked like a fish the first night he climbed in my window again. I miss him climbing in my window.

"I want to ask you something," I eventually say. "But you don't have to answer, because I know it's none of my business."

"Shoot," Levi says. "You can ask me anything."

I hesitate, then open my mouth and blurt, "I ... is there ... is everything okay with your dad?"

Levi stares at me for a long moment, and my heart beats faster. I hold my breath, because I think I know what he's going to say. I've seen the evidence, but I don't want it to be true.

"My dad is ... you need to read the letter from the day of Mason's funeral." Levi looks down at our hands, across the room, back to our hands. He runs circles over my skin with his thumb. "Just promise me one thing." Levi finally connects his gaze with mine again. "Remember I'm a different person now. I have everything to live for. I have you."

I'm puzzled by his words, and what could be in his letter, but I nod my agreeance.

Karen and Yvonne return with the hot chocolates, and Levi's mum leaves Karen and I to talk to Levi for a bit longer. I tell him about what happened with Mum and my uni letters, and that I still haven't followed up with any of my acceptances because of everything that's been going on.

"Mum was going to bring my letters in today," Levi says. "She doesn't want me to miss the cut-off date."

"Surely they can make a special consideration for you if you do," Karen says. "It's not like you *could* reply before now."

Levi shrugs. "We'll see. It will all work out."

The nurses haven't enforced the two visitors rule today since Levi is awake, and Yvonne pops in and out. I'm grateful she's letting Karen and I have so much time with her son. After lunch though, a nurse comes in and says it's time for us to leave.

"Now that you no longer need heavy sedation, we'll be moving you out of the ICU soon, maybe even as early as tomorrow," she says to Levi. "The doctor wants me to give you a good check over, and see if you're up to getting out of bed."

I stand from the chair. "I'll come see you again tomorrow, okay?"

"I'd like that," Levi says, squeezing my hand.

I lean down to hug him, and Levi reaches up to touch my hair. I stop and look into his eyes. He caresses my cheek with his fingertips, then slips his hand behind my neck and gently pulls me to him. I close my eyes. His kiss is chaste and soft. When I pull away, heat lingers on my lips, and I want to kiss him again, but there are other people in the room.

His hand falls away from my neck and I straighten. "See you soon."

"I'll be here." He smiles.

Karen and I say goodbye to Yvonne on our way out and head home.

"Need another lift tomorrow?" Karen asks as I get out of the car.

"Thank you. If it's no trouble?" I lean down and look through the window. "But I can catch the train home."

"Whatever." Karen waves her hand and smiles. "We'll sort it out later."

I wait for her to pull onto the street before turning back to the house. I have an hour or so before Mum should be home from work, so instead of going inside I go over to Levi's yard and make my way to the treehouse.

Once I'm at the top, I settle in with my back against the wall and pull the box out, flicking to the letter from the day of Mason's funeral. I run my fingers over the outside of the envelope before pulling the contents out and reading.

Dear Katie,

Today was Mason's funeral, and it has been one of the hardest days of my life. I still can't believe Mason isn't here anymore. But him not being here isn't the only reason today was difficult.

When I saw you, I just wanted to come over and hug you, and tell you how much it meant to me that you were there. Having you near was so comforting, and it helped me get through the day when all I wanted to do was run.

All the Things

Over the past week I've been thinking about how much easier everything would be if I wasn't here. If I didn't have to face my dad every day. How if I wasn't here I wouldn't feel the guilt over Mason's death. Because that guilt is tearing me apart.

The way Dad looks at me makes me want to be with Mason. He has to be in a better place now, because anywhere my father isn't would be better.

When we got home from the funeral, Dad was the worst I've ever seen him. No one knows what he's really like. He's always been so careful, but tonight I think he forgot I was there.

I'm so scared for her. I tried to protect her, and he hit me as well. Now I'm sitting in the treehouse with a bottle of bourbon, wishing I could climb in your window and tell you everything. Thinking about how much easier everything would be if I just disappeared, but wanting to say goodbye to you first, and then feeling guilty because I would be leaving Mum behind.

I can't leave her here on her own.

She needs me even more now that Mason is gone.

Now that he isn't here to protect both of us.

I have to protect her.

I hate my father.

I hate what he does to Mum.

I hate that my brother is dead.

I hate myself.

Levi.

Through blurry eyes I fold the letter closed. My heart hurts at what Levi has been through, and I sit staring at the box of letters on the floor in front of me. How many more has he written like this? How much pain and sorrow exists on these pieces of paper?

How am I supposed to help him?

How do I take his broken pieces and put them back together again?

My fight

Last night I stayed in the treehouse and read every single letter Levi wrote to me. I cried so many tears while on that platform in the trees, and it wasn't until Mum called my phone asking where I was that I realised how long I had been up there. When I'd gotten home and she had seen my puffy eyes, I'd explained them away as happy tears because I had finally spoken to Levi.

I'm not sure if she believed me.

This morning, I don't feel much better. I didn't get much sleep, and there's a hollow in my chest at the thought of talking to Levi about the letters today. There's someone else I want to talk to first though: Yvonne. I'm not sure how that's going to go.

"Are you going to the hospital again?" Mum asks.

"Yeah. I've made Levi a picnic basket. Figured hospital

food usually sucks, so I'd take him something nice."

"He hasn't been awake long," Mum says. "He might not be able to eat much."

"We'll see." I pick at the piece of toast in front of me. "Karen said she'd drive me in."

Mum smiles, then says, "We didn't get a chance to talk about uni last night."

I look up at her as she sips her coffee. "Can we not do this right now?"

"Well … I was going to say that I think you should do the course you have your heart set on." Mum smiles over the top of her mug.

I frown. "You don't want me to do law?"

Mum sighs. "I want you to be happy, Katie. And if that means doing a fine arts degree, then … I won't stop you."

"But I missed the interview. I'll have to wait until the mid-year intake."

Mum sets her coffee cup on the counter, and goes out to the dining room. She comes back with an envelope in her hand and passes it to me. It has the SCA logo in the top corner.

I rip it open to read the contents. As I scan the words, my mouth turns up into a smile and I jump up from the stool I've been sitting on at the counter.

"Thank you." I squeal and hug Mum.

She laughs. "You're welcome."

"How …?" I pull away and look at her.

"I emailed, and told them what you've been going through. They decided, due to extenuating circumstances, to allow you a reschedule date."

"Thank you," I say again.

Mum gives me another hug, then finishes her coffee. "I have a work thing this afternoon, so I'll see you tonight. Dad should be home this afternoon though."

"Okay." I watch her walk to the door then sit back at the counter.

I spend the next ten minutes in a state of happiness, staring into space as I finish my toast.

"Morning, space cadet," Daniel says from the other side of the counter.

I blink at my brother. "Hey."

"You looked like you were ..." Daniel waves his hand above his head, "somewhere else."

"Mum just gave me a letter from SCA. They've rescheduled my interview, so hopefully I haven't missed out on a place."

"That's great news," Daniel says. "How's Levi?"

Levi. I take a deep breath, because I'm not sure how to answer. My moment of happiness is gone as I think about what I need to talk to him about today. What I want to talk to Yvonne about, too.

"He's ... awake. And it's so great to hear his voice." I force a smile for my brother. "How's Jess after ... the other day?"

Daniel shrugs. "She's not great. I think Bridget has booked her into a psychologist."

"Oh," is all I manage to say. Then I think about all the stuff Levi wrote in his letters. "You have to promise me you'll do what you can for her. Look after her. Let her know that it's worth being here, and there are people who love her, even if she doesn't love herself right now."

"Wow, that was deep."

"I'm serious, Daniel." I stare at him. "Promise me you'll

tell her that."

"Yeah, I promise." He regards me for a moment. "What's happened, Katie? Did something happen?"

I shake my head. "It's okay. I just … I need to go and talk to Yvonne. I'll be back soon. Karen is taking me to the hospital." I get up and put my plate in the sink, then I hug my brother. "I love you."

He hugs me back. "I love you, too. Are you sure you're all right?"

"I'm good." I punch him on the arm then walk towards the front door. "I'll see you this afternoon. You'll pick me up, yeah?"

"Of course."

"You're the best."

"I know," he calls as I shut the front door.

I cross over through the garden to Levi's place, hoping Yvonne is still home and hasn't gone to the hospital yet. With a shaky hand, I knock on the door. Then I freak out because, seriously, what am I going to say? I go to turn around and leave when the front door to Levi's house opens.

"Katie?" Yvonne says. "How are you?"

"Hi." I give a pathetic little wave. "I … um … can … Is Mark home?"

Yvonne shakes her head. "No, sweetie. He went to work a couple of hours ago."

I take a deep breath. "Can I come in?"

"Of course." Yvonne steps aside and lets me through. "Would you like a drink?"

"Oh, no. I'm fine. Thank you." I follow her through to the kitchen, and it feels like an eternity since I've been inside Levi's house.

Yvonne sets two glasses on the kitchen bench anyway, and pours us both a glass of water from the jug beside the sink.

"Everything okay with you?" She raises a glass to her lips and takes a sip.

"I'm not sure. I mean … I'm all right. I just …" I sit at the counter and twist my fingers together. "I wanted to ask if you're okay?"

Yvonne smiles. "Yes, of course. I'm fine."

An uncomfortable quiet hangs between us, because we both know her words are a lie.

"I was in the treehouse again, the other night," I say.

"Oh, that's fine." Yvonne waves a hand. "You're welcome to go whenever you like."

"Thank you, but … I saw … I'm not sure what I saw. I just … he …" I stare at my hands. "I know Mark hits you."

Yvonne is silent for a few heartbeats, and I hold my breath. She's probably thinking, *what's this eighteen-year-old busybody doing in my house?* She's probably going to ask me to leave.

"Please don't worry about me, Katie," she finally says. "It was nothing."

"You know you can get help?" I say, not knowing if it's true or not. I've never experienced domestic violence before; I wouldn't know where to start. But there has to be some organisation or place she can turn to. Maybe even the police, if it came down to it. "And what about Levi? Has Mark … has he hit him, too?"

"Katie, really. We're fine."

I'm not sure what I expected her to tell me when I

thought coming over here was a good idea, but it's not okay. What her husband is doing to her is not acceptable.

I stand from the counter, anger at her calmness rising into my chest. "Did you know after Mason died, Levi thought about suicide? Did you know the only reason he's still here is because he wanted to protect you?" My voice gets louder at the last few words, and I clench my fists.

Yvonne's mouth drops open, then she closes it again. Her hand goes to her lips, and she squeezes her eyes closed. She takes a deep breath, then a big gulp of water from her glass.

"Did he tell you that?" She stares at me now, tears glistening in her eyes.

"Yes," I say, because even though Levi hasn't told me out loud, he wrote it in a letter. More than one, and I have to listen. I have to help him.

Yvonne presses her lips together. "I'll talk to Levi."

I nod, because what else can I say? Kick your husband out? I'm just a kid in her eyes. She's probably standing here thinking that she's the adult, and that I don't know anything.

A car horn sounds outside, and I look at my phone to check the time.

"Karen's here. I have to go. Thank you for the water." I turn to walk to the front door.

"Katie," Yvonne calls after me, and I face her again. "If you're going to the hospital now, he's been moved from the ICU."

"Thanks." I clutch my phone. "Are you going in?"

"I have some things to attend to this morning, but I'll be there this afternoon."

"Okay." I nod and turn back towards the door.

"Katie?" Yvonne says again when I put my hand on the doorknob. I face her. "I'm trying to … It's not easy after twenty years of marriage. I'm …" She pauses and attempts a smile. "Please don't worry. I'll sort it out."

I nod, and offer her a small smile. "I hope so."

And I do, because how can she be happy? How can Levi be happy having to live with what his father is doing to them?

When I get outside, I wave at Karen to wait while I run inside to grab my tote bag and the basket I put together for Levi. Seconds later the basket is on the back seat, I'm in the front with Karen, and we're driving to the hospital. The day I don't have to make this trip again will be a good one. I can't wait until Levi comes home so all I have to do is walk next door to see him.

"What's in the basket?" Karen asks.

"Nothing too exciting," I say. "Just something I put together for Levi."

Karen smirks, but doesn't push me to elaborate. She drops me off, and I tell her I'll see her later. Inside the hospital, I go to the front desk to ask where Levi is now.

"Up one floor then about halfway along," the nurse behind the desk says. "Room fifty-three."

"Thank you." I follow her instructions to Levi's room where I find the door open. I peek in, and he's not in his bed. The sheets are crumpled.

"Levi?" I call. "You here?"

I go into the room and set the basket on the table that slides up and down the bed. A toilet flushes, and the door to the adjoining bathroom opens. Levi comes out, dressed in his hospital gown and clutching his drip stand. He grins as he shuffles towards me.

I rush to him and take his arm. "Should you be up on your own?"

"I'm fine, Katie." He's shaky on his feet as I help him to the bed.

"What are you doing out of bed?" a nurse asks from behind us. "I told you to call me."

Levi chuckles. "And I told you I can manage on my own."

"Boys." The nurse shakes her head. "You haven't walked for a long time. I know you had physio every day while you were sedated, but it's not the same."

"You've told me this already." Levi sits on the edge of the bed and scoots back so he can swing his legs up.

"Slow and steady," the nurse says. She comes and takes his blood pressure and temperature, checks his drip, and writes something on his chart. "You need to keep an eye on this one." She smiles at me before leaving.

I look at Levi, and I can't help grinning. We grin at each other, and we must look like idiots, but I don't care. I'm so happy he's awake, and alive, and that we have another chance.

"What's in the basket?" he asks.

I tuck my hair behind my ears. "I brought you something."

I move the basket to the end of the bed, careful not to put it on Levi's feet, then move the table up the bed a bit so it's over his thighs. I go to the window and spin the rod so the venetians close a little. Then I flip the lid to the basket open and get to work.

Levi watches me in silence while I take out a small blue tablecloth and dress the hospital table. I line up five electric tea-light candles, because I figured the hospital wouldn't allow open flames, and then I set a bougainvillea clipping in the middle of the table. I glance at Levi from the corner of my eye, and he's still watching and smiling.

Next, I take out two wine glasses and a bottle of non-alcoholic champagne. Then I set down a plate and arrange some cheese, crackers, and dip. I pop the cork on the champagne bottle and fill the glasses, all while Levi doesn't say a word.

I pick up the glasses and hand one to Levi. "Cheers."

"Cheers," he replies.

We bump glasses before both taking a sip. The flavour is too sweet, and the bubbles shoot up my nose. I cough, then laugh.

"So …" I set my drink back on the table. "When can you get out of here?"

"I think I'm stuck for at least another week." Levi reaches out and pulls the table towards him, diving into the crackers and cheese. "The doctor said I'm not steady enough on my feet, and I need some more physio sessions before I can leave."

"How do you feel?" I ask, using a cracker to scoop up some dip.

"To be honest, really sore. My whole body aches."

"You were asleep for a while. I don't think you're going to feel perfect again overnight."

"I guess." He runs a hand through his hair, and my insides melt. "But enough about me. What's going on with you?"

"Oh, the usual," I say. "I read the letter you told me to … and the rest of them."

Levi raises his eyebrows. "You read all the letters?"

I sit on the edge of the bed with one leg under me. "Yeah, and I ... There's something ... I need ..." I twist my fingers together in my lap and stare at them. This is harder than I thought it would be.

"You want to talk about the stuff I said," Levi says.

I chew on my lip and look at him. "You don't ... you're not having those thoughts anymore, are you? Because I don't want you to go anywhere. Not after ... you came so close to ..." I stop again, because my throat is thick with emotion, and I have to hold my breath to stop the tears from coming.

Levi leans forward and takes my shaking hands in his. "I'm not thinking like that anymore."

I let out a long, shuddering breath and nod, because I still can't talk properly. And now I'm even more scared of the other thing I need to talk to him about. How do I tell him I saw his dad hit his mum? How do I ask him if he's being abused?

"Is everything ..." I lick my lips. "Wow, I'm not doing so well with the talking thing today."

"It's okay." Levi squeezes my hands. "Take your time. I could tell you had a lot on your mind the minute I saw you today."

"I'm that transparent?"

"Like an open book."

"Okay," I say, then take yet another deep breath. "Your dad. I know everything is not okay between you and him, but ... there's something I should tell you."

Levi rests back against his pillows. "What is it? Dad and I haven't gotten along for ages. From the letters, you should know what he's done to me."

"I'm more worried about what he's doing to your mum."

"Yeah, he treats her pretty badly."

"He hits her." I stare at him, and Levi looks at his hands. "He hits you." Saying the words out loud hurts more than I thought it would, but I can't even imagine what those words are doing to Levi. "Levi, look at me." He raises his head, and his eyes glisten with tears. "I'm not going to tell you what to do. I'm just worried about you, and … I'm not sure how to help other than talking to you about this."

Levi frowns and shrugs. "What's there to say?"

Now it's my turn to look away, because I'm not sure I can stare Levi in the face when I tell him what I need to. There's already too much pain in his eyes.

"The other day I was in the treehouse, and … I *saw* your dad hit your mum."

"What?" Levi's question comes out with a puff, and he sucks a deep breath back in.

"They came out to the back deck when I was in the treehouse, and I didn't mean to pry, or intrude, but I couldn't leave." I pick at a thread on the blanket on the bed. "I went to see your mum this morning."

"Why?" Levi asks.

"Because I'm worried about her." I look at him again. "I'm worried about you." We stare at each other for a few heartbeats, and it feels like a million years. The moment stretches out between us. "You have to … stop him somehow," I finally say.

Levi presses his lips together. "I'll talk to Mum. But I don't think it's going to help."

"Report him to the police."

"It's not that easy, Katie." Levi shoves both hands into his hair and pulls. "He's my dad."

"You shouldn't have to make excuses for him. You shouldn't have to protect your mum from him." My voice rises, and I stand from the bed. "You shouldn't be thinking about suicide."

"I'm not!" Levi says, his hands falling back to the bed with clenched fists.

"You should be able to feel safe in your own home," I say quietly.

"Katie is right," Yvonne says from the doorway, and I spin to face her.

"I'm sorry ... I—"

"Don't apologise." Yvonne holds her hand up. "You've given me the push I need to ..." She takes a deep breath. "To sort out ..." Yvonne swipes a tear from her cheek.

"Mum," Levi says, his face crumpling.

"I know, sweetie." She comes into the room and hugs her son.

Levi grips her tightly, and sobs into her chest. I back away towards the door, giving them some space.

"Katie, where are you going?" Levi asks, pulling away from Yvonne.

"You need to spend some time with your mum," I say, stopping in the doorway. "You've got a lot to talk about."

"Will you be back tomorrow?"

"Of course." I smile. "There's no chance of keeping me away."

He nods, and I give a nervous little wave before turning around and walking out to the corridor. I concentrate on putting one foot in front of the other, and I try not to think about how hard this is going to be for Levi. For Yvonne. I wish there was something I could do for them, but as much as I want to help, this time it isn't my fight.

12

Coming home

Over the next week I go to the hospital to see Levi every day. We spend our time talking mostly about the good stuff, and sometimes about the real issues that need to be talked about. Levi assures me his mum is taking steps to sort their shit out. I really hope it's true, because today he's coming home. And I'm a nervous wreck. I've spent the morning organising a surprise for Levi in the treehouse, and now I'm freaking out.

"What if he can't climb up there?" I say to Karen, twisting my fingers together. "He might not be able to climb the steps."

"I'm sure he'll be fine." She puts her hands on her hips, standing in the middle of my room. "Would you stop worrying?"

"It was a stupid idea," I say. "I shouldn't have done

anything."

"Oh my God, stop it," Karen says. "Stop fidgeting."

I clench my fingers and go to the window, kneeling on the window seat to stare out at the yard below. Yvonne told me she was picking Levi up late this morning. They should be home by now. I'm about to point this out to Karen when Yvonne's car pulls into the driveway.

I freeze.

What do I do?

Should I go down there? Or will he want to go inside first and get settled? He hasn't been home for a month and a half.

"What are you doing?" Karen asks.

I turn from the window and sit on the seat. "What if he doesn't—"

"Get up," Karen says. "Of course he'll want to see you."

When I don't move, she grabs my hand and yanks me to my feet. I follow her downstairs to the front door, catching a glimpse of Mum in the kitchen as we pass.

"Levi's home," Karen says as we go outside.

"That's great," Mum calls after us. "Say hi for me."

Before Levi is out of the car, Karen and I are standing on the lawn. Yvonne gets out of the front passenger side and comes around to the back passenger door on the driver's side. The trees in the driveway cast shadows over the window, so I can't see Levi's face. His mum opens the car door, and it's like everything happens in slow motion. I wait eagerly for Levi to stand, and when he does, I grin like an idiot. Yvonne helps him out and then leans into the back seat, coming out with a bouquet of flowers before closing the door. They're really pretty.

The driver's door opens, and Levi's dad gets out. He glances at Karen and me, a scowl on his face. I bite my lip. He slams the car door, looks at his wife and son, then turns and walks towards the front of the house.

I let out a breath I don't realise I've been holding.

Levi is walking, but his steps seem laboured and slow. He makes it to the front of the car, his gaze fixed on me. I wait for a few heartbeats before stepping through the garden to his side of the boundary.

My throat thickens, and I can't talk, even though I want to tell him how good it is to see him home. But I don't have to say anything, because Levi comes straight to me and wraps me up in a big hug.

"Hey, you," he whispers in my ear.

"Hey," I finally manage. "Welcome home."

He kisses the top of my head and rubs my back. "It's good to see you ... here. Not in the hospital."

Yvonne places a hand on Levi's shoulder, and he pulls away from me slightly, keeping one arm around my waist. She passes him the bouquet of flowers, and he grips the base of the stems with one hand.

"I'll be inside." Yvonne pats Levi's arm.

He glances towards the house where his dad has stopped on the veranda. "I shouldn't be too long."

Yvonne smiles. "Take all the time you need."

My heart lurches as she walks towards the house and her abusive husband. I really hope what Levi told me about her trying to fix things is true. When she reaches the veranda, Mark holds the door open for her, but she doesn't look at him or speak to him.

"It's great to see you out of that bed," Karen says.

She's still standing in my front yard.

"You have no idea." Levi tightens his grip on my waist.

"Well … I'll let you catch up." Karen points to her mum's car. "I'm going to head."

"Can I ask a favour first?" Levi says.

I look between my best friend and my boyfriend, trying to guess what he wants, because I'm itching to take him to the treehouse. I also can't help wondering when he's going to give me the flowers.

"Sure," Karen says. "What's up?"

"I'm not really ready to, you know … drive myself anywhere," Levi says. "And Dad wouldn't stop on the way home. I'd rather go with Katie anyway. So I was wondering if …" He glances at me sideways. "I … um …"

"Spit it out." Karen laughs. "Where do you want me to take you?"

Levi looks at the flowers, then at his feet, then at Karen. "I want to go to … I want to …" He sighs. "The accident site. I haven't …"

"No problem," Karen says. "Get in." She heads towards the car.

I look up at Levi. "The flowers are for Josie?"

He bites his lip. "Oh God, I'm sorry. You thought they were for you?"

"No, don't be sorry," I say. "I think it's really nice … you wanting to go and see her … where … you know."

"The accident happened?" He kisses my temple. "Come on. I'm not sure I'll be able to go without you beside me."

I totally agree, so I don't say anything. The one time I went to the accident site with Karen was really, really hard. I haven't been back since.

Under Levi's insistence, I take the front passenger seat and he gets in the back. We take the back route from my place towards the highway, and the drive to where Josephine ran the stop sign takes less than five minutes.

Karen pulls over to the kerb before the intersection and kills the engine. The three of us sit in silence for a moment, and my heart hammers against my ribcage. From where we're stopped I can see the mass of tributes and flowers on and around the telegraph pole on the corner. I'm not sure I want to go and see it again.

But I'm not the one who wants to be here. Levi is, and he needs me.

I turn in my seat and look at him. "Ready?"

He picks up the bouquet of flowers from the seat beside him. "I guess."

"I'll wait here," Karen says.

I lick my lips and nod, then get out of the car. Levi joins me on the footpath, and we walk slowly towards the corner. It's as if neither of us wants to walk too fast because what we're walking towards is full of pain.

"I still don't remember that night," Levi says, stopping a few metres short of the telegraph pole.

"Maybe you don't need to." I slip my hand into his. "Maybe ... what you need to remember is that forgiveness doesn't come easy, but it does come."

Levi squeezes my hand, and then he sucks in a sharp breath. When I look up at him, tears stain his cheeks. I swallow the lump in my throat, and gently pull him forward until we're standing at the base of the telegraph pole. Levi lets go of my hand and crouches, laying the flowers beside another fresh bouquet.

Josephine stares at us from the photo in the centre of the cross nailed to the telegraph pole. More letters, notes, photos, and flowers have been taped and tacked to the wood around it. They're different to the ones that were here when Karen and I came all those weeks ago. I wonder where they've gone, if someone collected them. They must have. Maybe Jessica has read some of them. If she has, I hope people's words have helped ease her pain.

I place a hand on Levi's shoulder as he stays crouched, his forearm resting on his thigh. He wipes his face with his other hand, then reaches out and touches a photo of Josephine with him, Jarred, Rachel, Veronica, and Geoff. It's the first time I've realised how much Josephine's death must be affecting them all. Like their group has been ripped down the middle.

Levi straightens and puts an arm around my shoulders. "Thank you." He pulls me close.

I'm not sure what he's thanking me for, so I just nod and press my cheek to his chest, wrapping my arms around his waist.

We head back to the car and Karen takes us home.

"I'll call you later," I say to her as I get out of the car.

"Whenever." Karen waves her hand.

Levi and I wait in the driveway until she pulls away and is driving down the street before turning back to each other.

"Now I can show you your surprise," I say.

"A surprise?" Levi raises his eyebrows.

I open my mouth to reply, but raised voices come from Levi's house, and my words die in my throat. We both stop and stare at his front door, waiting and listening. The shouts come again, and Levi rubs his face with his hands.

The front door bursts open, slamming against the wall of the house, and Yvonne comes out clutching her phone in her hand. She runs to the bottom of the steps.

"I'm not leaving," Mark yells, appearing in the doorway.

"Like hell you aren't." Yvonne turns and faces him. She looks so small standing at the base of the veranda steps. "I should've thrown you out a long time ago."

"This is my house." Mark points a finger at his wifc.

"I will call the police," Yvonne yells, shaking her phone at Mark. "I'm not going to take any more shit from you."

Levi and I stand in my driveway, watching. I've never heard Yvonne raise her voice before, let alone swear. I have no idea what to do. I feel like if we move, they'll see us, but how can they not see us anyway?

"What … Should we do something?" I ask, pressing into Levi's side and gripping his hand.

Levi moves towards his yard, but his steps are laboured. When he lets go of my hand, my skin is cold, as if he's taken the memory of his touch with him. I follow close behind because I want to help, but I don't know how.

Mark moves down the steps, his face red and scrunched. "You'll do as I say and get inside the house."

"No." Yvonne stands her ground.

"Leave her alone," Levi says when he reaches his parents.

Mark's gaze flicks to Levi, then me, then back to his son. "Stay out of this, Levi."

He shakes his head. "No, Dad. I'm not going to let you hurt Mum anymore." Levi takes Yvonne's hand then positions himself between her and Mark. I stride over and stand with them, touching Yvonne's arm in a way I hope is reassuring.

"Get out of my way." Mark comes down the rest of the steps and grabs Levi, shoving him to the side.

Levi stumbles and falls, clipping the railing on his way down. He lands half on the path and half in the shrubs beside the steps.

"Levi!" Yvonne yells, reaching for her son.

I race forward to help Levi up. Mark lunges at Yvonne and grips her upper arms, throwing her up the stairs and onto the veranda. She cries out when she hits the wooden boards and bounces into the doorframe. Her phone skitters along the wooden surface.

"Mum!" Levi scrambles up the steps, but his movements are slow. "Don't touch her." He shoves his dad, but Mark is bigger than his son, and he hits back.

Levi stumbles. I reach the top step just as he misses it and falls past me, knocking me to the side. I turn to help him, but someone grabs my arm.

I face Mark. His fingers dig into my skin. "Let go of me," I yell, trying to yank my arm away. But he only grips me tighter.

"Let her go, you bastard." Levi pushes himself up and stands.

Mark drags me towards Yvonne and the door. I try to fight, but he's too strong. I struggle to look over my shoulder.

"Levi!"

"Katie!"

Levi makes it to the top step as Mark forces me into

the house. I stumble over Yvonne and fall into the foyer. Mark steps on his wife and comes into the house, turning his back to me. I run at him, but his big frame blocks the doorway as he leans down to grab Yvonne. *What the hell is this psycho doing?*

"Katie!" Levi calls my name again.

He reaches the door and grabs Yvonne's arm. She struggles in Mark's grip, and he and Levi use her like a tug-o-war rope. All the while Levi and Yvonne are yelling at Mark to let go. I can't get out through the blocked door. I can't reach Levi. I can't help Yvonne.

I can't do anything.

Mark twists and shoves Yvonne at me, and we both tumble onto the floor of the foyer.

"What are you doing?" Levi yells at his dad. "Let me in."

Mark doesn't reply. He grunts as he forces Levi back onto the veranda.

"Levi? Mark?" I hear Mum's voice. "Is everything okay?"

"Mum!" I scream, scrambling to my feet. "Mum!"

"Katie?"

I catch a glimpse of her as she reaches the top of the veranda steps, then Mark gives Levi a hard shove, sending him towards Mum, and slams the door, twisting the lock home.

The click echoes through the foyer.

"Levi!" Yvonne screams from behind me.

Levi pounds on the door. "Mum! Katie!"

Mark turns to face us, and I back away towards Yvonne who is standing at the bottom of the staircase. She grabs my arm and pulls me behind her, shielding me from

Mark. I quickly glance around. I haven't spent much time in this house over the past few years, but I still know it like the back of my hand. I thought I knew Levi's dad, too, but I guess not.

The only exits are the front door, the back door to the yard, and the glass sliding door upstairs to the deck. There are windows in the front lounge room big enough to climb out, but I can't see if they're unlocked.

"You need to get out," Yvonne says to Mark.

What do I do? I can't get past Mark to the back door, he's blocking the way. I have my phone in my back pocket, but I don't want to risk Mark seeing it.

Yvonne presses her back into me and it forces me onto the first step of the staircase. I stumble and fall onto the carpeted step with a thud.

"This is my house," Mark says. "I'm not leaving."

Yvonne takes a shuddery breath. "Then why don't we go and sit and have a drink."

"I don't want a drink." Mark lunges at Yvonne.

She tries to race up the stairs but falls on me. I should've gotten out of the way. Mark grabs her hand and pulls her off the steps.

"Stop," I say, trying to grab for her. "Please, stop."

Mark turns and backhands me across the cheek. My head whips to the side and hits the banister rail. Stars dance across my vision. I grip the wood to stop myself from falling.

"Run, Katie," Yvonne says, her voice a whisper.

I blink to clear my sight. Mark throws Yvonne to the floor and kicks her. Tears fill my eyes and spill over onto my cheeks, blurring my vision again. I scramble backwards then turn to climb the stairs. It's the only way I can go. When I reach the top I head straight to the door leading onto the deck. My hands are shaking so badly, I can't work the latch. I press my forehead to the cool glass and close my eyes, taking a deep breath.

The glass shudders and my eyes fly open.

"Katie!" Levi is standing on the other side. "Unlock the door."

His eyes go wide and he waves his hands, banging on the glass. I glance over my shoulder and Mark is coming towards me.

"Where are you going?" he asks, his voice low and gravelly.

A siren wails.

My heart explodes with panic as my fingers slide over the latch. *Why won't it open?*

"The other way," Levi yells. "Push it the other way."

I flick the lock, and a hand clamps down on my shoulder. Levi rips the door to the side. He grabs my hand and pulls me outside, slamming the sliding door closed onto Mark's arm. He grunts.

The sirens are louder.

Levi races towards the back steps that lead from the deck to the yard, his palm sweaty in mine. I have to concentrate on not tripping. I glance over my shoulder at the door and Mark turns the lock, pulling the curtains closed.

"Levi, your mum," I say when we reach the bottom of the stairs. "I think she's hurt."

"We called the police. Dad won't open the door." He pulls me along until we're in the front yard.

Two police cars are parked on the street, their lights flashing, and an ambulance is in the driveway. Mum and Dad are standing near the boundary, and when our gazes connect, I let go of Levi's hand and run to them. They both wrap their arms around me and smother me with their hugs.

"What happened?" Mum asks.

"Are you okay?" Dad pushes me to arm's length and looks me up and down, his eyes wide.

Levi reaches out to touch my forehead. "What did he do to you?"

"Your mum ..." My breath hitches. "They need to get inside."

"You're hurt, Katie," Dad says. "Can we get help over here, please?" he calls.

"I'm fine. Yvonne is the one who needs help."

An ambulance officer comes over to us. "Did you hit your head? Why don't you come and sit down?" She touches my arm.

"No," I say, moving away from her. "I don't want treatment. You need to get Yvonne out of the house. He ... he hurt her."

I look at Levi, and he has tears in his eyes.

"Katie," Dad says.

"Just get her out!" I yell, looking frantically from Dad to the police officers who are doing nothing but standing in the yard. "Get them to break the door down."

Mum grabs my hands and makes shushing noises. "It's okay, honey. I told them Mark and Yvonne's history. The police will get her out."

I frown. Levi runs a hand through his hair and grips

the back of his neck. He stares down at his feet. The lights from the police cars flash red and blue.

"You told … their history?" I stare at Mum. "You knew? You knew he was doing this to her? Why didn't you help her?"

"Katie." Levi grabs my arm. "Calm down."

I don't understand. I look from my parents to Levi, and then back again. If they knew, why didn't they do something? How could anyone let something like this happen?

Two police officers come over to us. They look too calm, like they're here for a cup of coffee. The male officer is tall and skinny, all angles. The female officer has short hair with tight curls.

"Hi. I'm Officer Beck and this is Officer Samson. Were you in the house?" the policewoman asks.

I nod. "But I'm fine—"

"How did you get out?"

"Back door," I say. "Up the top."

"Is he armed?" Officer Samson asks.

I shake my head. "No, but he's hurt Yvonne pretty bad."

"You need the ambulance officers to check you out," Beck says.

"I'm fine. You need to get Yvonne."

"Please. Go with the ambulance officer," Samson says. "We'll handle this."

They join two other police officers on the front veranda. They're just standing there though, and I want to scream at them to break the door down.

Levi turns me towards the ambulance in the driveway.

I go with the paramedic and sit on the open back of the ambulance. She shines a light in my eyes and checks me over, swabbing the cut on my forehead and putting a butterfly Band-Aid on it. I keep moving to look around her though, trying to see what's going on.

"Police. Open the door," one of the officers says, banging on the wood with a closed fist. "Mr White, you need to open up."

I hold my breath and will the door to open. Mark has to open the door. I'm not sure if he hurt Yvonne more after I ran. I squeeze my eyes closed, and the image of him kicking her fills my mind, so I open them again.

"Open the door," I whisper.

"I'll be back," Levi says, then jogs across the yard and up onto the veranda.

One of the policemen steps in front of him and says something. I can't hear their conversation. Levi puts his hands up, then points to the far corner of the veranda. The police officer goes in that direction, but I can't see what he's doing. When he comes back to Levi, he gestures for Levi to go down the steps.

"Mr White, we're coming in," one of the police officers says. "This is your last chance to open the door."

I stand from my seat on the tailgate of the ambulance and wrap my arms around myself. Levi comes back to my side.

"What's taking them so long?" I ask. "Your mum …"

Levi puts his arm around my shoulders and pulls me close. "I know. It's okay, I told them where the spare key is."

"We're coming in," one of the police officers calls, and

the door to Levi's house finally opens.

Seconds later, an officer calls, "Can we get a paramedic in here now?"

Levi lets go of me and runs across the lawn. The two ambulance officers race after him to the house, medical cases in hand, and disappear through the front door. I feel helpless, unable to do anything but wait. All the police are inside. Levi is inside. Minutes pass and they feel like hours.

Mum and Dad come to stand with me near the ambulance. A few of the neighbours have come into the street, but they all seem to be keeping their distance. One of the paramedics comes back to the ambulance and gets a stretcher, rolling it to the bottom of the stairs.

Moments later, Yvonne comes out supported by Levi and the other paramedic. She's clutching her arm to her stomach, and blood covers one side of her face. She's helped onto the stretcher and rolled slowly to the ambulance. Levi walks beside her, clutching his mum's hand. Mum, Dad, and I step out of the paramedics' way.

"I'll go with her," Levi says, then he looks at me.

I nod and hug myself. "I'm fine. Go."

Levi climbs in beside his mum, heading for the one place he probably never wants to see again.

So much for coming home.

13

Our future starts now

They arrested Levi's dad.

The police brought Mark out of the house, handcuffed, not long after the ambulance took Yvonne away. They put him in the back of one of their cars, and I haven't seen him since.

Yvonne was treated for a fractured wrist, cuts, and severe bruising.

We all had to make statements.

They offered me a counsellor, but I told the police as long as Mark was never allowed near Yvonne and Levi again, I'd be fine.

That was four days ago.

Mum and Dad have been keeping a close eye on me. They think I haven't noticed, but they're acting as if I'm going to crack and fall apart at any moment. I won't. I don't think. They've even resorted to getting Daniel to suss me out whenever he can. He thinks I don't know what he's doing every time he asks if I'm okay.

Mark didn't hurt me as badly as he hurt Yvonne, but the look in his eyes and the memory of watching what he did to her will stay with me for a while.

The police put out a temporary restraining order on Mark so he's not allowed to go near Yvonne, at least until it goes through court properly. I might have to testify, especially since Mum and Dad want to press charges for what he did to me. I don't know what's going to happen there though. I guess we have to wait and see.

I'm not sure what any of it means for Levi. I know it's not the end of it for him or his mum, but at least it's a step towards getting Mark out of their lives. I'm still so angry at myself for never realising what was happening to them.

After Levi had come home, Mum offered for him to stay with us, since Yvonne was in hospital. I'd wanted to take him to the treehouse, but with everything that had happened, the surprise I'd planned didn't seem so important anymore. Instead, we'd spent half the night out in my back yard, lying on the grass and staring at the stars. The lights from the marina down the hill had been winking, and we'd talked about the time we bashed through the bush all the way down to the road at the bottom, then walked to the ferry.

We don't do that this time though. We take Mum's car and drive down the windy road, parking on our side of the river, before jumping on the ferry to go across to the marina. Being on the ferry on foot is so much better than sitting in the car. It's as if the trip goes in slow motion, and there's more of a chance to take it all in. The grinding of the gears as the cable feeds through the pulleys. The dark water beneath us. The feeling of moving while standing still.

When we reach the other side, Levi and I sit on the wall beside the boat ramp, our toes dipping into the coolness below. I rest my head on his shoulder, and let the warmth of the sun soak my face. The water from the river laps against the shore to our left, and jostles the boats in their pens to our right.

I haven't come down here since we were kids.

I miss it.

There's something about the sound of the water, and the birds in the surrounding bush mixed with the low hum of voices from the marina café, that's soothing.

"We should do this more often," I say, with my eyes closed and my face tilted to the sky.

Levi rests his head against mine. "We can do this as much as you like."

I don't open my eyes, but I know he's smiling. I can hear it in his voice.

"Did you sort uni out?" I ask.

"I'm going to do mid-year intake. So until then, I'm free." He laughs.

I chuckle and straighten up so I can look at him. "I can't believe I have to start in a few weeks. I feel like this summer has disappeared, and we didn't get ..." I stop because my voice starts to shake, and a lump rises into my throat. I stare out at the water, looking for a way to say all the things I want to say but can never find the right words.

Levi nudges my shoulder. "Everything will work out."

I turn back to him and he puts his arm around my shoulders, pulling me closer for a kiss. His lips are soft and gentle, and I never realised how much I missed him while he was in hospital. Missed the way his lips would curl when he smiled at me. Missed how when he ran his hand through his hair it made my belly flop. Every time I hear the sound of his voice, and feel the beat of his heart under my fingertips, I'm so scared it will be the last time that it makes me want to cry.

I pull away and press my palm to his chest. "We have so much hanging over our heads."

Levi puts a finger to my lips. "The past is done with, okay?"

I nod, unable to speak because the lump in my throat is still there.

My phone buzzes in my back pocket, but I ignore it. I know it's going to be Karen, and I hope she's finished with what I asked her to do, but I can't check because I don't want Levi to read the text message over my shoulder.

"We can still see your house from here." I point to the top of the hill across the river.

Levi looks up at the bushland. "Dad always made sure the trees were cut back enough not to lose the view." He smiles, but then it falters.

We go silent, and my heart lurches. I hope that it's not always going to be like this. That at some point in the future we'll be able to talk about him and not have it hurt. But that time isn't now. My dad never worried about the view, and I like that I know my house is there, too. It's hidden behind the screen of bush.

"Want to go back and look at the view?" I ask.

"If you're with me, I don't care where we are." Levi gets up and stands so his toes hang over the edge of the wall. He holds his hand out to me and I take it, letting him help me to my feet. He pulls me close and I shut my eyes, savouring the feeling of his arms around me, the sunlight on my skin, and the calmness I feel being here with him.

We put our thongs on, then walk slowly back towards the ferry, hand in hand. My phone buzzes again, and this time I take it out to read the messages. I pull my hand from Levi's and cup it around the screen so he can't see.

Karen: All set. Treehouse ready n waiting

Karen: When r u home?

Karen: UR obvs having 2much fun!

Karen: Going 2 C Jess

I smile at her words, but my heart lurches a little at the mention of Jessica. She's still not doing so well, and I'm grateful now that she has Daniel. The idea of my brother being with one of my closest friends has grown on me, and I figure if he can help her through the pain, then that's a good thing.

I flick Karen a quick reply.

Me: Heading 2 ferry now. Thnk you. C U 2morrow?

Karen: Of course

"Let me guess," Levi says. "Karen?"

I smirk and pocket my phone. "Who else? But you have my undivided attention now." I slip my arm around his waist and tuck myself into his side as we walk the last twenty metres to the ferry.

It's on its way back across the river, so we have to wait a few minutes before we can board. I lean against the railing overlooking the water and stare into the depths below. It's like thinking about the future. I've no idea what lies beneath the surface of the inky water, just like I don't know what lies ahead of me. The thought scares me, and I worry that something terrifying will launch itself out of the darkness. I've survived so much already. Levi has, too. If we can make it through all the days that have led us to this point, then we can make it through many, many more.

"You okay?" Levi asks. "You're quiet, and staring into space."

"Yeah." I smile, looking up at him. "Just thinking."

I don't know what the future holds, and as scary as it might be, I have to remind myself that at least now Levi and I have a chance at a future together. At least now I know I have him, and we have to make the most of every second, because no one knows when everything will end.

The ferry grates along the concrete as the ramp slides up, and it comes to a stop. The ferry master runs out and presses the button for the boom gate to let the cars off. We walk onto the ferry along the pedestrian path and stop about halfway, leaning against the railing. I stare out across the water, standing beside Levi so our shoulders are touching.

We don't talk for the ten minutes it takes the ferry to get to the other side. We just stand there, letting the breeze play with our hair, and enjoy the quiet and peace of the river.

I drive us back up the hill towards home. Levi isn't comfortable getting behind the wheel of a car. His BMW was a complete write-off. Even though he can't remember what happened on the night of the accident, I think guilt over Josephine's death still plagues him.

I pull Mum's car into the driveway and turn the engine off, nervous about what's going to happen next. When my surprise for Levi fell through on the day he came home from hospital, I never thought I'd have another chance to pull it off. Considering the treehouse is in his backyard, it was going to be hard to go out there without him noticing or seeing me.

That's where Karen came in, and I hope she did a good job.

This time it's going to be a surprise for both of us.

"I have something to show you," I say, curling my fingers through the door handle.

Levi opens the car door and sticks one leg out. "Really? What is it?"

I smile. "If I told you, it wouldn't be a surprise."

We get out of the car, and my chest tightens. I break out in a light sweat, nervous and shy, and suddenly worried this is stupid. What if Levi thinks it's a bad idea? What if what I want him to do is too much for him?

Get a grip, Katie. It's just paper.

And he told me the past was done with.

I meet Levi at the front of the car. "It's in the treehouse." I fidget with the car keys. "Think you can climb the steps?"

"For you, I could climb a mountain with two broken legs."

489

"I'm serious." I swat him on the arm. "I don't want you to hurt yourself. You're not supposed to be overdoing it."

"I'll be fine." Levi gently takes my hand and we walk towards the side of the house.

His steps are slower than usual, and cautious, as if he's done too much today, and I have doubts about him being able to make the climb. But he says he can, so I'm not going to stop him. When we reach the bottom of the tree, Levi looks down at me.

"It's been a while since we've both been up there … together," he says.

"It has." I smile, and remember when Levi chose truth at Veronica's party. We were always innocent in this treehouse. Maybe that will change today. "You first." I gesture to the pieces of wood nailed to the trunk that make the steps.

Levi sets one foot on the bottom piece of wood and grabs another with his hands. Slowly, he works his way up, and when he reaches the top he stops with the edge of the platform at his waist. At first I think he's stopped because he can't go any farther, but then he glances down at me, his eyes wide.

"Katie, this is amazing," he says. "When did you do this?"

"A good witch never reveals her secrets." I chuckle. "Now get in so I can come up, too." My smile widens, and my cheeks hurt. I'm not about to admit I have no idea what it looks like in there.

Levi pulls himself up the rest of the way and I follow. At the top I sit on the edge of the platform and swing my legs onto the wooden floor. I have to hold in my gasp. When

I told Karen romantic, I never thought she'd go this far.

Levi is sitting on the table in the corner, gazing around at the fairy lights strung up across the two walls, the tea lights set at regular intervals around the edge of the floor, and the bougainvillea flowers scattered around.

"Did you get new curtains?" Levi asks.

"Yep." I shuffle away from the edge of the platform. "The old ones were a bit gross."

"They're great." He reaches out and touches the bright purple fabric. "It's all great, Katie."

"Look under the table." My voice shakes a little, and I hope Levi doesn't notice.

He raises his eyebrows but does as he's told. He pulls out the box of letters, and a mixing bowl. The lighter I put inside the bowl moves, scraping against the metal sides.

"What's this for?" He holds the box in one hand and the bowl in the other.

I take a deep breath and close my eyes for a second, hoping that when I say what I want to say, he'll agree with me.

"That box ... everything in it is in the past. It's full of pretty sucky memories for both of us, and I'm not sure about you, but I'm done with all of that. I want to move forward with nothing hanging over my head. I want to put all that stuff behind me. Behind us, and start from now." I stare into Levi's eyes and smile. "I don't want to waste another minute, because you ... you're my everything, and ..." I can't keep talking because a sob rises into my chest.

Levi gets off the table, sets the box and bowl down, and kneels in front of me. "I know," he whispers, and then he kisses me, my tears falling onto our lips.

Levi pulls away and sits back on his heels. He sets the bowl between us and picks up the lighter. Then he opens the shoe box and grabs a handful of the letters, putting them into the bowl. He strikes the flint and holds the flame to the corner of the envelope sitting on top.

The fire spreads quickly, and we stare into the flames. They flicker between us, and as the pile crumples, Levi feeds more letters into the bowl until all of them are nothing but pieces of black, wispy ash.

He looks at me and smiles. "I love you, Katherine Sullivan."

Another tear rolls down my cheek. "I love you, too, Levi White."

He reaches out and wipes my tears away. The rough skin of his fingers anchors me in the present, and I press my cheek into his palm. We've been through so much, and come so far, from when I thought Levi and I had something, to when he made me feel like nothing, and back to him being my everything.

We've come out the other side together.

The past is where it should be ... in the past.

Our future starts now.

The End

Acknowledgements

Very special thanks to two amazing authors who I am proud to be able to call my friends. They are awesome beta readers, and my partners in crime. Selina Fenech and Serene Conneeley, you have both pushed me to be and do my very best. You give me support, make me focus, and encourage me to take action. Thank you so much for all the things. (See what I did there?)

My family: thank you for loving me no matter how crazy I can be, and for supporting my need to have my own space in the house where I can work and write.

To my wonderfully patient and supportive husband, Brendon, love you lots.

Thank you to my two beautiful children, for reminding me what life is about when I'm lost in my own imagination. You both keep me grounded when I need it most.

Lauren Clarke, editor extraordinaire ... thank you so much for all the time and effort you put into my manuscripts. I love your face.

Thank you to the Story Queens. I couldn't ask for a better group of writers and friends. Each of you has supported me in different ways, and I'll be forever grateful for the influence you've had on my writing journey.

And finally, to my readers, I hope Katie's story touched your heart, and I'd like to thank you for sticking with her and Levi until the end.

About the author

K. A. Last was born in Subiaco, Western Australia, and moved to Sydney when she was eight. Artistic and creative by nature, she studied Graphic Design and graduated with an Advanced Diploma. After marrying her high school sweetheart, she concentrated on her career before settling into family life. Blessed with a vivid imagination, K. A. Last began writing to let off creative steam, and fell in love with it. She is currently studying her Bachelor of Arts at Charles Sturt University, with a major in English, and minors in Children's Literature, Art History, and Visual Culture. She now resides in the countryside on the mid-north coast of NSW with her family and a menagerie of animals.

Connect with K. A. Last

Website www.kalastbooks.com.au
Facebook www.facebook.com/KALastBooks
Instagram www.instagram.com/kalastbooks
Pinterest www.pinterest.com/kalast
Goodreads www.goodreads.com/KALast
Twitter www.twitter.com/KALastBooks

**Scan the code to subscribe to
K. A. Last's newsletter.**